The Singularity series:

Redshift
The Observer Effect
Uncertainty Principle
Quantum Entanglement
Event Horizon
Point Singularity

Prequel
Ani, or, the care and feeding of your great tree-
dwelling venomous tentacled land-devil

THE OBSERVER EFFECT

R.M. OLSON

ISBN-13: 978-1-990142-13-0

Cover by MiblArt

"One thing that must be taken into account in every observation is the Observer Effect—the fact that observing a situation or a phenomenon will necessarily change the thing being observed, whether in large ways or small. The observation itself affects the outcome."

-From an introductory physic textbook, Sao Martim University, Vila Nova do Sol, Colorida

1

Aran

The alien jungle was all but silent, even the harsh, unfamiliar cries of the strange birds and the buzz and hum of insects muted.

Aran noticed it in the back of his mind, but most of his brain was focused on the threat in front of him.

And considering the survival of the entire ragged band of injured survivors behind him depended, more or less, on him not dying right at the moment—or at the very least, him getting the damn force-field back up before he died—he couldn't exactly complain.

He crouched carefully, staring into baleful yellow eyes that were almost the size of his entire face. "Easy there, big boy," he whispered, trying to keep his voice as low and unthreatening as possible.

The massive jungle cat's tail lashed, and it snorted, hot breath washing thick and heavy over Aran's face. It smelled like rotted meat—which, honestly, was probably a good thing. It meant the animal had eaten recently, at least. Which meant he'd probably been right when he guessed it was more curious than hungry.

Although that was still something of an open question.

The beast crouched a little, the rippling muscles under its skin as smooth as water, and Aran felt an awed smile spreading across his face, despite … well, everything. "You're beautiful, aren't you?" he murmured, keeping his head turned away to avoid direct eye contact. The creature snorted again and crouched lower.

Aran dropped slowly to all fours, trying to keep his body language submissive. His heart was racing, with terror or excitement or both. There were no cats even approaching this size back on Colorida. And despite the fact that it might actually eat him, he could hardly breathe from the sheer, lethal beauty of the animal.

"Easy there, beautiful. I don't want to hurt you, I just need you to give me back that force-field controller. It's not really good for you, anyways," he whispered.

He'd never interacted with this particular species before. Unless you counted inspecting the dead body Ani, his pet land-devil, had left after their crash the previous day, when one had tried to eat Aran and discovered, rather permanently, how bad of an idea starting a disagreement with a protective great venomous tree-dwelling tentacled land-devil was. Aran still felt guilty over it, honestly—the thought of the kind of impact Ani would have on this new ecosystem had woken him from nightmares the previous night. But he'd spent enough time around red-frilled mountain cats back on Colorida that he had a basic idea of how the creature might react.

"Alright," Aran whispered, stretching his hands out ever-so-gently towards the cat's mouth, which was now within easy arm's reach. "This is going to be the complicated part. But you're so smart, I'm sure we'll figure it out."

His hand was close enough to the huge muzzle that he could almost touch it, the soft breath against his hand hot and strong.

He drew in a quick breath, released it slowly, and, as gently as possible, placed his hand on the soft fur.

The cat snarled and sprang forward, massive paw slamming into Aran and sending him sprawling in the thick vegetation. He rolled to lay stomach-up, tipping his chin backwards to expose his throat and turning his head away, his pulse pounding in his ears.

The beast, still snarling, lowered its head towards his exposed stomach, and his muscles clenched involuntarily at the imagined pressure of those knife-sharp canines, the length of his hand at least …

"Um, Aran?" Ines's shaky voice came from somewhere behind him. "Um, should I—should I shoot it?"

Very, very carefully, Aran squeezed his hand into a fist to activate his wavelink. "No," he murmured, trying not to move his mouth. "Don't … do anything … yet. I've got everything … under control."

He hoped, desperately, that he was telling the truth.

Something bumped his side, and he tensed involuntarily, braced for the stabbing agony that was sure to follow the moment his nerves recognized the puncture wound—

But it didn't come. He opened one of the eyes he'd squeezed tightly shut, and from the corner of it, saw the beast drop its head back to nudge him again with its nose.

His heart was pounding so fast he was dizzy with it.

"That's my sweet boy," he whispered. "I'm not going to hurt you, I promise."

The animal snorted again, its breath washing over him, and despite his pounding heart, Aran realized there was a giddy grin on his face.

The beast was a juvenile, he was fairly sure, judging by its conformation and its behaviour. If it had been an adult, this interaction might have gone quite differently. But it was young, and still more curious about the world than defensive.

Again, Aran eased his arm upward. "Now," he murmured, "let's try this again. I promise I don't want to hurt you. But that's a force-field module you've got in your mouth, and it'll give you a stomach ache."

With glacial slowness, he raised his arm. The cat stiffened, and Aran stilled. "Alright," he soothed. "We're on the same side, you and me."

The cat bumped him again with its nose, and then, with an odd sort of growl, opened its jaws and caught his upraised arm between them.

"Aran?" Ines's voice was a terrified squeak.

"It's fine," he murmured, his voice shaking slightly. "It's fine, everything's under control."

If the beast closed its jaws, even gently, it would snap Aran's arm like a twig—but for the moment, at least, its mouth was soft, the knife-sharp teeth barely pressing into his skin.

And inside its mouth—

Yes. He had to bite back a grin of triumph.

The module for the force-field was wedged between two of the animal's back teeth, within reach of his grasping hand.

He closed his fingers around it carefully. "This would definitely have given you a stomach ache," he whispered. "Now, I'd really, really appreciate it if you didn't eat me as I get it out. We were getting along so well. It'd be a shame to ruin it."

He'd found the module, and he was still alive, which, all things considered, was a minor miracle. He just had to not think too hard about the fact that right now he was lying on the ground with his arm in the mouth of a creature easily ten times his length, with teeth sharp enough that they punctured skin almost on contact. Because if he did, he would lose his actual crap.

The cat moved its head, and Aran let his body go limp, moving with the cat's motion to avoid having his arm torn off at the shoulder. He managed to clamp his fingers around the sensor, and the beast gave a low, coughing snarl, pushing its paw down against his chest.

He froze.

"Aran …"

"I can't talk … right now …" he muttered through gritted teeth. "I'm kind of … in the middle of …"

"I'm—I'm sorry, it's just that—"

"Aran, what the actual hell!"

Aran almost whipped his head around, and refrained himself just in time. Istvay's voice was strangled.

Dammit.

Istvay was his best friend. He and Istvay had worked expeditions together for years now. There was no one Aran would rather have on his side. But … Istvay had a tendency to overreact to things like this.

"Pishti, it's not … what it looks like—" he managed, still without moving his mouth. "Keep Ani … in the backpack."

"I can't bloody leave you alone for five damn minutes," Istvay grumbled. "Here, hold tight, this'll help."

Aran paused, trying to relax as the beast rolled his arm between its teeth. "Istvay?" he tried after a moment.

"Give me a sec," said Istvay tersely.

There was a rustling off to one side. The cat tensed. Then, abruptly, it dropped Aran's arm, and the weight on Aran's chest lifted as the animal bounded into the jungle after whatever distraction Istvay had thought up.

For moment Aran just lay there, limp. Now that the danger was over, every muscle in his body had turned to water, and his heart was pounding so fast he thought he might throw up.

There were running footsteps, and before he could turn, Istvay had dropped down beside him, sharp worry on their face. "Aran. Talk to me. Are you—"

Aran groaned, and with an effort, rolled over into a sitting position. "I'm fine, Pishti," he said weakly. "Um. Thanks, by the way."

Istvay let out a long breath, then took him by the shoulders, looking him up and down. "You're bleeding. How badly are you hurt?"

Aran glanced down at himself, and realized there were thin trails of blood tracing down his arm where the cat's teeth had broken the skin. He managed a shaky grin. "I'm fine. It's just a scratch. It wasn't trying to bite me or anything, or—"

"Or I'd be picking up your limbs off the damn jungle floor, I don't need a reminder," Istvay sighed. "Come on, let's go before it comes back. I tossed it one of those slug things that Ani killed when I was on my way back, but I doubt that'll hold its attention long." Istvay slipped an arm under Aran's shoulder and pulled him to his feet.

Ines was waiting a few steps away with a pulse pistol held in her shaking hand, and Aran managed an encouraging smile in her direction. "Thanks, Ines. You did really well back there."

The girl gave him a tremulous smile, and the three of them started back across the small clearing towards where the huddled survivors, everyone they'd been able to find from the wreck of the diplomatic ship, waited.

"Ines told me what happened," said Istvay as they walked. "Did you get the module?"

Aran nodded, wiping the drool-slime off against his trousers leg.

"Let's hope it still works, after all that. We don't have any other force-field modules, and with the shape everyone's in, we won't last a standard hour out here without the damn field." He tapped the battered module a couple of times and, holding his breath, hit the button.

Across the clearing, the blue force-field that had previously made a translucent wall around the survivors flickered up, and then steadied.

Aran breathed a long sigh of relief and turned to his friend with a grin. "There. See? I didn't—"

He trailed off.

Istvay was watching him, their face smudged with dirt and a small streak of blood, eyes dark with concern and focused solely on Aran. And suddenly, Aran was much too aware of the pressure Istvay's arm around his back, the way their dark lashes brushed their cheeks, the rough hint of a beard on their chin, the wisps of black hair pulling out of the ponytail and falling across their face …

"Aran?"

He blinked and forced himself to look away, only then remembering to breathe. "Um. Yeah. Sorry."

He was being stupid. Like always.

Istvay was his friend. And Istvay had made it very clear, over the years, that that was all they wanted to be.

"I'll—I'll just go inside," Ines said quickly, her eyes flicking between Aran and Istvay. She stepped up to the force-field and tapped her wavelink, and the translucent blue field parted to let her through.

When she was gone, Istvay shook their head, turning back to Aran with a wry smile. "Should I even ask what happened?" Their voice was still just a little shaky.

Aran swallowed, and managed a small laugh. "The force-field

went down, and when I went to check out why, I found that little fellow playing with the component. When he saw me coming, he grabbed it in his teeth, so I had to—"

He trailed off again. Istvay was giving him their familiar look, half of exasperation, half of fondness. "You had to go and stick your damn arm in its mouth." They paused. "You know, some people might have just, I don't know, shot it?"

Aran frowned, and Istvay chuckled ruefully, still shaking their head. "Sorry. But … next time you plan on getting yourself almost eaten by a jungle cat, would you mind at least waiting until I'm close enough to help or something?" Their tone was a forced calm, but Aran could hear the tight worry under it, that flicker of almost-panic.

"Pishti, I'm fine. I promise. Okay?"

Istvay managed a wan smile, and Aran sighed to himself.

If there was one thing he'd learned over the past few weeks on the diplomatic ship, before it had broken up and stranded all of them here, it was that he'd take almost being killed by dangerous animals any day over the helplessness of watching his best friend fall apart.

But the problem was, Istvay seemed increasingly on the verge of falling apart every time it looked like Aran was in any danger at all, which didn't exactly help matters.

"So. Did you find anything?" he asked at last.

Istvay nodded, but Aran could still see the tension around their eyes and mouth. "I found the alien settlement we saw on our equipment. It was right where the sensor said it would be. And whatever lives there, they're definitely a sapient species—they've built a full-on city." They paused. "I didn't try to go in. I thought it would be wiser to come back here first and let everyone know, in case they —in case something—" They stopped, and Aran felt his own jolt of terror at what might have been, if Istvay had been discovered on their own.

"Anyways, whatever they are, they have a complex social structure and enough ability to communicate to build a city that could rival any back on Colorida. If Alba wanted someone to negotiate with, I think we've found them."

"And you're alright? Nothing happened to you on the way?"

Istvay snorted softly. "That depends on what you define as 'anything.' But considering Ani was acting as my guard dog, nothing was able to hurt me."

"And … how are you feeling, after—"

Istvay gave him a small smile. "I'm fine. Just a little slower than usual. But, I suppose, still fast enough to get back here in time to see you in the actual mouth of a jungle cat."

Aran closed his eyes in relief.

It had been four days since Istvay had been poisoned.

He could still remember the way his friend's face had looked as they lay on the floor in the diplomatic ship's corridor, foam speckling the corners of their lips, skin greyish, heart stuttering weakly as their body fought to keep them alive.

And he wasn't sure he'd ever be able to forgive his former-classmate-turned-mutineer, Emeric, for that.

Even after the mutiny, even after the ship breaking up, even after Emeric's attempt to kill Aran as he fled the dying ship, it was the remembered sight of Istvay lying still in the corridor, eyes closed, skin greying, that made Aran want to throw up.

Emeric had been killed when the ship had gone down. At least, he probably had—they had no real way of knowing. But he hadn't been among the survivors Aran had brought back to the clearing the previous day, and anyone who'd tried to face the alien jungle on their own was almost certainly dead by now.

"Well, I guess the others are lucky you were with them," Istvay said at last, their joking tone slightly forced. "Here. Let me—" they took Aran's injured arm, hands gentle as they probed the cuts.

Aran tried to convince his lungs to keep breathing, but there was something about Istvay's touch that made his shoulders relax and his stomach tighten, and something catch in the back of his throat.

At last, Istvay let go of him and looked up with a small smile of relief, and again, Aran forced himself to look away.

"Looks like just surface cuts. But we should disinfect it. No point having your arm swell up like a damn balloon, like that time in the Spider-Rim Basin."

Aran chuckled despite himself.

There was a questioning chirrup from Istvay's backpack, the fabric of it bulging and wriggling, and Aran's smile turned genuine. "Hello there, Ani. Did you miss me?"

He reached over Istvay's shoulder and unhooked the clasp on the backpack. The tip of a tentacle, striated with a bright, uneasy orange, emerged first, then another, and then Ani pulled her bulbous body delicately from the pack.

She gave Istvay a look that, even from her protuberant eyes, could only be called disdain, and tiptoed over Istvay's shoulder until she could grasp Aran's hand with her tentacle suckers. Then she swarmed up his arm and settled herself firmly on his shoulder, grumbling to herself.

Aran shook his head ruefully and reached up, stroking her. "Hey there, sweetheart. I missed you, too."

Istvay snorted. "She spent the whole time trying to get me to turn around so we could go back and find you." They paused. "On the bright side, there were about half-a-dozen jungle creatures that thought I looked like a tasty snack, and discovered they were no match for a land-devil. So I'm grateful nonetheless."

Ani had relaxed now, her grumbling turning to a slightly sulky purr.

"That's my good girl," Aran murmured, tickling her under the chin. Her tentacles changed slowly from irritated orange to a contented dark green, and Aran turned his attention back to Istvay. "Well, I guess we should go tell the others," he said reluctantly.

Through the force-field, he could make out people watching him, and their awed expressions made his stomach tighten with discomfort.

Istvay followed his gaze, then shook their head and chuckled, placing a hand on Aran's shoulder. "You can't exactly blame them," they said, their tone fond and amused. "I keep telling you this, but as much as you hate your heroic reputation, you do end up deserving it most of the time."

Aran scowled at his friend, and Istvay chuckled again and pulled him forward, holding up their wavelink so that the force-field parted around the two of them as they stepped through.

At least there weren't reporters. At least there was that, Aran thought to himself, trying hard to tamp down the irrational panic as the press of people crowded around him.

Istvay stepped in front of him, smoothly pushing back the crowd. "He's got a scratch, best to stand back. He needs to stay away from any possibility of infection until we can get it cleaned up." They managed to inject just the right blend of lightness and sincerity into their tone to make everyone back up a few paces.

Ani, who'd been growling uneasily on Aran's shoulder, relaxed as the people made room, and Istvay shot Aran a wink over their shoulder. Aran's heart stuttered just a little as he followed them back towards where the tiny diplomatic corps, consisting of Chief Justice Alba, the mission's head diplomat and Joint Head of the Joias System government, Feliu, her clerk, Yosip, the diplomatic aide, and Ines, the mission's linguist, had gathered.

Alba looked up at their approach. Her face was strained, but she still wore the arrogant expression Aran had grown accustomed to.

"Aran," she said briskly. "I suppose thanks are in order."

He blinked at her in surprise, then glanced over at Yosip, who was sitting next to her. The older man's face was solemn, but his eyes twinkled, and Aran found himself grinning.

"Alba," said Istvay. Their tone was short, and it would be a stretch to call it anything like respectful, but at least the hostility in it was more muted than usual, and again, Aran glanced at Yosip.

He wasn't entirely sure how the man did it, but the tension seemed to diminish palpably whenever he was part of the conversation.

Istvay gave a brief report of what they'd found—more or less what they'd already told Aran. When they'd finished, Alba nodded brusquely.

"Our first priority must be getting these people to safety, and getting assistance for the injured. Which means, of necessity, ascertaining the aliens' attitudes towards us. I will go, of course, and I believe Yosip and Ines must accompany me, as I will require their skills." She paused a moment. "I believe we will also need a guide, and the two of you are by far the most qualified. So I would like to request that one of you come as well." There was a tone in her voice that said she didn't like having to ask the question, and would much have preferred to have made an executive decision.

Aran and Istvay glanced at each other.

"I know what you're going to say, Aran, and the answer is no," said Istvay grimly. "The last time I left you alone without Ani, I came back to find you halfway inside the mouth of the jungle cat. Ani is staying with you."

Aran scowled at them. "I'm not staying. I'm not the one who was poisoned, what—four days ago? You're right, Ani's staying, but you're damn well staying with her."

"I'm the only one who's been to the settlement. If one of us is going—" Istvay's face was set into the stubborn expression Aran knew far too well. He opened his mouth to cut Istvay off, but before he could, Yosip held up a hand.

"Pardon my interruption. But Aran, you and Istvay work well together. It seems a shame to separate you. And this morning we learned exactly how easy it is for this jungle to eat us, force-field or no. Ines told me what happened out there." He gave a small, wry smile. "We're not safe here, not even with one of you two to protect us. I doubt, at this point, that there's a safe place to be had on this planet. It may be our best option to bring everyone along." He turned to the Chief Justice. "Madam? What are your thoughts?"

Alba sighed, glancing over the assembled group of them.

There were fewer than two hundred, said and done, from a ship of thousands, and Aran could see the strain of that knowledge in the lines of the woman's face.

At last, though, she nodded. "I believe Yosip is correct," she said, her tone softer than Aran remembered. "If there's no safe place, at the very least we should stick together."

Istvay sighed, following Alba's gaze. Then, at last, they glanced over at Aran, and the corners of their mouth turned up a little in a rueful grin. "Well then, I guess we'd better get everyone ready to go."

2

Alba

Alba glanced over her shoulder at the small, ragged group behind her. The only ones left, out of a ship of thousands.

In her seventy-three years of life, Alba had never imagined herself in a situation such as this one.

There may be other survivors scattered around the planet, or others who still hadn't landed. But they had no way of knowing, and no way of finding them. For all she knew, these were the only living humans in light-years' distance. And after the portal had closed, breaking their ship to pieces—there was no chance of getting back without the assistance of whoever or whatever lived in this place.

They'd reached the edge of the jungle without major incident, mostly thanks to the venomous murder-beast purring on Aran's shoulder. Now the landscape transitioned abruptly from thick trees to cleared fields, a flat, open area maybe a kilometre or so around outside edge of the alien settlement. The city Istvay had told them of.

The city itself loomed ahead of them. She couldn't see it clearly through what seemed to be a massive, shimmering force-field, glowing an icy blue and refracting the light from the planet's sun. But she caught a vague impression of towering buildings, oddly tall and narrow, and gleaming so brightly in the reflected light that the entire scene was a vague haze almost painful to look at.

She shivered.

Diplomacy and peaceful negotiations were their best chance for survival. All the theorists back on Colorida had agreed.

But the theorists weren't the ones leading this tiny remnant of survivors to what could be their death.

"Madam? Are you alright?"

She glanced over. Yosip had come up beside her, and his friendly eyes were crinkled in concern.

She forced a small smile. "I'm perfectly well, thank you."

Yosip glanced back at the survivors, following her gaze. "I know," he said softly. "But at the moment, all we can do is our best to keep them, at least, alive."

She took a long breath and nodded briskly. "You are correct." She raised her voice slightly. "Istvay? Would you be so kind as to lead the way? We'll come back for the others as soon as we're certain it's safe."

Istvay nodded, and she and her small, hand-picked party—Istvay, Aran, Yosip, and Ines—set off towards the city gate.

Alba could feel the eyes of the others on their backs, following them.

They'd made it barely halfway across the open area before they were spotted. A group of creatures, bipedal and uncomfortably humanoid, stepped onto the well-worn track the humans had been following and stopped abruptly, staring.

Istvay and Aran, in the lead, came to a halt as well.

The creatures ahead of them were smaller than the humans—the tallest barely matched Alba in height—and wearing simple tunics that came to about their knees. Their bodies were covered with a fine fur, their eyes large, with darker fur patches around them that made them appear constantly surprised. They had thin, prehensile tails, long, delicate fingers, and small, rounded features, and they reminded Alba of nothing more than a larger version of the lemurs from the southern Rim Mountains back on Colorida.

But there was something uncomfortably human in their expressions and movements, and an undefinable hint of threat in the wary way they watched the intruders.

For a moment, the two groups stared at each other.

With the aliens' diminutive size, their large eyes and delicate, perpetually surprised expressions, the overall effect should have made for something cute and harmless. But seeing them standing only a few metres away, Alba was struck by the sharp intelligence in those large eyes, the hint of canines peeking through their lips, how easily those long fingers would be able to grab and twist.

The small group had drawn back protectively and was chattering in a language that was entirely unintelligible. One of them held something that was likely a weapon, and Alba was surprised by the obvious technological sophistication behind it.

When they appeared to have finished speaking, Yosip glanced at her, a question in the look. Alba hesitated, then nodded, ignoring the tight worry in the pit of her stomach.

He stepped forward, hands spread in a non-threatening gesture, and the aliens drew back in alarm, watching him with obvious suspicion.

"We're not here to hurt you," Yosip said. They almost certainly wouldn't understand his words, but his tone was calm and soothing. "We were stranded, and we need help and medical assistance." He pointed to the sky, and pantomimed an object falling and impacting on this ground, and then drew back his sleeve and to show the bandage on his arm, crusted with dried blood, and made an expression of pain.

For a few moments, the aliens watched him. Then, at last, one of them gestured Yosip back with a sharp, grunted command, pointing its weapon at the humans in a way that required no interpretation. It said something over its shoulder, and three or four of the aliens ran off, chattering excitedly among themselves.

"Well, I guess that solves the problem of getting their attention," Istvay muttered dryly.

The heat hung over their small group like a heavy blanket, insects buzzing around their heads. Istvay shifted their weight from foot to foot, and beside Alba, Ines clutched her religious icon, her eyes closed, and recited litanies under her breath.

Then, at last, the alien watching them stiffened, its hand on its weapon tightening, and Alba looked up sharply.

From the direction of the city, a grim-looking troop of aliens approached their ragged band, each of them carrying a large weapon.

She drew in a deep breath.

At this point, it was too late to change her mind.

The aliens surrounded them, weapons held threateningly. The leader of the newcomers stepped forward, consulting quietly with the alien who'd stayed behind as guard. Then it turned to the group of humans.

It spoke loudly and slowly, pointing at them, the sky, itself, its weapon. When they simply stared, it shook its head in disgust and turned its weapon towards a small bush. It pulled the trigger, and the bush … vaporized. There was no explosion, it was simply that one moment the bush was there, and the next it was not.

Alba caught the glance that passed between Aran and Istvay, the sharp worry in it. "What the hell—" Aran began quietly.

The alien gestured to the weapon, the place where the bush had been, and back at the humans. Even without understanding the language, the threat was abundantly clear. Then it growled something at them.

Alba glanced at Ines, but the girl shrugged helplessly. The alien tried again, clearly growing impatient, and gestured into the jungle. At last it turned away in apparent exasperation, its tail puffed, and growled something to its subordinates. Alba couldn't read its expression, but its posture showed agitation.

And then Aran swore, and she glanced over, following his gaze.

Her stomach dropped.

The rest of the survivors were being herded across the open ground towards them, surrounded by grim-looking aliens, their weapons trained on their human captives.

When they reached the diplomatic party, Joska, the woman they'd left in charge, said in a low voice, "I'm sorry, Chief Justice. I thought it better to go with them than be shot down."

"You did exactly as you should have," said Yosip, smiling, but Alba could see the tension under his smile. "At this point, we're all at their mercy in any case."

The alien who seemed to be in charge barked another command. Two of its subordinates stepped forward, pulling half-a-dozen people from the edge of the group and arranging them in a line.

"What are you—" Alba began, stepping forward, shocked out of her caution. One of the aliens grabbed her roughly, shoving her backwards. She stumbled, shocked at the unexpected violence, and Yosip barely caught her before she could fall.

The alien in charge grunted to its subordinates again, and to her horror, Alba saw them raise their weapons to point at the struggling human survivors.

"No!" snapped Istvay, stepping forward. "You're not doing this."

Aran stepped up beside Istvay, planting himself between the aliens and their captives, his hands raised placatingly. "Listen," he began. "I'm sure we can—"

One of the aliens grabbed for him, and Alba heard Istvay's sharp intake of breath.

Ani hissed, the pouches under her eyes puffing up and her colour changing to a bright orange.

"Ani! No! It's fine, sweetheart, we're just meeting some new friends," Aran whispered frantically, stroking her tentacles.

The alien stepped forward again in irritation, bringing up its weapon.

Ani struck. Alba wasn't sure what else to call the whip-crack motion as the tentacle-beast reared back and spat.

"Ani—" Aran began, his voice horrified.

And the alien … melted. There wasn't even time for a scream, its face simply dissolved into a bloody, gruesome mess, its weapon falling as the specks of bloody foam hit the ground, steaming.

Aran was holding Ani with both hands, apparently trying to keep her from a full-scale rampage. Istvay stood beside Aran, tensed to do … something, although Alba wasn't certain what they'd be able to do in the face of an irate land-devil and a group of heavily armed aliens.

One of the aliens leapt forward, and Ani pulled free of Aran's grip, landing on the creature's face. The alien screamed, high-pitched and terrified. One of the other aliens yanked out its own weapon, turned it on its compatriot, and fired.

Aran gave a wordless cry of distress, and Istvay grabbed his arm, holding him back as the alien dissolved under the weapon fire.

When the smoke cleared, Ani sat in the centre of a small pile of debris. Her colour had gone a wavering, psychedelic pink and green, but she seemed to have suffered no other ill effects.

If a land-devil could look smug, this one did.

"Ani!" Aran gasped, his voice choking. "Ani, come here sweetheart, come, I'll find you a treat. No one's going to hurt us, at least, probably not anymore …" He trailed off, but Ani made her delicate way across the ground and swarmed up his side, perching herself on his shoulder and growling in discontent, eye pouches bulging.

Everyone else stood shocked and still, watching the bloody mess that was left of the one alien, and the pile of debris that was left of the other.

One of the aliens stepped forward quickly and grabbed the arm of the captain, whispering desperately in its ear and pointing back towards the jungle.

If Alba recalled correctly, Ani had left something of a mess around the place they'd left the others, in the form of one of the massive jungle cats which had tried to ambush their company.

The alien in charge glanced reflexively at Aran and stepped quickly back.

It gestured to its subordinates, and they lowered their weapons. At another command, they shoved their captives back towards the main group.

Slowly, Ani's hissing died down as Aran and Istvay stepped back to join the others.

The aliens consulted for a few moments. At last, the captain stepped forward cautiously, and gestured for them to follow.

Yosip hesitated, glancing at Alba.

"I think it's best we go with them," she said, trying to keep her voice from trembling. "Aran?"

"We should go," he muttered. He seemed to be making no attempt to hide the shakiness in his voice. "Maybe Ani can't be killed, but the rest of us damn well can."

"Well, I think they'll have second thoughts about killing us outright now, at any rate," said Istvay, their voice grim. "If they try to split us up, we'll deal with it then. But we're not going back to the jungle without a fight, if I'm any judge."

Alba glanced around at the weary, ragged group of survivors.

They wouldn't survive a fight. They could barely stay on their feet.

She took a deep breath, lifted her chin, and started forward after their captors.

She'd been the one to bring them here.

And it was starting to look like a terrible, terrible mistake.

3

Savina

Savina tried to blend herself in with the other survivors as the alien guards prodded them through the break in the city forcefield. But as she stepped through and into the city properly, she had an uncanny flashback of stepping through the gates of the Corpus Dai compound as a young child, back in the Rim Mountains where she'd grown up.

It wasn't a pleasant memory.

She took a deep breath and looked around her, peering through the stifling press of terrified survivors, to shake the strange feeling of déjà vu

The city they'd entered was as alien as their captors. But in one other way, it felt more like the compound than she liked to remember—the pervasive, cloying, sickening stench of fear.

She shook her head at herself.

It would be fine. She'd been in tight places before, and she'd always managed to charm or murder her way out.

Yes, this was terrifying. But it was familiar. She knew how to survive. She was good at surviving. And she certainly could find a way to escape, and then put a knife to the throat of whoever was in charge of opening the portal. She couldn't speak the aliens' language, but she'd always found her knives spoke a dialect universally understood.

She glanced reflexively over her shoulder to where Nicolau followed behind her, shoved along with the press of humans. He was gazing around him at the alien cityscape, and she could still see traces of tears on his cheeks. She'd heard his choked sobs the previous night, when they were all supposed to be asleep.

She and Beni had saved his life when they'd dragged him off the diplomatic ship as it broke up. But they hadn't had time to save the lives of his friends. And he still had no idea why they'd done it. No idea he was their brother.

As far as he knew, he was completely alone here.

And behind him, the ship's captain Joska followed, her apparent nonchalance marred by the wry look on her face as she watched Savina.

Savina hadn't told the woman she still intended to kill Alba, just as soon as the Chief Justice was no longer necessary for getting them home. But Joska must have guessed it. She was keeping an eye on Savina as if she were a farmer and Savina a hawk circling her precious chickens.

Savina scowled.

She'd hijacked the damn woman's ship and threatened to murder her more times than she could count. You'd think the bastard would be worried about her own life. Instead, Joska seemed intent on treating Savina like a troubled youth entrusted to her care.

She turned away with a sigh and followed Nicolau's gaze around their new environment.

The layout of the city was like nothing she'd ever seen in her life.

The buildings thrust upwards into the sky, with a height and solidity that belied the delicate, graceful curvature of their architecture. They looked like something fanciful, like something a doting Orthodox mother might spin from sugar for a child on their birthday. The height of them should have made the streets below almost a tunnel, but the buildings were constructed of glass and thin bands of metal, and the light from the sun shone through them, illuminating the streets in a sunburst of stripes and shadows.

It was hard to believe the creatures who'd built them were the same creatures who, a short time before, had tried to shoot their human captives down in cold blood.

The streets themselves weren't bustling with foot traffic, like she was used to in the larger cities on Colorida—the inhabitants seemed to prefer to stay indoors. A network of tunnels spread between the buildings, connecting them in an elegant maze that sparkled in the diluted sun through the force-field as if made of precious gems, and the skyways, where the transports buzzed back and forth, seemed to take up most of the streets themselves, the transports flying low to the ground and crowding out the space for pedestrians, rather than high overhead as they did in Vila Nova do Sol.

But at the street level, it looked much more familiar—dirty streets, narrow alleys, dirty-looking aliens peering from behind alley walls, faces pinched and hungry.

It seemed that no matter how advanced these aliens were, they hadn't solved problems like children starving to death in the streets.

Their captors shoved the group of humans down a wide street and into a large, open space that looked like a transport hub. They herded their captives into the centre and then stepped back, eyeing the hideous-looking tentacle-beast on Aran Romeu's shoulder suspiciously, their weapons held at the ready.

Savina glanced at the creature and gave a small shudder.

She'd watched the ease with which the thing had taken out the aliens, and, more unsettling still, its apparent complete immunity to the alien weaponry.

She would simply have to make very sure that, in her attempts to kill Alba, she never got on the scientist's bad side. He seemed simple, and almost painfully naïve. But if half the stories she'd heard about him were true, he was more dangerous than he looked.

Even without taking his horrifying pet into account.

Savina studied their captors carefully from the corner of her eye. They were small, lithe-looking creatures, with delicate bone structures and fine features.

Of course, when someone had a weapon that could vaporize you, it was almost irrelevant how physically strong they were.

"Savina?" Beni spoke in a whisper from beside her, their voice small and frightened. "What are they like?"

It had been a long time, Savina realized, since she'd heard Beni sound frightened.

She turned back to Beni quickly, smiling. Beni might not be able to see, but they'd always been able to read Savina's expressions in her voice.

"They're—I don't know. Not as strange as I thought they'd be," she whispered. "They look—almost human, but … not. A little like the lemur-monkeys in the mountains around the compound."

Beni cracked a smile. "You're not giving me a very intimidating picture of them."

Savina shivered slightly. "I don't have to."

"That weapon they fired?" Beni's voice was serious now. "I heard it, and I got my wavelink sensor to send me through the specs. We don't have anything back on Colorida that could stand up to a weapon like that."

"I know," said Savina grimly.

Overhead, a small aircraft was approaching. It was large and flat, with sleek, smooth sides, and it made almost no noise as it came to a hovering halt over them.

Their alien captors chattered at the humans, gesturing them out of the way to make room for it to land, and Savina and Beni were shoved backwards until Savina's back was practically pressed against the wall of one of the buildings.

She glanced around quickly, and let out a quick breath of relief. Beni had ended up beside her in the crush, up against the corner of an alley, and Nicolau was standing close by.

She tried to ignore how her eyes flicked over to find Joska and Rafel.

She didn't need to be worrying about those two. They'd be fine.

But she couldn't help the flicker of relief in her chest when she saw that they, too, were close by and unharmed.

And then, from the corner of her eye, she caught a quick flash of movement, heard a startled exclamation, quickly cut off.

She spun in time to see Nicolau, face blank with shock, being dragged into the alley behind her.

Savina swore through her teeth and dived into the alley after him.

"Savina? What's wrong?" Beni's voice followed her, but she didn't have time to answer.

The alley was empty, but Savina caught another flash of movement disappearing around a corner. She yanked out her pulse pistol and started after them at a run.

She rounded the corner in time to see an alien dragging Nicolau back towards a group of two others. Nicolau's captor looked up as Savina rounded the corner, alarm on its face, and jerked Nicolau around in front of it. It was holding a weapon, the same type she'd seen earlier, to Nicolau's head.

Another alien had its own weapon drawn, pointing at Savina.

Nicolau's eyes were wide with shock.

And for a moment, Savina's vision went red.

No one was going to hurt her baby brother.

She took a deep breath, fighting back the quick surge of rage. She'd have to work this carefully if she wanted to keep him alive.

But then, she was good at this sort of thing.

She stopped where she was, widening her eyes as if in fear. She bent carefully, laying her pulse pistol on the ground, and held out her hands in front of her to show they were empty. She didn't know anything about these aliens, their body language or their culture or their weapons, but she could see the moment where the tension in the posture of the one holding Nicolau began to relax.

And as it did, Savina took a small step forward and, in a smooth motion, yanked three throwing knives from her belt.

Two of them went through the throat of Nicolau's captor, and blood sprayed across Nicolau's face as the creature dropped to the ground, choking. The third went through the shoulder of the alien who'd been pointing its weapon at Savina, piercing its flesh and lodging deep in the wall behind it.

Before the alien could react, Savina was across the alley to it, an electric tranq in her hand. She slapped it against the injured alien's shoulder, and the creature froze as the current jolted through it.

Savina grabbed Nicolau by the arm and shoved him behind her, turning to the third alien. The alien grabbed for its weapon, but before it could bring it to bear, Savina grabbed the front of the creature's tunic and yanked it forward, off its feet. She slammed it against the wall, and it yelped in pain, but the sound was cut off as

Savina yanked out another electric tranq and slapped against the side of the creature's neck.

It froze, immobilized, and Savina let go, letting it fall to the ground as she stepped back. Then she bent over its prone body, her eyes hard and cold.

"Maybe you don't understand a word I'm saying," she purred, menace dripping from her tone. "But know this: Nicolau is mine. And you are going to stay away from him."

Nicolau was standing where she'd left him, as frozen as if she'd used an electric tranq on him, too.

Savina pulled three more knives from her belt. She smiled, letting her dimple show. "And you will stay the hell away from me," she whispered. Slowly, deliberately, she pushed the needle-sharp knife through the alien's shoulder, feeling the muscles and tendons separate under the smooth edge of her blade.

The alien's eyes were wide with pain and shock, but it couldn't move, couldn't even make a sound.

She shoved the blade the rest of the way through, jamming the point into the rough cement of the street below, and let her smile widen, just a little. Then she took the second knife, and worked it, just as slowly, through the creature's other shoulder.

She might not always be here to protect Nicolau. May as well give these aliens a lesson they wouldn't forget.

From behind her, Nicolau made a sound like he was going to be sick.

The alien was still staring at her, frozen and horrified, eyes brimming with pain.

She pulled out her third knife, and very gently traced it across the alien's throat. A thin line of red blossomed up in its wake.

"I'm not joking," she said, her voice pleasant and low. "I'm not playing around. And I can make you hurt in ways you can't even imagine." She dimpled prettily. "Maybe you don't understand my words. But I hope I've made my meaning clear anyway."

She stood, wiping her bloody hands clean on the alien's tunic. It didn't take its eyes off her the whole time, the tendons in its neck tight and the whites visible all the way around its eyes.

When she turned around, Beni had reached Nicolau, grabbing him by the shoulders, feeling down his arms, checking for injuries. "Are you alright?" they asked, breathing hard.

Nicolau didn't answer, just stared past Beni at Savina as though he was staring into the Void itself, his face deathly pale beneath his brown complexion.

Savina gave him her most charming smile.

It wasn't a bad thing for her baby brother to learn some respect.

There was a noise from behind her, and Savina spun in time to see the alien she'd pinned to the wall with a knife double forward. It must have knocked the electric tranq loose somehow, because it caught its balance and stumbled off at a run, clutching its bleeding shoulder. Savina swore and sent a knife after it, but it clattered off the wall of a building as the creature disappeared around a corner.

Savina narrowed her eyes and shook her head in disgust.

It probably wasn't worth going after, not in a city where she didn't know the unspoken rules or speak the language. Besides, the point of all that was so that one of the creatures would pass on the message to its little friends that Nicolau was off-limits.

"That was … efficient. Horrifying, but efficient," said a dry, amused voice, and Savina turned back, cursing. Had the entire damn crew followed her here?

Joska stood at the entrance to the alley, arms crossed on her chest, one eyebrow quirked. Rafel stood beside her, glowering.

"I'm starting to think Rafel and I are unbelievably lucky to still be alive, honestly," Joska said.

Savina glared at her. "Stay out of this. It's none of your damn business."

Joska raised her eyebrow higher. "I think it is, at least until we get off this planet and back through the portal." Her voice had grown, if possible, even more dry. "I'd hate to see anything happen to my two favourite thieves and murderers before you give me my ship back."

Nicolau was looking back and forth between Savina, Joska, and the fallen aliens, his expression a combination of terror, nausea, and utter bafflement. "Look," he said finally, swallowing hard and turning to Savina. "I'm … very grateful to you for saving my life. But shouldn't we—" he gestured back up the alley.

Savina rolled her eyes. "Yes," she snapped, glaring at Joska. "We should all get back to the others, considering the good captain here seems very uncomfortable leaving us alone." She strode over, grabbed Nicolau's arm, and started hauling him back down the alley the way they'd come.

Beni fell into step with them. "Are you hurt, Vina?" they asked in a small whisper. "Is Nicolau hurt?"

"No," said Savina brusquely. "Everyone's fine."

"Except for the aliens," Beni said.

"Except for them." Savina allowed herself a small smile.

Nicolau was glancing between her and Beni as if he was now unsure which of them he should fear more.

They rounded a corner of the alley that led to the main street.

The last of the stragglers were being herded into the transport, and Savina hesitated a moment.

Still, probably safer to be in the group for now, at least until they figured out what the aliens wanted. It wasn't like she had any desire to go back into that nightmare of a jungle.

"We should be able to slip back in without them noticing—" she began, speaking just loudly enough for Joska and Rafel, behind her, to hear.

Then she stopped short, icy fingers tightening around her chest.

Across the open area where the human survivors were huddled, she caught the faintest flicker of movement in the shadows of an alley.

It was barely visible, unless you were watching for it. But Savina had been born watching. And now her entire body went ice cold.

She recognized that odd grey colour that her eyes wanted to skip over, the lean, elegant form. And she didn't need to see the figure's face to picture the hatred in those icy, slate-hazel eyes, or the thin, dangerous knife-edge of a smile.

Reka Solar. The government agent who'd been pursuing her, armed with a government warrant. Who'd followed her through the damn portal.

Savina stepped backwards quickly, pulling Nicolau and Beni after her out of sight behind the walls.

How the hell had Reka followed her here? Reka was supposed to have died on the diplomatic ship when it broke up.

Her breath was coming oddly quickly, her hands trembling.

"Savina? What's wrong?" There was concern in Joska's voice.

Savina closed her eyes and took a deep breath. When she turned, she was somehow able to keep her voice steady.

"The government agent," she said in a flat tone. "She's followed us."

Emotions flickered over Joska's face—fear, concern, worry—but her expression settled, finally, into that familiar, slightly ironic resignation. "Well," she said at last. "You can't say she doesn't take her job seriously."

Rafel was scowling, his expression even more irritated than was its wont. "Don't expect sympathy from me," he grumbled.

Savina shot him an icy glare. "Believe me," she hissed, "I don't need sympathy from a useless one-legged man with a paunch."

He stared at her for a moment, his expression odd, and there was something under the irritation—something that could have been hurt.

"Savina," said Joska, her voice sharp. "You and I are going to have a talk, very soon."

Savina had seen Joska upset before. But now there was a cold anger in her face that made Savina swallow, and she stared at the captain a moment longer, almost as shaken by her sudden anger as she had been by the sight of Reka.

Joska took a long breath, visibly restraining her temper, and Nicolau cleared his throat.

"Um. I hate to interrupt, but could someone please tell me what the hell is going on?"

As one, they all turned to glare at him.

He looked faintly uncomfortable, but there was a stubborn expression on his face that told Savina her baby brother had no intention of just shutting up and going along.

"I mean, don't get me wrong, I'm very grateful to you for saving my life back on the ship, and then coming after me when that alien grabbed me, but—"

Savina grabbed him by the shoulders, even though he was significantly taller than she was, and turned him to face her. "There is a government agent after me," she said in an icy undertone. "She followed me here, and she's going to try to kill me. I assume she'll try to kill everyone with me as well. Which includes you. So if you like being alive, I suggest you shut the hell up and do as you're told." She grabbed Beni and her brother by the arms and shoved them farther back into the narrow, dirty back alleys of the alien city, well out of sight of the rest of the group.

She wasn't sure if she was irritated or relieved to hear Joska's and Rafel's footsteps following.

"What's the plan, Savina?" the captain asked in her low, calm tone, when at last they came to a halt. "We're not in the Joias system anymore. There's nowhere to run, not if we plan to ever make it back."

Savina glared at her, hoping irritation in her voice would hide the shakiness. "No one asked you to follow me," she snapped.

Joska raised an eyebrow again. "As I recall, someone stole my ship and put me into the crosshairs of that very government agent. I think I have as much vested interest in this as you do at this point."

Savina scowled harder, fighting down the twinge of guilt. "Alright, what do you suggest?"

Joska sighed. "You're not going to want to hear this. But I think our best bet is to talk to Alba. We're behind the portal, trapped in a city full of aliens. Perhaps she won't be impressed by your previous activities, but I sincerely doubt she'll be overly worried about punishing you as things stand. She's the one who issued the warrant against you, and she can put it in abeyance until the issue of the aliens is settled."

Savina stared at the woman, struck speechless for a moment. "You think I should turn myself in to Alba Espina? The Chief Justice?" she said when she'd regained her power of speech. "You honestly think she won't just have me killed where I stand? And what about Beni? And Nicolau, and you, and Rafel? She'll figure out pretty quickly that you're with me."

Joska shook her head. "I'm not saying it's ideal. But from what I hear, Alba has a sense of fairness, at the very least. You've saved several of the ship's crew when you pulled them off the diplomatic ship, and you helped protect the others in the jungle. She may be willing to let bygones be bygones, or at the very least, commute your sentence somewhat when we get back."

Savina was still staring. Her heart beat far too quickly.

Alba Espina. The Judge of Heresies. The woman who had haunted her nightmares since she was a child.

The woman she'd sworn to kill.

"Savina." Joska leaned forward, just a little, and laid a hand on Savina's arm. There was a sympathy in her eyes that almost made Savina sick. "I don't know what got you to where you are," she said quietly. "But the world isn't quite as desperate a place as you seem to believe it is."

Savina took a deep breath, narrowing her eyes.

For Joska, and for people like her, the world wasn't as desperate a place, perhaps. Joska was Orthodox. She was a ship's captain, of a ship she owned herself—or had, until she'd met Savina.

She was the type of person the system was built for.

She had no idea what desperation meant. She had no idea how it felt to spend your childhood terrified, so afraid you could hardly breathe, knowing that any moment the world could come crashing down on you. That if you were ever found, you'd be killed. That if anyone knew who you were, you'd be killed. That there was no one, anywhere, who'd protect you.

She reached up and grabbed Joska's wrist, wrenching the woman's hand off her jacket. "If you plan on talking to Alba," she said through clenched teeth, "you'll have to kill me first."

Rafel gave her a disgusted look that said, as clear as words, that if that happened, he wouldn't regret it.

And then Beni said quietly, "Savina?"

There was a tone in their voice that made Savina look up.

Beni's face was taut, their body tense, and they wore the look of concentration they always had when they were interpreting an unfamiliar reading from their wavelink's echolocator.

And even before Savina turned, she knew, with a heavy dread that sat in the pit of her stomach, what she'd see.

She turned anyway.

She and the others were standing in the intersection of two alleys. And now, three of the alley entrances were filled with the strange, monkey-like aliens.

Each of them carried one of their deadly weapons. And every weapon was pointed at Savina and her companions.

And at the very front of the group, lips pulled back from their teeth in a menacing snarl, shirt stained and dripping with blood, stood the alien that, only a few minutes before, Savina had pinned to the wall with her knife.

4

Alba

By the time the transport reached their apparent destination, a massive cluster of buildings in the centre of the city, Alba's entire body ached. There had been no comfortable seats, and the survivors were practically piled on top of each other.

Ines and Yosip had done their best to make room for her—Istvay seemed mostly focused on keeping Aran from an actual panic attack in the crowded space, with inconclusive results—but her body, already battered and bruised from the escape from the dying ship and then the night in the jungle, felt as she'd imagined a stick-fighter would feel after a particularly bruising competition bout.

She didn't dare look back to see how Feliu and the rest of the injured were doing. There was nothing she could do about it now. And besides, she wasn't certain she could stand to see the pallor of her old clerk's face and the pain in his eyes.

She was here to keep them safe. She was a diplomat and a politician, and everything she'd told the Council back on Colorida, when she'd proposed this mission, was still true—better to meet these aliens with an offer of peace and friendship than a threat. She was still the person best positioned to find a way to keep these survivors alive.

She'd been the reason, or at least part of the reason, so many had died, a tiny voice in the back of her head reminded her.

She had to save these survivors, at least. She had to be able to do at least that.

And she refused to let herself think about how desperate a litany that thought had become.

When the transport finally came to a halt, Alba pushed herself painfully to her feet. She had to lean on Ines for a few steps before her aching legs condescended to hold her up. And then she stepped down the ramp and out into the alien city, blinking at the light after the dimness from inside the windowless transport.

She'd grown up in Vila Nova do Sol, back on Colorida. She'd grown used to the ancient, beautiful stone buildings, the cobblestone streets, the charcoal fires at the corners of alleys where people huddled for warmth in the damp winters or cooked their food in the sultry summer heat. The very age and history of it had sunk into her bones, and she'd always felt the city was a part of her as much as she was a part of it—the minerals in her bones the ones leached off the ancient buildings into the watershed in the heavy spring rains.

This city, though, was something entirely new.

They'd been brought to a long, massive cement courtyard, surrounded by low-roofed buildings and broad streets and lined with towering jungle trees, carefully pruned. The broad main walkway was arched over with a thin, transparent plex, and ended in a large, shallow set of stairs leading up to a massive cluster of buildings.

The buildings were a work of art in and of themselves, towering spun-sugar confections of things, all glass and soaring arches and dizzying height. The metal struts that gave them strength were barely noticeable by a trick of the architecture and the way the light refracted from the glass, so the structures looked to be made of sunlight and air. At street-height, the building walls were a latticework of glass and steel, just enough to keep the interior of the building from being visible, but offering tantalizing glimpses of colour and light from within.

Alba had expected a focused, intense heat under the plex of the courtyard, like the inside of a greenhouse. But something about the way the material fractured and reflected light must have negated the greenhouse effect, because it was no warmer here than it had been in the jungle, and a cool, likely artificial breeze, carrying with it a thick, heady scent of flowers, wafted gently through her sweaty hair.

The faces of the others were drawn with terror or shock as they stumbled from the transport after her, their filthily, blood-stained clothing and exhausted expressions a sharp contrast to the clean, elegant lines in every aspect of the alien city. They stood in a huddled mass until one of the alien guards beckoned them roughly forward.

No one seemed willing to move, so Alba straightened painfully and stepped out ahead.

Her heart was pounding strangely.

For all she knew, these aliens were taking them somewhere to kill them—shoot them with their odd, terrifying weapons or eat their flesh as a delicacy. Every frightening tale parents told their children back on Colorida to frighten them into good behaviour rose nebulously from her memory, like silt stirred up from the bottom of a pond.

It was all nonsense, of course. These creatures, as Istvay had said, were clearly sapient. They had a functional language, and an obvious ability to collaborate in order to accomplish tasks as a group.

And furthermore, their degree of technological advancement equaled or exceeded that of the Joias System. A peaceful communication, a mutual learning of each other's culture, was not only possible, but likely.

Still, the six-year-old version of her, shivering in bed after a night-time story, refused to be convinced.

The alien in the lead gestured impatiently across the courtyard to the large stone steps, and Alba tried not to let a limp show in her walk as she strode forward. Ines jumped after her, sticking to her side like a shadow, and Yosip stepped forward as well. His face was grave, but there was that familiar twinkle of good humour in his eyes, and the sight was unaccountably reassuring.

The others hesitated, but followed at last, taking their cues from her.

She looked around surreptitiously as she made her slow, painful way down the cement walkway. The trees lining the courtyard were large, with gnarled branches spreading a lacework of shade across the bare cement. Unfamiliar, brightly coloured insects and birds fluttered through the air, their songs alien, but the sound vaguely comforting.

When they reached the long, low stairs, the guards brought them to a halt and stopped to confer among themselves in low voices.

Even with the thin, lacy shade from the trees, the sun reflected against the glass of the buildings and glowed through the city force-field, turning the air into a heavy, wet blanket. Sweat dripped, sticky and damp, down the back of Alba's neck, and itched uncomfortably in her hair. The droning chirp of insects was monotonous, and overhead, she could see the progress of the planet's sun, already dipping towards the horizon.

At last, an alien emerged from the building in front of them, the glass seeming to melt open for it to step through then reform behind it. It crossed quickly to the guards and said something sharp. The guards responded respectfully, gesturing at the group of humans while speaking quietly in their chattering language, and at last the newcomer turned to the group.

The creature's eyes roved over the group, and then, after a moment of consideration, it gestured to Alba forward.

She took a deep breath, raised her chin, and stepped out alone from the crowd.

There was something vulnerable and almost naked about standing alone in front of those odd, intense alien gazes, all of them fixed on her.

The newcomer gave a peremptory gesture for her to follow.

Istvay made a sound of protest, and from the corner of her eye she could see Aran step forward as well. The aliens jumped back at his approach, raising their weapons.

"No," Alba snapped. She took a deep breath. "No. Please wait here. I believe it's best to see what they want."

"If I may, Madam," said Yosip quietly from behind her, "it would be prudent to have others accompanying you."

Alba turned, and so did her guide.

Yosip turned to the alien and gestured to Alba, then to himself, then pointed to one or two others. The alien watched him in confusion for a moment, and he tried again, stepping forward and miming following Alba.

Alba's heart was still pounding strangely fast, her pulse thrumming in her ears.

She should protest, probably. They could be merely taking her away to kill her, and in that case, best they take her alone.

But … Yosip was right. Having more people along increased the chances that someone would be left alive to tell the others what had happened. And, she reminded herself, in the more likely case that this was a simple introduction, having more people along would increase the likelihood that they could accomplish their primary objective of, at the very minimum, conveying to their hosts—or captors—their party's urgent need of medical supplies and food and water.

But she couldn't ignore the sick, guilty flood of relief at the thought of not having to step into that wondertale-building alone. She'd read far too many stories, as a child, of what happened in wondertales to the lone child lured into a building of sunlight and spun sugar.

At last, the alien gave a grunt of what appeared to be acquiescence.

"I'll come, of course, Madam," said Yosip in a low voice. "And who else?"

"You—you brought me here to help with the language," said Ines in a small voice. "I—I should probably come too."

"I'm coming," said Istvay bluntly. "None of you are scientists, and you might need me."

"Pishti," Aran began, starting forward after Istvay.

Immediately, their guards jumped back again, their faces taking on an expression of what could only be called terror as they chattered over their shoulders to the newcomer.

Ani, still perched on Aran's shoulder, was growling softly.

Perhaps, Alba thought wryly, the uniting characteristic that bound all sapient life forms in the universe was, in the end, being afraid of Ani.

The other guards raised their weapons, pointing them at the remainder of the survivors, and Aran hesitated.

"You stay here, Aran," said Istvay quietly. "I'll go. Ani's never going to let you leave her here without you, and the aliens aren't going to let her anywhere near them, not if they're smart. Besides, we don't want them to change their minds and vaporize the rest of the group while we're gone." Istvay's face was grim, but they didn't appear particularly frightened. At least, not of the aliens.

Aran looked more than a little unhappy, but Alba didn't give him time to protest. "Istvay is right," she said briskly. "Someone needs to stay here and protect the others, and you're best positioned to do so, as long as you have that nightmare-beast on your shoulder."

Istvay shot her a look that was almost gratitude, then turned back to Aran. "I'll be fine, I promise," they said in a low voice. "If they'd wanted to kill us, there are a hundred ways they could have already." Then Istvay stepped up to join the tiny diplomatic party.

"If you're not back by nightfall, I'm damn well coming in after you," said Aran, his jaw set.

Istvay glanced around at the alien guards. "I'm not going to argue with that," they muttered.

Alba couldn't help a quick glance backwards at Feliu as she turned to follow her alien guide.

He'd be furious she was going without him, if he was in any state to know about it.

He likely wasn't. His eyes were closed, his face drawn, and he looked either asleep or unconscious. He'd be of no use to anyone, including himself, unless she was able to somehow convey their desperate need for medical care, food, water, and shelter.

Their alien guide looked at the four of them skeptically, but at last made a small motion that could have been a shrug and gestured again for them to follow.

Two other guards fell in behind Alba and the other three, their weapons held ready.

Alba forced the tension from her posture. She'd been in politics long enough to know how dangerous it was to show fear.

No matter how much fear you might feel.

They followed their guide to the blank glass of the building. The creature rubbed the pad of a finger along the surface, and the glass seemed to dissolve, opening up an entrance a little wider than a doorway back on Colorida.

Alba stepped through after the alien, despite visions of the glass reforming through the centre of her body.

It didn't, but somehow, that fact didn't calm her nerves as much as it might have.

The inside of the building they'd entered was a massive open space, with hallways leading off to each side. The ceiling was of that strange, refracting, glass-like material that let through light and glimpses of movement from the upper stories of the building, but no clear sight.

She had to bite back a quick, absurd snort of laughter at the thought that if the glass did give you a clear view, it would necessitate either a different uniform than the loose tunics for the aliens walking on the floors above them, or an entirely more intimate view of the alien civilization than she'd really wished for.

The wide, airy hallways stretching out from the main floor of the building seemed almost more passageways than interior hallways, connecting the buildings together seamlessly like tunnels in an anthill.

"They don't seem to like the idea of being out under the sky, do they?" Istvay whispered from behind her. "Between the tunnels and the force-field and the canopy over the courtyard, it seems like they're avoiding it as hard as they can."

Their alien guide brought them to a circular patch of floor in one corner that seemed to be made of a mosaic of glass tiles, and when they'd all stepped onto it, their guide licked its finger and made a complicated gesture in the air.

The air surrounding the mosaic turned to a solid tube, closing them in, and Alba's stomach dropped as they shot upwards.

Despite the fact that the feeling under her feet was almost of something solid, their pace was rapid, and the floors of the building around them flashed by. At last, however, they slowed, and at another gesture from their guide, another mosaic floor formed under their feet at what appeared to be floor-level several stories farther up, and the transparent tube around them melted away.

Their guide gestured them forward, and again, they followed.

"Ines," said Alba in a low voice. "Do you have any sense at all as to what they're saying?"

Ines shook her head mutely, her eyes wide. "If—if I could even get a few words to reference, I could find something, maybe, but—" She trailed off.

The hallways through which they were being led made Alba almost dizzy with vertigo. She wasn't one to be afraid of heights, but here, where the walls, ceiling, and floor were translucent as glass, it was difficult not to feel that you'd been pushed off a slide, and were in that breathless, heart-stopping instant before your body realized what had happened and your stomach dropped with the fall.

The alien leading them came to a halt, and again traced a pattern on the glass. It dissolved, and the aliens stepped through, beckoning Alba and her small retinue after them.

The inside of the room was as unfamiliar as everything else on this planet: translucent walls and floor, cushions rested upon delicate stepped tiers that wound their way around the back of the room and up towards the ceiling.

Other aliens, the fineness of their dress leading Alba to believe that they were even more important than a group that had led her here, sat comfortably on the tiers, watching her small company as they stumbled inside. The guards gestured the humans to a handful of stools, squat, but covered with cushions that looked luxuriantly soft after the two days of nothing but the damp jungle floor.

Alba hesitated a moment, then took her seat, and Yosip and the others followed suit.

For a few long moments, the humans and the aliens studied each other.

Alba couldn't tell the aliens' ages. Even if she'd been able to, she had no idea what would be considered old on this planet. But the creatures seated in front of her had a certain dignity to their bearing that seemed to denote a high social rank. Their tunics were fine and gauzy and covered in delicate embroidery, and Alba was acutely aware of her own filthy, stained travel clothing, the tangles in her hair and the dirt and grime caked on her skin.

At length another alien came in, bearing a platter of what looked like fruits of some sort. They stopped in front of Alba and hung the tray on a hook cleverly concealed on the wall. The alien seated on the highest stool in front of them made a low, humming sound, watching them, and gestured to the platter, then mimed putting food in its mouth.

"Istvay?" asked Alba, after a moment of hesitation.

Istvay took a fruit carefully and sniffed it. They broke the skin with their finger, licked it, frowning, and gave a small shrug. "I don't have the equipment with me to test it. But it's not bitter, and it looks like it's the same thing they're eating. Based on their physiology, I'd be willing to risk it."

The alien gestured again impatiently, then pulled a fruit off its own platter and bit into it.

"I suppose it's eat or starve at this point," said Yosip. "And my stomach is informing me it would prefer to eat." He turned to Alba. "With your permission, Madam?"

She nodded, and he took one of the fruits off the platter, and, following the example of the alien, pulled back the skin and bit into it. A sharp, sour, tangy-sweet smell burst in her nostrils at the small spray of juice, and Alba found her own stomach growling painfully.

Yosip chewed and swallowed, then turned back to them with a small grin. "At the very least, it doesn't seem to cause immediate death," he said, that ever-present twinkle of humour in his voice.

Alba hesitated again for a moment, then took a fruit as well, and Ines followed suit.

The fruit was as delicious as it smelled, cool and tangy and sweet, and by the time she'd finished, Alba found she wasn't quite as shaky as she had been.

The aliens on the other side of the room watched them as they ate, talking and gesticulating amongst themselves at the party of humans as if they were inanimate objects being haggled over.

And then a doorway appeared in the back of the room, the glass melting away, and everyone fell silent.

Another group of the white-clad aliens stepped inside, their heads downcast, their movements almost subservient. They were followed by a smaller alien, its clothes so pale they appeared almost to glow. Its movements were slow and careful and its face was creased with deep wrinkles.

The servants stepped back, and the alien approached their party, steps slow and deliberate. It paused in front of Alba, studying her carefully, and again, she was painfully aware of her filthy, desperate state.

The alien widened its eyes in the gesture that seemed to serve as a greeting. After a moment's hesitation, Alba did the same.

The alien made a soft humming noise. And then it opened its mouth and, in slow, careful tones, said, "Welcome, humans. We would very much like to know why you have come."

For a moment, Alba couldn't believe her own ears.

She glanced at the others, who looked as flabbergasted as she did. Then she turned back to the alien.

The words it had used were an older form of Common Dialect, mostly recognizable from ancient texts and classic literature—the unofficial common tongue that, stories had it, had been passed down from the language understood, at one time, by all the inhabitants of the generation ships. They still used it now and again in their periodic broadcasts to their sister-ships' colonies, messages that would take up to a decade to be received and then another to be answered.

As a politician, she knew the dialect well.

What she didn't know was how the aliens knew it.

5

Aran

Aran stood abruptly, unable to force himself to sit even one second longer.

Damn Istvay to hell. They knew damn well going into an unknown alien edifice with Alba could get them killed. They just didn't care. They were set on finding a way to open the portal again, Aran and his opinions be damned.

One of the guards shifted uneasily at his sudden movement, and Ani's growls increased in volume, her bulbous eyes fixed on the alien. The alien stepped back quickly, its expression stiff with fear.

Aran sighed heavily and reached up, rubbing Ani's head. "It's alright, sweetheart," he said, trying to reassure himself as much as her. "Istvay'll be fine. They won't do anything stupid."

At least, he hoped they wouldn't.

Three weeks ago, he would have been confident in his assessment. Istvay wasn't like him, liable to get so caught up in what they were doing that they forgot practical considerations. Istvay was the steady one, the solid one, the one who remembered things like packing food, and how much water they'd need for a three-day expedition.

But …

He drew in a long breath and stroked Ani's tentacles, her tight, nervous grip on him relaxing a little at his touch.

He'd never seen Istvay like they'd been since the two of them had started this mission. He'd never imagined Istvay standing in their cabin, eyes closed, fists clenched, clearly on the verge of breaking down completely.

Istvay was falling apart. And Aran had no idea what that even meant, or how to deal with things if Istvay wasn't the patient, stoic, practical one. He wasn't sure he had it in him to be that person, if Istvay lost it.

He took a deep breath and forced himself to kneel next to the unconscious Feliu. The man was laid prone on the hard concrete, along with the other badly injured members of their group, their heads pillowed on jackets donated by the other survivors.

The old clerk looked terrible, his face wan, his breathing shallow. He'd been doing much better that morning, but the combination of the heat and the lack of shelter seemed to have whittled down his strength to nearly nothing. Aran pressed his fingers to the side of Feliu's throat, the injured man's pulse thrumming weak and rapid under his hand.

Beside him, one of the crew members looked up, exhaustion on her face. "He's not going to last much longer, not if we don't get help," she said quietly. "Nor will the others."

Aran nodded. "I'll try again to get us some supplies. None of the injured are going to last much longer like this."

The woman watched him with dull, pleading eyes, and he rose wearily to his feet.

The guards stepped quickly back as he approached, raising their weapons with expressions of something like panic. He frowned, then realized they were staring at Ani, who'd puffed herself up and was starting to hiss menacingly.

He sighed and held out his arm, and reluctantly, Ani slithered down to envelop his forearm, the bags under her eyes puffed out angrily.

The guards took another step back, and Aran shook his head. "She'd—she'd perfectly tame. She won't to hurt you, not unless you provoke her." He reached out, keeping his movements slow and careful, and stroked Ani's head, then lifted her up to his face, rubbing his cheek against her warm, bulbous body to demonstrate how harmless she was.

The guards still had their weapons drawn, but now they were staring at him instead of Ani, as if they thought he might be insane.

"She's tame, see, she's very friendly," he tried, tickling her under the chin.

She growled, tightening her tentacles around his arm, and he said sharply, "Ani! Cut it out."

She was still hissing, but reluctantly, she loosened her grip. He shook his head at her in disapproval, and she slunk sulkily back up his arm and onto his shoulder.

The guards were looking at Aran as though he'd become more terrifying than his pet.

He sighed again and gestured to the huddled groups of humans. "We need water," he said slowly. He spoke the same way he'd speak to an unpredictable animal out in the field—it wasn't the words so much as the tone of voice, calm and unthreatening. "Water," he repeated, then mimed drinking from a bottle.

The aliens were staring at him, but they whispered back and forth, pointing at Ani in obvious fear. At last one of them stepped away, returning a few moments later with a soft jug. It placed it on the ground and backed away carefully, its eyes fixed on Ani.

Aran shook his head in resignation, but stepped forward to retrieve the jug.

Among so many, the jug of water was emptied quickly, but when Aran returned and placed the empty container on the ground, the aliens replaced it with a full one with impressive alacrity.

Whatever they'd decided he'd do to them if they didn't cooperate seemed to be a potent threat.

Every time there was a movement from the direction of the buildings, he found himself jerking his head up, his gaze pulled unconsciously to where Istvay and the others had disappeared. After about the seventeenth time, he shook his head and pushed the heels of his hands against his eyes.

He was being ridiculous. Istvay was fine.

He couldn't seem to convince his nerves of it, though.

Finally, he stood and paced restlessly along the base of the stairs.

The open courtyard they'd been brought through must be some sort of public square or park, because the area had grown crowded with pedestrians. The aliens stayed a respectful distance back from the guards, but they were clearly curious, watching the strangers with their large, wide eyes.

He didn't realize how tense he was until he felt Ani's tentacles tightening along his shoulders in response.

"Ani," he said warningly, and she loosened her grip with reluctance.

She was just as nervous as he was.

Then he frowned, cocking his head to the side.

In the courtyard, a small group of alien children were playing a sort of clapping game.

And the song they were chanting was hauntingly familiar.

He listened closer, frowning.

It was almost exactly the same as a song he had Istvay and their small, ragged handful of friends had sung in the streets back in Colorida when they were kids.

He had to be imagining things.

He glanced back at their alien guards, feeling suddenly very cold.

Two different cultures. From two entirely separate galaxies.

There was no way that their children would know the same tune by coincidence.

And as he listened more closely, he could pick out words— garbled, almost unintelligible unless you knew what to listen for, but words nonetheless—in the old form of Common Dialect, the one they used to share scientific discoveries between the colony ships.

"River rock, cold as stone, where's the place you call your home? Charcoal brick, hot as fire, who's the one that you desire? If you're sweet you get a kiss, if you're not you end like this: turn around, touch the ground, we will kick you out of town."

His breath was coming too fast, and he recognized it absently—he was either afraid or excited, his endocrine system didn't differentiate.

He could vaguely make out, through the crowd, the circle of children singing and clapping. Alien children, from an alien planet, singing the same words he and Istvay had sung years ago and light-years away.

And then one of the children jumped up, and the song broke off as they ran. The child in the centre grabbed the small ball used to tag the others out and threw it after the fleeing child. It hit a tree limb, bounced, and soared up into the air, landing in the courtyard next to Aran.

Aran bent to retrieve it automatically, and then almost dropped it again in cold shock.

There was a mark on it. A manufacturer's mark, just like the marks on the toys and books used by the children through Colorida.

The mark wasn't familiar, but the lettering underneath was. He'd seen that name not long ago, the last time he and Istvay had come back to del Sol to purchase supplies for their trip to the outer-rim volcano.

Labirinto.

The name of one of the colonies from a sister generation-ship. The colony they hadn't heard from in decades.

No one knew what it happened to it, or why the people there weren't answering. The hope had been that it was simply a matter of malfunctioning equipment. But he'd seen on the faces of the other scientists that, despite their optimistic words, they feared it was something much worse.

Who knew, really, what lurked in the outer reaches of space?

His hands were shaking slightly. He slipped the ball into his supplies pouch and reached up to rub Ani's head. "It's going to be alright," he whispered. "Everything's going to be alright."

But this time, he didn't even try to pretend it was Ani he was trying to reassure.

The brilliant orange-red streaks of sunset had flared upwards against the deepening blue of the sky when a small group of aliens, dressed in white shifts with embroidered hints of delicate, subtle blues and greens, stepped out of the building where Alba and Istvay and the others had disappeared.

Aran jumped up from where he'd been seated near Feliu, and Ani, who'd settled into a dejected lump on his shoulder, perked up with a low, growling hiss.

The newcomers conversed quickly with the guards, then stepped back, revealing Istvay standing in the centre, their eyes frantically scanning the crowd.

The relief that flooded Aran's body at the sight was almost enough to make him weak.

"Istvay!" he called, and Istvay's head jerked up.

Their posture relaxed visibly when they saw Aran. "Is everyone alright here?" they asked, their voice tense.

Aran shrugged helplessly. "We managed to talk the guards into giving us water, at least, but Feliu and the others aren't in good shape. You? What did—"

Istvay shook their head shortly. "We can talk later. They brought me out so I could fetch the rest of you. They said … they said since we're here on a diplomatic mission, they'd like to put us up in some more comfortable quarters."

Aran crossed over to his friend, and the guards stepped back at his approach, raising their weapons.

He ignored them.

"Istvay," he said quietly. "There's … something I need to tell you. Something here isn't right."

"I know," said Istvay, lowering their voice. "I know. But—" They glanced around at the others, and Aran followed their gaze.

He drew in a long breath.

Istvay was right. Even if they could escape, where would they go? The badly injured were unlikely to last the night without care.

"Yeah," he said at last. "You're right. We'll talk inside."

"Come on, help me get them up." Istvay's tone was grim.

Together, Aran and Istvay and the rest of the able-bodied members of the crew got the injured to their feet.

"Where's that woman, Joska? She was helping earlier, wasn't she?" asked Istvay, glancing around.

Aran frowned. "I haven't seen her since we got here."

Istvay shook their head, lips tight. "Maybe she saw her chance and made a break for it. I can't blame her. We'll just have to hope it's that, and not that she got herself killed somehow between the jungle and here."

Aran nodded, biting the inside of his cheek.

But there was nothing they could do about it now.

The aliens waited patiently, and when they were all on their feet, gestured them forward. They were led through the courtyard and into one of the low-roofed buildings off to one side, and it wasn't until they were inside, with hazy, floating lights illuminating the passageways, that Aran realized how dark it had grown.

He glanced over at Istvay as they walked, but Istvay seemed lost in their own thoughts, the worry that had never really left their face since the moment Aran had told them about this damn mission cutting a sharp line between their brows.

The survivors were deposited at last in a large, circular room, with short, dead-end hallways running off to each side, with doors along them—likely bedchambers. There was another room, rectangular and encased by glass so that it could easily be seen from the rotunda, with what were unmistakably medical cots and equipment laid out. Two of the aliens stepped forward, taking Feliu and the other injured members of the party from the rest of the crew, and situated them comfortably onto the small, sterile-looking cots.

"They've sent in … I don't know, veterinarians, from what I gathered," said Istvay, a wry note in their voice. "Probably the best option, considering I have no idea how similar their physiology is to ours." They sighed and laid a hand on Aran's arm. "Come on. Alba and the others are in the far room."

There was something in their voice that made Aran look at them sharply.

He followed Istvay into the small room where Alba, Ines, and Yosip waited, seated on the ubiquitous cushioned stools. Istvay gestured him to a seat, and sat as well.

"What happened?" asked Aran, looking around at the tense faces of the others.

Istvay shook their head uneasily, glancing at Alba. "The aliens had an interpreter who could speak our language. Ines says it's hypothetically possible they could have a translation program that could pick up our language and translate it in a matter of hours, but this seemed like—something else. And even if they'd had a program, the dialect they were speaking wasn't the one we use."

Aran nodded absently, chewing on the inside of his cheek. "It was the old dialect, right?"

Istvay turned to him, frowning. "What—"

"Pishti," he said. "Do you remember that generation-ship colony in the Labirinto System, the one we missed our last contact with?"

Istvay's frown deepened. "What are you saying?"

"I heard some alien children outside the gates this afternoon. They were playing a clapping game." He hummed the tune, and Istvay started violently.

"Are … you sure you weren't mishearing?" they asked at last.

Aran shook his head again. "I don't know their language, but I'm pretty sure it doesn't have words in it like this." He sang a few bars of the ditty.

Istvay was still staring at him, their face pale. From the corner of his eye, Aran could see the others staring as well.

"That's not all," he continued. He reached into his pouch and pulled out the ball with the maker's mark, and tossed it to his friend.

Istvay stared at it, turning it over and over in their hands. At last they handed it over to Alba, their face drawn with shock.

For a few long moments, as Alba handled the object then handed it on, there was utter silence in the room. Aran forced himself to focus on Istvay, their familiar, concerned brown eyes framed by dark lashes, because if he didn't, he wasn't certain that the terror of this whole thing wouldn't simply rise up and swallow him whole.

When Alba spoke, her voice was sharp. "I suppose, then, we must assume these aliens have been in contact with humans prior to us."

Istvay's expression was grim. "I don't think that's all we can assume. There are aliens here who understand our language, and their children play human games. But I haven't seen a single sign of a human besides us since our arrival. If they'd wanted to speak with us, sending out a human to open communications would be their easiest option, if there were humans here. Living ones, at any rate."

There was another long moment of silence, and the unease that had been twisting, formless and insubstantial, in Aran's chest, crystallized into a cold, sharp dread.

"You make a valid point, Istvay." Even Yosip's friendly face was creased in concern. "But we can't assume, necessarily, that they attacked or killed the Labirinto settlement. It's possible they had peaceful contact with them, and that's where their familiarity with humanity comes from."

"Possible, yes. But even you must admit it's unlikely," said Alba.

Yosip gave her a small smile. "Perhaps you're right. But I don't believe in borrowing trouble until we need it." He glanced around the room. "And right now, I don't think we need any more trouble than we have. We're trapped here until we find a way to get them to open the portal, and even if they'd let us go, I don't think much of our chances in the jungle."

Alba nodded slowly. "However the aliens learned our language, our original mission must be paramount. We must negotiate with these creatures, and do our best to persuade them to interact with our society on peaceful terms. That, obviously, is our first objective. However …" she paused a moment. "However, before we negotiate for the reopening of the portal, we must find out what they truly want. Because if they did, in fact, enter into hostilities with another human settlement—" she closed her eyes for just a moment, and for just a moment Aran could see the exhaustion and weariness and something that was almost despair written across her features.

But when she opened her eyes again, her voice was firm. "If they have hostile intentions against humanity, our mission must be to find a way to keep them from reopening the portal at all."

There was a long moment of silence.

At last, Yosip nodded. "I agree with your caution, Madam," he said. "We'd do well to be wary of their motives. But the portal was open for several days, and besides the box, nothing was sent through. We were the ones who came to them, not the other way around. This gives some credence to the idea that this might be no more than a misunderstanding. And if they can reopen the portal, as we assume, then we may not be able to prevent them from doing it if we wished to. Diplomacy may be the only hope, not only for those of us stranded here, but for the Joias System itself."

Istvay raised their head. The gesture was so weary that Aran reached out an unconscious hand to steady them. They gave him a brief smile, then turned to Alba, their face set in its familiar stubborn lines. Their eyes were dark with worry, their hair pulling out of its ponytail and plastered to their skin with sweat, smudges of dirt across their face and the dark circles under their eyes making them look younger than they were, tired and uncertain.

"I honestly don't know that we have another choice, at this point," they said quietly. "Have you seen the shape some of the people in our party are in? We're at these aliens' mercy, whether we like it or not. So I guess if diplomacy can keep us alive …" They gave an exhausted shrug.

"Aran? What's your verdict?" asked Yosip quietly.

Aran took a long breath.

He had no idea whether the aliens would be ultimately hostile, or friendly. But at the end of the day, none of it changed one cold fact: what these creatures had sent through the portal weeks earlier had shown that they were familiar with the genetic defect that was slowly killing Istvay, and that they'd found a cure for it. And for that—well, he'd happily ignore everything else.

His verdict had been set from the moment he'd agreed to come on this mission.

"I agree," he said in a flat voice. "We stay."

He could feel Istvay's eyes on him, and he could picture the worry on their face.

It didn't matter, though. He'd told Alba, back on the escape pod— he was here to find a cure for the defect. A cure for Istvay. Anything else was irrelevant.

"Very well," said Alba at last. "I'm meeting with their ambassador tomorrow. Tonight we should eat and rest, and regain as much of our strength and our wits as we can. If the fate of the Joias System and every person living there depends on our making the correct decisions, I'd prefer those decisions be made with all our faculties present." She paused, then added, in a voice so low she could have been talking to herself, "And may the Great Mystery keep and preserve us all."

6

Savina

Savina stepped forward quickly, her heart beating hard and fast, to shield her baby brother with her body—well, as much as she could, since he had about twenty centimetres on her in height.

"Beni," she whispered into her wavelink. "I'll take out the leader. You grab Nicolau, and—"

Someone touched her arm, and she looked up, startled, her hand gripping the knife at her belt.

Joska stood beside her, face grim. "Listen to me, Savina," she said quietly. "You've seen what their weapons do. If you fight, you'll die."

"And if I don't fight, we all die," Savina hissed. She forced her innocent smile. "Besides, you have no idea how efficient I can be when I need to."

Joska shook her head, something so close to sympathy in her eyes that it made Savina's stomach twist. "You'd be sacrificing yourself for nothing. There's no guarantee any of us will get out either way, but if they'd wanted us dead, they'd have killed us already. It's worth seeing what they do want."

Savina hesitated.

Joska gave her a wry look. "Some of us don't use killing as our go-to option in our day-to-day interactions. It is possible to negotiate tricky situations without anyone dying. Trust me on this, okay?"

Savina tightened her fist around the knife.

The aliens gripped their own weapons tighter.

Damn it to hell.

She didn't trust Joska. She couldn't trust her.

And yet—

Slowly, she loosened her grip on her knife, dropping her hands back to her side.

Joska gave a faint nod of approval. She stepped up beside Savina, her own hands empty of weapons, and Savina noticed how Joska's movement had positioned the woman between Nicolau and the aliens as well.

As if she understood how important it was to Savina to keep him safe.

She bit back the traitorous trickle of gratitude in her chest.

Damn Joska to the Void.

"Beni," she whispered. "We'll have to do what the good captain says, since we've just given up our other options. Let's hope she's as smart as she thinks she is." She made no effort to disguise the sarcasm in her tone.

The alien in the front of the group, blood still running down its shoulder and soaking its tunic, gave a growling command. Its eyes, fixed on Savina, were bright with hostility, but it didn't fire its weapon.

Two aliens came forward and patted the humans down with brusque efficiency. They removed several of Savina's knives, her pulse gun, her pistol, her pouch of electric tranqs, a bolas, three restraints, and various other accoutrements.

Joska watched with raised eyebrows, and Savina glowered at her.

"If we die because of you—" Savina hissed, as the aliens turned their attention to Beni.

"From what I saw there, if you'd tripped, you'd have killed every last one of us on accident," said the woman dryly.

The aliens disarmed Joska next. It was a much shorter process—a pistol and bush-blade, and a couple of restraints stored carefully in her jacket pocket.

Nicolau carried no weapons except for the ship's utility blade strapped to the belt of his uniform.

"One utility knife. Hard to believe he's our brother," Savina muttered into Beni's line on her wavelink.

Beni gave her a small smile, but Savina could see the fear in their expression.

When the aliens had finished disarming the five of them, they wrenched the humans' hands behind their back and bound them together with some sort of clip-on restraint.

"What the hell do you want?" growled Savina to the alien who was binding her—the one with the bloody tunic. It glared back and snarled something in its own language that could have been an answer, or could have been a threat.

Then a thick strip of fabric was tied over Savina's eyes, blocking out all but a faint sliver of light from the gap where it lifted over the bridge of her nose. The alien barked a command, and Savina was shoved forward, the hard muzzle of an alien weapon pressed against her back.

The streets, as pretty as they looked from a distance, were neither smooth nor clean, judging from the number of times Savina stumbled.

She could hear the others stumbling along beside her.

"So, Captain, how many times have you negotiated with people who couldn't speak your damn language?" Savina snapped at Joska through her wavelink. "Maybe your brilliant idea wasn't so brilliant after all."

"Considering the alternative was instant death, I'm comfortable with my choice."

Savina could almost see the woman's wry expression, the twitch of amusement in the corner of her mouth.

She scowled harder.

At last the aliens pulled them roughly to a halt. Savina could feel bruises rising along her entire damn body from where she'd bumped into walls or stubbed her toes against detritus in the street.

Their captors were consulting, not bothering to keep their voices down. Not that it mattered. She couldn't understand a word they were saying. But they seemed to come to a decision at last, because again someone barked a command, and she felt herself shoved forward once more.

"Vina, it's—"

Beni's voice through the wavelength was a moment too late. Savina stumbled as the ground disappeared from under her, and would have fallen all the way down what appeared to be a flight of stairs had one of the aliens not grabbed her arm roughly and yanked her back upright.

She stepped more cautiously this time, feeling for the next stair-step down with her foot.

Her whole body was trembling, from the shock of the near fall, and—well, and everything that had gone before it.

She bit down hard on her teeth.

This wasn't the time to fall apart. That could come later. Right now she had to keep herself and her siblings and that idiot ship's captain and her crew alive.

Behind them, she could hear the *click* of a door latching shut. The air here was cool and clammy, a sharp contrast from the thick, suffocating heat of the city streets. She was prodded down a corridor, and then another, and then another long set of stairs before she was at last jerked to a stop and the blindfold yanked from her eyes.

She barely had time to catch a brief, confused glimpse of a small, dank room, and then she was pushed towards a rope ladder that led into a hole in the ground.

Disarmed and disoriented, she hardly had a choice. She went, and the others followed.

When she reached the bottom, she blinked in the darkness, trying to orient herself to her surroundings.

They were in a small, bare space that seemed to have been hollowed out of dirt and rock. It was cool, and unpleasantly clammy, and the only feature it seemed to boast was the trap door above them.

Rafel, the last one down, stepped unsteadily down onto the floor. The rope ladder was pulled up and the trapdoor slammed closed, and even that bit of light disappeared.

For a while, none of them spoke.

"Well, one similarity between these bastards and humans," Rafel grumbled at last. "We both have similar ideas on what to do with people we don't like."

"Let's hope so, anyway," said Beni. "There was—I mean, I've heard stories about aliens eating people they captured."

Savina rolled her eyes in the darkness.

Beni and their romance stories.

"Beni," she asked. "What's the cell like?"

Beni paused. "It's not very big—four metres by four metres,

maybe? The walls are rough enough that it seems like it was just hollowed out of the ground. The roof is maybe two metres or so over my head if I was standing up, and the trapdoor seems to be the only entrance or exit."

"Thanks," said Savina shortly.

Thank goodness for Beni's echolocator. Sometimes, knowing your surroundings was as good as a weapon.

And—Savina reached down gently to touch the thin, needle-like electric blade tucked into the seam of her trousers, on the inside of her calf.

It wasn't much. But at least it was backup, for when Joska's stupid plan failed.

"Well, I don't know about the rest of you, but I'd almost be okay with the aliens eating us, as long as they fed us first." Nicolau's voice was trying to be stoic, but there was a note to it that told Savina his feigned nonchalance was mostly an attempt to stave off panic.

She turned her head towards him in the dark.

He seemed hardly changed from the child he'd been at five years old. Aside from his height and the way his voice had deepened, he had that same naïve, cheerful innocence that made her want to both grab him in her arms and protect him, and hit him in the face for being such an idiot.

"I'd trade all the food they'd give us in exchange for eating you for a bottle of water anyway," she grumbled at last.

There was a moment of silence, then Nicolau laughed, a surprised, friendly, pleasant sound. He seemed startled that she'd deigned to speak to him at all.

She rolled her eyes and settled back against the clammy wall of their cell.

"Captain," said Rafel at last, quietly. "Do you suppose they'll just leave us in here to die?"

Joska shifted, and when she spoke, Savina was surprised at the weariness in her tone.

"They'll take us out, eventually," she said. "They wouldn't have taken the trouble of bringing us here alive if they didn't want something with us."

Savina realized, suddenly, that she hadn't seen the woman take even a moment to rest or eat since they'd fled the dying ship, however long ago that had been. And Joska certainly wasn't superhuman.

Rafel grunted. "Let's just hope Beni isn't right about their intentions."

Joska chuckled. "After the last few days we've had, I doubt anyone would look at us and start drooling."

Savina found she was smiling unconsciously at the familiar, friendly banter.

It had been so long—almost her whole life, really—since she'd had anyone other than Beni she could talk to. That she could trust enough to banter with, and not calculate every word that came out of her mouth.

The thought sparked a strange jolt of longing, and she pushed it away determinedly.

There was a reason she couldn't trust anyone.

She tamped down the strange, uneasy restlessness at the memory of the holodiscs she'd found in Alba's safe, while she was lying in wait to kill the woman. Before the mutiny had sparked, dragging her and the others down with it.

It wasn't true. There was no way that what she'd read there was true—that the stories she'd heard her whole life in the compound, of how the Orthodox Church was lying in wait with secret plans to murder the Corpus Dai Old Believers, were no more than stories. The discs had to have been a lie. A trap of some sort, something planted there to get her to let down her guard.

But that didn't get rid of that small, nagging tug of unease in the back of her brain.

She gave an exasperated sigh, tipping her head back against the cold cell wall.

It didn't matter. Until they got out of whatever the hell situation they'd gotten into here, none of it mattered at all.

Nicolau cleared his throat uncomfortably. "I'm—sorry."

Savina looked up, startled.

"I—if that thing hadn't have grabbed me, or you hadn't come after me—"

"Shut up," said Savina, rolling her eyes.

There were a few moments of silence. "And Savina," he continued at last. "Um. I mean, I'm very grateful, but why did you —"

"I said, shut up!" She scowled at her brother in the darkness, even though he probably couldn't see.

This was neither the time nor the place to break the news to him about who his real family was.

She'd prefer never to break that particular news to him, if she could help it.

For a while, no one spoke.

And then a sound from above made Savina jump, and she looked up in time to see an outline of light edge the trap door as it was pulled back.

The ladder was dropped down again, and the aliens barked something from above.

Savina looked around at the others and stood, but Nicolau

stepped in front of her, jaw set in determination. He hoisted himself easily up the ladder, and Savina followed, clenching her teeth to keep from swearing at her brother's stubbornness.

The others followed, and at last they were standing in a huddled group in the corridor.

The alien waiting for them at the top was the one Savina had injured. It had changed its clothing, but there was the bulk of a bandage under its tunic, and it held its arm as if it hurt.

Savina met the creature's gaze, and smirked. The alien narrowed its eyes, glaring at her with enough hostility she could almost feel the heat of the glare.

At least some languages seemed to be universal, even in this hellscape.

The alien grabbed her by the arm and turned, snapping something over its shoulder. It shoved Savina, and she stumbled forwards, the muzzle of the alien's weapon firmly between her ribs.

She could hear the others stumbling after her.

They went up two sets of stairs, and then another, and then another, until last they were being pushed down a corridor that had once, probably, been brightly lit. It was built of a glass-like substance that reflected the light strangely, but it was old and grimy, as if it hadn't been cleaned for some time.

Savina's guide pulled her roughly to a halt in front of a door and called in a respectful singsong. The tone was repeated back a moment later, and her captor shoved the door open and pushed Savina inside.

Savina glanced around quickly as she entered.

In front of her, there was a rising, winding column of seats in a stair-step pattern, the design as airy and delicate as the rest of the architecture in this city. The seats were empty, except for the one in the centre.

And Savina knew at once that this was who they'd been brought to see.

There was something universal and unmistakable about the lazy slouch of the creature's posture, the half-lidded eyes, the way it lounged back, watching the room. Guards stood on each side, weapons levelled at Savina and her companions, but the figure on the seat seemed unbothered.

The seated alien gestured lazily to a cluster of squat stools on the floor, and Savina's guard shoved her into the seat. The other humans were directed, with a little less roughness, to their own seats.

Savina's breath was coming quickly, but she forced herself to appear relaxed.

It wouldn't be easy to get at her concealed blade, bound as she was. But not easy didn't mean impossible. If she could just tuck her leg far enough back, she could lean down as if she was scratching an itch or rubbing a bruise and palm it. And then she only needed to get herself close enough to the alien boss—

The alien who'd taken her captive and the boss were apparently having a detailed discussion—the boss kept making the small humming sounds, while Savina's captor was clearly growing more and more irate.

Savina let herself slump a little, as if she was too weary to sit up straight, and tucked her feet under the stool as far back as she could.

Not quite close enough.

She let her shoulders drop lower, yawning hugely. The guards stiffened at her movement, then relaxed.

She hid a smile.

And then a light, singsong voice said, with an air of command that was almost incongruous to the delicacy of the tone, "Human. It seems you and I have some matters to discuss."

Savina jerked her head up, blinking in complete shock.

The alien looked down at her from its seat, an unmistakable satisfaction in its posture at her discomfiture.

"What, human? Do you not understand your own language?" The creature's accent was strange and unfamiliar—closer to a Mountain Dialect accent, although wasn't really that, either—and its manner of speaking was stilted and odd. But the words were unmistakable for all that.

Savina blinked out of her shock and said, her voice only a little unsteady, "I don't discuss things with people who are trying to kill me."

It was childish, probably, but she was too surprised to think of a better retort.

The alien hummed softly. "If I'd wanted to kill you, you'd already be dead. So I suggest you talk while you have the chance."

"What do you want to talk about, then?" snapped Savina. She could feel Joska's warning gaze, but between the strain and the exhaustion and fear of the last few days, she could hardly be bothered to care.

"We saw a group of humans being brought through our city, and I instructed my people to bring one of the bigger ones here so I could make them an offer. I could use their help with our ... business." There was a tiniest hesitation before the word.

"Your business. You're a crime boss," Savina said, her voice flat. "And you tried to kidnap him."

The alien tipped its chin back. "Perhaps I am. Although from what my people tell me, you're not someone who shies away from killing. If I understand human customs correctly, murder is frowned on. So what does that make you?"

"Why were you trying to take Nicolau?" she countered.

The alien hummed again, and Savina realized, with shock, that the sound must be the alien's equivalent of laughter. "You have quite a belligerent attitude for someone entirely at my mercy."

Savina took a deep breath, struggling to regain her composure. She could still play this. In fact, this was probably advantageous—if the aliens knew their language, it would be easier to fool them.

She wouldn't let herself think too hard, right now, about the implications of the aliens' knowledge. Or of their obvious familiarity with humans.

She let her lips curve into an innocent smile.

The reactions of the aliens around her seemed almost reflexive— the guards took a quick step back, hands tightening on their weapons.

Interesting. Not the reaction she'd expected, but perhaps something she could use …

She widened her eyes instead, as she'd seen the aliens do when they greeted each other. "I'm sorry. I didn't mean to kill anyone, I promise. I was just so frightened, and they were hurting my friend—I didn't know what they were going to do with him. I never wanted to hurt anyone. If there's something I can do to pay you back—" Her tone was one of frightened innocence, her expression terrified and sincere.

The guards, at least, seemed to relax a little.

Savina smiled to herself.

They'd let her and the others go back to the main party, eventually. Or if they didn't, they'd let down their guard just enough. And then she'd kill them all, slowly and painfully. And she'd enjoy every moment, every scream.

"I'm afraid I can't let you back to your friends just yet," the boss said. "We have some unfinished business, you and me. You killed one of my people and injured two others. That requires an answer." The alien boss leaned forward a little, hands on its knees, and studied Savina with open interest. "I've seen people kill others by accident. They don't drive the point of a blade through both their opponent's shoulders, so they'll bleed out slowly. They don't nail their victims to the wall and then laugh in their faces. So. Let's be honest with each other. Let's say we made a bargain—the lives of you and your friends in exchange for your service." The alien gestured towards Nicolau. "I told my people to capture one of the bigger humans, like that one behind you. You humans are good for intimidation, with the sizes you grow to. But when I heard what you'd done, I realized I'd miscalculated. I think you are what I need, instead. There are some upstarts challenging my territory. You go out, do some tasks for me. Just some simple kills, nothing you'd find difficult, I think. And in exchange, I don't kill your friends." The alien shrugged. "Perhaps one day you even buy back your freedom, if you're useful enough."

Savina had slouched a little farther as she listened, and her fingertips brushed the end of her needle-thin electric knife.

A jump to her feet, a quick lunge—

And then what?

There were guards all around the room. The others would be dead before she had time to throw her knife.

She gritted her teeth.

Sometimes you had to be patient. Sometimes a job took more finesse than you'd been anticipating.

But one day … one day, this mob boss would regret the moment it had laid eyes on Savina.

"I … I guess like you said, I don't have much of a choice," she said, widening her eyes innocently.

From the edge of her vision, she could see Joska relax, and it was only then she realized how tense the woman had been.

"I'll do kills for you," said Savina. "And you'll keep my friends safe." She leaned forward, just a bit, and smiled. The aliens around her tensed, their weapons coming up, and for a moment the room was frozen.

"And if you don't," she said into the silence. "If I find even one of them hurt, or injured, or mistreated—know this. I will kill you all. You think you have the upper hand here. But the moment I lose my reason not to hurt you …"

Her fingers closed around the hilt of the knife.

She jerked it out, flipped it between her fingers, and sliced through the restraints binding her wrists, and stood quickly.

The guards jumped backwards, their weapons trained on her, and she raised her hands, still smiling, and lowered the knife to the ground.

"So," she said. "Now that we understand each other, I suppose it's just a matter of working out details."

"I suppose it is," said the mob boss. But the alien's eyes, as it watched her, were cold and calculating, and Savina had to fight back a shiver.

They were alone on an alien planet. The only person who'd noticed her disappearance was a woman sworn to murder her. And for all her bravado … she was at these aliens' mercy. And so were Beni, and Nicolau, and the others.

And if she didn't find them a way out, they would all die. Of that, she had no question.

7

Alba

Alba stood at the back of the airy, spacious room, with its arched ceiling and graceful, rising coils of seats stair-stepped like leaves on a climbing vine, and watched as the aliens—the yibo, they called themselves—move through their odd morning rituals, one of them chanting a sentence in their language, and the others repeating it back.

It was something like a call-and-response in an Orthodox ceremony back on Colorida, although the light streaming through the windows, the spare, minimalist furniture and the stylized greenery surrounding them, spilling over pots and draped from the ceilings, couldn't have formed more of a contrast with the heavy stone walls of the Orthodox churches, the ancient holographic projections glowing against the Mystery's altars and the stylized star-maps drawn out on the ceilings, surfaces darkened with centuries of brasier-smoke, the half-holy, half-claustrophobic feeling that had gripped uneasily at her chest since her first hazy memories from childhood.

But here in the light-drenched room, she found her mind

wandering just as it had in the Orthodox ceremonies, the ritual chanting forming a backdrop for her uneasy thoughts.

These aliens had been in contact with humans. That much was clear. How or why, she had no idea. But Istvay hadn't been the only one who had noted the chilling lack of living humans besides themselves among their yibo hosts.

She took a deep breath, forcing back the fear and panic that insinuated itself into her every thought.

They were here now, and despite the near-disaster at their first meeting, since then the yibo had been more than solicitous—caring for the injured, providing food and shelter for the ragged band of survivors.

But there was a bright thread of unease running through every interaction.

If the yibo were familiar with humans, why had they tried to kill them at their first meeting? Had it been a simple misunderstanding? Or were the yibo on unfriendly terms with whatever humans they'd encountered in the past? And if so, why had they suddenly decided to treat Alba and the others with such deference?

Today she was meeting with the yibo ambassador who spoke the human's Common Dialect. The yibo had told them that the ambassador and various select others could speak the human tongue on account of an expensive, and therefore rare, universal translator they'd developed. But Alba had seen no sign that the ability had anything to do with a technological device.

Her mind jerked back to the present as the last of the yibo diplomatic aides chanted the call of their call-and-response, and the others answered, finishing with a sort of shout.

The circle of lemur-like aliens dissolved into a chattering, milling group for a moment, and another group of yibo, servants of some sort, it appeared, stepped through, bearing trays of a steaming drink poured into vessels that resembled miniature pitchers.

The yibo took their drinks, still chattering, and the servants paused, then came to stand before Alba and Yosip, their eyes downcast, holding out the tray.

Alba hesitated, but a glance at the ambassador showed he was watching her, his eyes sharp.

She took a cup with a brusque nod of thanks, and Yosip took one as well. She hesitated, then brought it to her lips, sniffing the steam rising from it.

It had a sharp, clean smell, not unpleasant. Similar, perhaps, to the bush tea people drank in the Rim Mountains.

"It is nothing dangerous," the yibo ambassador said, his tone amused. He'd maneuvered his way through the crowd to stand beside them. "It's simply our morning drink. Not an intoxicant or anything of the sort, a mild stimulant at best."

She nodded, and sipped delicately at her cup.

The aftertaste was a touch bitter, but not unpleasant.

"You have eaten this morning, I hope?" the yibo man—at least, he'd introduced himself with male pronouns, so Alba assumed he was male—asked. "Ah. That is excellent. Seat yourselves, please, and I'll ask the younger ones to take their morning libations elsewhere. I am desperate to hear your story."

He called something to the other yibo, and reluctantly, the chattering group dispersed, leaving, finally, Alba, Yosip, the yibo ambassador, and a small handful of nervous-looking aides.

"Now," said the ambassador, seating himself gracefully on one of the rising tiers of seats across from the stools the yibo seemed to assume that humans preferred. "I am Harroch. I have been asked by Kachik, our head of government, to represent the yibo in our negotiations, as I am able to speak your language."

The name from his lips wasn't exactly "Harroch," but that was the closest sound Alba's mind could translate.

He leaned forward a little. "I am devastated by the tragedy that brought you here. Let me first tell you our regret for what you have been through."

Alba closed her eyes, glass-shard fragments of memory enough to suck the breath from her lungs—the claustrophobic press of terrified humanity bumping and shoving into her, ready to trample her and the injured Feliu under their feet in their blind, helpless panic, a woman's face turned to bloody ruin as a soldier's pulse gun went off point-blank, the terrified mass of people pushing for the escape shuttles.

The glittering, expanding cloud of wreckage, ship parts and bodies mingled and cast out into the frozen void of space, to drift forever in the icy nothing.

Her breath was coming too quickly, and to her horror, she found there was a tear was tracing its way down her cheek.

Harroch made a sound of distress. "I'm truly sorry for bringing that to your memory. Please, allow me to offer my sorrow for your loss."

Alba took a deep breath, trying to push the images from her mind.

It was harder than it should have been. She'd slept poorly the previous night, and the night before that in the jungle hardly bore considering. And when she was tired, the horror the memories dredged up was almost too much to push back.

"Thank you for your kind words," she managed at last.

Harroch tipped his head to the side in a gesture she'd learned meant acknowledgement. "Of course. Now, I understand you had come here to negotiate, is that correct? But perhaps let me reassure you first—we were distraught at the portal failing, and we have people working to restore it as soon as possible. I expect it to be done soon—perhaps twenty days? But in the meantime, please, tell me your purpose in coming here, and perhaps we can create some good from this tragedy. At the very least, it has been a great pleasure to find another species that is … sapient, I think is your word? We wish very much to have excellent relations with your people upon the portal reopening, and I believe an alliance would be mutually beneficial." His face was pleasant, and his words everything Alba had hoped for.

But he was lying to her.

The ball Aran had found, with its human makers-mark, sat heavy in her small reticule.

"We are your first contact with other sapient species?" she asked at last. "With technology to create a portal like you have, I would have imagined otherwise. And we are lucky indeed that your technology was able to translate our language so easily."

Harroch gave a close-lipped smile of amusement—it appeared these aliens viewed showing one's teeth as more a threat than a gesture of friendship—and tipped his head again. "Of course. We have various dialects in our system, and this makes it easier. The implant is difficult and expensive to program, so only a few of us have it, but it's enough that we can get by. And while you are not the only sapient species we've discovered, we have found they are rare."

"I see," said Alba. "And what were your relations with these other sapient species?"

The yibo made an amused humming. "It was over a century ago —before my time. But my understanding is, they were aggressive, and so my predecessors simply decided to close the portal so as not to allow them through." He twitched his tail in a gesture Alba had come to recognize as the equivalent of a shrug. "We are more wary of newcomers now. And so it is a delight to hear from you that your intentions are nothing but peaceful. Despite the misunderstanding with your pet … land-devil, was it?"

She'd been certain the aliens did not understand human sarcasm. But there was a note in Harroch's voice that made her look at him more closely.

She paused a moment. "Harroch," she said at last. "I understand you are wary of newcomers, and with some cause. But I believe, and always have, that negotiations are best carried out with as much frankness as possible between the two parties. I regret the unfortunate misunderstanding when our people first met yours. I'm not certain you were informed, but the incident you referenced came about when the yibo who found us pulled out half-a-dozen of our group in what appeared to be an attempt to shoot them. Our scientist stepped in front of the others to prevent this, and it was only when the yibo attempted to put their hands on him that his animal attacked."

Harroch watched her for a moment. His eyes were hooded, but there appeared to be a hint of unease in his posture. "I … was not informed of this," he said at last. "If it is true, I will ensure the perpetrator is punished."

Alba gave a dismissive shake of her head. "It is not my intention to ask for a litre of blood in exchange for our injuries," she said. "I simply wish this negotiation to proceed on the terms that will lead to the highest chance of success. And that, I believe, is a mutual understanding of the underlying factors." She paused a moment. "I understand our presence here is perhaps unexpected, but certainly it must not have been a complete surprise, considering the greeting you sent us through the portal."

Harroch frowned. "The greeting we sent?"

Alba exchanged a quick glance with Yosip, who had been listening to their exchange quietly. When she caught his eye, she saw the small crease of concern between his eyebrows.

"The container you sent through. Filled with samples from your system," she said, turning back to the yibo ambassador.

If she hadn't been watching his expression as closely as she was, she may have missed the quick shudder of—something. Unease, perhaps.

Or possibly fear.

"Ah, of course. We were not certain it had arrived at its destination." His face smoothed over, quickly enough that had she not been watching, she might have assumed nothing was wrong. But the tip of his tail, draped delicately over his arm, twitched slightly, and there was a tension in his posture that had not been there before.

He was hiding something.

She managed to keep the close-lipped smile on her face. "The item you sent contained objects of interest to our scientific community," she continued pleasantly. "Some of our world's best scientists accompanied us on our mission in the hope that they could speak with your scientists, and perhaps exchange knowledge. I understand that with circumstances as they are, this is not the most pressing matter, but at the least, our sharing of scientific knowledge could act as a token of our mutual goodwill while we negotiate."

Aran was correct—finding the cure for the defect was important. But that wasn't the reason she'd asked.

Her mention of the box had made the yibo ambassador deeply nervous. And Aran, she knew, would find out everything he could about that box, or die trying, if it held even the slightest chance of keeping Istvay alive.

The thought sent of twinge of guilt through her, but she pushed it resolutely aside.

Harroch watched her for a moment longer, then tipped his head in agreement. "I'm certain we could equip someone with our translation program to act as interpreter. Give me the evening to work out the logistics."

"You are too kind," Alba murmured.

"It is no difficulty," Harroch said, although the tension in his posture said otherwise. "The sharing of scientific knowledge must be a priority among all sapient species, if we wish to peacefully interact." He shifted in his seat. "And now that we have, as you said, a common understanding of your history and ours with respect to our meeting, let us—"

Alba leaned forward slightly. "With all due respect, Harroch," she said quietly, "I think perhaps we do not yet have a full mutual understanding. We are trapped here at the moment, although I am gratified by your assurances that your people are working on rectifying that situation. However, if we are to proceed with our negotiations, I must be frank with you. My people are not entirely powerless. We have technology which, while different from yours, is highly valuable, and the contributions we could add to any alliance or negotiated settlement are not insubstantial." She paused for just a moment, just long enough to let him hear the threat she did not utter. "With that in mind," she said, reaching into her reticule, "I had hoped that you would explain to me when you last interacted with humans."

She pulled the ball out of her reticule, the maker's mark clearly visible.

For a moment, the room was entirely silent. Even the aides had stiffened, glancing around as if they wished to be anywhere other than here.

At last, Harroch picked up the ball with his long, delicate fingers. There was tension in every muscle of his body as he turned it over and over.

"I'm afraid you are mistaken," he said at last, laying the ball down on the table. "We have never met humans before now." He was watching her, his eyes never leaving hers.

She frowned. She could feel the tension in her own muscles, the tightness of a headache at the base of her skull. "Harroch," she said, lowering her voice. "If you are at odds with this group of humans, perhaps there is something we could do to broker peaceful relations. But we must be honest with one another for this negotiation to have a chance of success."

For a long time, Harroch was silent. The tip of his tail was twitching nervously, but his expression remained a polite mask. At last, his mouth lifted into a small smile, but Alba noticed that this time, just the tips of his sharp incisors were visible between his lips. "I assure you, Alba. You are mistaken. You are the first humans we have encountered." His eyes flicked quickly from side to side, then returned to her. "I am devastated to disappoint you, but I believe this topic will be of no use to any of us. Now. Would you like to return to our earlier discussion?"

After her decades on the Council, Alba was used to long days of negotiations. But by the time she and Yosip were escorted back to the diplomatic quarters, uncomfortably full after the lavish meal they'd been served, Alba was bone-weary.

When they reach their rooms, she sank down onto one of the low stools and let her shoulders droop for just a moment before she straightened.

Yosip sat as well, and she could see, under his friendly smile, the same core-deep exhaustion that she felt. "What do we do now, Madam?" he asked quietly.

She took a deep breath. "We cannot negotiate with them in good faith if they refuse to be honest. And their dishonesty does not bode well for us, I'm afraid." She paused. "I don't understand—if they have hostile intentions, why bother with this farce? For all I wish it was not the case, we are currently all but helpless. And if they intend to make some agreement or alliance with us, why lie so blatantly?"

"I don't know," said Yosip, his voice weary. "But I agree that it does not bode well."

"According to Harroch, for as much as his word is worth, we have twenty days to figure it out."

And then there was a pounding on the door, and her head jerked up in surprise.

"Yosip!" someone was shouting, their voice harsh with panic. "Madam Chief Justice! You need to get out here, right now!"

She exchanged a look with Yosip and pushed herself to her feet.

When they reached the rotunda outside, the human survivors were milling about in panicked confusion.

"Alba," said Istvay, striding over to her. Their face was grimmer than she'd seen it in a long time. "One of the crew was shot."

"What?" she snapped, panic lurching in her stomach. "What happened?"

"They … said he'd wandered outside, and one of the alien guards saw him and panicked," said Aran quietly. He was staring at the ground, like he usually did, but his jaw was tight, and he was stroking his murder-beast absently. "But he was unarmed. Judging from what we've seen, I doubt the guard saw a threat. I suspect they just saw he was far enough away from Ani that she wouldn't be able to stop him."

"And have the guards tried to come in here? Threaten anyone else?" asked Yosip.

Istvay shook their head. "Not as far as we know. They were nothing but apologetic. But apologetic won't bring him back."

"I'll send for the ambassador immediately," Alba snapped, but there was something tight and sick in her stomach. "Ines, please find me an interpreter at once."

Something about her presence and her authoritative tone seemed to calm the crew somewhat, and for that, she could only be grateful.

But it meant, of course, that she couldn't allow the cold fear slithering through her to show in her face or her posture.

She took a deep breath and imagined herself standing in front of the Council.

She had plenty of experience with high-stakes negotiations. But she was not accustomed to the consequences of her negotiations being enacted so suddenly, or so permanently.

"Ambassador Alba."

She turned to see one of the yibo standing at the door to the room.

She drew herself up and strode over. "Yes. I would like you to inform your ambassador, Harroch—"

"I have come from Harroch," said yibo. "He has asked me to inform you that he has heard of what happens, and deeply regrets it. He has told me to tell you he will look into it personally. And ..." The interpreter hesitated a moment. "And he asked me to please tell you that Kachik as well conveys his regrets, and hopes with all his soul that such awkward questions as came up in your conversation with Harroch today not delay your negotiations. He said it would be devastating to him should such misunderstandings breed more fear between the yibo and yourselves, and potentially lead to more incidents."

Alba stared at the interpreter for a long moment, her heart pounding.

It did not take an experienced diplomat to hear the threat in the message.

She had asked the wrong questions today. And in retaliation, the yibo had ordered someone killed.

Whatever the yibo were hiding in regard to their prior interaction with humans, they had no wish to open the matter for discussion.

She took a deep breath.

Twenty days before the portal reopened.

If they survived that long.

8

Savina

"Savina."

Savina glanced up quickly. Joska had moved to stand beside her, and the woman's voice was low. "Are you going to be alright out there?"

Savina paused for a moment, nonplussed, then, with an effort, pasted on her brightest smile. "As you always say, this is my forte."

The look on Joska's face told Savina the woman wasn't fooled by her bravado, but she only nodded. "Good luck, then."

Savina refrained from looking after her as the woman turned away.

It wasn't like Joska was actually cared about her. She'd stolen the woman's ship and gotten all of them stranded here. It was absurd to imagine Joska's concern was for Savina's wellbeing. Given the right excuse, and the woman's pretended kindness would melt more quickly than a late spring snowfall in the southern Rim Mountains.

"Are you ready, humans?"

The words had a harsh, scornful tone to them, and Savina turned. The alien speaking to her was smaller than the mob boss, Yuur, but not by much—a young male, she understood. The dark fur around his eyes was an unusual light brown, his tunic the dull greens and greys that seemed to be the gang's trademark colours.

She hadn't spent long enough around the aliens to know their body language well. But she could sense the arrogance rolling off this one in waves.

She turned her most charming smile onto him. "Of course. Beni and I are ready whenever you are."

She enjoyed, for a moment, the flicker of uncertainty in his expression at her smile, and then she let it drop and widened her eyes. "Oh, I'm sorry. I forgot. Humans smile to be friendly, I wasn't thinking."

He grunted, but it was clear that she unnerved him.

Which meant he wasn't quite as stupid as he looked.

"Let's go, then," he growled, and she began a nod, then caught herself and tipped her head to one side to indicate agreement.

He grunted again, calling out something in that stupid chattering language the aliens had, and they started out the door.

The streets outside were as hot and muggy as they'd been the day before, when Savina and her companions had been dragged here blindfolded.

No need for blindfolds now. Joska, Rafel, and Nicolau were back at the gang's headquarters, hostages in fact, if not in name.

Beni came up beside Savina as she walked. "The aliens gave me a scan of the building where they think their target will have taken shelter, and my link gave me a verbal diagram," they said quietly. "I've marked up the exits and entrances for you, and calculated which ones are most likely to be used for defence, and which for escape. I'm sending it through now."

A moment later, something flashed in the corner of Savina's left eye. She blinked twice to bring up the retinal screen and studied the translucent diagram as she walked.

It was a small building, but multiple stories, which always made things more difficult.

"Do you have a plan for keeping them on one floor?" she asked, blinking again to banish the image.

"Yes," said Beni. "We'll send someone in to lock down the upper floors. There's a type of chemical bomb that should get them to shut everything down themselves."

"Not bad," said Savina, pulling up the diagram again and studying it carefully. "We'll just have to make sure that it's not enough to cause an evacuation."

"We'll have people in place beforehand," said Beni. "We should be able to do it without causing panic, but just in case, we'll have people at the exits."

"Good." Savina paused a moment. "Thanks, Beni," she added quietly.

She wasn't talking about only the job, and Beni probably knew it, but they just gave a quick nod and kept walking.

Savina watched them, worry growing in her chest.

She'd never seen Beni so quiet as they'd been the last few days. Not that she could blame them—it had been a lot for anyone.

But—

She and Beni had been through so much together. Much as she'd tried to protect her sibling, she and Beni had been through plenty of crap. And she'd never seen it affect Beni like this.

She'd fix it all, eventually. Somehow, she'd find a way to fix all of this, get herself and Beni and Nicolau away from these aliens and back through the portal, kill Alba, and kill that government agent— for a moment, her traitorous brain flashed her first view of Reka

Soler across her memory: her muscular back and shoulders, her figure, the curves of her body …

She shoved the thought away.

The point was, she'd find a way to get them safe. Now they had Nicolau with them, maybe they didn't even need to go back to the compound. Maybe they could find another place to hide, just the three of them.

Thought sent an unexpected ache through her chest.

She'd never let herself think about her own freedom. She couldn't. She couldn't let on, even to herself, how badly she wanted to be away from the compound. To be free. It would have put Nicolau in danger, and she and Beni had both agreed that was something they'd never do. They'd let him live his own life, happy and free, out in a world that hadn't yet learned to hate him.

Of course, that was hardly a consideration anymore. As much as she'd tried to protect to him, in the end, it hadn't mattered. He'd lost everything, because of her.

No. Because of that stupid Chief Justice, and her stupidly attractive attack-dog, Reka Soler.

Savina smiled to herself, her fists clenched.

She'd get away from these aliens. She'd find a way. And then she'd kill Alba and Reka. It really shouldn't be difficult.

"We're almost there," said the young male, falling back beside Savina and Beni. He was watching the two of them with open hostility.

Savina gave him her most innocent smile. "Good. Now. I'll go in. You'll do whatever Beni tells you to. Once I take out the target, your people can come in afterwards to sweep up the stragglers."

The alien returned her smile with one of his own, showing his pointed incisors. It was clearly not meant as a conciliatory gesture.

"Explain to me why I should take orders from you," he said, the words taking on a singsong tone. "You do the job, or we kill your friends. That's the bargain."

Savina blinked at him in innocent confusion, and he hesitated, just for a moment.

And in that moment, Savina stepped past his defences and slammed her wrist up, knocking the gun from his fingers with one hand while with her other she slapped the electric tranq she'd palmed earlier against his shoulder.

He froze as the current coursed through him, his eyes wide with shock.

Savina pulled out a long knife and tickled it under his chin.

The other aliens were beginning to turn, having realized, suddenly, that something had gone wrong.

Savina smiled at them. "If any of you takes so much as one step towards me, or even pretends to go for your weapon, I'll give this idiot a brand-new smile," she said.

She had no idea if they understood her words, but she was certain her gesture was unmistakable.

They hung back, and Savina turned back to her captive. "Rach is your name, isn't it?" she purred. "Well, Rach, I could slit your throat from ear to ear, right here in the street. I could leave you to bleed out, and the interesting thing about an electric tranq is, your body would just stay standing, because your muscles would be too tight to release. I've done it before. Takes a little longer for anyone to realize you're dead. I could do that, if I wanted to, and not one of your friends would be in time to stop me. But I won't, this time.

"You asked me why you're going to take orders from me? Because you want me to do the job, and this is how I'm doing it. You have your hostages. You have me under control. But don't ever make the mistake of thinking that means you've drawn my fangs, you bastard."

She bent and picked up the alien's gun, turning it over in her fingers. "I'm going to take the electric tranq off you. But if you so much as think a threat at me, or Beni, or any of my friends, I will kill you. Do you understand?" she paused, then gave a small, amused laugh. "Oh, silly me. You can't answer, can you? Because you can't move."

She stepped in closer. Fear burned in his eyes as she brought up her knife, and for a moment she stood there, basking in his terror. Then, with a quick motion, she reached forward and tapped the electric tranq from his shoulder with the tip of the blade.

The alien's body jerked as he regained control of his muscles. He turned shakily to glare at Savina, but there was terror behind his belligerence now, and he spat a word she didn't recognize.

She tucked it away in the back of her mind. People said things when they were angry. Things they didn't want you to know.

But now wasn't the time to worry about it.

"Beni," asked Savina. "Why don't you tell them where you want them to position themselves?"

The aliens didn't protest again, especially after Savina handed the confiscated weapon to Beni and instructed her sibling to use it at the earliest sign of insubordination.

Then, satisfied Beni had things under control, Savina stuck her knife back into its sheath, retrieved the electric tranq, and took a deep breath, smoothing back her hair with her hand.

The fact that she was a human would cause some interest in the streets, according to the mob boss. But not too much confusion.

Apparently, humans weren't completely unknown in the system.

She'd been tempted to find out more—but in the end, it didn't matter. What mattered was getting away from the aliens, killing Reka, getting the portal open, and killing Alba. Not necessarily in that order.

She widened her eyes and put on her most innocent expression as she stepped out of the alley—no smiles, she didn't want to frighten anyone—and pulled open the door to the small, seedy drinking place their target frequented.

A dozen pairs of alien eyes turned towards her as she entered, and she blinked at them in helpless bewilderment. "Are you—are you Kiritz?" she asked, pointing towards a squat alien in the corner.

The alien, who was staring at her more in calculation than surprise, said something in a curt tone, and two of his people moved around the edges of the room to flank her.

Just as she'd hoped.

She took a faltering step forward and tried again, pointing at him and saying his name in a questioning tone.

He was watching her with a predatory stare, and for just a moment, Savina felt a shiver travel up her spine.

Nicolau was right—none of them had any idea how these aliens saw humans; as an oddity, or a threat, or a meal.

He said something in his own language, and she took another couple of steps closer, as if trying desperately to understand his words.

She was quite close now, maybe two metres away. He'd never have let her get that close if she didn't look so innocent and helpless.

And it was the last mistake he'd make, unless you believed in an afterlife.

She crossed the remaining space too quickly for anyone to react, then her knife flashed out, sharp enough that it hardly caught on the thick knot of muscle and artery and trachea. Blood sprayed across the room and the aliens shouted in alarm, going for their weapons. Savina had her pulse pistol out in her free hand, and she fired off shots in rapid succession. Two more aliens dropped before any of them were able to free their weapons.

She caught the hint of movement to her right and spun, dragging the lifeless body of her target in front of her. He vaporized at the shot, the limp blood and flesh of him glowing briefly, then dissolving. She yanked out her knife and grabbed another of the aliens, one who hadn't had the sense to step far enough out of the way, and pulled him around in front of her, her blade sliding through his rib cage to find his heart.

It was lucky, she mused as his body twitched and stilled, that the aliens' anatomy was similar enough to that of humans that her usual techniques still worked.

Another shot, and her second shield dissolved in her hands.

"Beni. Send in the others," Savina hissed, and dropped to the floor just in time to miss another bolt. She rolled under the table and aimed her pulse pistol at the shooter, and he went down with a high-pitched scream of agony.

And then the doors burst open, and Rach's people flooded in, weapons drawn.

It took less than a minute to finish off the rest of the tavern's inhabitants—a brutal, efficient bloodbath that left disturbingly few bodies behind.

Savina shivered. Whatever those weapons were made of, and whatever they did, they were more than anyone in the Joias System had ever dreamed of.

When was over, they piled the bodies in a heap, and one of the aliens aimed their weapon, firing until the pile had dissolved into ash and fragments. Aside from the blood smeared across the floor and spattered along the walls, you'd hardly know there'd been a fight.

She took a deep breath and closed her eyes for a moment.

Violence didn't frighten her. She wouldn't have lasted long in this profession if it did. But there was something about the way the bodies were simply gone, dissolved as if they'd never existed …

Rach stepped up close to her. "You did your job," he said coldly. "Good. But don't make the mistake of thinking that makes you irreplaceable."

She smiled at him, showing her teeth, and blinked innocently when he flinched back.

He hissed the word he'd said earlier, and she watched him thoughtfully as he turned on his heel, gesturing her to follow as they started back for the safehouse.

She stepped up beside one of the other aliens as they walked. The alien turned, her posture uneasy.

"What is this?" Savina asked, whispering the word in the alien's ear.

The alien started, turning to her with an expression of terror, and made a quick, sharp gesture as if to ward off evil, babbling something incomprehensible in the alien tongue.

"What?" asked Savina, pasting on her most innocent expression. "I don't know your language. I just heard someone say the word, and I wondered what it meant."

The alien shuddered and turned away.

Savina watched her as they walked.

If there was something out there that these aliens feared, so much they'd spit it at her as an epithet when she tried to kill them, so much so that the mention of it made them wary—

Well. That was certainly something she could use. She just needed a little information, and a little time.

9

Aran

Aran stared at the group of aliens who, he'd been told, were scientists.

They stared back at him.

He shifted uncomfortably and cleared his throat. Ani gave a soft, low growl, and he reached up to stroke the tentacle that was draped down across his chest, and gently push aside another which had crept over his chin.

Ani had a tendency to get clingy when she was nervous.

The yibo scientists were still staring at him. Although, he noticed, some had stepped slightly back at Ani's sounds of discontent.

He cleared his throat again. "Um. She's. Don't worry, she's very friendly."

The interpreter, who had edged inconspicuously away to position herself on the side opposite Ani, as far out of reach as a possible while still being able to hear Aran's words, addressed herself to the scientists, presumably repeating his reassurances.

They did not appear to reassure anyone.

Aran cleared his throat again. "I—"

Dammit. He was rubbish at this. Why the hell hadn't he let Istvay come instead?

Of course. He bit back a sigh. Because Istvay was losing their damn mind right now. They'd determined, in their bullheaded way, that their number one mission was getting the portal back open, and they weren't going to contemplate anything else until that happened. If Istvay had come, this entire enterprise would boil down to them asking the scientists, in tones of ever-increasing irritation, what the hell they had to do to get it through the yibo's damn heads that the yibo needed to reopen the portal, immediately.

The fact that in this instance, Istvay might actually be worse at this than he was, did not, however, change the fact that Aran was rubbish at this.

"There was—there was a box you sent through the portal," he said finally. "There were some samples inside. Plants, voice samples, a blood sample."

The interpreter was watching him, and he could see from her posture, if not from her face, that this was not what she'd been expecting him to say. But she tipped her head in acquiescence and turned to the scientists, speaking rapidly in their language.

Aran had spent enough time observing animals that he was used to watching for the most minuscule reactions—not expressions, exactly, but the way muscles tensed, posture shifted, eyes widened.

Animals didn't lie. They told you, through their starts and shudders and growls, exactly what they were thinking, and exactly what they were going to do.

It seemed these aliens, from what Istvay had told him, were as adept at lying as humans were.

But he could see, from their small, subtle shifts as the translator spoke, that whatever she was saying made them deeply uneasy.

At last, one of the scientists stepped forward and spoke a rapid sentence to the interpreter. The interpreter tipped her head to one side in acknowledgement and turned back to Aran. "He says he's very happy to answer questions about the box, but since it was prepared with a great deal of care and has given you a good deal of information on our system, while they have had access to nothing at all from your planet, he would take it as a gesture of goodwill if they could ask you questions first."

Aran frowned.

But if they weren't going to talk, he wasn't exactly in the position to make them. He sighed, started to nod, caught himself, and tipped his head to one side. "You can tell them I'm happy to answer some questions, if we can talk about the contents of the box afterwards."

The interpreter conveyed that, then waited as the alien scientist asked something, gesturing to Ani.

"He would like to know what that animal you keep on your shoulder is. He wishes to know if it is common practice to keep such animals as pets on your planet."

Aran glanced guiltily at Ani. "She's, um, she's … her species is the great venomous tree-dwelling tentacled land-devil. She's—I mean, she's not native to our main planet. So they're not exactly a common pet, but—but she's very well behaved. Generally speaking," he amended.

The interpreter conveyed this, and the scientist cocked his head at Aran, his eyebrows raised in question.

Aran sighed. "She, um, is native to an uninhabited planet a little ways away from Colorida," he continued reluctantly.

With any luck, they wouldn't ask the next question …

They asked the next question.

"And is there a reason this planet is uninhabited?" the interpreter repeated.

Aran sighed. "They … Well, they—" he shifted slightly. "If land-devils are threatened, they can become—mildly aggressive."

He could see by the looks in the aliens' eyes as the interpreter repeated his words that they weren't going to be satisfied with the explanation.

"They're—venomous," he said last. "And, um, also poisonous. And they can inject you with digestive fluids, which will essentially melt your insides. And they can fly with their skin flaps. They're quite fast, actually. And they spit acid, which, I guess, you already know. And, um, they're impervious to most weapons. Including radiation. I think when we first came to the Joias System, the humans tried to, um, destroy the planet with a nuclear weapon after the first group of settlers encountered the land-devils. The, um, the land-devils seemed to—eat the radiation. So it didn't exactly work out. And they didn't dare try anything else." He was stroking Ani unconsciously, and as the interpreter repeated his words, he could see the looks of growing horror on the faces of the alien scientists.

"But that was before we realized how peaceful they were, generally," he added hastily. "As long as we leave them alone and don't go onto their planet, there's absolutely no reason why they would show any sort of hostility—"

The scientist was speaking rapidly to the interpreter.

He did not appear comforted by Aran's words.

"He would like to know why you've chosen to bring this creature with you, if the only way to halt their aggression is to entirely abandon any planet that they inhabit."

Ani had sensed Aran's discomfort, and was growling a little more threateningly now, the pouches under her eyes starting to puff out.

Aran stroked her comfortingly. "We—we generally don't. Ani's just—she's my pet. I raised her from an egg, she's very well behaved, and almost entirely harmless."

"You've removed her venom, then?" the scientist asked cautiously, through the interpreter.

Aran stared at him, shocked out of his awkwardness. "What? No, of course not! I'd never do something like that!" He rubbed Ani's tentacle reassuringly. "That's her only form of defence! Well, one of her only forms of defence."

He realized, belatedly, that perhaps a less emphatic response might have been more reassuring.

"But she's never … killed anyone. Besides …" The interpreter let the sentence dangle.

"Um." Aran shifted again. "Well. I mean, not very often. And it was always provoked, so—"

From the looks on the faces in front of him, his explanations were not actually helping the situation.

There were a few moments of uncomfortable silence.

At last one of the scientists asked, cautiously, through the interpreter, "This land-devil, then—she is the most dangerous creature in your system, yes?"

Aran frowned, holding Ani's tentacle defensively. "Well, maybe she's the only one that has all those modes of defence, but there are plenty of venomous animals on the planet. The crested herrings, for instance—I was bitten by one once when I was trying to observe their feeding patterns, and it knocked me out for three days, which is almost as much is the first time Ani stung me. On accident, I mean," he added hurriedly.

If anything, this revelation had left the scientists looking even more shocked than before.

"And then there's the red-frilled mountain cats," he added.

"They're notorious for hunting humans, and not only do they have five-centimetre claws, their newborn cubs also have venomous spurs on the inside of their front legs, which disappear as they reach adolescence. And—"

"The venomous spurs—who was it that discovered those?" asked one of the aliens, in a tone of voice that was somehow both terrified and resigned.

Aran shifted again. "Um. Well, I—I did, I suppose, when I was out doing fieldwork—" he surveyed the faces in front of him, then shook his head. "Look, why don't you tell me something about the fauna on your planet? I noticed the jungle cats have ridges in their back teeth, and I was wondering—"

The scientists were staring at each other now, their faces completely aghast.

"They—do," said the first scientist who'd spoken. "They do have ridges on their back teeth. But you've been on the planet for—what, three days now? How did you—" he stopped speaking abruptly. "Your—your land-devil killed one, didn't she?" His voice was now completely flat. "Do you know how much of our livestock, let alone our own people, those jungle cats kill every year? And your pet just —"

"She only killed one or two," said Aran defensively. "And anyways, that wasn't how I found out."

There was a string of words that the interpreter simply neglected to translate.

"How did you find out?" she translated at last.

There was a long silence that Aran didn't feel like breaking.

"You—" the scientists were all staring at him now. "You. You had your hand in one's mouth. Didn't you? While it was still alive. You had your arm in the mouth of a jungle cat while it was still alive."

Aran resisted, with difficulty, the urge to swear. "It—it wasn't really like that, it was just—I was—"

He trailed off, realizing nothing that he could say would salvage the situation at this point.

"Perhaps—" said the scientist at last. "Perhaps it would be best if we moved onto a different topic."

They asked some basic questions about the typical flora and fauna on Colorida, and the type of subjects that the human scientists were researching.

Aran answered as best he could, but he watched the scientists as they spoke. It was easy enough, since he always had to wait for the interpreter, so he was free to simply observe them.

They were obviously highly uncomfortable about—something. He couldn't tell what. And it wasn't just the unfortunate reaction to Ani's natural defences, either. They'd had the same air of unease even before the conversation had taken that unfortunate turn.

It was well past midday, and Aran's stomach had started to protest from hunger, when he finally turned to the interpreter. "I'd be very interested in seeing the scientific research they've been carrying on, and observing some of their experiments," he said. "I'm more than happy to share what we've been doing as well. But the thing I'm most interested in is who put together the box that they sent through the portal. There's information in it that could be immensely helpful to us."

There was the slightest moment of hesitation from the interpreter, but at last she turned and relayed his message to the others.

Again, Aran picked up on that odd sense of unease. The scientists glanced at each other, and then the lead scientist made a small, nervous humming sound.

"He says, he's sure there are some matters of interest from the box, but he can't imagine that they would be of more import than the scientific studies that are happening in the laboratory," said the translator, turning back to Aran. "He invites you to observe them first, and then perhaps your questions about the box will answer themselves."

Aran frowned slightly. "My question isn't a complicated one," he said. "I just want to meet the person who prepared the box. I have some questions for them." He paused a moment. "There's—there was some genetic information in it that might be the key to a cure for a genetic illness that's been plaguing us. I'm sure everyone back in Colorida would be grateful if … if you could—" He broke off quickly, a tight combination of fear and urgency choking in his throat.

He blinked hard, watching the scientists as the interpreter repeated his words.

There was irritation in their postures, and under it—something like fear.

But—

He frowned deeper.

At the back of the group of scientists, there was one who was watching him. They hadn't dropped their eyes like all the others had at the mention of the box, and there was something in their posture that made Aran think that they were at least somewhat sympathetic.

"He says, while he does appreciate your interest, he's quite certain you will get your questions answered in the labs much more easily than here. It would take some time to track down whoever it was who prepared the box, as it was likely one of hundreds sent out, and then they would have to determine which box was the one you were sent … while he's more than happy to help you, it will be a long process. In the meantime, he invites you to follow him down to laboratory."

Aran sighed and tipped his head.

It seemed this was the best he'd get at the moment.

The relief in the lead scientist's posture was clearly evident. He gestured, and Aran followed the scientists from the room, Ani still grumbling discontentedly on his shoulder and the interpreter walking, if possible, even farther away from him that she had when they'd entered the room.

The laboratory was indeed fascinating, and he was so caught up in observing the yibo's experiments that when the interpreter cleared her throat, he jumped.

"I believe there will be a dinner provided in your rooms, if you're hungry," she said.

"Oh. Um, yes, I'll be there in just a minute," he said distractedly, looking up from the microscope he'd been peering through.

The scientific theories the yibo were working on were fascinating, and had the potential to improve science in Colorida by leaps and bounds when brought back. And in turn, he'd been able to nudge them in the right direction in various experiments of theirs. But—

He couldn't help but notice how any topic of genetics or DNA was subtly sidestepped.

As he stood reluctantly to leave, he caught sight of the scientist he'd noticed during the meeting, the one who appeared sympathetic, standing next to the door as if waiting for something.

They caught his eye as he approached, and he realized with a jolt that they were waiting for him.

They touched his sleeve as he came up to them, and said something in their chirping language.

"She said she was interested in what you'd said earlier. She said she hopes you don't mind her asking, but are you affected by the genetic illness? You seemed distressed."

He cleared his throat. "Not me," he muttered. "My …. my friend." His voice wanted to choke again.

The scientist watched him for a moment, then at last said something to the interpreter, gesturing Aran to follow her as she stepped into the hallway.

"Her name is Ree." The interpreter rolled the "r" heavily, making the name a sort of chirp. "You said you were interested in the centrifuge experiment they were performing in the lab. She realizes it may not have been explained clearly, and said it may be easier if she illustrates the process for you."

He frowned in confusion as the scientist pulled out a writing surface and a writing stick.

She bent and sketched a quick diagram, supporting the surface against her knee, and Aran peered over her shoulder.

She'd drawn out two graphs that he could recognize fairly easily, and then …

And then, in the corner—something else. Something that didn't look like an experiment at all.

A long, thin box that was instantly familiar. And in front of it, a gash that looked like it could possibly be the portal.

He stared at the drawing, then back at her. "And this is, um, a subject you have particular expertise in?" he asked, gesturing casually at the drawing of the box.

She looked up at him, meeting his eye.

"It's not my specialty, no. But I know people who might specialize in it," the interpreter translated from behind him.

The scientist's voice betrayed nothing, but Aran could feel his heart racing.

There was something there. She might actually be able to get him some information.

It was only the beginning. It was only a start, and he forced himself to clamp down on the hope that bubbled up in his chest.

The scientist studied him for a moment, then seemed to make up her mind. "There is a group of scientists going out into the jungle to check the experiments in our field lab and collect samples tomorrow," the interpreter translated. "She is wondering if you'd be interested in coming along to watch."

He stared at Ree, trying and failing to read her expression.

But there was a reason she was asking him to come, and it had to do with the box. And that was enough for him.

"Tell her I'd be very interested," he said.

The interpreter translated, then turned back. "She says she'll pick you up outside the diplomatic quarters at sunrise."

Ree watched until he'd tipped his head in acknowledgement, then turned and strode back towards laboratory.

Aran watched her go.

Finally, he turned back to the patiently waiting interpreter and followed her back to the diplomatic quarters, his heart pounding quickly enough that he was dizzy with it.

10

Alba

"Harroch," said Alba coldly, sitting down on the proffered stool. Her pulse was pounding quickly, a mixture of fury and cold fear.

"Alba. Allow me to offer you something to drink." He came over to hand her one of the delicate cups of steaming liquid.

"Thank you, but I'm not thirsty," she said, ignoring the proffered cup.

Harroch studied her for a moment, then nodded politely, handing the cup to an aide and turning back to his own seat.

Alba sat in icy silence, watching him. The tip of his tail twitched slightly, but even had it not, she could see the tension in every line of his posture.

"Alba," he said again, settling himself and turning back to her. "You must allow me to express my apologies for what happened last evening. I truly had no knowledge of the danger until after it had occurred." He paused, and added, lowering his voice, "As a friend, I would advise you to warn your people against wandering alone in the streets until we have worked out an agreement between us."

"Believe me," she said sharply, "they have now been advised. But it escapes me how you expect me to enter into negotiations that will bear fruit if my people are terrified of your people, and, it would seem, for good reason." She took a deep breath, reigning in her fury.

A misstep could mean the death of another of the small group that was looking to her for their survival. And she couldn't ignore the sick guilt sitting hard and heavy under the fury.

She'd been the cause of the death last night. Of that, she had no doubt at all. Another person lost, with not even a body to bring home to his family.

"I … had hoped we could speak of that today," Harroch said. His posture broadcast his nervousness. "As you know, there are some few of us who have the translation implant. And Kachik is extremely interested in the fruits of our negotiations." The emphasis he put on the words was odd, and he glanced at one of the aides as he spoke.

Alba kept her expression from registering her sudden unease.

Could one of the aides be a spy, then?

"Nonetheless," Harroch continued, lowering his voice still more, "I hope that you and I, at least, will be able to come to a mutual understanding. As I am aware of the various … topics of discussion that could cause tensions to arise between our people, I may be able to steer the discussion in more productive directions, while still assuaging your concerns."

She watched him for a long moment, fighting down the sickness in her stomach.

She hardly had a choice. They were at the yibo's mercy, at least for the moment. Perhaps the yibo were afraid of Ani, but as dangerous as the land-devil was, there was only one of her. And the yibo had shown, last night, that they could and would kill the humans if they felt so inclined, Ani or no Ani.

All it would take in some cases, she was uncomfortably aware, was a simple denial of medical aid.

And yet, they were still alive. Which meant that yibo needed them for something.

But what?

And was Harroch willing to help them? Or was he simply another spy?

She was entering into a negotiation with world-altering stakes, against opponents whose motives she didn't understand and whose ultimate objective was a mystery, and who could and would set the terms and the boundaries of the negotiations with no consultation on her part.

She drew in a long breath.

Perhaps the stakes were greater than she was used to. And perhaps the cost of a mistake was incalculably high. But this was a game she knew how to play.

This was politics, and she'd cut her teeth on politics.

"Very well," she said at last. "I sincerely hope that you are correct. I came all this way as part of a diplomatic mission because I had hope that we would be able to establish mutually beneficial relations. If you wish for the same thing, I am certain we will be able to come to some sort of agreement."

Harroch tipped his head to one side in approval. "I'm happy to hear it," he said.

"I have no wish to speak of topics that are uncomfortable, so please do let me know if I am treading on sensitive ground," Alba continued, feeling the words out as she spoke them. "However, I believe it would be in both our best interests if we were to be frank about what our people wish to achieve from this negotiation." She paused. "For our part, we are interested in a mutual sharing of knowledge and commerce. Opening trade, sharing scientific and technological data according to agreed-upon protocols. Over our time in the Joias System, we have learned that mutual cooperation can drive advancements and achievements that are impossible when one is locked into hostilities, and we wish to avoid that outcome. Some, even in my own government, believe cooperation is weakness, but we have advanced as far as we have in large part because we attempt first to negotiate before issuing threats, and our ability to defend ourselves when necessary has been greatly enhanced thereby."

Harroch, she knew, was not a native speaker of the Common Dialect, but she had decades of practice in emphasizing just the right word in an innocuous phrase to highlight the fact that, while she was not, in fact, making a threat, she could.

Harroch hesitated a moment, then tipped his head again. "An admirable goal," he said. His tone told her he was picking his way through a minefield with his words as much as she had been. "I am gratified to hear both of your peaceful intent, and of your … technological advancements that make such a peaceful intent possible."

He'd heard the warning, then, and wanted her to know it.

"My people, unfortunately, have not had the advantages yours have had in that matter," he continued, his tone cautious and measured. "As I told you, we had the encounter many years back with sapient species whose intentions were not peaceful. And in our own government, we have also encountered those who see force as a first option, rather than a last. However, there are those of us who share your ideals, and …" He paused a moment, casting a quick, involuntary glance at the aides. "And I believe that, if we were able to demonstrate to them the benefits of peaceful negotiation …"

"Peaceful negotiation to what end?" asked Alba again.

Harroch's eyes darted around the room again, then came to rest on her. "An alliance," he said quietly. "As you said. A commitment to sharing knowledge, information, technology, commerce, mutual protection … sibling nations, as it were. Something that would show those who are more concerned with war the strength that could come from peace."

Alba frowned, and stopped herself with an effort from glancing at Yosip. "Within negotiated bounds, of course," she said, her own words cautious.

"Of course, of course." Harroch tipped his head to one side. "But for the sake of both of our objectives, if your is truly what you tell me it is, it would be … helpful if we could negotiate this settlement before the portal is reopened."

"And what am I to tell my diplomatic aides and my associates back on-planet, coming back to them with a proposed agreement, if they have the same uncomfortable questions that had crossed my mind yesterday?" she asked, keeping her voice low.

Harroch's eyes widened in silent warning.

"Of course, I expect that if I present them with the explanations you gave me yesterday, they would be satisfied," she added, pitching her voice just a little louder so as to be overheard.

The words tasted sour in her mouth. But she did not intend to be responsible for another death.

Neither did she intend to allow Harroch to forget the entire matter.

He paused a moment. "That is excellent, of course, that there will not be such uncomfortable questions," he said at last. "I assume it is because you will not bring such uncomfortable matters to their attention, but rather trust our goodwill. As befits allies. I would hope our relationship would be one of trust. One of … family. Sibling species." There was an emphasis on the words that made Alba look at him more closely, but his face gave nothing away.

"Now," he said. "Shall you and I speak of what such a relationship might look like?"

By the time she and Yosip stood and took their leave of Harroch, the late afternoon sun was streaming through the airy windows, lending a soft, warm glow to the setting.

Alba's head ached dully, her muscles stiff from the hard seat, but for the first time since she'd arrived on this Mystery-forgotten planet, she felt as if she was beginning to find her balance.

She still had no idea of what the yibo didn't want her to know, or why. But she had at least something to go on.

Family. Sibling species

She watched the yibo ambassador as he left them at the door.

There were far too many similarities between the yibo culture and her own for it to be mere chance. And as alien as these creatures were, she'd expected them to be … more so. The differences here were skin-deep, more akin to the differences between Villa Nova do Sol and an obscure settlement in the depths of the Rim Mountains than between two unrelated species. And hadn't the Colorida scientists said something about the genetic sample that had been sent through the portal? Something about the genetics being strangely similar to humans?

It didn't answer the question definitively, of course, nor did it solve the problems. But it was a start.

"I will see you again tomorrow, Alba," Harroch said, dipping his head and averting his eyes in the yibo sign of respect.

"Thank you," she said, copying the gesture with rather less grace.

But it was possible that they had, at least, one ally in this place.

Not certain, but for once, possible.

She and Yosip didn't speak on the way back to their rooms. She was far too aware of the yibo guides behind them. Their presence was nominally a courtesy, to be certain Alba made it back to her rooms safely, but she'd seen the outline of weapons under their thin tunics, and the degree of plausible deniability was only a veneer barely substantial enough to deserve the name.

Yosip seemed to have come to a similar conclusion, because he too didn't attempt to speak until they'd closed the door to Alba's room.

"It would explain some things," he said quietly, when she'd finished laying out her thoughts. "If we're distantly related, perhaps through one of the generation ships we lost contact with centuries ago, it's possible the language was passed down through families. And if it were long enough in the past, it could also explain why we've seen no humans living here. If our two species could interbreed, it's possible that after enough years there'd be no one left who's fully genetically human. But the maker's mark on that ball?" He shook his head. "It's not enough. They're hiding something, still."

"I know," said Alba softly. "I intend to find out what before I agree to recommend any course of action as to an alliance to the Council upon our return."

He looked up sharply. "Madam. These people here—they're trusting their lives to us. We learned yesterday what happens if we step somewhere the yibo don't want us to. Is asking those questions a risk you're comfortable taking?"

"This is the fate of the entire Joias System at stake," she snapped. "Whether or not we ally with the yibo could affect our future for generations."

Yosip closed his eyes for a moment, the weariness evident in his posture. "Perhaps you're right. Perhaps I'm not as used as you are to putting aside the well-being of the one for a hoped-for future benefit. But this crew trusts us. They came on this mission because they trusted we'd keep them safe. These are more than just pawns in a political game, Alba. These are people."

"And so are the people back on Colorida," she said quietly.

There was a tap on the door, and Alba glanced up.

"I imagine that's Istvay," said Yosip, rising with an effort. "They told me they'd come check in on things when we got back, and report on anything they'd found."

He started for the door, but before he reached it, Istvay pushed it open and stepped through.

They wore their typical stubborn scowl, and the combination of the sweat and grime from a long day's labour, and the exhaustion in their face, made them look faintly piratical.

"Yosip," Istvay said, their scowl dropping momentarily as they turned to him. There was genuine affection in their tone, and Yosip smiled.

"Istvay. How did things go today?"

Istvay gave a quick shake of their head and dropped down wearily on one of the stools.

Alba bit back her irritation—she was accustomed to at least a nod of courtesy before someone took their seat in front of her. But she knew from experience that giving the slightest hint of her irritation to Istvay would only egg them on.

If she was back on Colorida—

She broke off the thought. None of them were on Colorida right now, and the chances of any of them getting back there were largely dependent on their ability to work together. Which in this case meant, she supposed, that she'd have to take Istvay's shocking lack of manners, or more likely, their intentional provocation, in stride.

"Did you find out anything important?" she asked after a moment, trying and likely failing to keep the sharpness from her tone.

Istvay glanced over at her in irritation, then sighed and ran a weary hand over their face. "It's difficult when we don't have any idea what they're saying," they said, tipping their head back. "Aran had his hands full with Ani, and Ines and I were trying to keep the survivors from panicking. Honestly, it's a bloody miracle they haven't yet, locked in here like they are." They tipped their chin towards the door. "There's food out on the table. Ines is out there, I think she wanted to talk with you, Yosip. She's been working on a translator program, and she said you'd have heard different words than she would have out here. She was hoping she could get some of the background recording from your wavelink."

Yosip glanced between Istvay and Alba with a faint raise of his eyebrow, but nodded and got to his feet. "I'll go find her then. You don't want to come with me?"

"I'll be there in a minute," said Istvay. There was something grim about the set of their jaw, and for a brief, absurd moment, Alba felt a flash of something that could have been fear.

Yosip hesitated, then stepped out the door, and Alba felt an irrational urge to call him back.

She didn't, though, just turned to face Istvay with her most forbidding expression as the door slid shut.

Istvay was slumped down, elbows on the low table, chin resting on their hands, but as the door latch clicked, they looked up.

"Did you tell the yibo to offer to talk to Aran about their science?" they asked quietly. "Is that why they approached him yesterday?"

She met Istvay's eyes, despite the odd urge to look away. "Yes, I did," she said. "It's what he told me he wanted."

Istvay's gaze held hers. "And you're hoping he'll find something out for you."

She nodded.

Istvay narrowed their eyes. "You're using him."

"He's using this expedition," she snapped. "Don't tell me you don't know why he agreed to come. He has no interest in diplomacy, but he agreed to help if he could get what he wanted. I don't see how that's any different than what I'm doing. The ambassador I'm speaking with is nervous about something to do with that box that was sent through the portal. If Aran wants to help look for information through other means—"

"Aran is focused on one thing right now, and one thing only," Istvay said in a flat voice. "And if you'd like to talk him out of it, you're welcome to try, and may the Mystery grant you more success than it's granted me."

They drew in a long breath and released it slowly. "Listen," they said, their tone softer now. "You're trying to keep everyone here alive. I get it. And I … appreciate your efforts." There was a stiffness to their words, as if it was taking an effort to get them out. "But— leave Aran out of this, okay? You've done enough to him already. Asked him to come along on this stupid mission, for one, not to mention everything you did before. And the thing is, Aran's nice. He's a hell of a lot nicer than I am. And he tends to forgive and forget, and believe the best of everyone. And—" they broke off, shaking their head. "And look, I just don't want you to hurt him any more than you already have. That's all." Their voice was low, and they didn't meet her eye.

She frowned. "I'm—not entirely sure what you mean."

Istvay was clearly too tired to be their normal antagonistic self, and she wasn't certain how to navigate this unaccustomed vulnerability on their part.

Istvay looked up again and met her gaze challengingly. "You don't know what I mean," they repeated in a flat tone. Then they shook their head and laughed, a short, bitter laugh. "Of course you don't know what I mean. You probably didn't even think about it, did you?"

Alba's frown deepened. "I assure you," she said tartly, "I have no idea what you're talking about. The first time I had any dealings with Aran, other than official Council business, was when I requested his presence on this mission. And you can believe me that I regret this turn of events as much as any of us." She paused. "Unless you're referring to the reforms that ensured he, and presumably you as well, were able to complete your education in the first place, and had the qualifications necessary to be asked to accompany me. And I hardly think you can blame me for—"

Istvay gave a short, incredulous laugh. "That's what you—" they stopped, shaking their head. "Your 'reforms' sent Aran and me to university. Sure. You did that. But do you know how many of the kids we grew up with they sent to prison? You, personally, sent to prison, with your damn 'reforms?'"

They'd leaned forward, and she fought the urge to lean away.

"I didn't send anyone to prison," she said acerbically. "I merely passed a handful of laws that were part of a holistic package to assist those living on the streets."

Istvay's eyes flashed. "Assist those living on the streets," they repeated. "I lived on the streets. I know you know that. The news packets make a big deal of it every time they write something about Aran. They call me a former homeless child. My mother was one of those people you were trying to get rid of, with your 'holistic package.' I guess you think people on the streets live there for fun?"

Alba was discomfited by the intensity of their gaze, and wished, irrationally, that Feliu was there.

"Living on the streets leads to a number of undesirable outcomes in children and adults alike," she snapped. "I'm not sure why you are trying so hard to find malice behind—"

"I'm not sure why you think that if we'd had a better option, my mother wouldn't have taken it instead. My friends wouldn't have taken it instead," broke in Istvay, their voice as sharp as her own. "Do you really think that people too poor to afford a home are also too stupid to know what's best for them?"

"Colorida isn't a backwater village in the Rim Mountains. There are shelters, and—"

"Shelters, yes, where you move every damn night, and you can't leave your things without someone stealing them. Where you sleep in a room with a hundred other people, and you don't get a moment of privacy. Would you raise your child like that, if you had a child? Do you really blame my mother? You really think she's stupid for raising me on the street, where at least we had our own space, instead of inside one of those hellholes? They do their best, I'm sure. They don't have much funding, but they do what they can. Because Colorida is a humane planet, just like you said, isn't it? Where you treat even lowly beggars right, you don't let even the worthless homeless kids starve. Happy to provide them a nice comfortable jail cell with three hot meals a day."

She just stared at them, shocked at the intensity in their voice.

"The choice you gave our friends, Aran and me—get off the streets, or go to prison. You think any of us wouldn't have got off the streets if we had a better option? Look, you think Aran and I are worth something because you can damn well use us. I promise you, even if Aran wasn't a damn genius, he'd still be ten times the person you are. But you could make that decision for us, because you, in your infinite wisdom, knew what we needed better than we did. Did you ever think to ask us? Even once? Or were we so far below your notice that there was no need?"

Alba was still staring at them. She felt, somehow, as though she couldn't pull in enough oxygen.

She'd gotten some pushback on that particular set of laws, she remembered, but no one had given her a convincing argument as to why they should be changed, although some of the councillors had grumbled at the cost. And she'd given those individuals with potential, such as Aran and this ungrateful, irritating friend of his, the chance of a better life—a university education, a steady job.

It had been for their own good—despite what Istvay said, every person who'd been taken to prison had been taken there only after they refused every other viable option.

"All they had to do to stay out of prison was get clean, move into a shelter, accept meaningful employment—" she began.

Istvay slapped their open palm down the table, and the noise startled her into silence.

"All they had to do was get clean." Their voice wasn't even angry anymore, just a sort of weary resignation. "Get clean, go live in one of your benevolent shelters, get a job. Simple as that, right?" They looked up, and again, she was startled by the intensity in those brown eyes. "Would it matter to you," they said softly. "Would it even matter to you if I told you that one of the girls Aran and I grew up with died in prison? She died there. Just get clean, right? That's all she had to do. Sounds simple. You have no idea—"

They broke off, shaking their head. "You just trample roughshod over everyone's lives for their own damn good, and you don't even bother looking back at the wreckage you leave the behind.”

They stood, leaning wearily against the table, then straightened with an effort. They turned back for a moment, measuring her with their eyes. “You never had to deal with someone drinking, or shooting up, because it was better than whatever the hell was happening inside their head, did you? I guess I should envy you.”

She drew in a sharp breath, and for a moment, a face danced in her memory—dark, mischievous eyes, laughing, teasing mouth, devil-may-care smile.

She shoved the memory away. “Perhaps not,” she snapped. “But a doctor doesn’t have to contract a disease to know how to treat it.”

Istvay was still studying her. At last, they turned away. “Maybe not,” they said bitterly. “But they’d be a damn poor doctor if they didn’t listen to their patient when they say the treatment is killing them.” They hit the door control, and the door whispered open. “I’m going to bed. If there’s anything else we need to talk about, we can talk in the morning. Just … just leave Aran alone, okay? That’s all I’m asking.”

Then they were gone, and the door slid shut behind them.

Alba watched after them for a long time.

She shivered, and pushed herself to her feet. The ache in her legs at the movement was almost welcome. At least the pain was enough to help clear the memories.

She’d been trying to help. It only made sense that someone with years of experience, someone with education and ability, would be in the best place to make such decisions. And most people agreed her measures had been a success, striking an appropriate balance between strictness and kindness. At the very least, it had curbed the population of homeless on the streets of do Sol, which had been growing increasingly out-of-control.

But—there was that look in Istvay's eyes as they'd stepped out the door, a mix of anger and mockery, resignation, pity. And under it, a sharp hurt, pain that even after all these years hadn't gone away.

She realized she was clenching her fists tightly enough that her fingernails dug into her palms.

Yosip stepped back into the room a short time later. When he saw her, his forehead creased in concern. "Madam? Are you alright?" He glanced around quickly. "Where's Istvay? They didn't meet Ines and me in the dining hall."

"They went to bed," she said.

Yosip nodded slowly and sat down on the stool across from her. "What happened?"

"Nothing," said Alba irritably. "Istvay expressed their deeply held belief that I was looking for a way to hurt Aran, who apparently hung the moon in the sky, and then left."

Yosip was watching her, and she looked away from him deliberately.

The two of them sat in silence for a few moments.

"Do you ever wonder," she said, almost to herself, "whether we're doing the right thing?"

Yosip looked up, startled out of his reverie. He studied her for a moment, his bright brown eyes creased with sympathy. "I wonder that every day of my life," he said at last, quietly. He rose. "And now, I suppose, we'd best follow Istvay's and Ines' example and get some sleep. I have a feeling tomorrow will be another long day."

She watched the doorway for a while after he left, and at last made her slow way into her sleeping chamber. But the strange unease brought on by Istvay's words, and the haunting memories they had conjured in her mind—memories she couldn't exorcise even after all these years—made her dreams restless and troubled.

11

"Savina. I hear you've been threatening my people when I send you out on jobs." Yuur's voice was cold and dangerous.

Savina dimpled at her, fiddling with the small, needle-thin knife in her hand.

The aliens had stopped trying to disarm her once she'd proved that she could be as deadly with a shard of broken glass as she was with her knives. At least one of these aliens—yibo, as they called themselves—would wear a scar to remember that lesson by.

"I don't remember threatening anyone," she said. "Although …" She tapped her chin with one finger. "Although I do remember one of your people trying to sabotage the hit. I explained to him very nicely that he shouldn't do that, and that was the end of it, I think." She glanced up, catching Yuur's gaze. "You've seen me work. If I'd wanted them dead, there'd be no one here to complain, would there?"

Yuur looked at her for a long time, her eyes bright with a mixture of distrust and fury. "You've been useful, Savina," she said at last. "But don't forget your place." She paused. "I don't have any jobs for you today. So you're out helping to bring in packages from the warehouse. And I don't want to hear another complaint about you."

Savina gave her an insincere smile, still fiddling with her knife. "I can't imagine you would."

The cargo they were supposed to bring in was from one of the warehouses near the centre of the city. Joska was waiting when she arrived, and one of Yuur's crew bosses, Yika, gestured Savina over to join her, scowling.

She sidled up beside her as they walked. "Yika," she said, and the woman turned with a start.

"What is it, human?" she asked at last.

"Why did Yuur saddle you with this job?" Savina's voice was light with sympathy. "I thought I'd heard that you were supposed to be a crew boss. How did you end up getting sent out like this, in the middle of the day, with two dangerous criminals?"

Yika glowered at her, and Savina blinked, widening her eyes. "I'm sorry. I really am just curious." She paused a moment and lowered her voice. "Aren't you afraid of the kari?"

As she'd expected, the yibo woman flinched almost unconsciously. "What are you talking about?" she hissed. "What do they have to do with anything?"

Savina widened her eyes further, hiding a small, triumphant smile. "I … maybe I misunderstood. I thought they only came out in the mornings?"

The yibo woman cocked her head in puzzlement, then gave a brief snort of annoyance. "Someone told you that? You don't even know what they are, do you?" She slowed, turning to face Savina, and her face was serious. "Trust me, human, you should count yourself lucky. It's not just us they hunt. Humans are a delicacy.

You're not the first human we've seen in this system, and you won't be the last. They wait. They sit on the sidelines and they wait, and when they see an opening, they stream through and hunt. And you don't have the protections we have. You don't have force-fields over your cities. We do, and even then they get in here sometimes—someone gets tempted by the profits, thinks they're smart enough to strike a bargain, and lets them through. And you? You think you're so frightening, I know. But you're nothing but livestock."

She turned away, and ignored any further attempts at conversation.

Savina moved back until she was walking beside Joska, her thoughts spinning.

"What was that about?" Joska asked.

Savina shrugged, and gave the woman her best smile. "I don't know. There was something they were talking about the other day that they seemed frightened of. I was just trying to make sure it wasn't something we needed to worry about."

Joska watched Savina. "I'm never going to get you to tell me what you're really up to, am I?" she said at last. "You know, sometimes having friends can actually be helpful?"

"We're not friends," Savina snapped.

Joska smiled. "Allies, then, at least."

Savina narrowed her eyes and looked away.

When they reached the warehouse, a good thirty minutes' walk from the safehouse, the yibo set Savina and Joska to work loading up the transport drones. It was late morning, and the sun was hot enough that sweat beaded on Savina's skin in the thick, humid air, prickling under her hairline and dripping uncomfortably down her face.

She was used to heat. But the heat in the Rim Mountains was dry and sharp, not the sticky wet of this place. The air here smelled of a strange mixture of refuse and greenery—the yibo, she'd gathered, had an obsession with trees and plants, and even if they hadn't, this seemed the kind of place where things grew whether you wanted them to or not—flowers sprouting through cracks in the cement, moss and vines creeping up the smooth surfaces of the buildings.

The yibo watched the humans as they worked, leaned back against the side of the alley.

It wasn't until they were almost finished, and most of the yibo had started back after the drones, that Savina felt that faint, tickling unease in the back of her mind, that sense of something wrong—

She dived out of the way, and only as she was rolling on the pavement, only as, in the back of her head, she heard the *ting* of a weapon, heard Joska's quiet grunt of pain, did she realize where she'd been standing.

In front of Joska.

She rolled to her feet, muscles tight with panic, and looked back to the wall she'd been standing against. Joska was leaned against it, and blood trickled down her collar—

Savina leapt forward, heart hammering, and grabbed the woman, shoving her down into an alley. Then she looked down at the wound, almost not wanting to see.

The spike had passed so close to Joska's neck that it had cut a thin line across the skin under her ear, but other than that, she was unhurt.

Savina let out a shaky sigh of relief. And then a wave of fury washed over her, so strong it almost left her lightheaded.

"I'll kill her," she muttered, turning to where their supervisor had been standing.

She was gone.

And then she glanced down at the spike in her hand, and the boiling anger in her blood turned suddenly to ice.

This weapon style was one that she recognized. Something she'd known back on Colorida.

Which meant—

"What in the system—" Joska began.

Savina shoved her pistol into the woman's hands. "It's Reka. You take this. I'm going to bloody well kill her."

She stepped out into the street quickly, tracing the path the weapon must have taken. From the corner of her eye she saw the briefest flicker of movement, visible for just an instant before disappearing around the corner of the alley. The figure's sensual grace still had the power to make Savina's throat dry and her pulse pound.

Reka Soler.

Savina took after her at a dead run.

She kept to the walls, dodging in and out of shelter, a mix of fury and guilt and sick attraction churning in the pit of her stomach.

Reka had almost killed Joska. And it had happened because of Savina.

When she'd endangered people before, it had always been part of the game—anyone stupid enough to get in her way deserved to be her shield against people who were too squeamish to use the tools they'd been given.

But for some reason, this suddenly felt far, far too personal.

She rounded a corner, and another spike hit the wall millimetres from her head. She dived to the ground and came up with a flare in one hand, tossing it overhand in the direction the shot had come from. There was a muffled explosion and a sharp gasp, and she rounded the corner in time to see Reka stagger, knocked off balance.

Savina yanked out her knife and threw it. It hit Reka, skidding against her grey suit, and embedded itself in the woman's arm.

Reka turned, and for just a moment, Savina's eyes locked with hers.

The cold, implacable hatred in those slate-hazel eyes pierced Savina, as sharp as the knife she'd just thrown.

Blood dripped from Reka's arm, where Savina's knife was still embedded. The woman didn't even glance at it, just reached down, her eyes never leaving Savina's, yanked it out with a quick jerk, and tossed it scornfully to the ground.

Even the disdain in the gesture was a magnetic pull Savina couldn't tear her eyes from. Her chest was oddly tight, and for just a moment, she couldn't breathe.

With a movement that was graceful and fluid and almost too quick to follow, Reka pulled out a small, hand-held crossbow, and Savina barely had time to dive into an alley before a bolt shattered on the wall behind her.

When she peered out, Reka was long gone.

Savina's heart was pounding as she got shakily to her feet.

She brushed the dust off of her tunic in irritation.

Of course her heart was pounding. She'd just been running, after all, and she'd almost been killed.

It had nothing at all to do with the way Reka had met her gaze, yanked out Savina's knife and tossed it down like a challenge, as if the blood streaming down her arm wasn't worth her notice.

Nothing at all to do with the fact that Savina would probably be cursed with another three days of tangled, restless dreams, of Reka's hands twisting in her collar, shoving her up against the alley wall, those cold hazel eyes boring into hers.

Savina sucked in a long breath, and turned back to where she'd left Joska.

Joska met her halfway there. She took in Savina's disheveled state with a raised eyebrow. "So. Your first reaction when you're faced with a murderous government agent is to run after them on your own?" she asked in a dry tone. Blood stained the collar of her tunic, but it was clear that it had been no more than a scratch.

It hadn't been serious at all. But for some reason, the memory of Joska with blood dripping from her neck, the crossbow bolt embedded in the wall beside her, still made Savina's blood go cold.

"Are you alright?" Savina asked brusquely.

Joska gave her a quick smile. "It's pretty clear she wasn't trying to kill me." She paused a moment, the smile reaching of the corners of her eyes. "If I didn't know any better, I think you were worried about me. And here I thought you were a heartless murderer."

Savina glared at her, then gestured down the street with a jerk of her head. "I am a heartless murder," she snapped. "But I don't know how to pilot a ship well enough to get us off this damn place."

The smile tugged at the corners of Joska's mouth again, but she nodded, and they started back down towards the safehouse.

Savina's heart was still pounding oddly.

Reka was still after her. Reka hadn't gone with Alba and the others. Somehow, she was out here on the streets. Stalking Savina. Waiting for her.

She shivered.

They had to get out. They had to get away, she had to get Beni and Nicolau and the others to safety. Then she could find a way to deal with Reka.

If Reka were dead, there'd be no one in the diplomatic party who would know who she was. She'd have time to plan her next move. But here, with Yuur, she was trapped. No way to keep herself safe.

No way to keep anyone safe.

She got out, or they'd all be killed.

"Even then they get in here sometimes—someone gets tempted by the profits, thinks they're smart enough to strike a bargain, and lets them through." Yika's words echoed in her mind.

She had no idea what these kari creatures were. But if it was true —if they were sapient enough to strike a bargain with—she'd do it. She'd find a way to let them in. Because as far as she was concerned —this entire yibo city could burn.

12

Aran

"Aran."

He looked up, startled, to see Istvay leaning against the door frame to his room.

Their face was drawn with strain, and there was exhaustion behind their expression, and Aran had to fight back the twinge of guilt that settled in his stomach at the sight of his friend.

He'd hardly spoken with Istvay since they'd arrived in the compound three days ago. He told himself it was because they were both busy, and they both had too many things to do, but—

Well, but the truth was, he'd been secretly hoping that their paths wouldn't cross, not yet.

He knew Istvay disapproved of what he was doing. He knew Istvay wanted only to get the yibo to release them, to open the portal, and that Istvay was on the verge of losing their actual crap.

He wasn't sure he was ready, just yet, to start a fight with Istvay about how much their life was worth.

"Istvay," he said, trying to smile. "How are the negotiations going?"

Istvay stepped inside, and, glancing around, sat down on one of the stools that the yibo seemed convinced that humans preferred as furniture. "I … don't know," they said quietly. "It's hard to say at the moment." They brushed a hand across their face in a weary, unconscious gesture that made Aran's chest hurt, just a little. "What about you?" They looked up at him, attempting a smile of their own.

Aran averted his gaze. "Um. I—it's going alright. I spoke with some of the scientists. We're … we're going out to collect some samples today, in the jungle."

Istvay glanced at the disarray of the room. "You're—just collecting samples," they said, and there was a quiet note in their voice that told Aran they knew he wasn't telling them everything.

He managed a small grin. "One of the scientists invited me to come along."

Istvay watched him for a long moment, and then they stood abruptly, a flash of frustration on their face. "Aran. I know you're not going to listen to anything I have to say. Honestly, I should be used to it by now. But I'm not stupid. Don't bloody lie to me."

Aran clenched his teeth against the sick feeling coiling around his chest. "I'm not lying to you," he said, more sharply than he'd intended. "I'm going out to collect samples."

Istvay was still studying him, and there was still that sharp flash of anger in their expression. "And that's all you're doing," they said in a flat voice.

Aran hesitated a moment, then sighed, looking down. "It is what I'm doing. But I—I hope that the scientist who invited me might be able to—to give me some information. About the box."

Istvay gave a quick shake of their head. "I don't have to ask what information you want," they said grimly. "But can't you at least wait until at we know we have a way off of this place before you try to get yourself killed again? Wait until at least we know what these yibo want, and we have a chance of surviving this?"

Aran glared back at them. "And if we do find a way back home? I have no guarantee anyone will wait until we find a cure before we leave here, do I? No guarantee that once the portal's opened, we won't just go back through and let it close behind us. Because as far as I can tell, you don't actually give a damn about this. Or am I wrong?"

He could tell from the tight press of Istvay's lips that his words had hit their mark.

"Listen, Aran," they said, their voice strained. "I get that this is important to you. And I'm touched, honestly. But you know damn well this is dangerous. They killed someone two days ago as a warning, remember? And now you're risking your life, recklessly, for —"

This time Aran stood as well, his heart pounding. "I'm being reckless?" he snapped. "And your life is worthless. You're acting like we could just walk out of here, I could just walk out of here, knowing that you're going to die within a year, and I should be fine with that. If you're not going to damn well care, Istvay, then who else is going to?"

"I'm not the reckless one here," Istvay snapped back. "I'm just trying to keep all of us alive."

"Not all of us," said Aran in a low voice. "Not you. And I'm not going to let you selflessly sacrifice your life for the greater good."

"And what's your alternative?" asked Istvay, their voice short. "You'll sacrifice your life for the greater good?" They paused a moment, clearly trying to regain control. "Aran," they said at last. "You say you want to save my life. But how do you think I'd feel, knowing that you'd been trying to save my life when you—when you

___"

They broke off, turning away.

Aran drew in a long, shaky breath. "And how do you think I'd feel, knowing that I could have saved you, and I didn't?"

For a long moment, neither of them spoke.

At last, Istvay turned. Their face was still strained, and their voice still tight with irritation, but they made an effort to smile. "I don't know why I thought I could make you listen to me," they said, and their tone cut Aran like a knife. "But if I can't get you to listen, and I can't get you to talk to me, can you—can you at least promised to be careful?"

There was something tired and vulnerable in their expression, and Aran wondered, suddenly, how much they'd slept in the last three days.

If they'd slept at all.

They were standing there, watching him, and he swallowed hard.

He could lie, of course. But Istvay had always been able to see through his lies. And anyways, with the look on their face right now, he didn't think he'd be able to bear to.

"I'll be as careful as I can," he said at last.

He didn't have to look at Istvay to know they'd heard exactly what he'd said, and exactly what he hadn't—he'd be as careful as he could, without risking his ultimate goal.

Istvay's expression hardened, just a little. "I suppose that the best I'll get out of you," they said, and there was a touch of bitterness in their voice that almost made Aran want to take it back.

Almost.

But even now, he could see the hollowness under their cheekbones, the dark circles beneath their eyes. How their hands shook, in a way that couldn't be explained by simple exhaustion or strain or stress.

So instead, he just nodded.

Istvay sighed. "Well, I hope I'll see you tonight, then," they said at last, their voice still bitter. "Although I guess that's not really important, right?"

They turned away, and were gone before Aran had time to formulate an answer.

"What are we doing, Ani?" he whispered, leaning his cheek against the comforting bulk of her on his shoulder. "What the hell am I doing wrong?"

Ani chirped, rubbing a delicate tentacle across his face, and he stroked her gently. But somehow, he couldn't make himself smile.

By the time he got to the courtyard outside, where he was going to meet Ree, he'd somehow managed to put the interaction far enough out of his mind that he could actually focus on the task at hand. But he couldn't stop his brain from turning the words over and over in his head, replaying again and again the hurt look on Istvay's face as they stepped out the door.

He hated hurting Istvay. He'd always hated hurting Istvay.

But as much as he hated it, watching them die, and knowing he might have done something to stop it, would be worse. It would be a million times worse.

Ree was already there, and she gave him that close-lipped smile that seemed to be a common greeting among the aliens.

Aran smiled back, remembering just in time to keep his lips closed so as not to turn the friendly gesture into a threat.

He couldn't speak her language, and she couldn't speak his, so he simply waved at his pack to show that he was ready. She tipped her head to one side and gestured to a small transport.

It looked—much smaller than he was comfortable with. Honestly, anything that was going to be picking him off the ground and hurtling him through the air would be smaller than he was comfortable with. But this looked closer to a bike than a transport.

She climbed on and gestured impatiently.

Aran swallowed hard and climbed on after her.

Ani's tentacles tightened on his shoulder as they started down the bustling streets. The transport was barely big enough for the two of them, but Ree drove it with every sign of competence. Still, the speed at which the ground flew past beneath them made Aran feel slightly nauseous, and he gripped the edges of the transport hard enough that his knuckles were white.

When at last they reached the city gates, Ree tapped something into the glowing gate screen. Two guards appeared a few moments later, and she handed them a token, which they scanned. Then they stepped back and beckoned the transport forwards, and Ree drove straight for the force-field barrier. Aran closed his eyes and clutched on tighter, squeezing one eye open just as they reached it.

But at the last second, the force-field shimmered and parted, and they were through.

He let out a shallow breath of relief and glanced down, then groaned.

Opening his eyes may have been a mistake.

As bad as it had been to watch the city streets slipping away below him, watching the dark green of the jungle rush by beneath them was somehow even more viscerally terrifying.

He swallowed hard, and Ree turned back to him, saying something in her strange, chirping language. He had no idea what she was saying, of course, but from the tone of her voice, he guessed it was some expression of concern.

He shook his head, and tried to smile, instead of looking sick.

She asked again, and he made an incoherent, panicked sound, pointing ahead of them. She made that soft humming sound that was the yibo equivalent of laughter and turned back to her driving.

He squeezed his eyes closed again.

He didn't care how much she laughed at him, as long as he survived this damn trip.

Ani tightened her tentacles down on his shoulder, picking up on his distress, and gave a worried growl. He didn't have to look to know her bulbous eyes were peering around, trying to find the source of the threat. He managed a weak smile. "It's okay, Ani," he whispered, stroking one of her tentacles. "I just—I don't like flying, is all."

She growled again, but settled a little, and he breathed a small sigh of relief.

At last, Ree brought their small craft down in a clearing, where a small group of scientists waited with clear impatience. She gestured Aran to follow, and walked briskly over to her colleagues, speaking to them quickly in their rapid, chirping speech.

After a short conversation, in which the other scientists looked at Aran skeptically, Ree came over to him and said something in a slow, clear tone. At his look of utter incomprehension, she sighed and made a motion with her fingers as of two legs walking.

Apparently, they'd be going on foot from here.

He glanced around, trying to figure out why. This part of the jungle looked no different from the part they'd driven through.

He made a questioning gesture, and she tried to say something, then stopped, shook her head, and gestured him to follow.

Maybe he could get a translator to tell him what she meant when they got back.

They didn't walk long before they reached a small dome,

constructed of the same odd, light-refracting glass that the city buildings were made of, and protected by a large force-field. The scientists' relief was palpable as they stepped inside, the visible tension in their bodies releasing once the sky was once again filtered through the faint, translucent haze of the force-field.

Aran stood watching for a few minutes as the scientists went about their work. He couldn't understand their words, and there was no interpreter along, but there was something soothing and universal in the way they checked their screens, examined their equipment, frowned down at the neat rows of plants in the raised beds.

"Psssst."

He started, and turned quickly.

Ree stood behind him, a furtive look on her face and obvious tension in her posture. She beckoned to him, making a gesture that he guessed meant "quiet."

He turned to follow, his heart beating faster now. She glanced quickly around, then stepped to the force-field, grabbed his arm, and, after tapping the tech device on her wrist, pulled him through after her. And then they were out, and into the jungle proper.

"What—" he began, but she repeated her gesture of earlier and beckoned him again to follow, pulling a smaller version of one of the yibo weapons from her knapsack.

Aran could feel Ani perk up as they ducked into the dense undergrowth. Ree held her weapon in front of her cautiously as they pushed their way through the heavy vines, and Aran pulled out his bush-knife, cutting through tangles of vines too thick for him and Ree to crawl through.

They couldn't have made it more than a few hundred metres before Ani's grumbling purr changed to an uneasy growl.

Aran glanced around quickly. "What is it, girl?" he murmured.

"What's the matter?"

Ree glanced up, her expression halfway between concern and irritation.

She might be right to be irritated, honestly—knowing Ani, this could be a wild animal preparing to attack them, or a funny-shaped leaf that she found insulting.

The volume of Ani's growl increased, changing towards her high-pitched, teakettle whistle, and she shifted on Aran's shoulder.

Ree was looking around warily now, but at last she gave a short shake of her head and turned back to the jungle ahead of them.

Aran almost didn't see it either. He almost thought, for just a moment, that maybe it was just a funny-shaped leaf.

And then something that had been niggling at the edge of his mind for a few moments now finally caught, and he realized the shadow on the ground around them was odd, and darker than it should have been, and not entirely tree-shaped …

He shouted a warning. Ree spun around at the panic in his voice, and then her mouth gaped open in a way that would, in another situation, have been almost comical. She grabbed his arm, yanking him after her as the massive shadow, which had been slowly descending, dropped on them like a falling stone.

He caught a glimpse of the massive, formless pancake of a body, absurdly tiny legs, and teeth—far, far too many teeth, far more teeth than should have been possible, even for a creature with a circumference roughly the size of an abandoned escape pod.

He dived at the last moment, shoving Ree forward, and they rolled, barely missing the outside edge of the creature which, now that Aran saw it in closer proximity, was much too bulky to look like a pancake. Then they'd both scrambled to their feet, and were off running.

The creature moved far, far too quickly for its bulk, and it would be around in front of them in a moment—Aran skidded to a halt, but Ree, ahead of him, wasn't quite fast enough. She tripped, sprawling out on the jungle floor in front of the creature. Aran grabbed for his bush-knife in a sort of hopeless panic … and then Ani had launched herself off his shoulder towards the creature.

"Ani!" he shouted, and then she was on top of it, eye pouches bulging comically, hissing so loudly half the jungle could probably hear it.

The creature, whatever it was, had retreated at her attack, and although he could see her lashing it with her tentacle spikes and burying the fangs of her second external mouth into its bulk, it hadn't yet succumbed to her venom. It was clearly mad with rage, though, thrashing and rolling, trying to buck her off, and liable to smash Ree in the process.

He grabbed the scientist by the jacket and dragged her back out of the way, then yanked her to her feet and pointed back towards the bio-dome. "Go," he shouted over the sounds of Ani's hissing. "Get out of here, I'll get Ani."

Ree grabbed his arm and tried to pull him after her, but he shook her off. "I can't leave Ani," he said through his teeth. "Go!"

He turned back to the struggle.

Ani clung on with all eight tentacles and probably her beak, but he could see by her little, jerking movements that the interaction was not playing out exactly as she'd expected. Still, she clung on grimly, every tentacle sucker suctioned down onto the amorphous body of the creature.

He wouldn't be able to pull Ani off the beast. Even if he did, as pain- and rage-maddened as it clearly was, it would likely lash out and kill him or Ani or both.

And in the state she was in, Ani likely wouldn't be up for listening if he asked her nicely to come.

There had been, he reflected ruefully, many situations over the last three years in which Ani hadn't been up for listening.

He bit his lip, taking stock.

The creature was thrashing wildly, but its movements were less coordinated than they had been. The venom must be taking effect, then, slowly. But—

Damn it to hell. One of Ani's tentacles was sinking into the creature's gelatinous body.

He swore under his breath and grabbed up a branch, starting cautiously towards Ani and her opponent.

He could hear, distantly, Ree shouting something. He didn't need to understand her words to have a fairly solid guess as to what that something might be. But damn it, he'd almost lost Ani just a few days ago, and he wasn't about to do it again.

He was close enough now to almost be able to reach out and touch the struggling creatures.

"Ani!" he whispered.

The pancake-beast spun, and he jerked up his stick just in time as dozens of teeth clamped down, the animal's full attention swinging to land on him.

He realized, in complete fascination, that the outside rim of the creature's entire body was covered in small eyes—a mesmerizing discovery, but somewhat unnerving when all of those … thirty? Fifty? A hundred? eyes were turned balefully on him.

Very gently, Aran let go his grip on the stick and held out his hand, making his posture as nonthreatening as he knew how.

"Hello there," he murmured. "Not having a very good day, are you?"

The thing pounced.

Aran snatched up another stick, jamming it into the creature's jaws as its massive bulk descended on him. Ani was hissing like a punctured air-cylinder.

"Ani! Leave it!" he shouted desperately.

The beast splintered the stick in its teeth, tearing it from Aran's hands with a quick twisting motion.

He noticed, vaguely, that Ree's shouts from behind him had stopped, replaced with a series of horrified, disbelieving squeaks, but he didn't really have time to pay attention.

"Easy, beautiful, I'm not going to hurt you," he yelped, rolling out of the way as it dropped to the ground right where he'd been standing. "Ani, come on, dammit!" He dived behind a tree as the beast lunged at him again, its attention split now between him and Ani.

Ani growled discontentedly, but was reluctantly trying to pull her tentacles free of the creature's body.

"That's good, just let her go," Aran panted. "Just let her go, and you can go sleep it off, we'll get out of your hair."

The tree he'd dodged behind opened a gaping mouth, and he swore again and leapt backwards.

Hell. He'd forgotten to watch out for smooth-barked carnivorous trees in the excitement.

"Ani! Come on!"

Both Ani and the creature now seemed more than willing to part company. Two of Ani's tentacles pulled free with the wet sucking sound, followed by a third, and she tugged her bulbous body towards Aran.

With a soft pop, the last of her stuck tentacles popped free, and Ani, rolling like a drunken sailor, hurdled across the beast's body towards him, launching herself off its back, her skin-flaps spread. Aran held out his arm to her, then realized, and hastily yanked down the sleeve of his jacket to cover his bare skin before Ani landed heavily and scuttled up onto his shoulder.

The beast in front of him bridled, straightening, its eyes snapping back to him and its posture going tense.

"It's alright," Aran gasped in his calmest voice, taking a step backwards. "It's alright, we'll just get out of your way now—"

The beast made another mock-charge, and Ani tensed. Aran grabbed desperately for her tentacle with one hand and a stick with the other, and somehow jammed a branch between the needle-sharp rows of teeth descending on him.

The beast bit.

The branch bit back.

Ani hissed.

And, his hand clamped firmly around Ani's tentacle, Aran ran.

Ree, who seemed almost dumb with shock, turned when she saw him coming, and the two of them fled as fast as their legs would carry them.

Aran risked a glimpse over his shoulder. The thing was gliding after them, its many legs propelling it along between the trunks of the trees as easily as they would along the ground. But there was an unsteadiness to its movements that told him it wasn't operating at full capacity.

Thank the Great Mystery itself—or rather, thank Ani and her venom—because he was pretty damn sure that there was no way they could have outrun that thing on a normal day.

Ree grabbed his sleeve and yanked him into a thick stand of trees, where presumably the creature's bulk would make it unable to follow. He just had time to notice the ruins of a large spacecraft lying on its side, the ground around it odd and lumpy, before she shoved him up the loading ramp.

Once they were both inside, she dropped to the ground and leaned back against one of the battered walls, shaking visibly.

Aran glanced around quickly.

Then he frowned.

This craft was an escape shuttle. From the diplomatic ship, he was almost certain of it. But he was also very certain he hadn't rescued anyone from this area of the jungle.

He glanced through the small entrance at the thick trees outside, feeling mildly sick to his stomach.

The shuttle was big enough to have seated at least a hundred people. It may not have been fully filled when it took off, but still … he glanced down at his scanner.

Not even the faintest sign of life inside, other than himself, Ani, and Ree.

Whoever had been in this shuttle could have found their way out, somehow. It was possible. But …

His mind flashed back to the small, incongruous mounds outside the door of the shuttle.

Mounds that would, he was pretty sure, be about the size of a human body, once the jungle had covered it.

He pushed back a taste of guilty nausea at the thought. There was nothing he could do for them now.

The pancake-beast prowled around the outside of the stand of trees for a while, its multitude of tiny eyes glittering pools of hatred, but even if found a way in, it would never get through the tiny spacecraft door. At last it seemed to give the whole thing up as a bad job, and vanished back into the treetops.

Now they were apparently out of danger, Aran's muscles had gone a bit shaky as well. He peeled his hand loose from Ani's tentacles, and it was only when Ree made a sharp sound that he realized that the skin on his palm had been eaten almost completely through, raw flesh showing through peeling, blistered skin.

The scientist snapped out something that was probably a curse, gesturing at him to take off his jacket, and then he realized what had must have happened and did as she asked, his fingers fumbling in haste.

Just in time, it appeared—whatever had coated Ani's tentacles had already eaten through most of the jacket, and would probably have eaten straight into his shoulders already if he hadn't been wearing his field jacket, made with three layers of muskox hide.

While he stripped it off carefully, Ani still attached to the shoulders, Ree fumbled in her pouch, pulling out a water bottle and a packet of powder. She grabbed Aran's wrist and jerked his hand towards her, dumped the contents of the water bottle over his hand, then ripped the pouch open with her teeth and sprinkled a white, chalky powder over the raw skin.

He watched with interest as she treated the injury. He didn't feel any pain, which meant whatever the creature secreted, it clearly had an anaesthetic quality to it. Perhaps it would be worth studying, if they could isolate some of it—

Then he saw the look on Ree's face. He swallowed hard, suddenly uncomfortably aware of how it would not have taken much longer before it was bone instead of flesh peeping through the blistered, broken skin of his hand.

As a shock of the cold water eased, he could feel sensation beginning to return—which, now he considered it, wasn't something he was particularly looking forward to.

Ree yanked a bandage out of her pouch and wrapped his hand

quickly and efficiently. When she'd finished, he nodded his thanks, then pulled a pair of gloves and a water bottle out of his own pouch and sprayed down Ani's tentacles. She made irritated noises and tried to squirm out of the way, but at last he finished, and gingerly, with a gloved hand, he examined one of her tentacles.

It was slightly swollen, but nothing he'd worry about just yet, as long as it didn't get worse.

He breathed a sigh of relief and turned back to Ree.

Then he groaned.

He was all too familiar with the expression on her face as she looked at him.

She said something, and something about her tone and told him that whatever it was, had he understood it, it would have made him unspeakably uncomfortable. Then she pointed at Ani and, her expression still a little awed, said something, at length, which he couldn't understand in the slightest.

He shook his head helplessly, and she sighed again.

She glanced around uncertainly, then got to her feet and peered out the spacecraft entrance. She gave a final furtive glance around before she came to crouch back down beside Aran.

She hesitated a moment, then reached into her pouch and pulled out a sheet of paper, unfolding it to reveal a roughly drawn picture of what must be the box that had come through the portal.

Aran's heart began pounding quicker.

She took another deep breath, as if bracing herself, and he could practically feel the nervousness in her posture. At last, though, she bent over the paper, and Aran did the same.

She pulled out a writing stick, and beside the box, made a quick sketch of a figure that was instantly recognizable as one of the yibo.

Aran frowned. Was he supposed able to recognize someone?

She shook her head in mild exasperation, grabbed the writing stick, and scribbled out the figure, making a sharp gesture with her hand that, he'd picked up, meant no.

His frown deepened.

She sketched out another figure, something he couldn't recognize—a shape of some sort. A vehicle? A ship? And then, with a nervous shudder, she started another sketch.

He leaned closer, eyes narrowed in concentration as he watched. A figure—a human, maybe? Certainly not a yibo. It was taller than a human, though, from the scale of it …

And then, over their heads, there was the soft hiss he recognized at once as one of the yibo transport bikes.

Ree made a small, frightened noise, and Aran cursed and scrambled to his feet. He reached for his own weapon, only to remember he didn't have anything but a bush knife. Well, and Ani, of course, but—

He glanced down quickly at Ree.

Her face had gone completely bloodless, and she was holding an incendiary to the paper.

Before he could protest, it had gone up in smoke.

She jumped to her feet and grabbed his wrist, and he resisted just long enough to snatch his gear and bundle Ani into the remains of his jacket, much to Ani's vocal displeasure. Then Ree was yanking him down the loading ramp and pulling him back through the jungle at a half-run, casting frequent glances over her shoulder.

She didn't stop until they reached the force-field around the bio-dome and slipped inside. Then she made a sharp gesture for him to stay in the corner, straightened her clothing, and with a visible effort to appear calm, she slipped back among the remainder of the scientists.

One of them turned to question her, and she responded with a casual gesture in Aran's direction, and a terse sentence in a tone that, even in the yibo language, Aran recognized as exasperation.

Aran sighed.

The other scientist turned to glance at him, frowning, then twitched his tail in the yibo equivalent of a shrug and turned back to the data collection.

Ree didn't speak to him again, and after what had happened, he thought it best not to draw attention to himself. So he sat back, watching idly as his mind went over and over the events of the day.

Ree's clear unease, the half-finished sketch, someone following them.

The transport, the jungle-covered mounds outside.

He still felt faintly sick.

How many others from the dying diplomatic ship had landed on this planet, and been killed before they could reach even the relative safety of the yibo city?

How many might the yibo have killed themselves, without a land-devil to deter them?

Maybe Istvay was right. They knew next to nothing about their hosts. Except … well, except for the most important thing.

That Ree, at least, could possibly lead him to the cure for Istvay.

The only important thing, really.

At last, as the sun was growing lower in the sky, the scientists gathered up their supplies, chattering back and forth to each other, and returned to their transports. Aran followed, and when they reached the transports, Ree shoved him onto hers, swung on in front, and made for the city along with the others.

He could still see the lingering fear in her face, the tight strain in her posture.

Whatever it was she'd been about to tell him in the wrecked escape shuttle, she'd clearly found it almost as terrifying as the beast that had tried to eat Ani.

And whoever had followed them—it clearly hadn't been entirely unexpected.

Ree didn't speak on their drive. She turned off from the others to bring Aran back to the diplomatic quarters, and when she arrived, pulled to a stop and gestured curtly for him to dismount. The moment his feet touched the ground, she turned away as if to leave.

"Wait," he called.

With obvious reluctance, she turned back.

"Can you—can we—" he gestured to the transport, then pointed out towards the jungle.

She made that sharp gesture with her hand.

One of the interpreters had seen them and come over, and was waiting politely just out of earshot. Ree beckoned him over and said something rapidly in her own language.

The interpreter turned to Aran. "She says she won't be going out into the jungle again anytime soon, as she has the data she needed and she's very busy with her work."

Ree was watching his face, and what she read on it when the interpreter stopped speaking was obviously sufficient. She gave a brusque nod and hit the throttle on the transport, not even glancing back at him over her shoulder. But he could still see that strange tension in her posture as she disappeared down the street.

He stared after her, feeling suddenly hollow.

His only lead so far, gone.

He took a deep breath and blew it out, feeling suddenly very, very tired. He thanked the interpreter politely, then turned and made his slow way back towards the diplomatic quarters.

When he reached his room, Istvay wasn't waiting for him, Mystery's mercy. He dropped down on his bed, dumping out his sorely abused supplies on the light bedsheet. Then he cursed.

Ani had climbed back up on his shoulders, which meant he'd left his damn jacket on the bike. Which, considering how the day had gone, wasn't the worst thing that had happened, but still …

As his fingers brushed through the mess, his eyes caught on a scrap of something mixed in with his supplies.

It was a piece of fabric. The type they made on Colorida, not the thin, gossamer stuff they wore here. It had probably come from the abandoned escape shuttle.

And—

He closed his eyes for a moment, feeling suddenly very cold.

He didn't usually pay attention to what people wore. But this particular pattern had been imprinted on his brain while its owner stood over him, pulse pistol aimed at his face, as Aran lay frozen by an electric tranq on the floor of a dying ship.

Emeric. Emeric had survived the explosion, somehow, and had made it to the planet.

Whether he'd gotten farther than the rotting mounds outside of the escape shuttle wasn't very likely, but …

Well, but the shuttle could easily carry over a hundred people. And there hadn't been nearly that many mounds outside the shuttle door. Which didn't necessarily mean anything, but damn it to hell.

Istvay was going to be bloody furious.

13

Alba

Harroch met her at the door of what she'd come to think of as the negotiations room the next morning.

"Alba," he said, with his close-lipped smile. "I would like to propose a walk around the grounds. It pains me to think that you have not seen any of our beautiful city."

Alba studied him for a moment, then glanced at Yosip. He gave the briefest nod, and Alba forced her own lips into a close-lipped smile. "Of course. You are too kind. I would be delighted."

"And of course, your aide is more than welcome to accompany us," he added. "My aides will be accompanying us as well." There was no change in his expression, but she could hear the hint of warning behind his words.

She nodded stiffly, and Harroch led the way out through the building.

When they reached the broad courtyard outside, Harroch led them around to a small inner courtyard, dotted with trees and lined with small paths that meandered through the greenery. There were a few moments as their party rearranged themselves to fit the walking paths, and when it was over, Alba, Harroch, and Yosip were walking side by side, with the yibo aides a short distance behind.

The sun overhead was bright, the light dimmed slightly through the double layer of force-field, but still enough that Alba found herself blinking at the brilliance. The shade of the trees was welcome, although it did little to modulate the sticky heat of the place, and sweat trickled between her shoulder blades and prickled her scalp.

"I've heard from Kachik, and he is very interested in the progress of our discussion," said Harroch quietly as they walked.

The cheerful chirping of birds overhead and the soft humming of insects did much to disguise the sound of their voices, but even so, Harroch had lowered his so that Alba had to strain to hear him.

"We've hardly had time to open our negotiations," she replied, her voice almost as quiet as his. "I can make no promises yet as to what I can recommend to the Council. But I feel we've begun working towards mutually satisfactory terms."

Harroch glanced quickly around. "This is … a matter of some importance," he said. "I must have something absolutely firm to take back with me when I talk to Kachik. He will need to be persuaded that negotiations are the most beneficial way to approach this."

"And as I have told you before, I am more than happy to work towards a draft agreement that I can recommend to the Council," said Alba. "But I simply do not have the authority to enter into a final agreement on behalf of my government without the Council's full approval."

"I am … concerned what will happen if you do not." Harroch's voice was barely a whisper.

"I must operate within the constraints set me," replied Alba, her voice sharp. "And without the answers to certain questions, it will be difficult for me even to—"

"Ambassador Harroch," Yosip broke in with a friendly smile. "I noticed this particular flower the other day, growing outside our quarters. It smells delightful, and I was wondering if you could tell me what it was."

Harroch looked over, his face clearing in relief.

Alba bit back both her irritation, and her first instinct, which was to cut Yosip off sharply.

Yosip was an experienced diplomatic aide, and …

And, she found, she trusted him, more than she'd expected to. Despite their earlier disagreement.

"It's a virflower," Harroch said, his posture still wary. "It's not native to the jungle here, so it has to be cultivated especially."

"It's beautiful," said Yosip, beaming. "Your gardeners must be talented."

"Well, we do like to ensure that those working here are skilled in their work," said Harroch, smiling slightly in return.

"I can tell," said Yosip. "I've been so impressed with how much care you've taken with us, ensuring we had food and accommodations that were suitable for us. We've felt like honoured guests."

"And we would always be sure to treat you as such," said Harroch, his smile growing a little. "As I've stated to Alba, I wish nothing more than peaceful relations."

"It must have been so much trouble, though, readying all the infrastructure that humans would need," said Yosip, his tone sincere. "I really don't know how you managed it in such a short time span. I am beyond impressed."

"It was nothing." Harroch waved a hand. "Most of it was gathering dust anyways, and it hadn't been long enough for it to have fallen apart since last time."

Alba had to bite back her quick intake of breath, but under Yosip's kindly gaze, Harroch seemed not to have realized what he'd let slip.

So humans had been here recently, then—at least, within a few decades, by the sound of it. There was more to this than ancient history.

"Well, trouble or no, I do appreciate it," Yosip was saying, the corners of his eyes creased with that friendly, kind smile. Then he glanced over at the government building, which they were once again approaching. "Oh, I am sorry, I apologize for the interruption. Although I would love to spend the afternoon quizzing you on the gardens, I'm afraid Ambassador Alba would remind me that's not what we're here for."

Harroch nodded, his smile indulgent. "It's no trouble at all." He turned back to Alba, and he dropped his tone lower again. "I am sorry. As I was saying, I appreciate your position. But I also am operating within constraints. As I told you, there are those of us in the government who advocate for peace. But we must be able to demonstrate the strength of that position."

Alba drew in a long breath. "I believe," she said at last, "that the terms we were speaking of yesterday will be broadly acceptable to my government, as long as I can give them certain promises in return. This afternoon, perhaps you and my aide and myself can find a set of terms acceptable to both our people and can have a draft document, at least, to present to your Kachik."

Harroch nodded, but Alba had spent enough time around the yibo ambassador to see the worry in his posture. "And I will pray that it is enough," he muttered.

* * *

"Madam," said Yosip in a low voice, as they walked back together later that evening. "What they're proposing is not unacceptable, from what I can see. But …" He shook his head, and she sighed.

"I know," she said quietly. She paused a moment, then cleared her throat awkwardly. "Thanks to you, we know perhaps a little more than we did about their history with humans—at least, you managed to confirm this was fairly recent history. But I'm afraid it's not enough. I still have no idea why they would have been in contact with the Labirinto System, or what happened. And while Harroch, at least, seems to be nominally on our side, I don't dare trust him fully. We can present our draft document to Kachik tomorrow, but I cannot in good faith recommend a settlement to the Council without more knowledge than we have."

"I know, Madam," he said. "I … have been trying to find information for you, as much as I can without arousing their suspicion. But what I've found has been contradictory—Harroch's slip today sounds like their contact with humans was recent. But other aides I've spoken with have mentioned that, as we originally guessed, speaking Common Dialect is something that's been passed down in certain yibo families for generations. I … don't know what to make of it. It could be two separate instances, but why? And why contact another human system now? But I don't dare push, for fear of what the consequences might be."

She glanced over sharply. His normally cheerful face was creased in a frown, and there was a weariness to his eyes that was almost startling.

"Yosip," she said at last. "I'm sorry. And … I appreciate your help." She paused. "I … shall talk with Ines tonight. If she's close enough on her translator program, it's possible that could assuage both my concern over the withheld information, and your concern over the dangers of seeking that information."

Yosip nodded, a small, tired smile flickering across his face. "Thank you," he said softly.

Their guide left them when they reached the door to the diplomatic quarters, and Alba slid it back, opening onto the large common room.

Most of the survivors, it seemed, had avoided outright panic. But they were, for all intents and purposes, prisoners—even if the yibo would let them leave the compound, there was nowhere for them to go. They didn't speak the language or understand the culture, and outside the city walls was only a jungle that seemed both intent on, and capable of, murdering them.

At the moment, the crew were clustered in small knots, talking quietly, arguing, playing some dice game or another they'd brought with them from the ship.

Alba had no experience with this sort of thing. She'd been in government roles most of her life, which had always involved a calm, dispassionate, impersonally divvying out of resources or punishments, not interacting with the people for whom such resources or punishments were intended. But she'd overseen enough junior clerks in her time to know that idleness, boredom, and fear were a potent and poisonous combination, and a group of people easily swayed into a mob or a riot.

Yosip, though, smiled as one of the small groups of crew members turned at their entrance, and called out their names cheerfully, as if he was genuinely delighted to see them.

And to Alba's small shock, they grinned back at him, their sullen looks lifting, and beckoned him over.

He excused himself from Alba's side with a polite nod. "I'll come find you for dinner, and we can talk further," he said, then made his way across the crowded floor to the group of people he'd greeted.

Alba watched him go. There was an odd ache in her chest, for reasons she couldn't quite put a finger on.

She'd never asked for friendship. She'd never wanted it, and she'd never sought it. But there was something about the comfortable, easy way Yosip smiled at these ragged, uneducated crewmembers, and the way they smiled back, how they welcomed him into their conversations and their lives, not because they needed something from him, but because they simply enjoyed his company, that left the taste of something almost like regret in the back of her throat.

But she wasn't their friend. She couldn't afford to be. What she was doing now was merely a weighing game—measuring the value of their lives against the dangers posed to the rest of Joias should the yibo come through the portal.

"Madam Chief Justice!"

She looked up, startled, to see Ines standing in front of her. The girl was smiling, her eyes bright with excitement, her dark hair framing her face. The sight of her like this was so unexpected that Alba blinked.

"What is it, Ines?"

The sharpness in Alba's tone was more instinct than on purpose, but the light in Ines's eyes dimmed, her posture drooping just a little. "I'm—I'm sorry to bother you, Madam Chief Justice," she said. "I just—I wanted to tell you. I was working with the interpreters today, and I'm much closer than I thought I'd be to getting the translation program set up. Once I can run it, we can add a patch to our wavelengths that will allow instantaneous translation."

Alba managed a small smile. It didn't have the warmth that Yosip's would have, she knew—but at least she was trying. "Thank you," she said. "You've done very well. You should be proud of yourself."

Ines stared at her for a moment, uncertain, then bobbed her head in a quick, nervous nod. "Thank you, Madam Chief Justice."

She turned, but Alba said quickly, "Wait."

The girl hesitated, then turned, shoulders hunched slightly as if she was expecting a scolding.

"How are you holding up?" Alba asked at last.

She wasn't entirely sure why she asked it, except that Ines had looked so young in that moment. Young, and alone, and Alba had been the one to bring her here.

Ines blinked in surprise, and gave a small smile. "It's—not that bad. No worse than when the civic guards brought me and the other village kids into do Sol for finishing school."

Alba frowned slightly. "When they brought you in for finishing school? But that was a benefit, surely."

Ines' smile held a trace of bitterness. "I guess it was. I mean, I'm sure the schools in do Sol are better than the ones in the Rim Mountains. But I—" she'd been looking at the ground, and now she looked up. And for the first time, Alba caught the flash of something in her eyes—anger, or defensiveness, or hurt, she couldn't quite tell.

"It's hard. To be taken from your parents when you're twelve years old. We couldn't see them, because most of them didn't have the money to bring us back for holidays, because you don't make that kind of money on the Rim. And they didn't keep the children from the villages together when they brought us in, either, so none of us knew anyone. It was—it was like this, but worse. Because we were just kids. And my mom and my dad—I'm not sure they ever really got over it, losing their kids at twelve. I was the oldest, but I had siblings. When I got older, and I could earn my own money and come back, I saw the way my mom looked at them. Like she knew she'd only have them for a little. Like you see parents look at their child who has the defect."

She paused a moment, staring at her feet. "I … I'm sorry. May I —do you need me for anything else, Madam?"

Alba shook her head silently.

She stared after Ines, though, after she'd left, her eyes following the girl's slight figure through the crowded floor.

There was a slight nausea roiling in her stomach.

The reform had been one she'd wholeheartedly agreed to—the children from the Rim Mountain farms were almost always far behind their Belt Sector peers when it came to academics, and it limited their prospects. She'd been told that parents would often pull children from school with the excuse of illness when instead they'd use them to help with planting or harvesting. Bringing the children into do Sol for schooling, and mixing their cohorts between villages to give the children a taste of something beyond what they knew, keep them from an insular and myopic worldview—it had been for the best. For children's own well-being. There had never been any rule that the children couldn't go home to see their parents, in fact, parents were encouraged to bring the children home over the holidays.

And she tried to ignore the fact that in the debates, the possibility of parents being unable to do so had never come up.

Anyway, it was the only way Ines had gotten to where she was, certainly—had she done finishing school in the Rim Mountains, she'd never have made it into the University of Sao Martim, no matter how intelligent she might have been.

But, a small voice in the back of her head whispered, was where Ines was now really all that enviable? And, given the choice, was it where she would have wanted to end up?

For a moment, she heard Istvay's bitter words in her memory. *"You didn't even think to ask, did you?"*

She turned away and started back to her chambers.

It had been for the best. And perhaps it would take a few years for people to become accustomed to it—Ines must have been in one of the first cohorts, because despite her looks, she had to be at least in her early to mid-twenties to have finished a graduate degree in linguistics—but once it was no longer a shock, it would catch on. And in the end, everyone on the Council, even those who were originally from the Rim Mountains, had agreed that the reform was for the best.

She tried not to recall the pain in Ines's face as the girl had turned away, the weary resignation in her eyes that belonged to someone much older than she was.

Surely it had been for the best.

Alba made the decisions because she was educated, and intelligent, and had earned her position and the public trust. She made them because she did know better than others what the Joias System needed. Just like she had been tasked with making the decisions in these negotiations.

She had to know better.

Because who was there to make the decisions otherwise?

14

Aran

Aran barely had time to put away his equipment before Istvay banged on the door, then shoved their way in without waiting for an invitation. When they saw him, they grabbed his arm, pulling him to his feet.

He fought back a flinch at the unexpected touch, and Istvay let go like they'd been burned.

"Where the hell have you been?" they hissed.

Aran blinked and frowned.

He hadn't realized until just now how strained Istvay's face had become, how much those telltale dark circles under their eyes had darkened.

He bit back the twist of guilt.

He was trying to save Istvay. That was the point of all this, and if he managed it, he could finally make those dark circles go away for good.

And if he didn't—

He gave a quick shake of his head. Those were thoughts he refused to contemplate.

"I told you—I was out in the jungle. Collecting samples."

"And what samples, exactly, did you collect?" Istvay's voice was icy, and they were staring pointedly at the raw burn on Aran's hand and at his torn shirt, where some of the acid from his and Ani's adventure had eaten through the fabric.

Aran closed his hand self-consciously, trying not to wince at the pain of the newly blistered skin. "We—ran into a creature of some sort, and Ani decided that she wanted to pick a fight. It wasn't anything, really. But honestly, I think there must be a topical anesthetic in the substance it secreted that we really should look into. I thought maybe there'd be enough left on my jacket that …" he trailed off at Istvay's expression.

"Well, it's good to know you thought that was hardly anything, really," repeated Istvay, their voice brittle. "Back here, things haven't been so simple. Apparently, the yibo ambassador told Alba and Yosip that the yibo head of government, Kachik, will meet with her tomorrow. You know, the one we all suspect ordered the killing. And Ines has been working her butt off to get her translation program functional before then, and I've just been trying to keep everyone else here from being murdered by the yibo. Well, except for you, since you decided to hare off into the jungle on your own with a yibo scientist who you'd met exactly once before."

"I had Ani," Aran protested.

"Well, I bloody hope you found what you were looking for, so that maybe we might stand a chance of, I don't know, keeping you alive for a few more days."

"Um." Aran paused, not wanting to continue the conversation, at least not with Istvay in this mood. "I. Um. While I was in the jungle, I found … look, there was a crashed escape shuttle in the jungle. It was empty, and I didn't see any signs of anyone left alive. But it looked like … it looked like Emeric might have been on it." He caught the look on Istvay's face and hurried on. "There wasn't any sign of him. He probably died in the jungle, or in the crash or something, honestly. But I thought—"

"You …" Istvay sounded almost too upset to form words. "You saw that, out in the jungle, and you didn't even think to come find me to tell me about it? Just if it happened to come up in the conversation? What the hell, Aran?" The tone in Istvay's voice was almost enough to make Aran flinch.

He scowled. "Listen, Istvay. I'm not stupid. This might surprise you, but I am capable of making some decisions on my own, and some of them might actually be good. I don't need a damn caretaker."

There was a look of mingled shock and hurt on Istvay's face, and again the guilt rose up in Aran's chest, twisting together with his anger in thick, choking strands, but he ignored it.

The two of them glared at each other for a moment, and something in Aran's chest ached.

He wanted, so badly that it hurt, to see Istvay's familiar crooked grin, the mischief dancing in their eyes, the way they smiled at him that made everything feel safe—like no matter what the two of them were going through, it would all be alright in the end.

He couldn't remember the last time he'd seen that look. Not since he'd agreed to come along on this damn mission, probably.

When had this happened?

He wasn't sure, anymore, what had gone wrong, or how to fix it.

"Is—is everyone here alright?" he asked at last, dropping his eyes.

Istvay turned away, and just for a moment Aran caught a glimpse of the weariness in their face. "No one's dead, if that's what you're asking," they said. "We've decided to set a watch, just in case. I'm taking the first shift, and Yosip and Ines will spell me off."

"I'll come with you," Aran blurted. "It'll be better with two of us."

Istvay just looked at him, and for one awful moment, Aran wasn't sure what they'd say. But at last they give a brusque nod. "Fine. Like you say, it's probably better with two pairs of eyes."

Neither of them spoke as they sat in the dark on either side of the doorway.

Aran wasn't unhappy with the silence.

He wasn't sure what he'd say to Istvay if they wanted to talk. He wasn't sure what Istvay would say to him, and he wasn't sure he wanted to know.

Over and over, his mind kept pulling up the sketch Ree had drawn out for him. The figure of a yibo, crossed out. Killed? Was there a threat he was unaware of in the box they'd sent? And then some sort of spacecraft. She'd seemed highly uncomfortable about it—was the craft something to do with the reason behind the force-field over the city?

Did they think, perhaps, that the humans were coming through to attack them? It didn't really make sense—the yibo may not have been friendly at their first meeting, but they'd never seemed particularly afraid of the humans. Well, unless Ani was there, and even then, Aran was pretty sure it wasn't the humans the yibo were afraid of. Or was there something that had come through the portal before?

He could still see, in his memory, those lines of data from the lab on the diplomatic ship—organic matter and inorganic matter mixed, remnants of destroyed spacecrafts.

Was whatever Ree had been trying to warn him of the thing that had destroyed the ships in the first place?

And what did that have to do with someone following them? Ree hadn't been nearly surprised enough for it to have been entirely unforeseen. There had been a reason she'd insisted they go so far into the jungle before she spoke to him.

But who was behind it, and why?

He hesitated, glancing at Istvay. But he couldn't talk to them, not when they were like this.

He'd never seen Istvay thrown so far off their balance. He'd never seen Istvay so tense, so out of control. He'd never dreamed Istvay, of all people, would shout at him.

And he knew, uncomfortably, that it was at least partially his fault. But the alternative—forgetting about the box, forgetting about the cure—was unthinkable. And mentioning to Istvay that he and the yibo scientist had been followed while they were out in the jungle would not do anything good for Istvay's state of mind.

He glanced at his friend again out of the corner of his eye. In the dim illumination from the lights of the city outside, he could see the tight lines of Istvay's face, the strain in their muscles, the tension in their shoulders.

Istvay was on the verge of breaking. And this might be the thing that would push them over the edge, and Aran wasn't about to do that.

When Yosip and Ines traded him and Istvay off, Aran and Istvay went back to their respective rooms in silence. Aran fell into bed, his hand aching and throbbing where it had been burned, his entire body exhausted from the day's exertion. But tired as he was, he tossed and turned on the hard cot, unable to get comfortable.

He must have fallen asleep at last, because when he opened his eyes again, faint light from the planet's sun illuminated his bedroom. He bit back a groan as he rolled stiffly out of bed, every muscle aching, and stumbled off to find the yibo equivalent of a steam cleanser—a sort of hot shower that used much more water than a steam cleanser, but performed the same function. At last, clean and dressed and feeling slightly more awake, he made his way down to the breakfast room.

He ate quickly, hardly noticing the food as he chewed and swallowed. Istvay wasn't there, but whether they'd woken early and already gone out, or were still asleep, he didn't know. Again, that sharp pang of loneliness twisted in his chest, but he fought it down.

If Istvay died, this was how it would be for the rest of his damn life.

Ani, perched on his shoulder, gave a questioning chirrup. He managed a small smile and handed her a scrap of his meal as a treat, and she subsided contentedly.

When breakfast was done, he made his way through the common room where the rest of the human refugees gathered, talking, arguing, and throwing dice, and out into the courtyard. Once he was out in the morning air, already sticky-warm despite the early hour, he glanced around quickly to make sure no one was watching, then slipped casually into a side street that led in the direction of the labs.

He glanced behind him as he walked to check whether he was being followed, but it was impossible to tell—the yibo gave him a wide berth, and whether someone was stepping quickly out of sight because they were trying to come after him, or because they were afraid of Ani, it wasn't easy to guess.

There was an uncomfortable prickling between his shoulder blades at the memory of the man who'd been killed in these streets days earlier.

Istvay would be furious that he was out here.

Istvay would just have to damn well not know about it.

Once he could see the towering shape of the science compound ahead of him, he turned to come around the back of the building. When he reached it, he checked the makeshift bandage around the still-tender burn on his palm, and placed his hands carefully on the wall.

There wasn't a force-field around the building itself, Mystery's mercy, and it didn't seem to be heavily defended. Although, considering the caliber of the guards' weapons, he wasn't sure it needed to be.

It only took him a few minutes to scale the outside wall and drop silently down inside. He scanned the courtyard, then ducked behind the trunk of an arching tree as a small knot of yibo scientists, talking loudly, came out through the walls of the building, the material dissolving and reforming around them.

One day, he'd figure out how the hell they did that. But likely not today.

He crouched where he was, studying the building's layout. If he remembered correctly, the lab was on the third floor, towards the back. It was impossible to see anything clearly through the strangely reflective glass, but he was pretty sure that in the corner over there, there had been a large storage closet.

He closed his eyes for a moment.

He hated heights. He bloody hated them.

He reached into his supplies pouch and pulled out his adhesive grips. He'd used them more than once for scaling next-to-sheer surfaces. Technically speaking, they should work just as well on the yibo buildings as they did on the rough rock faces he was used to— better, even—but ...

Well, he'd just have to not think about the 'but' for right now.

Ani gave a comforting little chirrup, and he pet her absently. She purred and touched his face delicately with the tip of one tentacle.

The yibo scientists were on one of the smooth walkways that criss-crossed the courtyard, partially obscured from view by the lacy branches of the trees.

The moment they were out of sight, Aran started at a running half-crouch towards the corner of the building.

When he reached it, he sucked in a quick breath of relief and glanced around.

It didn't look like anyone had seen him. And the portions of the courtyard still in view were deserted.

He fixed the adhesive grips to his hands and the toes of his boots and closed his eyes for a moment, fighting back the wave of panic.

He was doing this to save Istvay.

He opened his eyes, and started up the wall.

The grips gave just a little, like they always did, every time he shifted his weight onto one of them, and the sick, churning terror in his stomach spiked every damn time.

One floor up.

He'd have to hope that either the glass was thick enough that it would be difficult to make out from the inside a damn idiot human scaling the walls of the damn science lab, or that the surface he was climbing faced onto somewhere out-of-the-way enough that no one would think to look.

Two floors.

His palms were damp with sweat, and he kept himself from looking down with an effort. If he looked, he'd panic, and Istvay wasn't here to talk him down.

The thought of Istvay sparked another flare of panic, but this time, it wasn't at the thought of what he'd see below him.

He could do this. For Istvay, he could damn well do this.

Three floors.

He stopped, wiping his face against the shoulder of his shirt, and glanced down, just for a moment, on accident.

He felt his entire body freeze.

The ground looked a hundred kilometres away, and he was acutely, absurdly aware of how little was actually holding him here, and how easily his grips could fail, sending him plunging to the courtyard below—

Distantly, he felt Ani's tentacle-suckers latching down on his shoulder, heard her small, questioning little noise. He forced his eyes closed, his whole body shaking.

Istvay.

He wasn't going to let his best friend die.

Without opening his eyes, he carefully detached the grip from one hand and reached into his supplies pouch, pulling out a small, sharp cylinder designed for breaking the thick plex windows of a building or transport if you were somehow trapped inside.

Still with his eyes shut, he let his fingers slide across the smooth surface.

It didn't matter if he was looking, he wouldn't be able to see inside anyways. So he'd just have to hope he'd guessed right, or else he'd send himself and Ani sprawling out onto the floor of the lab. Which wouldn't exactly be the most subtle entrance.

He held his breath and, with a sharp motion, hit the pointed tip of the tool against the glass.

His fingers explored the small spiderweb of cracks, and he carefully felt his way to the centre of them, positioned his glass-pick, and tried again.

After years of fieldwork in places that utterly terrified him, he'd become surprisingly good at working with his eyes closed.

After three more strikes, the glass shattered with a delicate tinkle. He brushed his fingers across the long shards, gently enough to hopefully avoid slicing his finger open—that might be hard to explain to Istvay—and then cracked his eyes open a slit.

There were no furious alien faces peering out through the hole he'd opened, so either he'd guessed right, or no one was in the lab. But the soft murmur of voices from inside told him it wasn't entirely deserted, at least.

He took a deep breath and peered through the hole he'd made.

Sure enough, it looked like the inside of the supplies cupboard he'd seen the day before, and the equipment inside was clearly that of the lab.

He pulled a protective sheet out of his pouch and shook it out carefully, then laid it over the sharp shards of glass and cautiously pulled himself through the opening he'd made, trying not to think of how far the ground was below him.

Once inside, he glanced around the claustrophobic space.

Damn it to hell, the yibo didn't use doors in most of their buildings, he'd forgotten that detail. But … there was a small gap in the semi-transparent surface, where the edge of one of the large centrifuge machines had been caught, the glass had only partially reformed around it.

He knelt and peered through the gap.

He'd guessed correctly—outside was the lab he'd been brought to earlier. And …

He let out a quick breath of relief.

Ree was there.

From how frightened she'd acted the day before, he hadn't been sure she would be.

She was working across the lab from him, her back to the

cupboard. He glanced around irresolutely, then pulled a small water bottle out of his supplies pouch, the same one he'd used to spray off Ani's tentacles the previous day.

It fit through the gap, just barely, and he rolled it across the floor. His aim was good, and it bumped up against Ree's ankle.

She glanced down, half-turning, and frowned. Then, abruptly, she stilled, her body tense, her face taking on that same terrified expression he'd seen the previous day in the jungle. She glanced behind her, the movement quick and furtive, and he slipped his hand out through the small opening, just enough to be in view.

She must have caught sight of it a moment later, because her body went even stiffer, her head jerking up as if she were being hunted. She hesitated, then said something to her lab partner and crossed quickly over to the cupboard.

She stepped inside, pushing the centrifuge in with her so the gap in the glass closed fully, and turned to Aran. She was glaring, but there was stark fear behind her gaze.

She whispered something harsh, then made a quick, angry gesture with her hand.

"Listen," he whispered, even though he knew she couldn't understand. "I need to know more. It's … my friend is dying. Please." He reached into his supplies pouch and pulled out a drawing he'd made of the box.

She snatched it from his fingers and tore it up, then tossed the bits of paper out the hole he'd made in the glass, to drift to the courtyard below.

"Please," he said desperately. "I—"

She made another curt gesture and turned, retrieving his jacket from one of the shelves. She turned back to him and held the jacket out, speaking quietly in her chattering language.

He closed his eyes for a moment, despair sitting heavy in his chest.

He opened them to the sharp poke of a finger in his chest. Ree was watching him with narrowed eyes, and when he met her gaze, she hissed something, then pulled out a small scalpel and sliced a quick cut across the pad of one of her fingers. Then she grabbed his jacket and squeezed the injured finger with her other hand, and a drop of red, glistening blood fell onto the worn leather. She pointed at it deliberately, then gestured to the lab.

He frowned in puzzlement, and she made a gesture that, despite their lack of a common language, managed to convey absolute exasperation.

Someone called something from outside, and she shoved Aran back against the shelves and turned, her hand parting the glass like a curtain. She called something in reply, then snatched a pipet from the shelf beside Aran's head and stepped back out into the lab. As she went, she managed to bump the centrifuge, and it lodged itself in the parted glass once more.

Aran looked after her, still frowning.

The space now was big enough, barely, that he could squeeze his way through if he had to.

He glanced back at the glistening drop of red on his jacket and closed his eyes for a moment, his heart pounding.

She was trying to tell him something. And he was pretty sure he knew how to figure out what it was.

At last, the scientists began to filter out of the lab in ones and twos. Aran glanced at the sun through the broken glass. From the look of it, it was probably around the time the aliens took their midday meal.

And with any luck, no one would look up and notice the damn hole broken through the side of their lab building three floors up.

Ree left with the final group, but she cast a quick, nervous glance behind her as she went.

Aran waited until they were all gone, then a couple minutes more to be safe. And then, gingerly, he slid out from his hiding place and into the lab proper.

The equipment here was unfamiliar, and the readouts like nothing he'd seen before. But if he recalled correctly, from his earlier tour of the lab … yes. There. The DNA extractor.

He dropped his coat on the lab table and pulled a swab from his supplies pouch. He held it against the red stain, and as the blood soaked into the white fibers, he inspected the machine quickly. Istvay would be better at this than he was, because Istvay was the one that paid attention to systems and procedures. But Aran had spent enough time around lab equipment, familiar and unfamiliar, that he could make an informed guess as to what he needed to do.

He tapped the power on and fed the swab into the mouth of the machine, and waited as a hummed quietly to itself.

He glanced around the small lab as he waited for the analysis to finish. DNA sequencing was a time-consuming process back on Colorida, but if he'd guessed correctly—and he had to have guessed correctly—this was what Ree had been hinting to him about. Which meant either she hadn't thought it all the way through, or the yibo's DNA sequencing procedure was faster than the ones back home.

Or she wanted him to get caught, and was setting him up. Still, there were a hundred easier ways she could have set him up, if that's what she'd wanted.

At last the DNA-sequencing machine beeped, and after a few unsuccessful tries, Aran managed to pull up the screen with the readout.

He scanned through it blankly.

It was utterly unintelligible.

He groaned in frustration and glanced around again, helplessly.

How long did he have before the scientists came back?

Then he frowned, and on impulse, pulled out another small sample, a bit of what had come through the portal. He paused a moment, then fed it into the machine.

He already had a DNA analysis of the sample from back on Colorida. If he could run it through the yibo machine, perhaps he could compare the two readouts and come up with a key.

The DNA sequencer beeped a few endless minutes later, and he captured the data on his palmscreen. He shut off the machine and paged back to the previous readout.

He frowned, comparing the two images. Then he scanned back to the readout of Ree's blood, his heart pounding.

For a moment, he felt like someone had hit him in the stomach, hard enough to knock the breath out of him.

He'd need a lot longer to figure out a key for interpreting the scans, or to extrapolate any of the data. But one thing was all too obvious.

Whoever or whatever had provided the blood sample that had been sent to Colorida was an entirely different species from the yibo.

He stood staring at the DNA readout for a long moment. His brain was whirling too quickly to allow him to focus on any one thought.

An entirely different species.

No wonder Ines was struggling so hard to figure out the language —if he was right, she was trying to interpret a completely different language than the one she'd worked on from the portal samples.

And if it hadn't been the yibo who'd sent the box—had it been them who'd opened the portal at all? Or, for that matter, who'd closed it?

He leaned against the table, trying to gather his thoughts.

Ree's brief sketch in the jungle. This was what she'd been trying to tell him all along. The box hadn't come from the yibo at all. It had come from someone—or something—else.

Ships, the force-field over the city, her instinctive fear of something coming from above them.

How everything about the box made her nervous.

The sharp *ting* of something hitting the floor in the hallway outside caught his attention. He frowned, looking up, and then he realized he'd been hearing in the back of his brain the sound of approaching footsteps, the chatter of voices.

He recognized Ree's voice, loud and nervous-sounding, and he could see faintly through the glass a figure bending over, as if retrieving something from the ground.

He swore, and jumped for the supplies cupboard.

Damn it to hell.

The glass parted as a group of scientists stepped into the lab, and he saw from his hiding place the tension in Ree's posture, the way her eyes darted around the lab, and then how her posture relaxed on finding it empty.

And then one of the scientists started for the supplies cupboard.

Aran swore under his breath, scooping his supplies and data haphazardly into his supplies pouch. Ani growled uneasily, tightening her tentacle-suckers down on his shoulder. "No, Ani," he hissed.

Right before he had to climb three stories down the sheer side of a building was not a good time to be knocked dizzy by land-devil venom.

The scientist had almost reached the cupboard. Ree called out, and through the small gap in the glass he could see the approaching scientist pause, half-turning to call something back. Then he turned back, reaching out his hand to part the glass.

Aran hissed in a quick breath, slipped the grips back onto his hands—no time to pull them over his boots as well this time—and, sending up a prayer to the Great Mystery, slipped out the broken hole he'd made, pulling the protective sheet after him.

He could hear the moment the scientist stepped into the supplies cupboard. There was the crunch of glass underfoot, a moment of startled silence, and then a shout of alarm.

Damn it to hell, damn it, damn it, damn it.

He squeezed his eyes open for a moment, glancing down to judge the distance.

Too far to drop, that was for damn sure, at least if he didn't want to break both his legs in the process.

But someone would poke their head out any minute now …

He was dangling over the height from the grips on his hands like a fly dangling from a damn spider's web.

He gritted his teeth and sucked in a breath, and started lowering himself hand over hand, trying not to think of the distance between him and the very hard ground, very far below.

His shoulders ached and burned, the muscles in his arms shaking with the effort.

The grips were never meant to hold his body weight singly—it was supposed to be three-point contact, so no one link would have to hold the climber's full weight. Now every time he pulled a hand free to lower himself, the remaining grip slipped ominously.

From above him, he could still hear the yibo scientist's sharp tones, and he could see through the glass a vague shape approaching the broken hole …

He was half-way down by now, at least, he was pretty sure. Far enough that a fall wouldn't necessarily kill him …

He held his breath and, with a sharp yank, pulled both his grips free from the glass, shoving himself off the wall at the same time.

The sharp, panicking sensation of falling hit him like a wave, and he gritted his teeth, bracing himself … and then he hit the ground hard and rolled, Ani hissing in disapproval. A sharp pain shot up his ankle, but he scrambled to his feet and dived behind one of the trees as a yibo head poked through the shattered hole in the wall of the building.

The moment no one was looking, he sprinted silently for the courtyard wall and, with arms almost too shaky to obey him, pulled himself up and over, landing with a wince on the street below. Pain jabbed through his ankle with each step as he made his hurried way back through the streets, but his mind was spinning so fast he hardly noticed.

He slipped back into the courtyard of the diplomatic quarters, and through the mostly empty common room—at this time of day, most of the other humans were in their rooms, sleeping away the worst of the heat.

Istvay was pacing restlessly back and forth in front of the door to Aran's room. When they saw him, they grabbed him by the shoulders. "Aran! I've been worried sick about you. Where the hell did you disappear to? And—" They stepped back a pace, frowning. "And what happened to you?"

Aran managed a tired smile. His whole body was still buzzing with adrenalin, leaving a sick knot in his stomach.

"Pishti. Listen. I just got back from the lab. They—the scientist I went out into the jungle with gave me a drop of blood for a DNA analysis. And …" He squeezed his palmscreen, holding it out so

Istvay could see the parallel sheets of data. "Their analysis readout is different than ours, obviously. But this, here—this is the readout from the blood sample that came through the portal. And on the other side is the scientist's blood."

Istvay frowned at the readout for a long time. When at last they looked up, Aran could see the comprehension on their face. "They're —not the same species."

Aran nodded again, distantly.

For a few moments, he and Istvay stared at each other. Then Istvay reached out, supporting themself on the wall. Their face had gone very pale.

"What does this mean?" they asked quietly.

Aran shook his head. "I have no idea. But—" he paused, and met Istvay's gaze. "I'm going to find out."

Istvay closed their eyes, and there was a pain in their expression that made Aran look quickly away. "Aran," they said at last, quietly. "While you've been gone. Things are … they're not good. The yibo guards have been here three times looking for you. I don't know what they're after, but if I was going to guess, I'd say they don't like the idea of someone with the kind of firepower Ani gives you wandering around free. You know how nervous they are when she's around. We need to get out of here while we can. I'm afraid Alba's gotten herself in deeper than she realizes. If we can get out, there's a chance we can come back later and help the others. But if we're caught here …"

Aran stared at them. "Pishti. No. I told you, I need more information before—"

"Aran!" They made a quick, brusque gesture. "I'm not joking. You've got Ani, so right now if we try to leave, I doubt they'll be able to stop us. They're too afraid. But …" They glanced up, and swore.

"They're coming back. Aran—"

Aran glanced up, his heart pounding strangely.

A small group of frightened-looking guards, accompanied by an interpreter, were approaching. "Hello, Aran," the interpreter called as they approached. There was a tinge of nervousness in her voice.

"Hello," he said warily, turning to face them.

Istvay stood beside him, their entire body tense.

The interpreter cleared her throat. "Aran. I … have been asked to inform you that Kachik has requested that a separate quarters be prepared for you and your pet. And your assistant, of course, they are welcome to accompany you." She made a nervous humming sound. "I do hope you don't take offence, but your … animal has made some of the government ministers nervous. This way, we can keep her from disrupting their schedules, while providing you pleasant accommodations without the constant attention, which must be uncomfortable."

Aran watched her for a moment.

Istvay was right. They were trying to neutralize the threat he posed, put him somewhere that Ani would no longer be part of the equation. What little influence he had at the moment would be gone completely.

And Istvay was right about something else, too—if they ran now, he and Istvay and Ani could still get out. He could see it in the guards' postures—they wouldn't come after him, not as long as Ani was with him. They'd be free.

And he'd be back where he'd been on Colorida—desperately searching for a cure that might exist, but with no idea where to find it.

And that, he couldn't do. He couldn't bear to.

He took a deep breath and gave the interpreter a close-lipped smile. "Thank you," he said. "I'll follow you."

She turned, her shoulders slumping in relief, and the guards closed in around the two of them as Aran turned after her.

He deliberately avoided Istvay's gaze, but he could feel the fury rising off them like steam as they fell into step beside him.

15

Savina

Savina crouched in the dark of the alley, her knife at the throat of a trembling yibo woman.

"Yuur told me to kill you, just like I killed your co-workers," Savina whispered. "But I'm a merciful person. I'm willing to look the other way when you escape. But only if you tell me what I need to know."

The yibo's eyes were wide with terror, but she didn't tip her head in acknowledgement—the electric tranq on her stomach assured she wouldn't move a single muscle until Savina let her.

"Now," said Savina, lifting the knife from the woman's throat, "I'm going to take this off. You'll be able to move again. But you're going to be very, very quiet. Because if my little yibo helpers figure out you're here, and that you're not dead, they'll make sure to rectify that. But they won't need to, because by the time they get here ..." she smiled. "You will be dead."

She knocked the electric tranq free, and the yibo jerked, her body shuddering.

"Now," said Savina. "I asked around before I started on this job. I know you speak my language. That's why you're not dead on the street with the others. So let's see if you can stay that way. Tell me, what are the kari?"

The yibo's eyes were wide with shock and terror. "The …" She paused, as if gathering her thoughts. "The kari. Raiders, in your language. They're—they hunt us. They're the reason we put up force-fields around the cities."

"Are they sapient?"

The yibo shivered. "Yes. They're very intelligent. Most speak our language and yours, as well as their own."

Savina smiled. "Perfect. And how would one contact them?"

This time, the yibo woman just stared at her.

"I said," Savina hissed, raising her knife again, "How can I contact them? Because I know people do. I know people make bargains with them." She pushed the knife up against the yibo's throat, and red welled up around the blade. "I know your boss has made bargains with them."

"I'll tell you, please—" the yibo rasped.

Savina let off the pressure with a close-lipped smile. "Good. I'm so happy you're cooperative."

The yibo woman swallowed hard and closed her eyes for a moment. "There are communication devices you can use to contact them," she said at last. "They have an open channel. They can't get into the cities, normally, and we have defences outside the cities—weapons and so forth. They don't raid around major settlements like this, at least, not often. But there's a communications line open for bargaining. The lawmakers and the law enforcement pretend they don't know about it, but they use it too, if they have to."

"Savina! Did you find her?" Rach growled from around the side of the alley.

"Give me the communicator. Now. I know you have it. You're your boss's communications specialist." Savina grinned. "Or you were, until tonight. Hard to be a communications specialist for someone who's dead."

"Savina?"

"Now!" Savina hissed.

"You don't understand what these raiders are," the woman whispered. "You don't know what you're—"

Savina raised her knife, and the yibo woman yanked out a small device, shoving it into Savina's hands. Savina grabbed it, tucking it into her bra for safekeeping.

"Get out," she hissed. "But if I find you lied to me, I'll track you down. And believe me, I will make you hurt in ways you've never imagined."

The yibo woman tipped her head in a quick, desperate gesture, then scrambled to her feet and took off down the alley.

"I found her, but she got away," Savina called back. "I got a knife into her, though. I doubt she'll live long. Not worth going after, I think."

Rach rounded the corner, his weapon drawn and pointed at Savina. "You don't think?" he hissed. "Who gave you the right to make decisions?"

Savina took a deep breath and turned, pasting on a look of distress.

It was easier than it should have been.

The sight of blood running down Joska's throat, the memory of Reka's cold, disdainful gaze as she yanked the knife from her bloody arm and tossed it to the cobblestones, haunted Savina's memories and twisted uneasily through her dreams.

None of them were safe here. None of them would be, until she fixed this.

"I'm … I'm really sorry. I honestly thought I'd be fast enough to catch her. But she has one of my knives in her back, right here." She touched a spot just below her shoulder blade. "It went in deep, I saw it, and she was coughing blood by the time she got around the corner. I don't think she'll make it far."

Rach snapped something at two of the yibo, and they started down the alley in the direction Savina had pointed.

The wrong direction, and by the time they figured it out, the yibo woman should be long gone.

Yuur had grown accustomed to granting Beni access to her internal files in order to plan the raids, and even if you didn't know the language, it was surprising how much you could pick up from context. This yibo woman, for as pathetic as she'd looked under Savina's knife, was a killer, and good at it. She'd be fine.

"Alright, human. You've done your part. Come on, let's get back," Rach growled. "Yuur wasn't thrilled you suggested this raid, but she'll be happy enough now it's paid off."

Savina dipped her head humbly and followed, the communication device cold and hard against her skin.

It had paid off, indeed.

"Vina? Are you alright?" asked Beni as soon as the door to their room closed behind her.

Savina glanced around quickly. Joska and Nicolau weren't there, probably out doing some errand for Yuur, so it was just Beni and Rafel waiting for her.

Savina took a deep breath. "I'm fine. Listen, Beni, I need you to help me with something." She paused a moment. "Nicolau and Joska are—are they—"

"They're fine," said Beni. "They're downstairs washing up dishes. Rafel and I just got done." They paused. "Is … is Reka after Joska now, too?"

"No." Savina bit off the word. "Joska was in the wrong place at the wrong time."

She glanced over to where Rafel sat in the corner, but he seemed to be absorbed in whatever the hell he was doing. She reached into the front of her tunic and pulled out the communicator device the yibo woman had handed her. "Beni. I need you to take a look at this, see if you can figure it out. It's supposed to be able to connect to some open channel, but I don't know anything about the communication channels the yibo use."

"I … know a little," said Beni, frowning, their fingers brushing over the device. "I've been able to pick up some things while I've been planning the hits. What is this for?"

Savina hesitated. "It … could help us get out of here," she said, lowering her voice.

Beni was quiet for a moment, still running their fingers absently over the device. "I'll see what I can do," they said at last.

Savina looked at them more closely, frowning. There were dark circles under their eyes, and they looked exhausted.

"Beni? Have you been sleeping?" she asked abruptly.

Beni's cheeks flushed darker. "I—I've just been—"

"Have you been listening to those stupid romance novels all night?" Savina snapped.

Beni looked down, and didn't answer.

Savina gritted her teeth.

The last time Beni had been like this had been after a particularly messy job, and it had taken Savina weeks to pull her sibling out of it.

And Savina wouldn't ever admit it, but the sight of Beni growing more and more exhausted, their face drawn, the bones in their wrists more pronounced, terrified her. It scared her more than anything had scared her since she was twelve years old and she'd saved her brother, and burned five people alive to do it.

"I'm fine, Savina," said Beni softly. They couldn't see Savina's expression, but Beni and Savina had been a team for so long that Beni didn't need to. "I'm just—" they trailed off, as if unsure how to finish the sentence.

"You're damn well going to start sleeping, or I'll make you take sleeping pills again," Savina gritted out through her teeth.

Beni nodded, turning away quickly. "I'm going out," they said shortly, and left, closing the door behind them.

Savina stared at the door for a few moments, her hands clenched into fists.

This was spiralling out of control.

She swore viciously, and turned around.

Rafel stood against the wall, his arms crossed, watching her. When she caught his gaze, he sighed and straightened.

She narrowed her eyes at him, making no secret of the fact she was not in the mood for conversation.

He paid no attention. Because of course he didn't.

"Savina," he said bluntly.

She glared at him, and didn't answer.

"I don't think I've been subtle about the fact I don't like you," he said.

She snorted. "I'm not sure you could have more obvious if you'd written it on a sign. Don't worry, the feeling is mutual."

His mouth twitched in a reluctant half-smile, but the expression disappeared almost as soon as it came. He sighed again. "Your brother seems like … a decent person. And even Beni's not a complete monster. So because of that, I'm going to give you the benefit of the doubt. I'm going to assume you have the capacity for rational thought." He stepped closer to her. He was taller than she was, and his prosthetic leg gave him an odd, swaying limp. "I'm going to assume that somewhere in that black heart of yours, you have the capacity to recognize when someone's done you a good turn. So I'm going to tell you something about Joska."

Savina stared at him for a moment.

Rafel snorted at her expression. "What? You think I'm about to tell you she's an undercover assassin like you? Or that we're secretly lovers?" He shook his head. "Nothing like that. But … she's a good person." He hesitated, a distant look in his eyes. "I served in the military, before. I was one of those that got sent out to put down the uprising in the Rim Mountains ten years back." He shuddered, just a little. "Don't like to think about it too much. But that's where I lost my leg." He paused.

"I was in a bad way after that," he said at last, quietly. "Nightmares every night, hated the whole system. Couldn't go back to the military, not like this," he gestured at his prosthetic leg. "Didn't have the skills for anything else, either. They pay you if you get injured on duty, but it's just enough for a tiny apartment and a few cheap bottles of wine in the evenings. And they don't tell you how you go off your head crazy, sitting around replaying it over and over. Finally started taking on jobs on cargo transports, but never stayed long—no one wanted me. Don't blame them, either. I was a nasty bastard. Figured anyone who took me on did it out of pity, and I hated them for it. Got thrown off a few crews for fighting, then one day they were hauling me into the station brig to sober up, and I met Joska.

"She asked me if I wanted a new job, because she was looking for crew. I almost spat in her face, but I couldn't bring myself to. Figured it'd be another temporary post, but—" he shrugged, his gaze still distant. "It wasn't. I figured out, eventually, she wasn't much different than I was, far as her situation. Worked her whole damn life just trying to get ahead, but every time she almost got there, something slapped her down. Maybe if she'd been a little more ruthless, she would've made it. But it never seemed to matter to her all that much—least, I never heard her complain.

"Even after that storm broke up her ship five years back, and she lost every damn bit she'd been saving—oh, she swore the air blue when it happened, but even then, never really heard her complain. Just kept going, when I figure anyone else would have given up. And she'd have been in her rights to, I figure. She was just barely starting to get her feet under her again when you—" he made a brief motion with his hand, but Savina understood very well what he was saying.

She hated how the guilt gnawed at her insides at the thought.

"She saved my damn life," he said quietly, not taking his eyes off her. "I wouldn't have lasted more than another year or two. And I know you're not stupid enough to think she hasn't saved yours."

"It was just the easiest way to make sure she got her ship back," Savina snapped.

Rafel snorted. "Even you aren't that damn stupid."

Savina glared at him, trying to ignore the guilt curdling in her stomach.

His eyes caught Savina's, there was an unaccustomed gravity to his expression. "She's my friend. And she's saved my life, more than once. And you will not hurt her, any more than you already have. I know if I went up against you, I be dead in two seconds flat. But I'll do it, Savina, if that's what it takes to keep the captain safe. Do you understand me?"

His meaty hands were balled into fists, but he didn't look frightening. Just resolute, and maybe a little scared.

Savina narrowed her eyes and licked her lips. She wanted to snap a sharp retort, but she couldn't seem to bring herself to.

"You say she's so good," she said finally, in a low voice. "You felt like a victim because of what you did to a bunch of farmers and kids in the Rim Mountains. And you think Joska's some hero for taking you on in spite of that. You say she's been so benevolent, saving my life when she didn't have to. I could have killed her a hundred times, and I haven't. Am I a hero too? She took you on because you were Orthodox, and military, and had a sad backstory. She's kind to me because I'm Orthodox, and I'm young and pretty, and I remind her of her niece. How do you think she'd treat me if I was ugly? If I was weak? If I—if I was an Old Believer?"

Her heart was pounding. Because Rafel hated her, and that was fine. She hated him, too. And he'd have no reason to soften the truth.

Rafel was staring at her. At last he snorted, loudly. "After everything you've seen, and you think any of that would make a difference?" His voice was almost scornful. "I'm so young and pretty, with my leg and my attitude, and that's why she took pity on me? Pretty sure the captain didn't ask how you prayed before she saved your sorry butt from the government agent." He turned away in disgust. "You're stupider than I thought. But I'm warning you, I wasn't joking."

"Listen," Savina spat, "Like I said. I could have killed Joska a hundred times over, and I haven't. I still bloody well need her to get me off this dump of a place. So you don't have to worry about me not taking care of your hero. I have a vested interest in making sure she stays alive, and you know I look out for my own interests."

Rafel turned back and gave her an appraising look. Then, finally, he smiled, so briefly she wasn't sure she'd actually seen it. "I'm not like Joska. I don't give a damn about you, or your reasons, or your history, or anything else. I just want to know that we're on the same side as far as the captain is concerned. And if we are, that's all I need."

She stared at him for a moment as he turned away again.

Then she shook her head.

Easy for him to say. As if he deserved any pity for what he'd done up in the Rim Mountains.

Anyway, she'd been telling the truth—she couldn't kill Joska, not yet. And so the default was that she'd keep her alive.

But nor could she trust her.

"Be careful of what hides under friendly smiles." That had been one of the precepts they'd pounded into her in the compound, the ones she'd repeated daily at worship her entire childhood. And unlike the ones about the Great Mystery's existing in a corporeal body, that one she actually believed.

It was just a matter of waiting to see the threat under the smile.

Beni came back right around the time the yibo sent dinner in— something boiled and mashed and bland, as usual.

"Vina," Beni whispered, when all of them were done eating. "I think I figured out how to make it work. Here, I'll show you."

Savina led her sibling back to a corner as Rafel pulled out his pouch of dice.

"Savina," Nicolau called. "You going to play? I'm with Rafel, but Joska needs a partner."

"Beni can play in a minute," Savina called back. "I still have to work out some things for the next job."

"This is how you turn it on," said Beni in a low voice. "And I think you just speak into it here, and then this button transmits the call. If a message comes back, you hit this button to listen." They paused. "As far as I can tell, this has got to be black-market. The only reason they'd make something like this so low-tech is to avoid it getting tracked. Savina …"

"You're just going to have to trust me, alright?" Savina hissed.

Beni was quiet for a long moment. Then, at last, they nodded and stood, turning away from her. "Joska, you still need a partner?"

Savina could hear the laughter of the others in the background as she crouched over the communicator, typing out a message.

The raiders, whoever they were, would understand her language. At least, that's what the yibo woman had said. She'd just have to not think too hard about the reasons behind that.

It wasn't until much, much later that night, when the others were already in bed, that the communicator buzzed in Savina's hand. She pulled it out and crossed over to the grimy window, holding the screen up to the moonlight.

We'll send someone to meet with you, the message read. *Three days' time. The tavern I've marked on the outskirts of the city. Pay off your contact, and he'll pay off the guards.*

Savina looked up, staring sightlessly out at the grimy alleyway, still and cold in the moonlight. She allowed herself a small, satisfied smile.

The raiders may be dangerous. But they had no idea who they were dealing with. And nor did Yuur.

And if everything went as planned—well, maybe Savina and the rest would survive this after all.

16

Alba

"Madam." Yosip's voice drifted through the door. "It's me and Ines. May we come in?"

Alba glanced down at herself—as presentable as it was possible to be on this forsaken system—pushed herself to her feet and hit the door control. Yosip stepped inside, and, after a moment's hesitation, Ines did as well.

"How are you feeling, Madam?" Yosip asked. Despite the lines of exhaustion on his face, he was wearing his usual friendly smile.

"I'm fine, thank you," said Alba, and she realized the words had come out in a much softer tone than was her wont.

The smile-lines around Yosip's eyes creased deeper. "I'm glad to hear it." He paused a moment. "Ines has some news for us."

"I—" began Ines, visibly bracing herself. "I stayed up late working on the last of the translation program last night. And … and it's done."

Alba stared. "You … you've worked out how to translate yibo?"

Ines nodded timidly. "It's a program we can set into our wavelinks. I'll set it up for you, if you want."

Alba was still staring. At last she said, "Ines. If you've done that …" she shook her head. "Thank you. You may have saved us all."

Ines beamed. "Let me—I'll install it on our wavelinks, then," she said, with her usual puppy dog eagerness.

It was only a short time later when Yosip opened the door to three of the lower-ranking diplomats, plus an interpreter and a full complement of bodyguards.

"Alba," the interpreter said, ducking her head in respect. "If you'd follow me, please, Kachik is awaiting you."

Alba took a deep breath and followed.

Their guides led them through the courtyard and into the diplomatic building. When they reached the room, the bodyguards pulled back the doors and gestured them inside. Alba hesitated, then stepped through, the three yibo diplomats following behind. She was gestured to a seat, and Yosip and Ines sat down beside her.

The diplomats settled themselves on the other side of the room, and for a while, the six of them sat looking at each other.

The yibo didn't seem upset by the wait, but Alba could feel an itching impatience worrying at her. Ines' hand was clutched, white knuckled, around her icon, but Yosip sat serenely. When he caught Alba's glance, he gave her a small, encouraging wink, and she sucked in a breath of disapproval that only made him smile wider.

And then, at last, the doors behind them opened. The three yibo diplomats jumped to their feet as someone who must be Kachik stepped through the door, flanked by his own bodyguards and followed by Harroch. The ambassador's head was down, but he managed a small, reassuring smile at Alba.

Alba inclined her head graciously. Kachik returned the gesture with a close-lipped smile, but there was an unreadable expression in his large eyes. He walked to his seat slowly, and sat down, again with no trace of hurry.

"Ambassador Alba," he said, his accent making her name strange. "I asked to speak with you because I have excellent news. Our scientists have been working day and night, and it appears they will very soon be able to restore the portal, and restore you and your friends back to your own people. And in the interim, I understand that you and Harroch have come to an agreement. I must congratulate you."

Alba smiled, despite the tension twisting her stomach. "I'm very glad to hear it."

"Of course," said Kachik. He paused a moment. "I … understand there have been some concerns on your part. Stemming, I gather, from various aspects of our culture you find difficult to explain."

Alba stiffened. "I—" she began.

Kachik shook his head. "No, please. I apologize that this should have become an issue. I did not wish for it to distract from the negotiations. But as it seems you have reached an agreement—" he flicked his tail in the yibo equivalent of a shrug. "I have instructed Harroch that such matters are to be explained to you whenever you wish."

Alba frowned, staring at him.

Could it really be that simple?

"Thank you," she said at last. "I appreciate your consideration."

"Of course," he said, smiling. "We are delighted that our nations have met, despite the unfortunate circumstances, and that after all we were able to come to a negotiated agreement."

"As are we," said Alba, relaxing back in her seat just a little. She hadn't been aware how tense her muscles had been until now.

Kachik smiled, then paused a moment. "And just to be clear—this agreement you've made is binding on your government, yes? As the portal will soon be open, I would like to be certain of the state of things. A military alliance is something that must be dealt with properly, and I would hate for there to be misunderstandings."

Alba frowned.

Harroch hadn't mentioned a military alliance in particular, only an alliance in general. And while with a generous interpretation, the draft document would likely invoke mutual military aid once details were worked out, it hadn't been something they'd discussed with any specificity.

"I'm sorry for any misapprehension," she said, a sudden trickle of unease starting in the back of her mind. "As I explained to Harroch, I was sent here on behalf of my government to negotiate terms with you. However, I'm somewhat limited as to the scope and nature of my authority. Until I have the opportunity to present the agreement to the full Council and receive their ratification, I'm afraid this document can be nothing more than a draft."

Kachik's eyes narrowed slightly, and he made a brusque gesture with his hand. "That will not be enough. If we are to reopen the portal, we must ensure that your people do not intend to wage war on ours. The agreements we make must be binding beforehand, to assuage any potential threat."

He was speaking as if he feared a threat. But there was no fear in his posture, only a barely disguised impatience.

"You've seen the weapons we carry," Alba said carefully. "They're hardly superior to your own technology."

"But they are certainly not ineffective," said Kachik. "At the least, it would be proof of your goodwill. And as you surely have surmised, that must be our main concern."

Alba and Yosip exchanged glances. She could see the echo of her own concern in Yosip's eyes.

"I—can understand why you would ask for a binding agreement," Alba said slowly. "But as I have explained, my authority here is limited. As much as I might wish to, as an ambassador, I cannot bind my nation in an alliance with another without consulting the Council."

Kachik was studying her closely, and again, she couldn't read his expression. He turned to his aides and said something in a low voice, and when the AI voice in Alba's wavelink spoke in her ear, she almost jumped.

"They're lying," the cheerful AI voice translated. "This so-called ambassador is one of the most important people in their government. It's beyond the bounds of believability that she doesn't have the authority to enter into a binding agreement."

Alba's veins turned to ice as she stared at Kachik, trying not to let her horror show on her face.

She didn't need to glance behind her at Yosip and Ines to know their expressions must have frozen as well.

There was no way the yibo should have known who she was.

"She's delaying on purpose. Do you think anyone has spoken to them in secret?"

Alba schooled her expression into its usual stern, no-nonsense look, forcing her face still. But if they could have heard her heartbeat, it would have given her away in an instant.

"You would have me believe, then, that should you make an agreement with my people, your own government would refuse to acknowledge it?" Kachik turned back to Alba, a tone to his voice that was almost sly.

Alba lifted her chin and narrowed her eyes. "I am afraid I would be outside the bounds of my authority to enter into such a contract. I could not require my government bind itself to such an agreement without due deliberation."

Kachik nodded slowly, still watching her. "I see," he said. "You are telling me that under no circumstances are you willing to enter into an alliance with us."

Alba took a deep breath. "I apologize if I gave that impression. That is not what I meant to convey. My government, as I have stated, has an abiding interest in entering into peaceful relations with you. They would not have sent me to head this diplomatic mission otherwise. I am merely speaking to the limits of my authority." She hesitated, then continued, "I may say, in fact, that there is not a single member of government who alone is authorized to make such a decision. All such decisions must be jointly made, and must involve the majority vote of all three sections of government."

"They're hiding something," Kachik said to Harroch. "I thought you told me you'd managed to get an agreement. And now they're holding back."

"Perhaps—perhaps they're stronger than we thought," Harroch whispered back. There was nervousness in every line of his posture. "After all, we didn't know anything about the land-devil until they arrived. If their planet is populated with those beasts, and they've managed to harness them as weapons, this encounter could go very differently from the last."

Kachik snorted. "They're still playing coy. I hear from our scientists that that scientist of theirs was trying to convince them that the thing was harmless. And if my intelligence from the peacekeepers is correct, there is a human who's escaped into the city who's proving how dangerous their low-tech weapons can be. Without land-devils I doubt they'd pose enough of a threat to seriously concern us, but we don't have the time to deal with a situation of that kind."

"Exactly," said Harroch eagerly. "You must see how a negotiated solution—"

Kachik cut him off with a curt motion, and turned back to Alba. He watched her for a long time.

"You must understand my position," he said at last, speaking in accented Common Dialect once more. "You say you are operating under constraints—I am as well. And as it appears we are currently at an impasse—" he made a brief gesture. "I am a very busy person. I will allow you to go back to your quarters and rest. We can resume this conversation another time, perhaps when you've had some time to think things over." He gestured to the guards, and they stood, waiting for Alba and the others to rise.

As they turned to go, he muttered something to his aides, turning away from them.

"If she won't commit to a military alliance," the AI voice in her ear translated, "then we'll have to resort to the fall-back. And if that doesn't work … it would take more resources than I'm comfortable with, but even taking those land-devil creatures into account, I think we have the weaponry to force the humans to the table if we must. And if they refuse to negotiate even over the bodies of their people —" he made a dismissive gesture. "We destroy enough of their infrastructure that they can no longer communicate with the other generation-ships, and then move on to another settlement. We only need enough of them to keep our enemies' weapons busy. This is a temporary setback, nothing more."

Alba forced her legs to keep moving. She was trembling, just a little, but she refused to let the yibo see it.

It appeared the situation was more desperate even than they'd imagined.

17

Savina

"Where's Nicolau?" asked Savina, scowling at the room in general.

Joska, Rafel, and Beni were in the corner, a handful of dice on a low table between them. Rafel looked up, scowling at her. "Ask your boss friend," he grunted. "Rach had me and Joska serving all day, and he pulled Nicolau out for something about half a standard hour after we got on shift."

Savina swore under her breath, turned on her heel, and stalked out towards the room where she knew the crew boss was most likely to be.

"Savina? Where are you going?" came Beni's voice from behind her, but Savina ignored them.

She shoved open the door to Rach's office to find the man leaned back in his stool, sipping something that even from here Savina could smell was fermented.

"Where's Nicolau?" she growled.

The crew boss, who'd sat up in surprise as Savina burst through the door, gave her the look she'd come to recognize as something between disdain and fear. "I sent him out to help bring back some supplies," he said in irritation. "What's the use of feeding you humans if we don't use you for what you're good for?"

Savina let a slow smile start on her face and crossed the space between her and the yibo man in two strides. Rach flinched back, and the guards in the corners lifted their weapons.

Savina didn't touch him, though, just bent in close. "I agreed not to kill anyone here, because your boss agreed to keep my friends safe," she said quietly, making each word clear and distinct. "Didn't she?"

He didn't answer, just swallowed hard.

She smiled at him, showing all her teeth. "Didn't she?"

He swallowed again, and tipped his head to the side.

"And if one of my friends is killed because you were stupid enough to send them out in the streets in broad daylight after what happened just a couple days ago with Joska, then I promise you, I will kill you. And you can ask your friends exactly how efficient I can be."

He looked like he wanted to protest, but didn't dare.

"Now," she continued, the lightness in her voice not disguising the fury, "tell me where you sent him."

"I'll—I'll send you his tracking device signal," Rach muttered, and a moment later the yibo communications device on her wrist flashed with a location.

"Thank you," she said, with a pleasant smile. "I'm going to hope, for all of our sakes, that nothing has happened to him."

She turned on her heel and stalked from the room.

Beni was waiting for her outside. "Savina?" they asked.

"They sent Nicolau out into the streets. I'm going after him," Savina snapped. "You stay here. I'll be faster if it's just me."

Before Beni had time to protest, Savina slipped past them and out the door.

She started off down the streets at a jog towards the small flashing beacon indicating her brother's location. A stitch started under her ribs after a couple of blocks, and she pressed her elbow against her side as she ran, trying to ignore the painful ache.

She hated running. She'd always hated running.

Nicolau had damn well better appreciate this, that was all.

She slowed as she approached his location, gasping for breath.

She was overreacting, and she knew it. Chances were he was fine. But she couldn't help the tight snake of worry that had wrapped itself around her chest.

Reka Soler had proven herself a dedicated pursuer.

Ahead, Savina heard yibo voices, and mingled with them, her brother's cheerful, bright-copper tenor, and her shoulders slumped in mixed relief and irritation.

Nicolau was laughing at something one of his companions had said, sounding completely at ease.

Caution, habit from years of experience, kept her from stepping around the corner herself, but she peered out carefully.

Nicolau was leaned up against the wall of one of the buildings, the heavy bag he must have been carrying on the ground at his feet. One foot was crossed over the other, and he was talking easily with one of the mobsters, who'd also put down their loads for a brief rest.

And behind them, perched on a small ledge which jutted out from one of the buildings, but easily within pulse-fire range—

Savina's heart almost stopped.

Reka was lying on her belly, her eye to the sights of a pulse-rifle, elbow braced against the clear glass of the ledge.

Savina choked out a curse.

But it was Savina who Reka was really after. If she could just distract woman's attention for long enough to get Nicolau away—

She closed her eyes for a moment, muttering a half-remembered prayer. Then she yanked out her pistol and threw herself around the corner, lining up a shot as she ran.

She got off three shots before Reka had time to swing the barrel of her rifle around, and then Savina dived behind one of the buildings as the pulse from Reka's shot jangled off the stones around her.

Nicolau was staring at her in utter astonishment, and she shouted, "Run! Get out of here, get behind something!" Then she was moving again, rolling upright and snapping off another two shots.

She was too far away for her shots to be effective, but she was closing the distance quickly. And anyway, at this point, she just needed a distraction. She just needed to get Nicolau out of danger. That was all.

She heard Nicolau's muffled swearing, the yibo's excited chatter, and then fleeing footsteps. She let out a quick breath of relief, then fired twice more as another shot hissed over her head, dispersing against the building behind her.

Reka had dropped her rifle and rolled off the ledge, pulling out a small, deadly looking pistol.

Savina slipped into another alley. She was close enough that this time when she fired Reka had to duck out of the way, her movements smooth and deadly and graceful. There was the familiar hiss and clatter of a bolas, and Savina dived, rolling on the rough pavement as the weapon slammed into the wall behind her. When she straightened, Reka was almost on top of her.

Savina lunged upwards, catching the woman's wrist and twisting it she did so. She heard the satisfying *ting* of the pistol hitting the street, and then Reka's hand was around her throat, shoving her up against the building.

Savina stared into Reka's eyes, panic coating her brain as her breath was cut off.

There was something like triumph in the woman's icy gaze, a small smile on her sensual lips, her expression cold with hatred. Savina struggled, but her head was going fuzzy from lack of oxygen, and for a moment she just stared up at Reka, unable to pull her gaze away.

Reka's eyes narrowed, her expression growing even colder.

And then Savina's free hand found the knife she'd been fumbling for, and she brought it up in a brutal motion that should have opened Reka up from hip to breastbone. Reka gasped in surprise and dodged aside with almost inhuman grace, but her hand on Savina's throat loosened.

Savina twisted free and jumped back. Her throat was bruised and aching where Reka had grabbed her, but she still managed an innocent smile. "It's a little bit harder to go up against me instead of some defenceless kid, isn't it?" she croaked. "Did you get off on the thought of killing someone with my DNA, but without my skills? Would it have made you feel strong?"

Reka's face creased for a just for a moment in confusion. And then Savina lunged at her again. Reka grabbed for the hand with the knife, her fingers catching Savina's wrist and squeezing hard enough to make her loosen her grip, but Savina's other hand was digging in her pocket, and she yanked out an electric tranq and slapped it against Reka's ribcage.

The woman staggered slightly, but didn't freeze.

Savina swore. Reka's suit must be armoured against it. She tapped the toe of her boot to the pavement, and as the sharp, concealed blade sprang out from the toe, she kicked Reka's shin.

Reka stumbled back with a grunt of pain, cursing. There was blood dripping down her leg, but not as much as there should have been. She reached up, still swearing, and broke the electric tranq free, the small twist of pain in her face the only indication that she'd been affected by it at all.

For a long moment, the two women studied each other, both breathing heavily.

Reka's hair, damp with sweat from the fight, stuck to the side of her sharp cheekbones, the smooth black of it contrasting with the cold copper glow of her skin. There was nothing superfluous about the woman, her body lean muscle, her elegant features as sharp as if they'd been cut from steel, her eyes cold and ruthless. The only hint of softness about her was the full curve of her lips, and even that was offset by her knife-sharp smile. She looked dangerous, as beautiful and deadly as the slender ribbon snakes up in the Rim Mountains, and Savina found she was smiling, her heart pounding in a combination of fear and exhilaration.

The targets she'd been going after with the yibo were hardly a challenge. Most of the targets she had gone after since she started this job as a teenager hadn't been a challenge. And she'd never minded that—simple jobs were the ones that kept you alive. And you make sure that none of your jobs were challenging, because you prepared beforehand. With Beni providing backup, killing had been as humdrum and routine as making a pot of porridge in the mornings.

It wasn't until this moment, staring into Reka's cold eyes, that Savina realized how badly she'd been craving a challenge.

Reka moved first, the motion as swift as a striking snake, but Savina stepped backwards just far enough to avoid the blow. She grabbed Reka's upper arm and twisted backwards, using the woman's momentum to pull her off-balance. Then she jerked Reka upright and slammed her back against the building, and with her free hand, she yanked out her own bolas and swung it sharply. It wrapped firmly around Reka's arms and torso, the hard metal balls on the end of the cords smacking into the woman's solar plexus with enough force to make her grunt.

Savina pushed her further up against the wall, her forearm across Reka's throat, and pulled another knife from her belt. Her face was only centimetres from Reka's, the heat of the woman's panting breath hot against her skin.

"You came after me," Savina hissed. "I'll kill you for that, but I least I could respect it. But to hunt down a kid who's never hurt anyone, just because he's my brother—you're a damn coward. At least I only kill if I'm paid for it." She grabbed Reka's hair, dragging the woman's head back far enough to expose her throat.

Those slate-hazel eyes were steady, locked on Savina's face. There wasn't the fear in them Savina had secretly hoped for. Instead, there was that same disdain as when Reka had come after her on the *Dolphin*.

Reka tensed, and Savina grabbed her knife, bringing it up so she could slide across Reka's throat. And then the woman's foot swept Savina's legs from under her.

Savina fell heavily.

"If I'd wanted to kill your brother, you little idiot, he'd be dead," Reka gasped, her voice hoarse from the pressure of Savina's forearm. "It's you I'm after."

Savina yanked out her knife, twisting to meet the attack that was certain to come.

And then someone shouted, "Savina! Are you alright?" And from behind her, she heard running footsteps. She turned in time to see

Nicolau sprinting towards her, half-a-dozen heavily armed yibo mobsters on his heels.

Reka hissed out a curse and turned, disappearing down the alley.

When Nicolau reached Savina, he looked her over carefully, wincing slightly at the bruises and blood, then reached down to help her up. She ignored his proffered hand and rolled painfully to her feet, scowling at him.

His eyes were wide and innocent, and in his case, it wasn't even an act.

"Are you alright?" he asked again, his face creased with concern. Savina nodded, then sucked in a quick breath as she tried to move.

"Nothing serious," she said irritably, as Nicolau's concerned expression turned to one of alarm.

"Praise the Mystery's goodness for that," he said, his voice thick with relief. "Who was that woman? Was it that agent you were telling me about? I thought she'd kill you." He paused, his expression sobering. "I … guess she could have killed me, too, couldn't she?"

Savina glared at him. "That bastard isn't touching what's mine, not if she knows what's good for her."

Nicolau took a deep breath, and there was a look on his face as if he was bracing himself. "Um. Savina," he said, the slight tremor in his voice showing through his determination. "I think—I think you and I need to have a talk."

Savina glanced around quickly. Reka had taken off, but there was no guarantee she wasn't waiting in another alley, her sniper rifle perched on her knees. "Let's get out of here first," she said grimly.

The yibo were looking around warily as well.

Nicolau hesitated for a moment, then nodded. "As long as you promise when we get back, you'll—"

She grabbed him by the arm, turned him around, and shoved him bodily down the street ahead of her.

They reached the mob headquarters without incident. Savina marched into Yuur's office without knocking.

"If you or your people ever put my brother in danger again," she snapped at the shocked yibo woman, "I swear to you, I'll kill every person here. Do you understand me?"

She ignored the guards, and waited, eyes narrowed, for Yuur's head to tip to the side in acknowledgement. Then she left, slamming the door behind her.

And then, at last, she was back in their rooms with Beni and Joska and Rafel and Nicolau.

Nicolau waited at the back of the room, determination clear on his face.

"He told us what happened," said Joska, her face grave. "I'm glad you both made it out of that alive."

Savina gave the woman a brief nod. She was still too shaken and furious to dwell on what might have happened.

"Do you need to be treated? How bad are your injuries?" Joska continued.

"I'm fine," said Savina shortly. She closed her eyes for a long moment and drew in a deep breath.

Nicolau was still watching her steadily.

At last, she turned to him and raised an eyebrow.

May as well get this over with.

He cleared his throat, looking faintly uncomfortable. "Um," he began. He cleared his throat again. "Savina. You've—that's the second time you save my life. Third, I guess. But—" he seemed to be bracing himself. "But I … I don't want any misunderstandings. I'm very grateful to you, but—but I thought I should just make it clear. I'm … not interested in you in—in that way. In case that's what you were thinking." There was a flush rising on his cheeks, and his voice was thick with embarrassment.

Savina stared at him, for once in her life completely at a loss for words.

He took a deep breath and soldiered on. "I'm—I mean, I don't mean to be rude, and—and I'm sure you're a very nice person, but —but I'm just not—"

Savina was still staring.

From the corner of her eye, she could see Joska's mouth twitch.

"You." Savina began. "You thought. You thought the reason I was saving you was because." She couldn't continue, because her brain had completely shut down.

Nicolau scowled at her, embarrassment clear on his face, the flush risen all the way up to his hairline now. "I—" he began.

She held up a hand to stop him. "Listen. Nicolau." She took a deep breath. "I can't even begin to explain to you all the levels on which you are mistaken."

He stopped, and now it was his turn to stare at her in confusion.

She closed her eyes and drew in another deep breath.

This … had not been how she'd envisioned having this conversation.

She let out her breath and opened her eyes, giving him her most charming smile. "First." She ticked off the points on her fingers. "I'm attracted to women. Second, I'm too old for you. Third, you're my brother."

There was a long, long silence.

Nicolau looked like someone had hit him over the head.

"I'm your—" he began uncertainly. He took a deep breath and shook his head. "I don't have any siblings. I don't know who you've mistaken me for, and I'm very sorry to disappoint you, but—"

Savina's heart was pounding strangely.

She hadn't meant to tell him this way.

She had meant to tell him at all if it could have been avoided, but honestly, at this point, it probably couldn't.

She took a small step closer and reached up to put her hand on his shoulder. "You grew up, the first five years of your life, on a small farm outside Pine Ridge, in the southern Rim Mountains," she said, the words tasting strange in her mouth. "You used to have a dog, a little black one. Your mother was a farmer. She found you, wrapped up in dirty blankets, outside her door late one night at the end of summer. Your cottage burned down when you were five, and that's when your family left the mountains. You settled down in one of the smaller belt villages after that, and your mother never let you go up to the Rim Mountains, even to visit." She paused a moment, watching him. "Do you want me to go on?"

He was staring at her, the shock on his face sharp and bright. "How—" he began. His voice was slightly choked. "How did you—"

She gave him a small smile that couldn't quite hide the bitterness. "Who do you think left you on that doorstep?"

The flush had gone from his face now, replaced by a sick sort of shock. "Why—" he swallowed hard. "Why would you—why did—"

Looking at him, Savina could feel once more that tiny, squirming bundle in her arms, the round-cheeked infant, his face smeared with dirt.

She hadn't known, standing there in the moonlight shivering in terror, what path that one decision would put her life on. Where that path would ultimately lead.

But even if she had—she wouldn't have chosen differently.

She couldn't have. She couldn't have watched that tiny body be slowly covered in dirt, his wailing cries muffled, and not have frantically clawed him out, her fingernails bleeding, her heart pounding in her chest in panic. Not have brushed the dirt out of those tiny baby eyes and that soft round mouth. Not have heard that wavering cry he'd finally given, and known it was the sweetest sound she'd heard in her seven years of life.

And looking up at his open, innocent face, she knew she could never tell him. She could never explain to him exactly what had happened.

No one deserved that knowledge.

So instead, she said, "Our parents were … not nice people. Beni and I—it was the only way we could think of to keep you safe."

He was watching her still, cautiously, as if unsure whether or not to believe her. Unsure whether, if she was telling the truth, he should thank her for what she'd done, or hate her for it.

"It's true," came Beni's soft voice. "I was there too. It was the only way we could keep you safe."

Nicolau was still watching Savina, his face pale with shock. He looked, a little, like he might pass out.

She sighed. "Look, I know it's a lot. We can talk about it more later, okay?"

He nodded, in a stunned sort of sort of way.

Dinner that night was a quiet affair. Nicolau didn't speak much, and nor did anyone else.

"Listen," Savina said, after dinner was over, but before they'd all dispersed. "I … what happened today, to Nicolau, might have happened to any of you. You can't go out alone, not ever. If the yibo try to make you, call me on the wavelink."

"And what about you, Savina?" asked Joska quietly, concern in her tone. "You're the one Reka's after."

Savina hesitated just for a moment, oddly unwilling to say what she had to say next.

Her words to her brother echoed in her brain. *"Our parents weren't nice people."*

That hadn't been it, though. She wasn't sure, now, whether or not her parents were nice people. It hardly seemed to matter.

They'd loved her.

They'd loved Nicolau.

And that hadn't stopped them from letting him be buried alive when the Head Order demanded it.

It had been the Head Order of the compound. It had been him, ultimately, who'd coerced her mother into doing what she'd done. But it had been her mother who had made the final choice.

Just like Savina had made the choice to do what she'd done.

She'd never let herself feel bad about the people she'd burned to death in that fire in the farmer's abandoned cottage, when she'd killed them to save her brother and the family who'd adopted him.

They'd deserved it.

And she knew, deep down, that if she ever let herself feel regret, at anything—if she paused to look back for any reason at all—it would drown her. So she never had. Not when she was twelve, and not when she was a teenager and found she was good at killing, and people would pay her for it. That she could use that as a reason to leave the compound, get her and Beni out, for days or weeks at a time. And as long as the people she was killing were Orthodox, and as long as she sent the money home, no one cared.

Her whole life, she'd accepted that was the natural order of things —that as bad as it was in the compound, it would be worse outside. But looking at the open, friendly innocence of her baby brother's face—maybe she'd been wrong. Maybe that had been yet another lie.

Joska seemed to think so.

Joska would never agree with Savina's plan, not if she knew what it was. She'd insist there were other options. And maybe she was right. Maybe there were.

In the end, though, it hardly mattered. Joska wasn't the one who had to get them out of this. Savina was. And this was the only way she knew.

And, after today—after the shocking, horrifying sight of Reka's rifle pointed towards Nicolau, after the remembered panic at the blood dripping down Joska's neck—she didn't have time to argue about it.

"Listen," said Savina at last. "I can't keep you safe here. But I might have a way to get us out. I … made contact with the creatures these yibo are so afraid of, the raiders. I'm going to meet with one of them tomorrow night. And I'm … hoping I can convince them to make a distraction for us. But we'll have to be ready to go at a moment's notice."

Joska frowned at her. "How are you going to convince these raiders to help us?"

Savina smiled. "I'm very charming when I want to be. Besides, Beni's been looking into Yuur for me, and I have quite a lot of useful information on her."

Not that any of her information mattered—what she had in mind needed only Yuur's name, and a convincing argument that Savina worked for her. But no need for Joska to know that.

She'd almost lost her brother. She was going to get everyone out. She had to, if she wanted even the slightest chance of keeping him safe.

"We'll be ready," Rafel grunted sourly. "Just try to make sure you don't accidentally get any of the rest of us killed in the process."

"Oh, I have no intention of that," she said lightly.

18

Aran

For the rest of the afternoon, Aran and Istvay were left to their own devices. Aran didn't speak much, and neither did Istvay.

Istvay hadn't said a word to him since he'd followed the interpreter to the new out-of-the way accommodation, with its own separate force-field spreading over the top like a foam-bubble over seawater. Instead, they ignored him, pacing like a trapped animal.

Aran couldn't bear to watch them. He couldn't bear to be alone with his thoughts, either, not with the uncomfortable memory of the look on Istvay's face when the yibo guards had closed and locked the door behind them playing over and over in his head.

At last he pulled up the two DNA scans, as well as the DNA readout from back on Colorida, on his datapad, and began to go through the painstaking process of trying to create some sort of a key.

He was so engrossed in the task that when there was a tap on the outer door, one of the yibo bringing their dinner, he jumped.

He picked at his food, still not meeting Istvay's gaze. But he could see, from the corner of his eyes, the tension in their posture, the way their jaw clenched, and guilt twisted in his stomach.

The next morning, Istvay still wasn't speaking to him. The yibo came as usual, with the same polite attention as always.

"I'm terribly sorry, but there's been a break-in at the science laboratory," said the interpreter apologetically. "Until we figure out who is behind it, they've asked that we not bring anyone in. But I'll come fetch you the moment I'm permitted to, if you would like to continue your scientific discussions."

Aran managed a close-lipped smile that hopefully didn't look too guilty, and ignored Istvay's suddenly suspicious scowl.

"Aran—" Istvay began when the yibo had left, turning to him.

Aran sighed. "Pishti. It's … They didn't catch me, anyways, and —" he trailed off. He wasn't completely sure what to say.

Istvay watched him for a moment, then turned away abruptly. "Look, it's fine," they said through their teeth. "Talk to me when you feel like it, then. But don't bother talking to me tonight, because I plan on asking your interpreter friend to bring some damn alcohol, and then I damn well plan on getting too drunk to see straight."

Aran turned quickly, staring after them, but they'd already stepped inside and closed the door firmly behind them.

He took a long breath and closed his eyes, leaning against the wall of the courtyard.

He deserved this. He deserved it, and he knew it.

He wanted, more than anything else in the world, to talk to Istvay. But these days he couldn't mention anything without them blowing up, and besides—

Besides, he knew Istvay didn't approve of what he was doing. And he didn't honestly care. He couldn't afford to care.

There was a soft thud, and he looked up quickly, jerked out of his thoughts.

Something red and round had rolled to a stop along the courtyard wall—a child's ball, it looked like.

He walked over cautiously and bent to pick it up. He turned it over in his fingers, noting the familiar maker's mark—and then he noticed something else.

The ball was slit open, and there was something shoved inside.

He pulled it out. It was paper of some sort, folded over itself several times.

He unfolded it, his hands shaking just a little.

There were markings on the paper. And he recognized the drawing style.

"Ree?" he whispered.

"Shhhh!" came a familiar voice from the other side of the wall, followed by a quick burst of words he couldn't understand.

He glanced down at the pictograph.

It was the same diagram she'd drawn in the jungle—the box, the yibo figure crossed out, a ship.

And beside it, another figure. The figure she'd begun in the jungle, now fully filled out. It was humanoid, but much taller than the yibo —taller than a human, if he were to guess from the proportions— with long hair hanging loose down to its knees, sharp teeth, a vicious expression.

He stared at the drawing.

He couldn't be certain why she'd sent this.

But he could guess.

He pulled out his own writing stick, and added a planet to the drawing, up in the corner. He circled the planet, then the ship, then the strange, vicious-looking creature. Then he folded up the paper and shoved it into the slit in the ball, and tossed it back over the wall.

Apparently, the force-field around their compound wasn't built to keep out objects as small as a child's ball.

The response, when it came, was the picture he'd sent, but she'd added something—a picture of someone who was probably supposed to be him, since there was an odd, tentacled lump on its shoulder. He was holding the box. And something that looked like a knife was embedded in his throat.

He stared at the picture for a long moment. From outside, he heard an inquisitive noise.

The message wasn't particularly ambiguous. Whatever this box was, it was dangerous. And if he guessed correctly, she was asking if it was more important to him than staying alive.

Was letting him know those may be his options.

He circled the picture of him getting stabbed in the throat, trying not to think too hard about what he was doing, then tucked it in the ball and tossed it back over the wall.

She unfolded the paper, and he heard her grunt an affirmative. The ball came over the wall one last time, and then her footsteps faded away.

"Wait—" he called, but the footsteps didn't pause.

With trembling fingers, he pulled out the paper.

Inside was a map of the government compound, with an "X" marked in one of the more secluded walkways. Above, there was a drawing of the two moons, then another, with the second set circled.

She'd meet him tomorrow night, at the walkway. And either she'd betray him, or she'd tell him about how to find the creatures who'd sent the box. Who were clearly frightening enough that no one wanted to talk about them.

Well, assuming he'd interpreted her messages correctly.

He sank down against the wall of the courtyard, staring blankly at the pictogram.

His hands were shaking again.

Damn it to hell, why did she have to warn him? It was easier if he could pretend the information would be simple to find, and then deal with the dangers as they came up. Thinking about them beforehand made it a hundred times worse.

But he needed this information. And he wouldn't change his answer, no matter how much time he had to think it over.

At last, he stood and crossed through to their small apartment. Istvay was nowhere to be found—probably in their room, and probably avoiding him on purpose.

He sighed and made his way to his own room, pulled up his palm screen, and began scanning through the DNA sequences again, the soothing ritual of reading data finally enough to calm his spinning brain.

He thought he heard, once, in the corner of his mind, Istvay's irritated voice calling him, probably to come for a meal, but he hardly registered it, so focused on his data that the words didn't compute.

When he finally did look up, it was dark, and Istvay was nowhere to be seen.

He blinked, bringing his mind back to the present.

"Istvay?" he called, pushing himself to his feet. His muscles were stiff. He must have been sitting for longer than he'd realized.

He stepped out of the bedroom and into the small common room. There was a dish of food, now cold, on the table. The other must have been cleared away.

"Istvay?" There was a sudden panic rising in his chest. "Istvay, where are you?"

There was no light shining out from under Istvay's door, but he tapped on it anyways. When there was no response, he cracked it open to see if his friend was already asleep.

The room was empty.

Fighting back a sharp stab of worry, Aran closed the door and stepped out into the small courtyard.

It took him a moment, in the dim light, to make out Istvay's figure.

"Istvay?" he said cautiously, and Istvay turned towards him.

They were leaning back against the wall of the courtyard, a soft flask of alcohol, mostly empty, dangling loosely between their fingers. The moons were bright enough that Aran could make out their face, and Istvay smiled a little when they caught sight of him.

Aran's shoulders dropped in relief. "Istvay. Is everything alright?"

"Aran. Come have a drink." Their words slurred, just a little, and Aran gave a small, rueful sigh.

He knew exactly how drunk Istvay had to be before they started slurring their words.

He crossed the small courtyard towards them, and placed a hand on their shoulder. "Pishti," he said gently. "Come on, let's get you to bed."

Istvay shook their head stubbornly, glancing up at the double moons, then turned back to Aran and smiled that slow, sweet smile they had. "Stay here and watch the moons with me for a bit. They're pretty tonight."

Aran nodded, returning Istvay's smile. He couldn't say no when Istvay asked like that, even if he wanted to. And he found he didn't really want to. "Alright, Pishti. We'll stay and watch the moons for a bit."

Istvay tried to straighten, swaying a little, and Aran caught their arm. "Let's sit down, at least," he said, trying not to let his amusement show in his voice.

Istvay turned to stare at him for a moment, then nodded, swaying again. Aran grabbed their hand as they lowered themself gingerly to the ground, then he settled himself beside them. Istvay leaned back against the courtyard wall, pulling one knee up to their chest and stretching the other leg out in front of them, like they always did.

Aran smiled, watching them, and something in his chest ached, just a little. Istvay was still gripping his hand, and Aran tugged it gently. But instead of releasing it, Istvay tightened their grip, pulling Aran's hand into their lap.

Aran's heart was suddenly beating faster than it had been, and he took a long, steadying breath.

It was fine. Istvay was just a little drunk, that was all, and it was fine.

Istvay glanced over at the bottle in their other hand, then held it out to Aran with a quirk of their eyebrows.

Aran shook his head, swallowing down the tightness in his chest.

He was smart enough to know that any impairment of his faculties would be a very, very bad idea right now. Especially with Istvay sitting beside him, their shoulders touching his, Aran's hand clasped in theirs and those brown eyes watching him in the moonlight, for once soft and liquid instead of hard and challenging ...

Istvay studied him for a moment, then shrugged and brought the flask to their lips. They took a brief swallow, then corked the flask and dropped it to the ground beside them. Then they leaned their head back against the wall and looked up at the sky, where the moons glowed bright even through the faint glimmer of the force-field.

Aran took another deep breath, trying to steady his heartbeat.

They were just friends. That was all, and that was all he needed. No matter how badly it hurt, it was for the best. Because if he couldn't have anything more, at least he had this. At least Istvay was here, and when they were drunk and tired and vulnerable, he was the one they wanted to be here with them. Even if they were furious with him when they were sober.

Istvay's gaze fell to Aran's hand in their lap, and they smiled, just a little. They slid one hand down to circle Aran's wrist, and with the other, traced a finger gently across the lines of his palm.

Aran closed his eyes and bit down hard on his teeth, trying not to swear.

It didn't mean anything. Istvay was very, very drunk.

But the firmness of their hand encircling his wrist, the soft brush of their fingers across his palm, the warmth of their shoulder against his, was making something squeeze painfully in his chest, and a warmth pool in the base of his stomach that he had to focus hard to fight back.

Istvay traced their fingers along Aran's hand, their fingernails trailing down the soft hollow of his wrist, and Aran clenched his teeth harder and bit back a groan.

Damn it to hell—

"Aran?" asked Istvay softly.

Aran blinked his eyes back open and glanced over at them.

They were watching him, their expression open and vulnerable, and there was something hesitant in their voice that Aran hadn't heard there in a very long time.

"What—what is it, Istvay?" he managed, trying to keep the shakiness from his tone.

"Call me Pishti. I like it when you call me Pishti."

Aran swallowed. "I—Okay. Alright, Pishti. What is it?"

For a minute, Aran wasn't sure if they'd continue.

To be honest, it was hard to focus on anything at the moment except the soft, teasing pressure of their fingers against the skin of his hand.

They sighed, their shoulders slumping just a little. "Aran. I'm … sorry," they said at last, their words almost inaudible.

Aran frowned, trying to gather his thoughts. "Pishti. What are you talking about? Sorry for what?"

Istvay shook their head, not meeting his eye. "I—I guess I'm not much use after all," they said, with a small, humourless laugh. "I—I came along to protect you. That's the whole reason I came. I didn't want you to come on this mission at all, because I knew—I knew things could go wrong. And you'd be afraid, and it was dangerous, and you were only doing it because of me, and—" they shook their head in frustration. "I spent my whole damn life trying to keep you safe. Not that I don't think you're good at what you do—you're the best at what you do. I've never seen anyone who can do what you do, Aran. And I'm good for—well, for trying to keep you safe. And I couldn't do it. You're here, and we're trapped behind the portal, and I couldn't—" their voice choked off.

Aran drew in a sharp breath. "Pishti. Listen." He found he was stumbling over his words. "It's—it's not like that. Please don't say that. That's not all you're good for, you're—you're so much more than that, you're—and this isn't your fault. There's nothing you could have done, you couldn't have—"

Istvay raised their gaze until they were looking him straight in the eye. Their eyes were unfocused from the alcohol, but their expression was deadly serious. "That's my job, Aran. That's—that's all I ever wanted. For you to be safe. For you to be alright. That's the whole reason I came. And I'm trying, but I can't … I'm not good enough. I

—I shouted at you the other day, and I know you hate that, and I … I scared you. And I spent the rest of the damn night feeling like dirt, and trying to figure out how to apologize, but I couldn't find you in the morning when I came to look, and I can't even—you don't even talk to me anymore. You don't listen to me. And it's my fault, I know, but I can't …" They shook their head. "You won't even talk to me anymore. Probably shouldn't, because I'm a damn … I can't even —" they trailed off for a moment.

"I tried to tell you it's not worth it. What you're doing, I mean. I know you want to find a cure. But—but if you found a cure, and you saved me, and you died doing it—I don't think you know … You have no idea what you mean to me. And I don't know how to make you damn well understand." They gave a small, choking laugh. "You're so damn stubborn, Aran. You've always been. You get something into your head, and then you … But if something happened to you, I'd—I couldn't—" their words trailed off again, and Aran stared at them in a mixture of guilt and horror as they dropped their head, blinking hard against the bright shine of tears welling in their eyes.

"Pishti—" he choked. "Pishti, listen." He was talking frantically, trying not to think about Istvay's words. It wasn't fair of them to drop something like this on him when they were drunk and he couldn't talk sense into them. "Pishti. It's—it's not your job to keep me safe. If I get hurt, it's no one's fault but my own. You're—look, Pishti, I'm an idiot. You don't have to—"

Istvay looked up, shifting slightly against his shoulder. They were sitting too close, the warmth of them pressed up against him, the moonlight reflecting softly from their dark eyes as they watched him. The sight jolted through Aran's entire body, and he had to swallow hard before he could speak again.

"I'm sorry," he whispered, trying to make his dry mouth form words. "I'm sorry I made you feel like that. This isn't your fault, none of it is. It's mine, because I don't know how to do this. I've never known how to do this." He couldn't seem to pull his gaze from Istvay's face, and the moonlight on their skin, the way they watched him from under their long lashes, was making any semblance of focus next to impossible. "If I … if I did, maybe this would all be different. Maybe I could have actually explained myself so that you'd understand. How you're brilliant, and kind, and … and the one good thing in my life. The one thing that makes everything else worthwhile. And maybe you'd finally understand that I can't lose you. I can't. That if there's anything I can do, anything at all—"

Istvay was still watching him, their expression so intent that when Aran looked at it, he found he couldn't remember what he was trying to say.

At last, with a small sigh, Istvay turned their gaze back to the moons, their head dropping back against Aran's shoulder. They still had Aran's hand in their lap, their fingers tracing aimless lines on Aran's palm, following the outline of his hand, dipping between his fingers.

Aran's throat had gone completely dry, his pulse pounding like he'd been running. Istvay's head was leaned back into the hollow of his shoulder, their eyes half-shut and their hair pulling loose from its ponytail, and Aran had to fight back the urge to brush the stray hairs from Istvay's face.

He forced his free hand down into his lap, clenching his fist hard enough that his fingernails bit into his palm.

This was fine. It was all fine, and by morning Istvay would have forgotten about all of it.

But there was a heavy, choking ache in his chest that told him he wouldn't forget nearly so quickly.

He was almost tempted to take Istvay up on the offer of a drink. But he doubted even that would be enough.

And then, to his utter horror, he realized there were tears trickling down Istvay's cheek, and their shoulders were shaking, just a little.

He couldn't remember the last time he'd seen Istvay cry. Yes, they were drunk, but—damn it to hell, he couldn't actually bear it. He'd never been able to bear seeing Istvay cry.

He tugged his hand a little more sharply, freeing it from Istvay's grasp, and hesitantly, he put his arm around their shoulders. "Shhh, Pishti, it's alright," he murmured, fighting down the irrational panic that seeing Istvay upset always brought. "It's alright. You—you don't need to cry. Nothing's wrong, I'm fine, we—we'll be fine. Pishti, please—"

Istvay wiped their eyes on their sleeve and took a long, shuddering breath. Then they reached up and grabbed Aran's hand on their shoulder, lacing their fingers through his and pulling his arm down around their waist. They curled into Aran, nestling their head against him.

Aran's entire body had gone completely rigid, his mouth dry, every nerve sparking like he'd been hit with a jolt of electricity.

Damn it to hell. Damn everything to hell, he wasn't going to actually survive this.

Istvay shifted again, looking up at him in the moonlight. Their gaze was deadly serious, and Aran's heart stuttered painfully.

"I … know what you want me to be, Aran," Istvay said in a low voice. "I know how you feel. And I wish I could be that for you, hell, I can't tell you how much wish I could. But I … I can't." Their voice broke a little. "I can't. I want … I wish I …" they stopped abruptly.

"Pishti. I know," Aran whispered, and he had to swallow hard against the sharp pain of the words. "I've known that for a long time now. I don't know why. I don't know why you won't talk to me about it. But it doesn't change this. It doesn't change any of it."

Istvay's head dropped back against his shoulder, their eyes falling closed. There were still tears glistening on their cheeks, but their mouth curved up into a sleepy, contented smile. "You're so good, Aran," they murmured. "I know I don't deserve it. But you're so good."

Aran almost choked.

Their face was tilted up to him in the moonlight, and he had the sudden, almost unbearable urge to wipe away the tears glistening on Istvay's face, kiss the places where they'd been, and it hurt like a broken bone that had never really healed.

He closed his eyes and gritted his teeth and forced himself to stop thinking of how natural it felt to have Istvay curled into him, his arm around them, their fingers laced through his own, their face nestled into the hollow between his neck and his shoulder and their breath warm on his skin.

They were drunk. And they were his best friend, and he was lucky to have them. And he knew perfectly well that none of this meant anything, but he couldn't seem to convince his body of that, couldn't convince the tight knot in the pit of his stomach to loosen or force the shakiness from his muscles.

He cleared his throat, and when he thought he'd be able to speak, he said, "Come on, Pishti. You look tired. We should get you to bed."

Istvay blinked their eyes open again, and Aran had to look away quickly, the sleepy flutter of their lashes almost too much for him to handle. When at last he looked back, Istvay was staring up at him with a soft, trusting look on their face, and he had to swallow hard.

"'M sorry, Aran," Istvay mumbled, their words slurring more now, and layered with weariness. "'M sorry. I know you're angry at me. I deserve it. Should've—I should've—you're trapped here, and it's my fault, and I should've—"

Aran shook his head sharply, guilt tightening in his chest. "I'm not angry at you, for the Mystery's sake. Nothing here is your fault, and I'm an idiot, and if anyone should be apologizing, it's me. Come on, bed."

This time Istvay let him help them to their feet, and they leaned heavily against him as he led them across the courtyard through the door into their small apartment. At the door to their bedroom, Aran hesitated, then shook his head wryly.

Istvay was almost asleep on their feet at this point.

He pushed the door open with his foot and manoeuvred his friend inside, then lowered them gently onto their cot. They sprawled on the sheets, already half-asleep, and Aran managed a small smile of amusement despite the ache in his chest.

He arranged them in a comfortable position, head propped up on the pillows, then pulled off their boots and gently tucked the thin blanket over top of them. Istvay's eyes had fallen closed, but they blinked them half-open, watching him through their long lashes.

Aran hesitated a moment, then sighed and sat down on the bed beside them, reaching over to untie Istvay's ponytail. If they slept on it like that, it would give them a headache, and from the look of it, they'd have enough of a headache in the morning as it was.

He ran his hand along their hair, and tried to ignore how naturally his hand cupped around the back of Istvay's head, how soft their hair was under his fingers, how his stomach had tightened and his hand shook. He closed his eyes, because he couldn't look at Istvay right now, and fumbled with the hair tie.

The skin of Istvay's neck was warm under his fingers, the feel of their hair soft and silky, and his treacherous brain wouldn't stop reminding him of the one time in his life when he'd been able to tighten his fingers into Istvay's hair, pull their mouth to his—

Something grasped his hand, and he blinked his eyes open in surprise.

Istvay had reached up and captured his hand in theirs, and they were smiling up at him, a small, sad half-smile.

Aran found he wasn't breathing at all.

"Istvay—" he croaked.

"I know you're angry with me, Aran," they mumbled. "But—can you stay here? Just for a little?"

Aran swallowed again. He wasn't sure he'd be able to move even if he wanted to, with how shaky his muscles had gone. "Okay," he managed. "Okay, Pishti, I'm here. And I'm—I'm not angry with you." He paused, slipping into Mountain Dialect. "I love you, Pishti," he whispered. "I've always loved you. And I don't know how to be angry with you, even when I try."

Istvay sighed softly, their body relaxing. Their arm dropped, pulling Aran's hand forward until his palm was cupped around their cheek.

His heart was beating quickly enough that he thought he might pass out.

Very softly, so softly that it might have been an accident, Istvay pressed their lips sleepily to the side of his hand.

Aran's soul almost left his body.

Istvay's head relaxed against the pillow, their breathing slowly evening out.

For a few minutes Aran stayed there, not daring to pull his hand free in case he woke Istvay. He tried not to stare at them—the dark half-circle of their lashes against their cheeks, the sharp line of their cheekbones, accentuated by the hollows underneath, the salt glittering in tear-tracks down their face—but he couldn't seem to make himself look away.

The pain in his chest was a sharp, piercing, palpable thing, and it hurt so that he thought he might die from it. But he couldn't bear to pull his hand loose. So he stayed, until at long last Istvay's fingers relaxed, their hand sliding down to the pillow.

He pulled in a shaky breath and stood, bending to tuck the blanket closer around Istvay before he left the room. But he paced the courtyard under the glow of the double moons for a long, long time, and the moons had almost set before he was finally able to fall asleep himself.

19

Alba

No one spoke as the yibo guards herded them back towards the compound.

There was a sick feeling in Alba's stomach, a helpless tightness in her muscles, and her body ached with weariness and strain.

She glanced surreptitiously at the other two, following close behind her.

Even Yosip's normally cheerful face was tight with worry, and Ines's mouth was clamped shut, her eyes huge and frightened.

When at last the door to their quarters closed behind them and the lock clicked, and the three of them let out an almost-simultaneous breath of relief.

"Madam?" came a weak voice from one side, and she turned quickly to see Feliu seated on one of the cots. His face was still pale and drawn, but he no longer looked on the verge of death.

A tight, choking gratitude welled in her chest at the sight of him, and she found herself blinking back tears. "Feliu," she said. "It appears you've picked an unfortunate time to recover."

"Do—do you think—" Ines began, but Yosip gave a small shake

of his head, gesturing with his chin into the small apartment.

Ines clamped her mouth shut and nodded.

Their rooms were bugged, almost certainly. And Alba had lived long enough to know that letting on how much they actually knew was unlikely to be good for their health.

Yosip pulled a piece of paper out from a stack on the small shelves and sat cross-legged on the floor beside Feliu's cot, tearing it into a square. "Ines," he said, smiling, although Alba could see the tension behind his expression. "Have I ever showed you the paper folding they do up in the northern Rim Mountains?"

Ines looked at him, puzzled, but came to sit beside him. He gestured to Alba. "You might find this interesting as well, Madam," he said. Frowning, she pulled over a stool.

The rustling of the paper as Yosip folded and tore it was loud enough that Yosip's voice, when he spoke, was almost inaudible, and she had to lean closer to hear.

"I'm sure they're still listening in, and possibly watching," he said quietly. "We'll have to be careful what we say."

Alba nodded, and Ines bobbed her head as well.

Yosip gave a succinct summary of their conversation of that morning for Feliu's benefit, then turned to Alba.

"So," he said, in the same low voice. "What do you think, Madam?"

Alba narrowed her eyes in thought. "They haven't killed us," she said, in a voice that was almost as quiet as Yosip's. "That means they still want an alliance more than they want a war."

Yosip nodded. "It sounded like they were concerned about the resources for a full-on attack. And that even if there were a war, it would be to force us to ally with them if possible."

Alba nodded slowly. "Whatever it is they want from an alliance, it can't be good. Forces for military engagement, perhaps, against someone or something—it sounded as if their plan was to use the humans as cannon-fodder. We cannot let that happen. And they knew about the generation ships, and that there are other human colonies." She sighed. "You've seen the weapons they have. As well you know, I do not have the power to unilaterally agree to an alliance—my actions would always be subject to the review and approval of the Council. But even if I could, I wouldn't dare."

Yosip nodded, his face grave. "Yes. But if you've guessed correctly, once the portal has opened, there's no way we can prevent this from happening. They'll take what they want from us, or if they can't get it, they'll destroy us and take it from one of our sister colonies."

For a moment, there was no sound but the rustle of the paper Yosip was folding.

Alba's brain felt as frozen as the rest of her, her thoughts sluggish.

There were well over a hundred of people trapped here, behind the portal. Well over a hundred people who were looking to her to save them.

But … there were countless millions of lives on the other side of the portal.

She closed her eyes for a moment.

So many decisions she'd made over the course of her life. So many things she'd thought had been for the best, and she'd never stopped to worry about consequences she couldn't see. Now, seeing the consequences playing out in front of her own eyes—she found she'd lost the iron certainty she'd once held that her native intelligence and good intentions were enough.

But a decision had to be made, regardless.

"Very well, then," she said sharply, opening her eyes. "They already believe I am lying to them, and that I do have the power to make the agreements they wish. I shall attempt to convince them that I have reconsidered my position, and am now willing to do so, given a sufficiently attractive promise in return. Whatever their ultimate intentions, it seems they don't relish the thought of an outright confrontation with us unless there is no other viable option, and perhaps, given time and effort, we can convince them that an agreement entered into with mutual honesty will be more profitable for them in the long run than whatever this is."

She made a mental note to thank Aran—he'd likely never have any idea the service he and that murder-beast of his were providing, with his desperate attempts to convince all and sundry that Ani was nothing but a normal, harmless pet.

"And … and if not?" asked Ines, her voice breathless and terrified.

Yosip was simply watching Alba, as if he'd already guessed what she'd say next.

Possibly he had.

"We use the negotiations to give us time find the plans for the mechanism that opens the portal," she said quietly, forcing her voice steady. "And—" She took another deep breath. "We find a way to destroy it, before the portal can be reopened. We stop this war before it's begun."

There was a long, long moment of silence. The parchment rustled under Yosip's fingers, but he was no longer looking at it, only studying Alba's face.

"That would mean everyone here is trapped for good," said Feliu quietly.

"I know that," she snapped. "Do you have a better idea?"

Again, there was silence.

She couldn't bring herself to look at Yosip. Because he must know as well as she did—this would condemn everyone here to death. If they had no alliance to offer, the yibo had made it very clear how little they valued human life. And she would not be asking for the crew's opinion. The decision to sacrifice them would be hers alone.

And she'd learned, over the past weeks, how very hollow her imagined competency had rung.

"Madam," Yosip said quietly. "I am not a politician. As I told you, these are not decisions I am accustomed to make." He sighed heavily. "I will trust to your judgement, then, Alba."

Alba turned on him, frowning, but there was no mockery in his expression, only a deep, weary sorrow.

"Madam—Madam Chief Justice?" whispered Ines.

Alba turned on her in irritation. "Yes, girl?"

"They don't know the translator program is finished. If I act like I still need to work on it—get them to take me around so I can gather more data—it's possible they'll take me somewhere I might hear something. I could help you look for information."

Alba stared at the girl.

Whatever she'd expected Ines to say, this hadn't been it. But somehow, the girl always seemed to be able to surprise her.

"You know that this means—" she began.

"I know," said Ines, her voice almost inaudible.

And Alba realized, with a twist of guilt, that Ines knew better than any of them what it meant to be ripped away from everything you knew.

And that, too, had been Alba's fault.

"I think that would help very much, Ines," said Yosip, his voice warm. "Thank you."

Ines smiled at him, her smile as sudden and bright as a shaft of sunlight through the trees.

Yosip glanced down at his hands and made a final crease to the paper, then raise the small figure to his mouth and blew gently into it. It puffed up, and he held out, smiling. It was the figure of a red-tailed mountain squirrel, each small limb and delicate feature intricately folded.

"What do you think?" he asked, handing it to Ines. "These paper figures are funny that way—they always look like a hopeless mess just before they turn out."

Ines stared down at the paper, then back up at Yosip.

He smiled at her, familiar smile-wrinkles creasing through the worry in his face. But his eyes met Alba's as he rose, and she could see in his expression that she had not overstated the desperation of the situation.

But someone had to make a decision. And she was the ambassador. In this case, whether she wanted it or not, that someone was her.

She could only pray her decision was the right one.

20

Savina

The streets were dark, the light of the alien sun a fading memory that glowed faintly through the city's force-field, more notable for emphasizing the darkness than providing light.

Savina tugged on her balaclava, tucking it up with her hair inside. The dark, loose clothes did wonders to conceal her shape and form in the dimness of the evening.

Yuur had bought her deception: that there was going to be a member of a rival gang at the tavern tonight, one who owed a debt he hadn't paid.

She wouldn't have been able to sell the story without Beni's and Joska's help. Beni had found enough details to make the idea convincing, and Joska had agreed, reluctantly, to "pass along" the information she'd supposedly overheard when she was serving on cleaning duty.

Yuur had only sent two of the gang members to accompany Savina, which was fine by her. The job was supposed to be clear-cut —go in, take out the target, get back without being killed.

At least, that's what Yuur thought.

At last they reached the place marked by the coordinates on Savina's wavelink.

She frowned. The building abutted the edge of the city's force-field, and the street outside it was strangely empty.

It was unusual for anywhere this side of the city to be quiet, no matter what time of day or night.

She turned to her companions. "Wait here," she whispered. "Let me get inside and scout things out first."

She could kill them both before they had time to realize what she was doing, if it came to it. But easier not to.

They tipped their heads in acknowledgement, and she shot them a threatening glance. Then she turned and slipped out of the alley, pulling off her drab charcoal-grey robe and balaclava to reveal a simple tunic, indistinguishable from what anyone else on this planet wore.

She pasted on her most innocent expression as she crossed the street to the pub and pulled open the door. She stepped in, letting the door swing closed behind her.

Then she stopped dead.

She didn't need anyone to tell her who it was she was meeting.

And she no longer wondered why the yibo had spoken of the raiders in terrified whispers.

The creature that stood at the bar was definitively not yibo. It stood a full head and a half taller than Nicolau, and Nicolau already towered over the largest of the mobsters. There was no soft fur on its face or hands, no bushy tail looped neatly over an arm, and it looked, at first glance, almost human—except that its body was much thicker and more powerful, and there were claw-tips at the end of each finger. Its hair was long and hung down its back, and its face, too, was almost frighteningly human, which made the incongruences even more terrifying—the deep scarlet of its eyes, the long incisors, sharp as one of Savina's knife blades, visible through its smile.

It wouldn't have looked out of place in a drawing of a monster from a wondertale.

No wonder the yibo didn't smile with their teeth, not if they had this to look at.

She had no idea what the creature was, or where it came from. But that small part of the back of her brain, the part that had evolved from a terrified ape, screamed an interpretation at her that she was powerless to counter.

Predator.

She had stepped into the pub. And the moment she had, the moment its eyes had turned towards her, she'd become prey.

She took a deep breath to slow the pounding of her heart, and blinked innocently around the room.

Now that she had time to notice something other than her target, she saw the yibo, the servers and the owners, cowering as far from the creature as they could manage in the small confines of the space. As she watched, one of them approached, trembling with fear, and slid a large plate across the counter to the stranger.

It caught the plate deftly with one hand, its movements a fluid animal grace, without once taking its eyes from Savina.

"Hello," it said, its smile broadening. Its voice was deep and rich, the accent strange, but the words were clearly understandable. The corners of its mouth tipped up, the fangs peeking through. "I didn't realize your employer would send a human to talk to me. Trying to get into our good graces, is she?"

Its eyes were hypnotizing, the colour of blood, and its hair, long and luxurious, reached almost to the back of its knees, pulled up in a half-ponytail and braided through with a scarlet ribbon. The long length of scarlet swayed as the raider moved, hypnotizing in the way a snake's weaving body was hypnotizing.

Savina widened her eyes and smiled an entirely human smile—apologetic, open, innocent. "Yes. Yuur asked me to come specifically." She paused a moment, letting her eyes brush up and down the raider's form. "I'm sorry," she stammered. "I just—I've never seen—" she let her words trail off.

Her target seemed taken in by the act, his smile widening—at least, Savina guessed it was a male, and she didn't feel any need to verify further. "Very good. Why don't we talk, then?" There was a hint of amusement in the rich ripple of his voice.

Savina gave an eager little nod, then faltered, dropping her eyes. "Yes, please."

He gestured to a chair across from him, and she hesitated a moment, as if afraid.

It wasn't entirely an act.

"Come. I agreed to negotiate," he said. "It would be counterproductive for me to eat you until I know what you want." His teeth peeking through his wolfish smile made the words less of a joke than they should have been, and Savina had to fight back a shiver.

She came closer, her movements timid. "I … I'm sorry," she said again. "I …" She sat down, perched on the edge of her seat.

He watched her with a hungry, predatory gaze. And while what he wanted could be a sexual thing, if she were to judge from the pitying glances of the yibo around her, it was more likely something that had more to do with a more basic appetite.

"So," he said. "You said your employer has a message for me."

"Yes. I … have it here—" She stood, fumbling in her pouch.

Her heart was pounding, sick and fast.

He was wearing armour. But apparently, he hadn't been particularly worried about an attack. His jacket was pulled open a little at the neck, the hood dropped back.

She knew, gut-deep, that she could never trust a creature like this to negotiate, even if she had something to bargain with.

But then, her plan wasn't based on negotiation.

All she needed was an opening.

She took a step forward, still fumbling in her pouch, and stumbled, tripping over the floorboards.

He reached out, the movement inhumanly fast, to catch her.

And as he did, she yanked the pistol from her pouch, shoved it against his cheekbone, and, as his clawed hand closed around her elbow, fired.

The small hiss echoed in the suddenly silent room.

The pulse-waves of the shot had stopped where they met the raider's body-armour, but his face and upper chest were a ruined mess.

His body swayed for a moment, then toppled forward, his hand still clasped around her arm tightly enough that she had to brace herself against the counter to keep from being pulled over on top of him. He must be dead—nothing could survive that—but his grip was tight enough that his claws dug into her flesh.

When at last his hand released, she staggered backwards, almost losing her balance.

No one else had moved. Everyone in the room was entirely still, staring at her.

She turned, recovering her balance, and gave them a toothy smile. "If anyone asks, please tell them Yuur is tired of the raiders negotiating with our rival gangs."

She turned, and made her way out the door.

No one followed.

When she reached the alley, she grabbed the balaclava and grey tunic, glaring at her two supposed helpers. "The tip was bad. No one was there. Let's get out of here."

They grumbled, but followed her lead. By the time she got back to the safehouse, though, her shoulders ached with tension.

She'd done exactly what she had to. The raiders had a clear trail to follow. She'd been very explicit when she set up the meeting—Yuur had specifically requested it. And there was the yibo tavern keeper and his employees, who'd all vouch for what had happened.

But …

"Savina! Did it go alright? Did you manage to make a bargain with them?" Beni's voice was a frantic whisper as Savina stepped back inside their rooms. Joska, too, was watching her, concern in her face.

The woman had been skeptical enough about Savina trying to bargain with the raiders. If she'd had any idea exactly how Savina intended to get the raiders' help …

She'd killed him. It hadn't even been the hardest job she'd pulled. It should just be a few more days now.

But she'd lived long enough to know how thoroughly a situation could change in a few days. And the memory of those blood-red eyes, the fangs peeking through that amused, wolfish smile, heavy sheets of black hair hanging almost to the floor, made something small and animal inside Savina tremble.

"It's fine," she said, through the tightness in her throat. "I think they'll do what we need them to."

21

Aran

Istvay stumbled into the common room late the next morning, blinking and squinting against the light, with a surly scowl on their face. They dropped onto one of the small stools, and Aran hid a grin as he shoved a cup of coffee across the table towards them.

Istvay took it with both hands and didn't bother trying to speak until it was halfway empty. Then they put it down on the table with a *thump*, winced, and glowered at Aran. "Where the hell did you find coffee?"

Aran bit the inside of his cheek and tried not to smile. "I had some in my supplies pouch. Emergency stash. I thought this qualified."

Istvay sighed and pushed the heel of their hand against their forehead. "I'm getting too old for this," they muttered.

This time Aran did crack a smile. Istvay scowled at him, and then, suddenly, they swore, winced, and swore again, but more quietly this time.

"Oh hell. I made you come sit outside with me last night, didn't I?" They groaned. "Hell. I thought I was too drunk to have got back to bed on my own." They were quiet for a moment. "Did I—how badly did I embarrass myself?" Their tone was joking, but Aran could hear the stark panic under it.

He smiled, even though his chest ached a little at the memory. "Well, apparently I'm your very best friend in the whole world."

Best stick as close to the truth as possible, probably.

Istvay scowled at him suspiciously for a few moments. "Is that all I said?"

Aran chuckled. "You said it a few times. You were very emphatic about it. It was quite touching, actually."

Istvay glared at him for a little longer, as if trying to decide whether he was lying. At last, their mouth twitched up into a rueful smile. "I guess that's not the most embarrassing thing I could have said," they said finally. "I mean, I guess I could have gotten sappy about Ani."

Aran laughed despite himself, and Istvay joined in, then winced again and swore softly. "Ooof. That'll teach me to get drunk."

Aran grinned at them, and he was almost sure he'd been able to hide the sharp pain in his expression.

Istvay finished the coffee, and looked with distaste at the spread of fresh fruits and pastries laid out on the table. "I guess they don't do greasy eggs and fried ham in the mornings around here," they said ruefully. "I feel bad for the university kids on this planet." They blinked hard, scrubbing of their eyes with the heels of their hands, and sighed. "Well, I'm not going to feel human again for at least a few hours. So in the meantime, since we're here now, I guess it's probably worth talking about what we're going to do next."

Aran didn't miss the way their mouth tightened, their shoulders tensing just a little, as if they were preparing for an argument. And he remembered, suddenly, the tears trickling through their long lashes the night before.

He almost winced at the guilt the memory dragged along with it.

"Listen, Pishti," he said quickly, turning away so he didn't have to meet their eyes. "I—I'm sorry. I … haven't been acting like we're a team. And I shouldn't have done that. I shouldn't have agreed to let the yibo take us here without talking to you. I shouldn't have—I should have told you the whole truth when you were asking me about things, instead of trying to hide it. I—that wasn't right, and … and I'm sorry."

For a few moments, there was silence.

Aran risked a quick peek at Istvay.

His friend was staring at him, a complicated expression on their face. "Where did this come from?" they asked at last.

Aran shrugged. "I don't know, I just … I mean, last night—" he paused, then rushed on as Istvay's face once more took on an expression of vague panic. "No, I just mean—you said I was your best friend. And I realized—I realized this isn't how friends treat each other."

Istvay was still staring at him suspiciously, but at last they nodded. "Aran." They hesitated. "Thank you. And—" they visibly braced themself. "Dammit, Aran, why do you have to be all sweet and sincere when I'm in the middle of a damn hangover, and I just want something to yell at?" they muttered. They let out a long breath. "But, since you're going to insist on torturing me, I guess I should say that—that I'm sorry, too. I guess I've been … not very considerate lately. I've been behaving badly, and I … I guess I can't exactly blame you for not wanting to talk to me. I haven't been exactly—anyways, I'm sorry, and I'll try to be better, okay?"

Aran stared.

Istvay managed a small grin. "Sorry, that's as nice as I can possibly be when I'm feeling like this. You want anything more flowery, it's going to have to wait until the headache goes away."

Aran was still staring, but he felt a small smile growing on his face. "If it was any more flowery, I'd think you were trying to get me off my guard so you could throw me in front of a mountain cat or something," he said.

Istvay rolled their eyes, and for moment Aran couldn't breathe, his chest tightening with a mixture of happiness and pain at the familiarity of the teasing.

"So," said Istvay at last. "Now that we've made up, let's decide what we're going to do next."

Aran glanced around reflexively, and Istvay followed his gaze.

"You're right," they said in a low voice. "It's probably bugged. Courtyard?"

Aran nodded, and the two of them stood, pushing back the low stools, and stepped outside.

The courtyard was most likely bugged as well, but it was easier to make noise there—scuffing their feet along the concrete, kicking small pebbles, rubbing an arm along the roughness of the courtyard wall—that would make it more difficult for anyone to overhear. Besides which, Istvay's muttered profanities at the brightness of the mid-morning sunlight were probably enough on their own.

Aran gave Istvay a brief summary of what he'd learned from Ree the day before, and Istvay nodded thoughtfully. "So she's meeting with you tonight, then. What do you hope to find out from her?"

Aran hesitated. "I … well, I think she knows where I can find these—whatever they are. Although I hope she's a hell of a lot better at pictographs than I am, because that's always going to be the challenge."

Istvay was quiet for a long moment. At last they turned, their eyes catching Aran's. "We could always just leave," they said quietly. "If we can find a way to get out of this place to meet with your scientist friend—we could just get out, instead."

Aran's breath caught in his chest.

He couldn't. He was so close. He was finally starting to figure out where the hell he needed to go to find the mysterious blood donor—

Istvay was watching him, their eyes serious.

Aran forced himself to pull in a deep breath. "Istvay—" he began, and then he couldn't continue.

Istvay was still watching him, still with that strange look on their face. "How long will it take you to learn what you need to?" they asked finally.

Aran looked down, his heart pounding. "I—I don't know, for certain," he said quietly. "But … just give me one more day. Please."

Istvay shook their head. "Why are you even asking me? You're going to do it anyways, aren't you?"

Aran closed his eyes and forced himself to swallow through the tightness in his throat. "Because … because I want to know what you think. Even if we disagree. We're a team, and I won't go behind your back, not again."

Istvay was still watching him searchingly. At last, slowly, they nodded. "Fine." They paused. "Look. I mean—like you said, this is a joint expedition. So … so if you were asking what I thought, I guess I'd tell you that as long as you could promise you'd be careful, and you agreed to get out of here afterwards, we may as well go talk to Ree."

Aran nodded, unable to speak. He felt shaky with relief.

He hadn't known, until just now, how badly he'd needed Istvay's support.

"Alright, then," said Istvay. "We'll figure out a way to get into the government compound tonight, once it gets dark. We may as well stop by and check in on Alba and the others on the way. And then tomorrow, as long as we have the information we need, we'll make a plan to get out. Deal?"

"Deal," said Aran, and he was unable to stop the grin spreading across his own face.

By the time the daylight had turned the soft orange of early evening, he and Istvay had sketched out the best map of the compound they could put together. It wasn't much—they hadn't exactly been given a tour—but then, both of them had plenty of experience mapping out uncharted places.

"Do you remember doing this while we were getting ready for the expedition to observe the land-devil hatching? Where you found Ani?" Istvay's grin was a mixture of mischief and ruefulness. "I'm still not sure how you managed to talk me into that one."

Aran grinned back at them. "I think you said I was just too damn adorable, and you couldn't say no to puppy-dog eyes like that."

Istvay snorted. "I'm a hundred percent sure that I'm not that masochistic. I cannot believe that I would've encouraged your absolute shamelessness."

Aran laughed, and scratched Ani under the chin. "Well, there are two of us here who are happy you did."

"And probably the majority of the population of Colorida who aren't," Istvay muttered. They sighed and pushed away their drawing tool. "Well, it's the best we can do, I think. We'll just have to wait till after dark and hope we got it right."

The security in their tiny compound was tight. But clearly their captors had never dealt with something on the level of Ani. When they had tested little of her acid in a corner where it wouldn't be visible, it had eaten through the walls like warm water through a sheet of ice.

There was a bit of the courtyard just behind the house that was deep enough in shadows that he and Istvay should be able to keep their sabotage secret.

Once they'd gotten through the wall, they'd still have to get past the guards, of course—but the benefit of having spent the majority of the last seven years on unconventional expeditions to inhospitable places studying dangerous creatures was that both of them had plenty of experience moving quietly past things that wanted to kill them.

It had been easy enough to convince Ani to do what they needed of her—once she understood, she spat the acid enthusiastically, and Aran rewarded her with a pat and a little piece of his dinner at every spray.

Istvay watch the two of them, a small, fond smile on their face. "You and she make quite a pair."

Aran glanced up and grinned, then had to look away quickly, because the expression in Istvay's eyes reminded him far too much of the previous night.

He didn't think he could bear to think about that without at least a few years' distance.

They left the acid to do its work and went in for dinner, then played a few rounds of dice before Istvay got to their feet and stretched.

"I'm going to sit in the courtyard for a bit, if you want to come," they said casually.

Aran nodded and stood as well, picking up the flask the yibo had left them to go with dinner, and the two of them strolled outside.

Istvay sat down close to where they'd left Ani's acid to do its work, leaning back against the wall. They took the flask from Aran and took a swallow, then handed it back to him. Aran did the same, letting a trickle pass his lips, just enough to make it look convincing.

The part of the courtyard they'd chosen was already dark—the lights from outside hit the corner of the building and cast a sharp shadow over where they sat—but they waited until the first of the moons had appeared over the walls of their prison. They passed the bottle back and forth for the look of things as they waited, neither of them really drinking. Then, at last, Istvay winked at Aran, slipping out of their jacket. Aran struggled out of his own battered jacket and draped the two jackets over the pile of bedding he and Istvay had smuggled out earlier.

It wasn't much, but with any luck the dark shapes would be enough to make their captors think the two of them had simply fallen asleep, slumped back against the wall.

Istvay grinned, their teeth flashing white in the reflected light, and once they were concealed by the shadows, dropped onto their belly and wriggled through the hole over the protective sheet they'd thrown over the remnants of Ani's acid.

Aran followed, pushing Ani through ahead of him.

He'd rather Ani stay back, honestly. But that was an argument he wasn't going to win, and he knew it.

Istvay held out their hand to him as he scrambled out. He took it, and Istvay pulled him to his feet, and the two of them stood in the quiet of the outer courtyard, giving their eyes time to adjust to the dim light.

He and Istvay had come out into a patch of deep shadow—which was a good thing, because when Aran's eyes adjusted to the light, he saw the yibo guard standing only a metre or so away. He bit back a yelp of surprise and nudged Istvay, gesturing with his chin. Istvay followed his gaze and nodded, then flicked their eyes in the opposite direction.

The two of them crept along the edge of the wall, and Aran kept his breathing as quiet as possible.

This, though, was something he knew how to deal with. Istvay's strange mood, yibo diplomacy—none of that he was good at. But this was something familiar and simple. Keep quiet, keep whatever it was from seeing you and killing you.

They got around the corner of the wall and into a patch of shadow from one of the large overhanging trees. Cautiously, Aran stepped forward, staying low to the ground and making his movements as smooth and silent as the moon-shadow of the leaves in the faint breeze. Istvay followed close behind, and a few moments later, they were at the trunk of the tree. Istvay bent, cupping their hands, and Aran stepped into their palms. Istvay braced themself, then hoisted him up in a smooth motion, and he grabbed the lowest branch and swung himself up, flattening on his belly on the broad, smooth limb of the tree. Once he'd caught his balance, he lowered his hand for Istvay to grasp. They grabbed on and clambered up, impressively quiet despite their feet scrabbling at the rough bark of the tree.

Then the two of them inched out along the thick branch on their stomachs.

Thankfully, the tree was an old one, and the gnarled branch, worn smooth with age, plenty thick enough to support their weight. When they were far enough out, Aran stood carefully, crouched to disguise his silhouette. Istvay came up beside him a moment later, and the two of them surveyed the courtyard of the government buildings silently.

There was—an impressive number of guards. More than Aran really wanted to think about.

His heart was beating tight in his chest.

The two of them dropped down again, making their way along the branch until it became narrow enough to dip under their weight. Then he and Istvay jumped down, crouching in the deep shadows that pooled under the overhanging branches.

They made their careful way across the courtyard until at last they were crouched outside the wall of the building that, not long ago, had been their home.

Aran and Istvay exchanged quick glances.

This next bit was the part they hadn't worked out—they couldn't call in over the wavelink, not with the building's force-field in the way.

And then Aran heard, from inside the courtyard wall, the soft crunch of feet on gravel.

"Yosip?" he hissed, just loud enough that hopefully whoever was inside would hear.

The footsteps stopped abruptly. "No, it's—it's me, Ines," came a small voice. "Aran? Is that you?"

"Yes," whispered Aran. "Me and Istvay. Look, Ines, what's going on?"

"How did you get over here?" Ines' voice was soft and frightened. "I heard they'd locked you up. What—"

"They did, but we're … out, for the moment," whispered Istvay. "We wanted to talk to you, figure out what's going on. We found out that the yibo aren't the ones who sent that box through the portal, but we don't know more than that. Aran has a scientist friend who seems willing to help us, but since we can only communicate in pictographs—"

Ines gave a small, almost hysterical little laugh. "Well—I might be able to help with that, at least. You know that translation program I was working on? I finished it."

Aran and Istvay exchanged glances again, and even in the darkness, Aran could see the glint of interest in Istvay's eyes.

"I can give you a holodisc that should let you sync the program into your wavelink," Ines whispered. "Just a sec, I'll toss it over now."

A moment later, something dark and glittering arced over the wall. Istvay caught it and turned it over in their hands. They opened their palmscreen, typing in a command, and tapped it against the holodisc, then they passed it to Aran.

"Did you get it?" whispered Ines.

"Yeah, thanks," Aran whispered back as his own wavelink hummed, incorporating the new information.

"Once you activate it, it should translate directly into your earpiece when it picks up on their speech," she said. "If you have a retinal screen, it'll translate the writing as well. If you don't have a retinal screen, it should still translate on your palmscreen, but you'll have to scan the writing in."

"Ines." Istvay sounded impressed. "You're brilliant."

Ines gave a soft, startled laugh, sounding suddenly flustered. "Oh. Um. I—I mean, it's just what I learned in school—"

"You're as bad as Aran," Istvay whispered, their voice teasing. "Is that a thing with you geniuses, never accepting complements?"

"Oh. Um." She sounded even more flustered. There was a long pause.

"So," whispered Aran at last. "Do you have any idea what—"

"Just—just a minute," said Ines. "I think Alba's asleep, but I can get Yosip, if you want. He'll be able to tell you what's going on better than I can."

"Thanks," Aran whispered, and they heard her footsteps walking quickly off.

A few moments later, two sets of footsteps were audible across the courtyard. "Aran? Istvay?" came Yosip's voice over the wall.

"Yosip," said Istvay. "What's happening? Are you all alright?"

When Yosip answered, his voice was more grave than usual. "I'm afraid I don't have good news. We've discovered a little more about the yibo's intentions, and they're … not peaceful. We're still trying to figure out our next steps."

Aran glanced at Istvay. Their expression in the moonlight was grim.

"How did you get here?" asked Yosip. "I heard they'd locked you up."

"They did," said Aran. "But … I mean, it's not the first time we've ever had to get out of somewhere."

From inside the wall, Yosip chuckled softly. "That doesn't surprise me."

"We're going to try to get out of the city tomorrow night, after dark," Istvay whispered. "Do you want to come with us?"

There was a moment of silence. At last, Yosip said, "I'll … talk to Alba. But I suspect the answer is no. She still believes she can use diplomacy to find a way of dealing with the threat posed by the yibo. And as I agreed to come on this mission as her diplomatic aide, I can't in good conscience leave either."

Aran and Istvay glanced at each other. "Do you need our help?" asked Istvay quietly.

Yosip sighed, his voice going even more grim. "If you can get out, you should. If things go well, you being here won't help. And if they go badly—there won't be anything you can do to stop it. They already see Aran as a threat. If they can't kill him because of Ani, they'll find a way to neutralize him."

There was a moment of silence. At last Istvay said, "Alright. But if you change your mind and decide to come—" they reached into their supplies pouch and pulled out a small flare, tossing it over the wall. "Set that off. It's not big enough to alarm the yibo, but we should be able to see it, and we'll come for you on our way out."

"Thank you," said Yosip.

Around the corner of the wall, there was the faint sound of approaching footsteps.

"Someone's coming," whispered Istvay. "If we don't see you again before we go—good luck."

"And to you," Yosip whispered back.

Aran and Istvay glanced at each other, then crept quietly along the wall in the opposite direction of the footsteps, keeping out of sight against the smooth surface of the wall.

They made their way down the narrow, darkened footpaths, keeping to the shadows. There was the hazy glow of artificial lights, but the ever-present trees cast shadows deep enough that they were able to stay out of sight.

When they reached the place Ree had indicated on her map, the two of them ducked down behind a tree trunk.

"Where is she?" Istvay whispered, peering around. "If she's told someone, and they know we can get out of where they've put us—"

"I don't think she will," Aran whispered back. "She could have done that when I broke into the science lab, and she didn't. I think she wants to help us."

"You also refused to believe that Emeric wanted to kill you until he was literally pointing a pistol at your head," Istvay muttered sourly.

Aran sighed.

The moons glowed brilliant overhead, and from the corner of his eye he caught a flicker movement.

His pulse jumped, his muscles tensing involuntarily, and then he recognized the figure as Ree. She was creeping furtively along the path, clearly uncomfortable.

"Psst!" he hissed, and she jerked around, hands coming up defensively.

"It's okay, it's just me," he whispered, stepping out on the path, and she slumped with relief, muttering something in her own language.

The bland AI voice in Aran's earpiece almost made him jump, and it took him a moment to realize it was Ines' program, translating the scientist's words. "Scare me to an early death, why don't you?"

"Um," Aran began, and then realized that she wouldn't be able to understand him in return. He sighed, and pointed back into the trees where Istvay was still hiding.

Ree stiffened again.

"It's just my friend, they're fine," he said, hoping the reassurance in his tone would convey the meaning. He beckoned to Istvay, and they straightened, stepping out to join Aran and Ree.

Ree glanced between Aran and Istvay. "Is that your friend? The one you're so worried about?" the AI voice translated. Ree made a low humming sound. "I guess there's no accounting for taste."

Istvay and Aran exchanged glances, and Aran had to bite back a smile.

Ree had already crouched down, pulling a sheet of paper and a writing stick from a pocket in her robe, and Aran and Istvay crouched beside her.

Aran felt slightly guilty that he could understand what she was saying without her realizing it, but then again, he wasn't exactly sure how he'd explain it to her without her being able to understand him.

She sketched the box again and gave him a questioning look.

"Yes," he said, taking the writing stick from her and circling the box. "I need to know about this. I need to know where it comes from." He made a rough sketch of a ship, with one of the strange, dangerous-looking figures inside.

Istvay turned to him, raising their eyebrows. "Really, Aran?" they whispered, gesturing at the drawing. "I guess it's a good thing you didn't decide to go to art school."

Aran scowled at them. "You want to try?"

Istvay chuckled, and Ree, watching them, hummed in amusement. Then she sighed, taking back the writing stick, and hesitated for a moment, staring at the paper.

"I'm going to get into so much trouble for this," the AI voice translated in Aran's ear as she muttered to herself. "Humans are supposed to be so cowardly and vicious, and I run into the one that not only saves my life, but looks at me like a fledgling fallen out of its nest any time I'm tempted to tell it 'no.'"

Aran narrowed his eyes at Istvay, who looked like they were trying very hard not to laugh.

Ree sighed again, heavily, and pulled out a small metal sphere from her pocket. She drew what looked like a planet or a moon on the paper, then a line between the planet, the ship Aran had sketched, and the box. She tapped the drawing, then tapped the spherical device.

"A map or something, maybe?" said Istvay, frowning. They glanced at Ree for permission, then picked up the object and examined it.

After a moment, Ree took it back in exasperation, tapping sharply on the bottom. A glowing holoprojection sprang up around the object, something that looked like a starmap.

And in the centre of the map, a round, glowing projection that covered the metal sphere itself.

Ree touched the sphere, then touched the planet she'd drawn on the parchment, and Istvay nodded, caught themself, and tipped their head to one side in the yibo gesture.

"I don't know why I'm doing this," Ree grumbled, shutting the device off and handing it back to Istvay. "I'd be doing you a favour not to, honestly. I'm probably sending you to your death. I have no idea why the raiders would have sent a damn sample box through the portal in the first place. They eat humans. They'll probably eat both of you. And I have no bloody idea why they sabotaged the damn portal, instead of waiting until we were done with your planet, then going in afterwards and slaughtering their way through the leftovers like they usually do. But I guess anyone who walks around with a damn natural disaster on their shoulder doesn't think about things like that, do they?" She was still muttering to herself as she lit the paper with an incendiary.

The three of them watched it as it burned. When it was gone, Ree crumpled the ash under her boot, then pulled a small flask of water from her pocket and rinsed the stains off the stone surface of the pathway.

Aran bit his lip, trying not to let the excitement show in his expression.

So maybe Istvay was right, and these raiders, whoever the hell they were, weren't exactly the friendliest types. It didn't matter. Their blood held the answer to a question he'd been asking himself, desperately, for years.

There was the far-off sound of footsteps approaching, and Ree stiffened, jumping quickly to her feet. She made a sharp gesture to Aran and Istvay.

"I'm not going to be able to do this again. I'm risking my life at this point." She hummed ruefully. "Not that you understand anything I'm saying."

"Thank you," said Aran fervently, then repeated it in what he was pretty sure was yibo.

His accent must have been atrocious, because his wavelink didn't translate the sentence, but Ree seemed to understand. She gave him an amused, close-lipped smile, then she turned and was gone.

Aran's heart was pounding as they made their silent way back towards their compound, the starmap tucked into Aran's pocket. He felt almost sick with a mixture of anticipation and a sort of dread.

He'd been hoping for so long. And now that the answer was practically in his reach, he had the sudden, sickening fear that maybe he'd find it was a mistake, maybe it wasn't anything after all. Hell, maybe he'd wake up and realize the whole thing was a dream.

He had to swallow down the nausea in his stomach.

Istvay didn't speak, and in the dim grey light of the early morning, Aran couldn't make out their expression.

When at last the two of them and Ani were back inside the walls of their small prison, Istvay stood for a long time, staring at the courtyard wall.

Aran's heart was pounding so hard it was almost painful.

At last, Istvay turned to him. "Aran. Your cure isn't going to do anyone any good if we're dead," they said softly.

"Pishti. Listen." He could hear the desperation in his own voice. "We have the map. We know where to start. This is what we've been looking for this whole time, and we finally have it!"

Istvay sighed in familiar exasperation. "Are you forgetting the part where those raiders, or whatever the hell they are, hunt humans for food?"

Aran waved a hand. "Come on, you know how rumours spread. I

mean, land-devils are supposed to be vicious, bloodthirsty monsters, and look at Ani." He stroked her, and she purred contentedly, twining her tentacles around his upper arm.

Istvay stared at him for a moment, then sighed. "I don't think you're making the argument you think you are," they said through their teeth. They paused. "These raiders are clearly dangerous. Ree looked terrified to even talk about them."

"Everyone was terrified of coming through the portal, too," Aran retorted.

Istvay raised their eyebrow at him. "Again, I'm not sure that's the argument you think it is."

Aran sighed. "Istvay," he said at last, quietly. "I know you don't like this. But I don't know if you know how much—how important —" he broke off for a moment, dropping his face into his hands. "If you die, Pishti, I—I'll—"

Istvay was silent. When Aran looked up at last, they were watching him, and he couldn't read their expression.

Finally, they nodded, slowly. "Alright, Aran," they said at last, quietly. "Alright. We'll get out tonight, and we'll find a way back to the escape pod. And then we'll go and see if we can find this cure. I knew when we agreed to come on this stupid mission that that's what you were coming to do. And—" they sighed. "And I'm not letting you do it alone. Okay?"

Aran drew in a deep breath. There was something squeezing in his chest, a mixture of guilt and gratitude. "Pishti," he began, and then he found he couldn't finish for the knot in his throat.

Istvay gave him a rueful grin. "Have I really been that awful the last few weeks?" they asked. "I—" they paused, clearing their throat. "I'm … sorry. I—I didn't mean to—" they broke off, and Aran tried to grin.

"We do have Ani," he said. "I figure she'll even the odds, at least a little."

Istvay managed a grin in return. "Maybe you're right, at that."

22

Alba

A tap on her door jolted Alba out of a nightmare, and she sat up abruptly, covers clasped between her trembling fingers.

She forced herself to take a long, steadying breath.

"Madam?" It was Yosip's voice.

"What is it?" she asked, her tone sharp to hide the shakiness.

"Madam, if you're awake—I have some news from Aran and Istvay."

Groaning, she dropped her legs over the side of the bed, and when she felt steady enough, pushed herself to her feet.

She stared at her hands as she pulled on the simple embroidered tunic and removed her hair wrap. Her skin was faded and spotted with age, knuckles standing out knobbly against the frail, slender fingers.

They were an old woman's hands.

When had she become an old woman?

Perhaps, at last, she was getting too old for this. Too tired.

She fastened the ties on her tunic and straightened.

In the end, it hardly mattered. She'd accepted this responsibility, and capable or not, she'd see it through.

She didn't have another choice.

"Come in, Yosip," she called, and he opened the door, his face grave.

His gaze, when he studied her, was far too perceptive, and she narrowed her eyes at him. "You said you had some information?" she asked, voice tart.

"I spoke with Aran and Istvay last night, after you'd gone to bed," he said quietly. "They were outside the courtyard. Ines came and got me."

Alba raised her eyebrows in surprise. "They're not locked up?"

Yosip's familiar smile tugged at the corners of his mouth. "I … believe they had been, at one point."

It wasn't actually surprising, when she thought about it. She hadn't followed Aran's career closely, but from what she'd read, he and Istvay had been through enough difficult situations that they'd probably lost count.

She was still finding rather difficult to reconcile the shy, awkward young man she knew with the reputation he'd gained, apparently quite deservedly.

"And?" she prompted.

Yosip sighed. "And, they say they're going to try to get out, tonight." He hesitated a moment. "They offered to take us with them. Aran gave us a flare and said to shoot it off if we wanted them to come get us as they left. I—told them I doubted you'd want to go."

Alba glanced at him sharply. "You are correct," she said. "As much as I wish it were otherwise, it's likely a wise move for them to get out. With how uneasy the yibo are about that murder-beast of Aran's, I'm certain Kachik is already looking for a way to get rid of him and Istvay quietly. But the two of them were not tasked with ensuring that contact with the yibo would not destroy the Joias System." She paused a moment, drawing in a long breath. "I, however, was."

"Staying here could kill you," Yosip said quietly. There was something that looked like actual concern in his face.

And she realized it didn't surprise her as much as it would have weeks ago.

Yosip only had to meet someone to care about them.

"I appreciate your concern. But I can hardly see my way clear to abandoning my duty now," she said, her voice icy.

Yosip placed a hand on her shoulder. "I know. I wouldn't have expected you to."

She just stared at him, unable, for the first time in a long time, to formulate a response. His hand on her shoulder was warm, and he was watching her, the deep smile-lines carved on his face, concern creasing between his eyebrows, that genuine kindness that glowed through his every expression. His grip was firmer than she'd expected, and she wasn't sure why the realization sent a quick shiver through her body.

By the time she realized how long the silence had stretched and opened her mouth to snap something—anything, really—he'd already dropped his hand and stepped away.

She cleared her throat. "I—thank you," she said at last, awkwardly.

"Of course, Madam," said Yosip. "I suppose, then, that we'd best make our plans. Istvay mentioned some other things that may be of interest. I'll wait for you in the main room."

He stepped out the door, and she sighed, pushing away the strange shakiness in her muscles.

The room was still dim this early in the morning, full of shadows, but she turned to her closet and reached inside, letting her fingers slide across the thin cloth, choosing her outfit by feel.

There was no warning, not even a scuff of a footfall. One moment, she was staring vacantly into the closet. The next, someone had grabbed her from behind, grip rough and bruising. Before she could make a sound, something was clamped tight around her face, covering her eyes and mouth and nose and cutting off her breath.

She tried to scream, but the sound was muffled by the thick fabric covering her face. She kicked out, struggling, but whoever was holding her was far, far stronger than she was.

Here, she wasn't the Chief Justice of the Joias System. She was simply an old woman, muscles weakened by age and disuse, bones brittle and thin.

Alba was not accustomed to feeling powerless. She'd ensured that, lived her life in such a way that she'd always have the power of making the final decision.

But here, she was entirely helpless.

She couldn't breathe. She grabbed at the arm of the person holding the pillow across her face, the silky sheen of their tunic slippery under her gasping fingers, but beneath the soft fabric, the muscles in their arms may as well have been made of steel for all the good her prying fingers could do.

Her head was spinning, her lungs aching from lack of oxygen, her throat burning. Tears welled in her eyes, whether from pain, or fury, or fear, or from the humiliating, sickening helplessness, she didn't know. Her muscles, never that strong to begin with, were weakening. She wanted to scream, but even had the sound not been muffled, she no longer had the breath to do it. She thrashed weakly, her attacker's fingers pushing bruises into the papery skin of her arms and throat.

She bruised so easily these days.

Would they guess, when they found her here dead, what had happened?

And then her scrabbling fingers touched something cool and hard, something that must have fallen from her reticule as she'd dropped it in the shock of the attack.

The pistol Yosip had given her back on the ship, days ago that seemed like a lifetime.

She grabbed blindly for the small weapon, her fingers closing around it. She was too lightheaded to think, too lightheaded to remember the instructions Yosip had given when he'd first handed it to her. But she remembered enough to push back the safety, and then she shoved the tip of the weapon into the unyielding body of her attacker pressed against her, and fired.

Abruptly, the pressure around her mouth and nose released, the fingers around her throat loosening. She crumpled to the ground, gasping for air.

In the back of her mind, she heard stumbling footsteps crossing the floor, and she lifted her head in time to see the window falling closed, a smear of blood across the sill. Then she dropped back to the ground, gasping and panting. Tears ran down her cheeks, although she couldn't remember starting to cry, and the hard floor was bruising on her sore muscles and battered body.

She shifted a little, curling up around herself like a frightened animal. Her lungs burned, and her throat ached, and the places where her attacker grabbed throbbed with rising bruises.

But what hurt perhaps more than anything else was the sick realization that after everything she'd done, everything she'd worked for—she was still helpless.

Someone wanted to kill her. And they could have. They almost had. It could have been the yibo, or one of Cavaco's people hidden among the survivors, or one of the desperate survivors themselves. There was no shortage of people who had reason to hate her.

The memory of that sparkling halo of death spreading outwards from the ruins of the diplomatic ship lodged in her memory like a fishhook through the tender mouth of a fish.

She'd advocated for this mission with the best of intentions. And she'd killed them all.

And she might kill every person in the common room outside, every person looking to her to save them. Because it was for the best.

She wasn't sure how long she lay there, gasping and shivering, tears dripping off her chin and the tip of her nose and onto the floor. At last, though, there was a gentle tap on the door, followed by Yosip's concerned voice. "Alba? Are you alright?"

She took a long breath, and then another, and forced herself to roll over, her muscles shaky and weak. She pushed herself into a sitting position with trembling arms and wiped the humiliating tears from her cheeks.

She had to breathe for a few moments before she could speak. "I'm—I'm alright." Her voice, though steady enough, was hoarse and weak. "Wait for me, please. I'll—I'll be out in a moment."

It felt disturbingly close to begging, asking him to wait.

Carefully, she pulled herself to her feet, and glanced down at her wrinkled, filthy nightdress. There was blood on it—a brilliant, garish red stain flowering outward across her side and back where she'd shot her attacker.

She shuddered, glancing involuntarily down at the floor where she'd dropped the small pistol.

She'd shot someone. Maybe killed them.

She hadn't been able to when it was Feliu's life at stake. But here, choking her life out on the floor of her chambers in an alien city, she'd done it.

The warm, sticky wetness against her skin sent a sudden, visceral shudder through her body, and she yanked the nightdress over her head with more force than was necessary, dropping it onto the floor like it was poison. Then, slowly, every part of her aching, she moved back over to the closet and selected one of the plain tunics.

This was ridiculous, of course. The moment she stepped through the door, Yosip would be able to tell by the bruises, if nothing else, that something had happened. And she'd tell him. Surely, by that time, she'd be able to push the words out through her lips.

She lifted her chin and pulled the tunic down over her head.

Whatever had happened, at the very least, she would come to the morning's negotiations in clean clothing.

She tried not to think about how desperately she was clinging on to the small things that were still within her control.

"Madam. You must tell them you can't make it today." Yosip's face was dark with concern as he knelt in front of her, inspecting her bruises. "Ines is already out gathering information. Let her find what she can find. You rest."

"I must say I agree with him, Madam," said Feliu. "You cannot enter into a negotiation minutes after an assassination attempt."

She lifted her head. She knew the helpless anger boiling inside her was much less about their concern than it was about how very badly she wanted to agree.

"And if I don't go? I wish, gentlemen, that my duties were quite as forgiving as all that. But as far as I am aware, this attempt at an assassination did not create out of whole cloth another ambassador the yibo will agree to negotiate with."

"Alba," began Yosip softly.

There was a knock on the door, and they looked at each other for just a moment.

"If you would," she said, trying to keep her voice from shaking.

Yosip closed his eyes wearily for just a moment, and nodded. "Of course, Madam," he said, and stood slowly.

"Madam Chief Justice," said the interpreter, when Yosip had opened the door. "If you would be so kind as to join Ambassador Harroch?"

"Of course," Alba said brusquely, and, with Yosip behind her, she followed the interpreter as the guards fell into step beside them.

Harroch was waiting when Alba arrived in the comfortable room. He rose when they entered, and came over to greet them. By now, Alba was accustomed enough to yibo gestures that she could see the way his face creased and the tip of his tail twitched nervously.

He was worried about something.

Her entire body felt shaky and weak, and her breath rasped in her throat, but she forced her own face to a polite calm.

"Chief Justice Alba, we have a problem," he blurted in Common Dialect as soon as she was seated. "I'm very sorry to disturb you so early, but it is vital that we speak at once."

Alba didn't have to fake the frown on her own face. "What happened?" she asked.

He leaned forward just a little. "I don't want to understate our concerns, Alba. I have spoken with Kachik, and I must ask you again —can you commit to some military alliance?"

Alba took a deep breath, fighting back the thoughtless panic that slid through her muscles at the frightened tone in his voice. "Ambassador Harroch," she said, testing the lie as she spoke it. "Since we spoke yesterday, I have … rethought my position. I will need some time to consider the options, but if your people are facing an emergency, there are perhaps protocols that I could use. My chief of protocol, Feliu, is still recovering. I don't wish to give you false hope, but I am optimistic that once he has recovered …"

"Madam." Harroch leaned farther forward. "I don't think you realize the peril that not only I, but you, yourselves, are in. As long as you can give Kachik what he wants, you're safe. But they've locked up your scientist and his land-devil apart from the rest of you to remove the threat he poses, and they'll kill him soon. You must give me some agreement I can take back to Kachik, and you must do it urgently. If you don't—" His tail twitched again.

"Ambassador Harroch." Alba's voice was stern, and she willed it not to tremble. "If I were to purport to commit my government to a course of action without following the proper protocols, there is the very real threat that they would not follow through on the promises I have made on their behalf." She paused. "You must understand— the wheels of our government turn slowly, but once they are turning, they are difficult indeed to stop. Our nation in a peaceful one, but it cannot be denied that if there is a threat, they will act with a force that could ruin even you, with your advanced weapons.

"You must see that if I purport to enter into a unilateral agreement without proper protocol being followed, I may lose my own influence in the matter, and you, rather than be treated as valued allies, could be viewed as enemies seeking to take advantage."

Harroch watched her for a long moment.

Her heart was pounding strangely as she tried to read his expression.

Perhaps she'd failed the people on this mission. Perhaps she'd already sealed their fates. But she couldn't fail the remainder of the Joias System as well. In this, at least, she had to succeed.

At last, Harroch leaned back in his seat. The nervousness dropped from his posture like a mask, and he smiled at her, the expression cold. "I see," he said. "They told me this was how you would respond. I wanted to give you a chance before I parsed the competing offers and made my judgement. If the information I have from the street is correct, however, matters have arisen that force my action. There are rumours that … certain enemies of ours are approaching, and I can no longer afford to delay. And so, with nothing solid to refute it, I will have to reluctantly believe the others, that you never had any intention of agreeing after all."

"Which others?" Alba snapped. Her heart was pounding, her throat dry.

This entire situation—trapped, with hidden enemies, all of whom had agendas she did not know and couldn't anticipate or react to, the brutal half-spoken threats of physical violence—had shaken her very political ability, her steadiness and capacity to respond to the unexpected coolly and efficiently, in a way she was not sure would recover.

Harroch gestured to one of his aides, and behind her, Alba heard the doors slide open.

She forced herself to remain facing stubbornly forward, instead of spinning around to see who the newcomers were.

Something cold and sick in her stomach told her she already knew the answer.

"Madam Chief Justice."

The words were polite, the tone faintly ironic and far too familiar from her time on the diplomatic ship.

At last, she did turn.

The captain of the diplomatic ship stood there, flanked by a group of soldiers, in their lead the woman Ines had almost knocked senseless as Alba and the others had fled the dying ship.

"Madam Chief Justice," Captain Mattin repeated with a faint smile. "I'm so very pleased to find you alive and well. At least for the present."

23

Aran

When the yibo had taken away the dinner dishes, Aran stood, stretched, and wandered aimlessly out into the courtyard.

The hole they'd made the night before was still there, and apparently still undiscovered.

He strolled around for a few minutes, then turned back inside and headed into his bedroom. On the pretext of tidying up, he slipped his equipment into his supplies pouch, packing it in neatly. Whatever wouldn't fit, he'd leave—he hated to do it, but Istvay was right; they needed to get out. The yibo were clearly uncomfortable around them, and at this point, surviving long enough to get out of the compound was the main thing.

Istvay, he knew, was doing the same.

Once both of them were packed, they settled down on the floor of the apartment for a game of dice to pass the time.

Aran would have preferred to throw himself into analyzing data on his wavelink screen to avoid the thick fear tightening in his chest. But he knew far too well his tendency to get so caught up in research that he forgot everything else that was going on, and he didn't dare risk it, not tonight.

He found it almost impossible, though, to keep his mind on the game, and even Istvay had to be reminded once or twice to look at the numbers on their dice to come up with the score.

"We'll leave as soon as it gets dark enough," Istvay whispered.

Aran nodded, glanced over his shoulder through the window at the sun. It was just disappearing over the horizon.

They played a few more rounds of dice, the lights inside their small apartment illuminating as darkness began to fall, until Aran could see the first hint of a moon peeking out over the top of the wall.

He glanced at Istvay, who gave a barely perceptible nod.

"Give it another hour," they whispered. "We'll play a few more rounds, then we'll head out."

Suppressing a sigh, Aran gathered the pieces for another round.

The pounding on the door startled him so much that he jerked up, spilling dice across the floor. Istvay, too, was frowning.

"They never come at this time of night," said Aran, his voice tense.

What had gone wrong? Had the hole in the courtyard wall been discovered?

Istvay give a short nod, pushing themself to their feet. "I'll see what it is. You stay here, keep Ani calm."

Aran pulled the quietly growling Ani onto his lap and stroked her gently as Istvay pulled the door open.

"What do you—" they began.

Then they gave a startled exclamation as they were yanked through the door.

Aran scrambled to his feet, but the door slammed shut, and he heard the lock click.

He reached it in two strides, and pounded on it with his fist, Ani hissing on his shoulder. "Open this door right now, or I'll damn well melt it," he shouted, his words harsh with panic.

"We'll open it, certainly," came an accented voice, harsh and amused. "Just as soon as you convince that animal of yours to stay inside."

"Open the door. Right now. I'll let Ani kill every last one of you if you don't give me Istvay back, this moment," snapped Aran, panic pounding in his veins. He pulled Ani down from his shoulder, stroking her with trembling hands. "Ani," he whispered.

"I have a gun to Istvay's head. Would you be able to do that faster than I can pull the trigger? If you break out, there will be no Istvay left to save. Put your animal away, and then come out here. We only want to talk."

"Aran!" Istvay's voice was strained. "For hell's sake, get away from here! Don't try to come out, they'll just—"

Aran heard the unmistakable sound of something hard hitting flesh, and Istvay's voice broke off in a grunt of pain.

"Aran—" Istvay managed, and then there was another blow.

Aran's pulse was pounding in his ears, his mind buzzing with panic. "Just—just give me a second to calm her down," he snapped. "Leave Istvay alone, I'm coming, just give me a second. I swear to you, if you hurt Istvay, there's nothing that will stop me—"

"As long as Istvay keeps their mouth shut, and you don't try anything stupid, we have no reason to hurt them," came the accented voice, amused.

Aran's shoulders slumped in a mixture of relief and despair. "Ani," he murmured, lifting her gently. "Ani, I need you to stay in my room, you understand me? I'll be back in just a minute. Look, you stay in my room, and I'll get you a treat, okay?"

Ani growled restlessly, clinging onto his arm. She'd clearly picked up on his tension.

"Ani, please." His voice was choking in his throat. "Ani, I need you to listen to me, just this once—"

She was still growling, her tentacles tightening on his arms.

He lifted her, cuddling her bulbous body against his chest, trying to keep back the desperate tears that threatened to form in his eyes. "Ani. Please. You have to do this. You have to let me save Istvay. Please …" His voice broke.

She growled again uneasily, but for a wonder, she let him detach her from his arms and place her into her makeshift nest at the foot of his cot. He handed her one of the bright orange fruits she'd developed a taste for, and rubbed her head gently. "Stay there, and I'll bring you another when I come back," he whispered.

Then he closed the room door, took a deep breath, and stepped to the door leading outside. "She's somewhere safe," he said. "I'm alone. Now—will you let me out?"

"I'm unlocking the door now," said the voice. "Please know, we are standing far enough back that we'll have plenty of time to kill your friend if we find out you're lying to us. Even if you kill the one holding Istvay, there are more weapons than you can count pointed at their head. One of them will hit."

"I'm alone," said Aran again, his words choking. "Just—just don't hurt them. Please."

The lock clicked, and the door was yanked open.

Aran held out his hands to show he was unarmed, and stepped through the door.

Istvay stood a few metres away, held by two yibo guards. A trickle of blood ran down their temple. Istvay's eyes were fixed on Aran, their expression anguished, but they didn't say anything as he stepped outside. Aran saw at a glance that the person who had spoken hadn't been exaggerating—there were at least a dozen weapons pointed at Istvay's head.

"Very good," said the yibo who seemed to be in charge. "They told us you were intelligent. I'm pleased to see they were correct."

"Who told you that?" asked Aran, fear tightening in his throat. "And what the hell have you done to Istvay?"

The guard laughed. "We haven't done anything to Istvay. At least, nothing permanent. You were impressively quick at following orders. And as for who told us—" the yibo gave a close-lipped smile. "It seems the two of you have made some powerful friends." The guard stepped to one side.

Emeric smiled at him from across the courtyard.

The sight of that satisfied smirk brought back far too many memories—Istvay, pale-faced, shoved up against the corridor with a gun to their head. The tip of Ani's tentacle slipping loose as she was sucked out the airlock. The frantic hatred on Emeric's face as he tried to talk Aran into stepping out into the corridor to be shot, in exchange for his friends' lives.

"Aran." Emeric's voice was pleasant, but there was something vicious under it. "I'm so glad to see you made it planet-side safely."

"I'm surprised you managed to survive long enough in the jungle to get rescued," said Istvay, their tone thick with scorn. "Did you find someone smarter than you to protect you? I imagine you were wishing you had Aran along with, considering how—"

"Shut up, or I'll tell them to shoot you both, right now," Emeric snapped, his face dark with rage. "Believe me, I won't regret it." He paused for a moment, drawing in a deep breath and clearly trying to calm himself before turning back to Aran. "Aran," he said, trying and failing to strike a superior tone. "I had hoped to be able to speak to you alone for a few minutes. I thought we might be able to come to a mutually beneficial arrangement."

Istvay lifted their head again. "Why the hell do you think Aran would talk to you?" they snarled.

Emeric shot them a savage glare. "Because for some unaccountable reason, I think Aran wants to avoid seeing you beaten to a pulp in front of his face."

Aran stepped quickly forward, holding up his hands placatingly. "Just—can both of you just—Emeric. What did you want to talk about?"

Emeric glanced around at the guards. "Back in the courtyard," he snapped. "I'd like to talk somewhere private."

Aran shot Istvay a quick glance, but from Istvay's expression, they had no better idea of what Emeric was up to than he did.

Aran sighed. "Listen," he said. "I'll come talk with you. But Istvay comes with. I'm not leaving them alone out here."

Emeric's expression darkened, but with an effort, he gave a quick shrug of his shoulders. "I suppose that's alright, as long as they can keep their damn mouth shut. But they've never been very good at that."

Aran bit back a retort. There was already a bruise rising across the side of Istvay's face, and he damn well wasn't going to risk another, not while he had any say in the matter.

Emeric gestured the yibo guards forward, and said to the interpreter, "I need to talk to these two in private—it's a human tradition for discussing important matters. But tie their hands so they can't try anything. And if I'm not back soon, come looking for me. You have my permission to shoot both of them if they've done anything to hurt me."

The aliens stepped forward, and Aran held out his hands to be bound.

There wasn't any point in fighting, not with the odds they were facing right now.

The yibo guards clipped something around his wrists and Istvay's, then opened the gate between the front and back courtyards. Emeric gestured Aran through, but hesitated a moment at the doorway. "Ani's not—" he began, glancing around with a nervous, involuntary twitch to his movements.

Aran had to bite back a quick, grim smile. "No, she's not in the courtyard," he said. "If she had been, she'd have already climbed the walls to get to you, believe me. She's—very interested in renewing your acquaintance, I think."

Emeric gave a nervous, involuntary shudder, and again Aran had to bite back a grin.

When they were at the far side of the courtyard, out of earshot of the waiting guards, Emeric leaned towards him and hissed, "I know you know something about the cure, Aran. Tell it to me, and I'll get them to keep you alive."

Aran blinked at Emeric.

"Don't play stupid," said Emeric impatiently. "I know you know something about the cure. You're too bloody bullheaded not to have figured out something by now. So that's my offer—you tell me, and I'll get them to lock you up somewhere safe and not kill you. The captain wants to kill you, but I can talk him out of it."

"So, the mighty Emeric, come to talk to an actual expert," said Istvay, their tone dripping with sarcasm.

Emeric shot them a murderous glare, and for a moment, Aran thought he might hit them.

"If you so much as touch Istvay, you'll get nothing from me," Aran snapped, his voice sharp with panic.

Emeric glared at Istvay bitterly, then turned his attention back to Aran. "Go ahead, then," he said. "Tell me what you know."

Aran narrowed his eyes. His heart was pounding. "Why the hell would I?"

"Are you even asking that question?" Emeric's own voice was thick with sarcasm. "Aran Romeu. The selfless hero whose only aim is to help humanity. Surely you want to find a cure to send back. These aliens are going to ally with Cavaco, not your Chief Justice. So, you tell me, and I'll bring the cure back. I thought you didn't care about your reputation. I thought you hated being famous, isn't that what you always said? Or was that just a lie? Are you actually desperate for all that publicity, despite your demurrals?"

"And what would happen to the cure if you got your hands on it?" Aran's breath was coming too quick. "If you brought it back to Cavaco—would it really go out to people who needed it? Who would be able to access it?"

Emeric smirked. "Are you questioning my judgement? Cavaco's judgement? Surely those kinds of decisions should be left to people who are actually competent to make them. I'm sure everyone who merits the cure will be given it."

But as he spoke, he cast an involuntary glance at Istvay, undisguised loathing in his expression.

And Aran was suddenly, irrevocably certain that any cure that Emeric found would not be used for Istvay. Not if they lay dying on a cot in front of him.

"I—I'm sorry," he said, the words tight in his throat. "I don't know anything."

Emeric's eyes narrowed. "Don't be stupid," he snapped. "I know damn well that you know. You want to be a martyr? You're willing to die right here, and watch Istvay die too, rather than give up any of your glory?"

"It has nothing to do with glory," said Aran in a low voice. "I just don't want you or Cavaco to have it."

"You will tell me," Emeric hissed, stepping closer to him. "You will damn well tell me, Aran. I hear these aliens know how to make people talk."

Aran felt strangely calm. "That's fine," he said. "You might hate me, Emeric, but you can't deny I've learned how to deal with pain a hell of a lot better than you have. So, try me."

Emeric stepped in and slapped Aran across the face, the sharp sound of the blow breaking the silence of the courtyard. Istvay made a strangled noise and stepped closer, but Emeric whirled, yanking out his pulse gun.

Aran blinked back tears from his eyes at the stinging pain. "Sorry, Emeric," he said through clenched teeth. "You're going to have to do better than that."

Emeric flipped the pistol in his hand and drew his arm back, slamming the butt of it into Aran's temple. Aran staggered, and without his hands to catch him, fell heavily onto the ground of the courtyard.

His ears rang from the force of the blow, sharp pain knifing through his skull from where he'd been hit, and it took him a moment to refocus his gaze. Emeric was watching him, teeth bared in a vicious smile. "Go on, Aran. I can keep doing this for as long as you'd like. You're going to damn well tell me, or—"

"Or what?" muttered Aran. His teeth had cut through his cheek at the blow, and he could taste the iron tang of blood. "You think you can do this longer than I can take it?"

Emeric drew back his foot, eyes glittering with hate, and kicked Aran hard in the stomach. Aran doubled over, gasping.

Emeric crouched over him. "You've fooled everyone else, Aran. You've got that damn Istvay and everyone else on Colorida eating out of your damn hand. You think you're better than I am, don't you?" His voice was almost frantic. "You think that even here, on this damnable, forsaken planet, you're above me. You think you can just stand here and take away what should have damn well been mine in the first place. You think—"

"Aran!"

Aran jerked his head up, and Emeric paused.

Istvay's face was pale, blood crusted down their temple and clotted in their hair, and there was a look on their face that reminded Aran suddenly of the night when Istvay had been drunk and leaned up against his shoulder.

"Aran," said Istvay again, their voice quiet. "Just … tell him."

Aran stared at Istvay, not sure if the blow had affected his hearing.

"Please, Aran." Istvay's voice was weary. "Just—just tell him. If you die, it's not like you could get the cure anyways."

Aran opened his mouth to protest, a hundred excuses dancing on his tongue—it was still possible that they could fight their way out of this somehow, escape before Emeric killed the two of them. This was just getting beat up, and hell, he didn't like it, but it wasn't like he wasn't used to working through pain. He could take pain. He couldn't take bloody watching Istvay die. And if he told Emeric— gave him the map, since he'd certainly insist on it—that's what he'd be doing.

Istvay couldn't ask him to give this up.

But the look on Istvay's face held so much vulnerability, so much hurt, so much tentative trust—more hope, really, than trust—and suddenly, Aran realized he couldn't bear to hurt them anymore. He couldn't bear to see the pain in Istvay's eyes when he plunged recklessly ahead, like he usually did.

He took a long breath.

Anyways—Istvay was right.

As much as he wished for it, there wasn't a way out of this.

"The yibo won't tell you anything about the cure, because they're not the ones who have it," he said at last. "Whoever this blood sample belonged to, it wasn't them—I've done a DNA analysis."

Emeric was breathing heavily, their mouth twisted in a triumphant smile. "Who was it, then?"

Aran gave a one-shouldered shrug. "I don't know, exactly. Only that it's another species of aliens, and from what I've gathered, the yibo are afraid of them. As far as I can gather, they're dangerous—I think they're the reason the yibo keep force-fields around their cities."

"And where would I find them?"

Aran glanced at Istvay. They were watching him steadily, and they gave a small nod.

He closed his eyes for a moment. "I—have a map," he said at last, in a dull voice.

"Let me see it," snapped Emeric.

Aran pulled the sphere out of his pouch, and Emeric snatched it from his fingers. He studied it for a long time.

"Show me how it works," he demanded. Aran did. He felt like his body belonged to someone else, his fingers working almost without his instruction.

Emeric nodded, straightening. He seemed to have regained his calm. "See? I knew you could be reasonable, with sufficient persuasion." He glanced over at Istvay. "And you're right. I wouldn't have thought Istvay, of all the people in the world, would have been helpful, but I suppose even they have their uses."

Aran just stared dully at the rough ground of the courtyard.

Emeric's face was all pleasant smiles, but there was an unmistakable glitter of malice beneath, sharp as glass-shards. "Well, Aran, I'm so glad we had this little chat. I'll tell the aliens to keep you alive, just like I said. Your new accommodations might be a little less comfortable, but at least you won't be shot tomorrow morning, like we had planned. You made the right decision. And you'll have the satisfaction of knowing that when the cure comes back, and I'm successful—you were part of it." He gave a small, vicious smile. "Who knows, perhaps I'll even dedicate it to the memory of Istvay, the last victim of the defect before the cure was found."

Aran didn't even have the energy to look up.

24

Savina

Savina heard the shouts in her dreams, and it took her a few moments to wake up. And then it took her a few moments more of peering around the small room and blinking owlishly before she realized the shouts weren't from her dream, they were real. And they were coming from somewhere outside her bedroom.

She jumped to her feet, heart pounding, grabbed up her knives, and burst out the door.

The corridors were deserted. Whatever was happening, it had clearly attracted the attention of everyone in the crime boss's compound.

Savina swore and started down the hallway at a sprint.

She hated running. But it seemed like that was all she did these days.

The time she got to the main level, the indistinct shouting had resolved itself into words, and Savina groaned.

The shouts were in her own language. And she recognized Nicolau's voice.

"—talk that way about my sister!"

There was the unmistakable sound of a fist hitting flesh, and a grunt of pain.

Savina swore again, viciously, yanked out her pulse gun, spun the settings, and fired it at the lock.

The metal shattered, and as the door swung loose, she pushed her way inside to meet a scene of absolute chaos.

Nicolau stood at the far end of the room, facing off against three yibo. There was blood streaming from a cut on his cheek, and his expression was furious. He was standing over a fourth yibo, who was flat on the ground and bleeding from their nose. As Savina watched, the other three rushed him at once, two grabbing his arms and jerking him around while another pulled back their fist.

Savina yanked out a throwing knife, but before she could send it flying, a grim-faced Joska shoved her way through, grabbed Nicolau by the shoulder, and pulled him out of the way of the blow. His attacker staggered, caught off balance, and Joska stepped forwards and calmly brought a bottle of liquor down on the back of the yibo's head. He slumped, and the other two turned on Joska—and then stopped abruptly as she brought her pulse pistol to bear.

"Stand back, please," said Joska, and Savina caught the cold anger under her tone. "Back where I come from, four on one is considered a bit unfair."

Behind the captain, Nicolau was scowling in fury, but Joska's hand on his arm held him back, so scowling was the best he could do. There was a bruise rising on his cheekbone, as well as the cut under one eye, and his fists were bloody.

The other yibo backed slowly away, but they weren't leaving—Savina could see them pulling out their own weapons, forming a wide half-circle around Joska and Nicolau. Joska had obviously noticed it too, and there was that wry look on her face that always appeared when things were going even farther sideways than usual. She took in the situation quickly, then leaned back to whisper something to Nicolau, not taking her eyes off the yibo.

Nicolau shook his head angrily. Joska rolled her eyes upwards and give a long-suffering sigh.

Then Savina stepped forward, clearing her throat. One by one, the yibo turned to look at her.

She smiled at them. Then she grabbed the nearest by the back of the collar, yanked them towards her, and buried her knife up to its hilt in their thigh.

The yibo screamed, eyes going wide with fear and pain, and Savina, still smiling broadly, pulled out a second knife, holding it at the alien's stomach. "I know you don't much care for humans," she said, giving them all her best dimpled smile. "That's alright, I don't blame you. But if even one of you touch either of those people, your friend here is going to have to hold his guts in with both hands. I think you understand me, whether you speak my language or not."

For a moment, no one spoke or moved. They were all staring at Savina in a kind of shocked, dazed horror.

She ran the knife gently along her captive's belly, the cloth parting under her blade and a thin line of blood beading up along its track. "You have three seconds," she said pleasantly. She held up three fingers, her knife dripping blood onto the floor.

The yibo dropped their weapons and scattered.

When they were gone, Savina jerked her frozen captive around so they were staring into her face. Their expression was thick with horror, blood beading and dripping from the thin line on their stomach, blood already soaked through their thin tunic where Savina's knife was still buried in their thigh. Their eyes were glassy with shock and pain and fear, and when Savina reached out and patted them gently on the face, they trembled at her touch.

"We had a deal," she said pleasantly. "Your boss told me we had a deal, and part of that deal was that you leave my friends alone. I hope I'm not being unreasonable, but I do expect that when I agree to deal, the other side keeps their part of the bargain." She let go her grip on the mobster's arm, and they whimpered softly. She yanked the knife out with a sharp tug. "I'd get that looked at, if I were you," she said sympathetically, her eyes wide and innocent. "It looks nasty. Hate to lose too much blood."

The yibo staggered from the room. Savina glanced around, then picked up a napkin from the bar and wiped the blades off her knives before re-sheathing them.

When she turned, Joska and Nicolau were both staring at her. Joska's face bore a complicated expression, somewhere between disapproval, resignation, and amusement. Nicolau looked like he was staring at the monster under his bed.

Savina gave him her prettiest smile. "What happened?" she asked. She could hear the dangerous calmness in her own tone, but at this point, she was too angry to really care.

Joska was still watching her. At last, she shook her head and gave a small smile. "I came in halfway through, I'm afraid."

Nicolau was still scowling, which made him look a little like a sulky child.

"Nicolau?" Savina asked, turning to him.

He glared at the ground, and didn't say anything.

"Nicolau," she said again warningly, stepping over to him. She was still holding the knives, and there was still blood on her hands, and she saw his eyes widen just a little.

She smiled with a slightly bitter satisfaction.

He may as well learn to be afraid of her, at least a little.

"They were—" he muttered, then trailed off.

Joska sighed. "From what I heard," she said, shooting Nicolau a meaningful glance, "there was some talk among the yibo about hoping you'd be killed on one of your hits."

Savina looked between her brother and the captain blankly.

She would have expected this, maybe, from Beni. She and Beni had always been a team. But—Nicolau? And Joska?

Her brain didn't seem able to compute this new development, and honestly, she wasn't sure she wanted it to.

She managed a smile anyway. "Well. I suppose I'd better go talk to Yuur. She and I had a deal, I think, and it didn't involve four aliens trying to hit my baby brother."

Nicolau flushed, and she had to bite back a grin of genuine amusement.

Joska was shaking her head, but she had a small smile on her face.

Savina glanced around, and took a deep breath.

She would have to talk to Yuur. She had no idea when the raiders would make their move, but she was very certain they would. And until then, she couldn't let Yuur wonder why she'd suddenly become so very complacent.

Yuur was waiting for her as she stepped through the door. "Ah. Savina. I was hoping you'd come," she said.

She was leaning back in her seat, and something about her relaxed posture made Savina's scalp prickle.

The woman should have been furious after what Savina had done. Instead, she smiled and gestured to a stool.

Slowly, carefully, Savina sat.

From the corner of her eyes, she noticed Yuur's bodyguard stepping into the doorway, blocking the exit.

He'd been doing that more and more frequently when she met with Yuur.

"Your people were trying to beat up one of my friends," Savina snapped. "I thought we had an agreement."

The mob boss studied her for a few moments, and then smiled. But it wasn't the yibo's typical close-lipped smile—this smile showed her teeth, and there was no mistaking the menace behind it. "Savina," she said. "I thought we had a deal as well." She paused a moment. "But perhaps we both misunderstood what that meant."

Savina frowned.

Then, behind her, the door creaked open, and she could hear soft footsteps, barely audible on the hard floor.

They were a different cadence than the quick, light footsteps of the yibo, and too quiet to belong to anyone on her team.

Something cold and terrified clutched at Savina's throat, and for just a moment, she couldn't make herself turn to look.

Maybe was nothing. Maybe she was imagining things. It had been a long few days, and she'd been under a lot of stress—

Slowly, unable to help herself, she turned.

The woman in the doorway was as coldly, breathtakingly alluring as she'd been when Savina had almost bumped into her in the moonport back on Rochesa, weeks ago and light-years away. As she'd been in Savina's restless, disturbing dreams—sometimes of those strong hands tipping her head back, those sensuous lips on hers, and sometimes those hands around her throat, inexorably choking the life from her as she gasped and struggled and pleaded.

Reka was more gaunt than she had been, her hair not quite as sleek, her undershave starting to grow back in a prickly shadow. But she was still able to draw Savina's eyes like a magnet.

Reka's grey-green eyes were as sharp as ice and hard as steel, and her lips curved up the smallest hint of a smile. "Savina Moya."

Savina shivered at sound of her name. Reka's voice was quiet, but there was a note to it, like the sound of struck iron—cold, unyielding, with a clear timbre that resonated in her bones.

And then Savina came out of her trance, and leapt to her feet.

The yibo guards seemed to have been waiting for just such a move, because they'd surrounded her in a moment.

She could kill as many of them as possible before she went down. It was tempting, honestly.

But Reka just stood there watching her, with that cold, mocking expression, as if Savina was a bug scraped off the sole of her shoe. And those cold eyes told her that all Reka needed was an excuse.

"I wouldn't try anything," came Yuur's voice from behind her, breaking through her thoughts. "Your friends wouldn't survive it. I have someone watching them. The moment you make trouble—" She left threat hanging.

Savina took a long breath, and let her fingers relax on the hilt of the knife she'd grabbed instinctively.

"Reka," she said in a flat voice. "What are you doing here? Bounty hunting wasn't exciting enough, so you decided to get a job with the alien underground?" Her voice wasn't quite as steady as she wanted it to be, her heart pounding in a mixture of fear and fury and something else she didn't want to name.

Reka was still smiling that mocking smile. "No, Savina," she said, and the name on her lips sounded like she was tasting something rotten. "I'm not like you."

The scorn in her words could have curdled milk.

"So what, then?" asked Savina, putting on her lightest, most innocent tone. "You sleep your way into their good graces? A pretty thing like you, it would be easy. I heard rumours you were willing to do anything for a job, but I didn't expect that. Still, when you're not skilled enough to take what you want, you just kiss up to someone who—"

Reka stepped forward and grabbed Savina by the collar, yanking her up in a movement too swift for Savina to react to.

The yibo guards brought up their weapons, and for the barest second, the two women glared at each other. A sick mixture of fear and desire sparked through Savina like electricity, and she stared like an animal caught in the beams of a fast-moving transport, unable to move even to defend herself.

Reka shoved her away scornfully, and Savina staggered, trying to catch her balance.

"You don't deserve an explanation," Reka spat. "But I'll give you one if it makes you feel better. I ran into people who were looking for you, and since we both have the same objective, we joined forces."

Savina frowned in confusion.

"Savina," said Yuur from behind her. "The raider captain sent Reka to contact me. I've worked with this captain in the past, and she wanted an explanation of why I'd ordered a hit on one of her people. I looked into it, and I realized at once that there was a solution that would make my problem and her problem both go away. And so—" she shrugged eloquently.

Savina spun to stare at the small yibo woman, sickness crawling in her stomach.

There was an insincere smile on the mob boss's face. "Reka is here to guard you until her allies come to pick you up. What they'll do with you after that, I have no idea. But then, I don't see that it's my business. Reka assures me that if you come peacefully, your friends won't be hurt—at least, not yet. But I told her it was important to lock all of you up, because as far as I'd seen, that was the only way to ensure that you'd behave yourself."

Savina stared, her chest tight, her heart pounding.

The others were locked up. The raiders were coming for her. And what arrangement Reka and the raider had worked out, she didn't know. But—

She remembered the raider man she'd killed, the deadly glint in his eyes, the understated menace in his every movement. The undefinable air of a predator about him.

Whatever it was, she was very certain she would not come out of it alive.

"Come along, Savina," said Reka coldly. "If you're dead, my allies have told me they'd take your siblings in exchange. And I don't think you want that, do you?"

Savina stood numbly as two of the yibo came to lock her hands behind her back. Her mind was spinning, and she had to fight the nausea in her stomach.

She should fight. She could fight, and maybe she'd get away.

But even if she did—Beni would die. Nicolau would die, and Joska and Rafel.

When Savina's wrists were tightly bound, Reka stepped over, looking her up and down as someone might inspect an unappetizing cut of meat. Then she jerked her head, indicating Savina to follow. "Let's go," she said, her voice cool and indifferent.

Savina clenched her teeth, and looked up at Reka with her most innocent smile, her eyes wide, her dimple showing. "I'd love to follow a pretty girl like you. But it's hard for me to walk with my hands tied behind my back like this. It knocks me off balance."

A flicker of annoyance crossed Reka's expression, but it was gone almost quickly as it had come. "You'd best get used to it, then," she said, turning.

Savina took a step, pretended to stumble, and fell forward.

If she'd managed it, she would have hit Reka just at the right angle to knock her feet from under her. But the woman seemed to sense her, and spun in a catlike motion, catching Savina skilfully and depositing her back on her feet so quickly Savina barely had a chance to take stock of the easy, lazy strength in the woman's grip before she was standing again, blinking dazedly.

"Be careful," said Reka, still in that cool, indifferent tone. "I'd hate for you to damage yourself before my friends come to pick you up."

Savina took a deep breath, trying to slow her oddly racing heart, and followed Reka.

Two of the yibo guards followed as well, but they were far enough back that it was clear they had every confidence in Reka's ability to deal with Savina.

It was—a little insulting, to be honest.

She scowled at Reka's back.

They came to a corridor, and Reka paused to open the door.

Savina stumbled again. Reka spun just in time to catch her, and for a moment, Savina blinked up at Reka from the woman's arms.

Reka was holding Savina as if she weighed nothing, but even considering Savina's slightly shorter stature and Reka's obvious strength, Savina was certainly not weightless.

She could see irritation on Reka's face now, cutting through the indifference, and the sight of it made something savage well in her chest.

She gave a small, helpless smile, letting her dimple show, and she caught Reka's almost unconscious flinch in response.

Her smile had always been a weapon, and she knew how to use it.

"Reka," she whispered, her eyes wide and frightened. "Don't hurt me. I'm so scared of the raiders, Reka. I'm just a girl from the Rim

Mountains, I don't understand any of this—" she made as if to blink back tears, her eyelashes fluttering innocently.

Again, there was that flash of hatred in Reka's face, and the woman stepped back abruptly, letting go of Savina.

Savina didn't try to catch herself. She fell awkwardly to the floor and looked up at Reka pathetically.

She knew what a pitiful sight she made. She knew how to make the most pitiful sight possible. It had been the thing that had kept her alive—no one wanted to hurt someone who looked so small and helpless.

There was a vicious, unreasoning anger burning inside her.

She wanted to hurt Reka. To break that indifferent expression, force the woman to do something—snap at her, hurt her, kick her— anything other than that cool indifference.

"Please help me, Reka," said Savina, letting her voice waiver a little. "Look at you, a government agent. Trying to hurt me by hurting my family. My younger siblings. They're almost babies, and you don't care, anything to get to me. Why don't you just kill me, leave them out of this? You're a monster."

Reka was still staring at her in disgust, and Savina rolled up onto one elbow, wincing as the restraints cut into her wrists. "Ouch! It hurts, Reka. These restraints are too tight. I can't even feel my fingers. You can kill me if you want, but please stop hurting me. Your masters won't want damaged goods."

"They are not my masters," Reka hissed, but she bent to inspect Savina's hands.

Savina waited until she was close enough, then she spat as hard as she could. Reka flinched back, and Savina flashed her a vicious smile.

"Of course they're your masters. You were Cavaco's lapdog until he threw you out. Then you were Alba's. You lost her, so you found another master. Were you lonely, was that it? Needed someone to pat your head and tell you you're a good girl? Look at you, crawling back to the people who kick you, whining for your dinner. What a good dog you are."

Reka stared at her, spittle glistening on her cheek. Then she grabbed Savina by the bound arms and yanked her to her feet, and Savina gave an undignified yelp of pain. Reka held her upright with one arm, and with the other reached into the pocket of her suit and pulled out a tissue to wipe the spittle from her face. She dropped it on the floor with a look of disgust, then turned back to Savina.

If her gaze had been indifferent before, now it sparked with cold fury.

Savina twisted in Reka's grasp, her heart pounding, her blood racing, something between fear and anticipation pulsing through her veins. Reka shoved her up against the wall, her forearm pressed against Savina's throat, gaze boring into Savina.

Savina's breath was tight, her throat dry. She couldn't seem to pull her gaze away from those eyes, cold and hard and sharp as knives and glittering with loathing, and a sick triumph pulsed through her at the sight.

She wanted to hurt this woman. She wanted to see her bleeding.

"Don't like hearing the truth?" she gasped. "At least I don't need a master. At least I make my own decisions."

Reka shoved her harder against the wall, so that Savina had to choke out the last words.

"How's that working out for you, Savina?" Reka purred. "Dragging your friends through the portal. Getting them caught up in the alien criminal underground. Putting a target on all their backs. Is that how you make your decisions, over the bodies of people who care about you?"

Savina tried to spit again, but Reka's grip was too tight, and all she could do was gasp for air.

For a long, long moment Reka studied her as blackness crowded Savina's vision. At last, the woman stepped back, releasing her, and Savina dropped to her knees, gasping through her bruised throat.

She looked up, shooting Reka a resentful glare. The agent seemed to have regained her composure, and just watched her with that cool look from earlier.

But despite her attempts at indifference, Savina could see the hatred glittering under that gaze.

Reka gestured with her chin, and when Savina didn't move to get up, drew back her booted foot and kicked her. Savina landed on her stomach on the filthy floor.

"Get up," said Reka calmly.

Savina set her jaw stubbornly.

Reka kicked her again. "Get up, or I'll pick you up and carry you over my shoulder."

For a moment, Savina was tempted to make her. But instead, she rolled painfully to her feet, shooting a glare over her shoulder at the woman behind her.

"Go," said Reka. "Your cell is down at the end of the corridor. If you fall again, I won't be catching you."

Savina gritted her teeth and didn't answer.

When they reached the cell door, Reka unlocked it and gestured her in.

After a moment, Savina dropped her head and went.

The door slammed close behind her.

It took her a few minutes, in the darkness, before she could make out the shapes of the others huddled against the back wall.

There was blood dripping down Joska's face, and Nicolau had a rapidly forming black eye.

So they hadn't been taken without a fight.

But they had been taken.

"Savina?" Beni's voice was tight with worry. "Are you alright? What did they do to you?"

"Nothing," said Savina softly.

She closed her eyes for a moment, and she could see behind her eyelids the hatred in Reka's stare, the dark, predatory gaze of the raider man she'd killed.

"Nothing yet," she added, through the sickness twisting in her stomach.

25

Alba

Alba glared at the captain in icy disdain, and didn't deign to answer.

Harroch glanced between them with a small smile of amusement on his face. "I see there is no love lost between you, then," he said. He sat back in his chair, and gestured casually to the three humans beside him. "We found Captain Mattin and a hundred or so of his soldiers outside one of the shuttles, just a day or so after you got here. They'd been trapped there, and enough of them had died in the jungle that they were very grateful to see us. As we were already in negotiations with you, and as Captain Mattin was able to show me sufficient proof that he was working as a direct representative of one of your other Joint Heads of Government, General Eniko Cavaco, we brought them in.

"Once they were aware of the situation, they asked to be allowed to negotiate without your … assistance. And after having spoken to them, it seems this General Cavaco is less wary of using his authority to enter into agreements for his and his system's benefit. These people promised me an alliance, along with all the weapons and military assistance we might require. And they've proved to my satisfaction their ability to deliver on such promises."

Alba's heart was beating quick and strange in her chest, and there was a light-headedness washing over her that made her unconsciously reach out for support. She could hear the words Kachik had spoken the previous day, the dismissal in them.

"We only need enough of them to keep our enemies' weapons busy."

Should they agree to a military alliance, the humans would be used as cannon-fodder, whatever Harroch had promised Cavaco's people.

Yosip caught her elbow inconspicuously, steadying her. She breathed a grateful sigh, but didn't dare glanced at him in gratitude. Instead, she kept her attention focused on Harroch.

"So you were negotiating with them behind our backs," she said, her own voice sounding strange in her ears. "And to what purpose? If you believed Captain Mattin could give you what you wanted, why the facade?"

Harroch smiled gently. "Madam Chief Justice. I would have preferred to negotiate with you. You came yourself, rather than send a representative. I admire that. I thought it bode well for our chances of reaching a mutually acceptable arrangement. And further, it's clear that Cavaco is afraid of you. But you were unwilling to negotiate."

"I was unwilling to roll over and concede to your demands, my responsibilities to my own government and my ability to carry through with my promises notwithstanding," she answered sharply. She let her icy gaze sweep over Captain Mattin's face, and was rewarded with his almost unconscious twitch. Then she turned her gaze back to Harroch. "Ambassador. Captain. This facade will benefit none of us. Neither I nor the General have the power to unilaterally enter into an agreement with a foreign entity without the consent of the Council."

"Perhaps," said Harroch, his voice soft. "But you yourself have informed me that the military is under Cavaco's command. If he chose to deploy it—"

"If he chose to deploy the military in disregard of the Council's instructions, he would be sanctioned, and the military operation recalled," Alba snapped. "And you would be traitors, and allies to a traitor."

"And yet—" the ambassador continued thoughtfully, still stroking the end of his tail. "And yet, it always takes some time to recall a military operation, does it not? Especially if the officer in charge takes time to be convinced of the necessity of such action. I'm sure that in that amount of time, if the military had engaged and a conflict had broken out—surely it would be almost impossible to pull back from something like that. Don't you agree with me, Madam Chief Justice?"

Behind him, the captain was smiling, a small, self-satisfied smile.

"You are putting a great deal of weight on the hope our government will not act quickly enough," said Alba shortly. "Please understand, should you choose this as your method of forming an alliance, such alliance would be very likely to end along with the military operation—both of which would be terminated by the sanction imposed on Cavaco. The chance of you forming a lasting alliance through these methods is next to nothing. Besides which, surely you understand that such assistance—coming, as it does, with the guarantee of illegal conduct—must carry with it a great deal of risk. I would strongly advise you to consider what you're agreeing to in return. If you are indeed suffering from internal tension, making an enemy of our system will not advance your interests. Rationality must argue for simply opening the portal, and letting our diplomats engage in legitimate discussions."

Harroch gave the yibo equivalent of a shrug again, a small twitch of his tail. "Perhaps it is as you say. But I have seen the wheels of our own government turn, and I doubt yours would be significantly faster. If I were to agree to your proposal, I would come away with nothing more than a promise of further discussions. Even if your government did eventually agree to an alliance, who is to say how far our internal situation would have devolved in the meantime? Who is to say, if your people saw us weakened, that they would not prefer to simply take what we have by force? No, I believe that of the two risks, the risk of waiting too long is the greater. Your General Cavaco has promised me exactly what I have asked for—weapons, soldiers, military assistance. If, as you say, your system would be willing to enter into an alliance, surely the fact that Cavaco has agreed to this would not automatically negate that willingness. And as far as the cost to us—" he smiled a little. "I've heard their requests. And they are not unreasonable. Nor even all that difficult to grant."

His words sent a chill up Alba's spine.

She took a deep breath.

All there was left, then, was to make her final, desperate play.

"Yosip," she snapped. "Would you please pull up a starmap of our system?"

Yosip frowned at her, but did as she asked, and the holographic map with the inhabited planets labeled spread across the empty space of the room.

It was a risk, but it was a calculated one. No doubt Cavaco's people had shown the yibo more than this already.

She gestured to the map. "These are the inhabited planets in our system. Now, please show me a starmap of your own system."

Harroch was frowning, but he gestured to an aide. Yosip's map flickered off as the yibo map appeared.

Alba's heart was beating far too quickly, nausea rising in her stomach, but she forced her expression to give nothing away. "And which planets of yours are terraformed and occupied?" she snapped.

Harroch gestured again, and the aide tapped a button on the map base. A handful of planets showed up, glowing a light red.

"That is the number of people we will both have to convince to make this alliance work," she continued. "Does that look to you like something that can be done by a ship's captain who tells you he's representing an army general from one of the many inhabited planets in our own system? Is that a promise you can trust?"

She wasn't expecting to convince Harroch, not anymore. He'd clearly already made his decision.

But then, that wasn't what she was after right now.

The moment Cavaco's people had stepped through the door, she'd known what she needed to do.

She flicked her eyes to one side in a gesture that was barely perceivable, and her retinal screen blinked for a moment in response, capturing the image of the starmap.

Harroch sighed, and the alien starmap flickered and died.

"I am sorry, Madam Chief Justice, I find I may be occupied in negotiations with Captain Mattin for the remainder of the afternoon. I'll ask my guards to escort you back to your quarters."

He turned to the guards. "Don't take her back to the quarters," Alba's AI translated into her earpiece. "Take them to the holding cells. I believe the discussion today has made our decision very clear."

"Of course," said the captain of the guards. "We'll take them there at once."

There was something cold and tight in Alba's stomach as she

turned to follow the yibo guards out the door.

She'd lost her gamble. She'd lost her chance to convince the yibo to negotiate in good faith.

And the cost of that failure was more than her numb mind could contemplate.

26

Aran

Aran could hear Emeric calling out instructions to the yibo guards as he left.

He didn't care.

He barely looked up when the guards grabbed him, and just nodded dully when they held a gun to Istvay's head and told him to get Ani, to keep her calm and under control while they took him Istvay to their new cell.

He didn't bother to try to fight—what use would it be? If Istvay was going to die anyways, there was really no point to him and Ani escaping.

He couldn't bear to look at his friend. He couldn't bear to think about what he'd just done.

Even if he and Istvay could escape now, he had no way of finding the raiders. He'd given the map to Emeric. Which meant that any value his cooperation might have had was gone. Any leverage he could have used to keep Istvay alive was gone. Any chance of finding the cure and using it to save Istvay was gone. The thing that had occupied his every damn thought for the past three years, that he'd almost died for more times than he really wanted to think about—gone.

He felt a little bit as if he was standing outside his own body, watching himself walk down the narrow pathways towards the prison.

He wasn't sure, if he had to think about it, that he'd remember how to move his legs. So it was just as well he was doing it on autopilot.

Istvay was silent as well.

The group of them reached the prison, finally, and the guards opened the cell door and shoved him in after Istvay. When the door slammed behind him, he dropped to the ground, leaning back against the cold, damp wall.

He pulled Ani down into his lap, stroking her automatically. She whimpered a little and tried to plaster herself against him, and some part of his mouth remembered how to smile.

"Hey Ani, it's okay," he murmured, but the words stuck in his throat.

It wasn't okay. He wasn't sure if it would ever be okay again.

"Aran."

It was Istvay's voice, and Aran didn't want to look at them.

He knew damn well there would be no accusation in their eyes—and he couldn't bear not to see it there. He couldn't bear to see Istvay smiling stoically at him, telling him that it was alright, that they'd known they were going to die anyways, and all the crap he'd heard over the last however many damn years.

He didn't need Istvay to be self-sacrificing. He didn't need Istvay to be resigned to their own fate. He needed Istvay to actually give a damn. And it would hurt more than he could possibly imagine to look at them, and see that they didn't.

"Aran?" The voice came from closer this time, right behind his shoulder, but he still couldn't bring himself to turn around.

His entire body was trembling, his hands shaking. If he hadn't been stroking Ani, he'd probably have been halfway to a complete meltdown right now, his mind spiralling out of control in panic, his muscles shaking, words sticking in his throat so he couldn't express himself at all. Ani being here helped—at least, she helped keep him from the worst of it.

But still—he couldn't do this, not right now.

"Aran." Istvay's hand landed on his shoulder, warm and firm. They knew how much he hated light touches, and somewhere in the back of his mind, he was vaguely grateful that it was them here, not anyone else. He couldn't have stood to be around anyone else.

"Aran? I need you to look at me. If you can't talk, that's okay, I just—I need you to look at me, so … so I know if you're alright."

Aran took a long breath, and Ani, seeming to sense his distress, tightened her tentacles around his wrist. The half-felt pain of the suckers against his skin did something, at least, to ground him. He managed another deep breath, and then, not wanting to do it—not daring, almost, to do it—he turned.

Istvay was crouched behind him, their hand on his shoulder, and they were watching him in concern.

He'd guessed right. There was no accusation in their face, and the realization sickened him.

"Aran," said Istvay again, quietly, and he forced himself to look into their eyes.

Then he blinked. Istvay's eyes were shiny with what could only be tears.

"Istvay!" he began in sudden, frantic panic.

Damn it to hell, he'd wanted—he'd wanted to see *something* in their eyes, but this— "Istvay, are you alright? What's wrong? Are you—Pishti, please—" His words were choking in panic.

Istvay grabbed his other shoulder, holding him steady. "Aran. Aran, look at me. It's alright."

He took a deep breath, his heart slowing a little at the calmness in Istvay's tone. "I'm sorry," he said at last in a thick voice. "I'm so sorry. I let you down. I should've—I should've—"

Istvay shook their head, squeezing his shoulders. "What you did back there—I know it wasn't what you wanted." Their voice choked just a little as well. "But I—I needed you to, and—I was so afraid, Aran. I didn't know if you would actually—and then … and then you did." They broke off, squeezing their eyes closed, and a tear trickled from the corner of one eye down their cheek. Aran stared at the wetness glistening on their lashes, unable to formulate a response.

Istvay blinked hard and gave a small, broken smile, then grabbed Aran into a hug that was almost tight enough to choke off his breath.

Aran stiffened in shock, blinking in astonishment at the press of Istvay's face against his shoulder.

"I—I didn't know if you'd listen to me. I didn't know if—I didn't know if you trusted me anymore," they said, their voice choking against his ear. "I was so scared, and I didn't know—"

Aran's muscles were relaxing unconsciously, and he found himself leaning into Istvay's embrace. He couldn't think about what this meant, if it meant anything at all, but Istvay was warm, and their quick, unsteady breaths pressed against Aran's chest, and somehow, in the circle of Istvay's arms, Aran's panic faded, just a little.

He took a deep breath, and found he was choking on tears as well.

And for the first time, he realized how much he'd been worried that Istvay would be angry. That Istvay would hate him, somehow.

That after all this time, all the decisions he'd made for both of them without Istvay's input—that it would have been one too many, and that now they'd hate him.

Something squirmed under his elbow, and he glanced down.

Ani was trying to shove herself between them, chirping plaintively.

"Ani," he began, but she ignored him, managing to flatten herself into an oddly shaped pancake and ooze into the almost non-existent space between him and Istvay. Aran yelped as one of her tentacles pressed into a particularly ticklish spot under his arm, and Istvay gave a groan of mixed irritation and amusement and stepped back, blinking the tears from their eyes.

They didn't let go of Aran's shoulders, though, as Ani pushed herself into the space, purring loudly.

Aran gave Istvay a wet smile, and released one arm to stroke her. "It's alright, Ani, we love you too," he whispered.

Istvay drew in a shaky breath, and Aran saw a relief on their face that made them look years younger, a bright, unconsciously happy grin he hadn't seen almost since they'd boarded the Firedawn weeks ago. Certainly not since they'd arrived in the alien compound.

And something inside his chest released, and he realized how much he'd missed that smile. How much he'd missed this—Istvay happy. Not worried, or stressed, or frightened, or angry, just—happy.

Istvay was laughing a little, wiping their eyes, and Aran took a deep breath and wiped his own.

"Pishti," he said, when could speak again. "Pishti, look. I'm—I'm sorry I made you think—"

Istvay shook their head, still blinking. "No," they said, and their voice had that familiar warmth that meant that somehow, no matter how bad the circumstances, everything would be alright. "I'm sorry, I'm fine. It just—it meant a lot to me. That—that you were willing to trust me. Because—" they took a deep breath. "Because I realize, looking back, that I really hadn't been doing a very good job at this friend thing since we got here, and—" they sighed, and gave Aran that small grin that always made him melt.

"And anyways, I—I hope you'll forgive me. Because, um. I told you to tell Emeric about the cure, and give him the map, and yes, part of it was I hate watching you getting hurt. But also—I spent most of the afternoon studying that map. I don't have a full copy of it, but I think I have enough that we can figure out what we're missing. And, um … I'm pretty sure I have a way out of here. And I'm pretty sure that between the two of us, we can find the answer before Emeric can."

Aran stared at them for a moment, hardly able to believe his ears. "I—" he began, and then wasn't sure how to finish the sentence.

Istvay chuckled, the sound still a little wet. "Aran. Listen to me." They leaned forward, catching his eye, and waited until he was looking at them. They were close enough that he could feel their breath against his skin, and their brown eyes bored into his, dark and intense. "Sometimes I'm a little—defensive about you trying to find something to save my life. I spent so long assuming it couldn't be done that I guess it's become a bit of a habit. But I realized, today, what would be like if the situation was reversed. And—" they took a deep breath. "And the thing is, if there's something that important to you, I wouldn't be much of a friend if I didn't support you in it, I guess."

Aran was blinking back tears again, and Istvay was as well.

Ani chose that moment to remind both of them of her presence by the simple expedient of wriggling up Aran's chest and shoving her bulbous body directly into his face.

He laughed, and gathered her back into his arms—something that took longer than it should have, with the number of tentacles she'd grabbed him with—and by the time he finished, he'd managed to compose himself.

Istvay, too, looked slightly more composed by the time he looked up again.

"So," Aran said, looking up at his friend. "You have a way to get us out of here?"

Istvay nodded, a hint of their familiar mischievous grin on their face. "I've been keeping an eye on the guards and their habits. The guards that came to our compound in the evening just before it started to get dark were the ones that were always a little bit less dedicated. They were usually on for only a couple of hours before someone came to relieve them. And that night I got drunk—I saw the way they were watching the liquor bottle when I went out to pick it up. The other guards didn't seem to care, but these ones were obviously coming off a rotation before they got to us. Which means, if someone wanted to, for example, get the guards a little drunk—" they reached into their jacket and pulled out a small flask of liquor. "I hung onto this from the night we both pretended to get drunk so we could sneak out. By the smell of it, it's pretty strong. And it looks like the evening guards come off one shift just to get dragged onto another for a couple hours before the night shift comes on, so I think they're our best bet."

Aran stared at them. "You just—picked all this up from watching?"

Istvay chuckled. "Aran. I spent four years in university studying systems. I might not be as good at science as you are, but I am good at this. Emeric's apparently not going to try to come in and kill us tonight, and he's probably going to want to keep us alive in case he gets stuck while he's looking for the cure. So all we need to do is get the guards drunk, get out of our cell, get to the courtyard, and then get over the outside walls. And Ani's acid should get out of the cell once the guards are drunk—I scanned the material, and her acid should melt right through it."

They grinned at Aran. "What? You're looking at me like I just grew another head."

Aran shook his head, unable to stop smiling.

He'd thought, when they'd been locked up, that the worst thing in his life was not being able to get the cure as fast as he knew he needed to.

He hadn't realized exactly how much he needed to see Istvay grinning again. How much he'd needed to know they were on his side.

Istvay was watching him, their expression soft. "Aran," they said quietly. "You're my best friend. I might have told you that a few times when I was drunk, if you're telling me the truth."

Aran smiled back, and found he couldn't speak at all.

Istvay winked at him. "I guess we'd better make sure this bottle gets somewhere our guards will see it. And then—" they spread their hands. "And then, I guess we go hunt down some human-eating pirates, and talk to them about genetics."

27

Savina

Savina slumped down against the wall of the cell, as far away from the others as she could get.

She should talk to Beni, see if they were alright, find out how badly Nicolau and Joska and Rafel were hurt.

But she couldn't. She didn't want to know. She couldn't actually change anything if she knew, and she would rather die not knowing.

Outside the room, she could hear Reka's footsteps, pacing back and forth for a few moments, and then the sound of someone sitting on one of the low stools, the creak of the wood as Reka leaned back against the wall.

Savina focused on that, and tried not to think of anything else.

Rafel had warned her. He'd told her she was putting people in danger, people who didn't deserve to be in danger. People who hadn't done anything wrong.

She'd always justified it before—she and Beni were a team. They'd both agreed to do this.

She'd never let herself think about how the only reason Beni agreed to come along was that Savina was their sister, and they'd never leave her alone. If she asked, they'd come, even though she knew—she's always known, if she'd admit it—that they didn't like what Savina did. And Nicolau—she'd always told herself this had all been to keep him safe.

But now here he was, locked up in a cell on an alien planet, and it was her fault.

Hot tears stung her eyes.

She shouldn't care. She'd killed enough people that she'd learned not to think about situations from someone else's perspective.

But this time, she couldn't help it. The thought of the look on Joska's face; curious, measuring—but not judgemental. Never judgemental, even when she should be.

She blinked hard, and shoved herself back against the wall.

She hadn't had a choice. She'd done what she'd done because she had no choice.

But—it was always a choice, wasn't it?

"Savina?" It was Joska.

She didn't answer.

"Savina? You alright? What did they do to you?"

There was concern in Joska's voice, and the sound of it made to Savina bite down hard on her molars.

It wasn't fair. Why couldn't Joska bloody well leave her alone?

"Savina." It was Nicolau this time.

Savina gritted her teeth and looked up, pulling in a shuddering breath. She glared at Joska and the others.

"I'm fine," she bit out. "There. Are you happy now? I'm fine, and you aren't, and you're all here because of me. I ... I killed that raider. I wanted his captain to come after Yuur, but she sold me out. So you're right. This is all my fault. Fine. At least I accept it now. That's what you wanted, right?"

The bitterness was entirely undeserved, and Savina knew it, but she couldn't help herself.

It hardly bloody mattered anyway.

There was a long moment of silence, and Savina glared down at the dirty, mouldering floor of their cell.

At last, Nicolau cleared his throat in the silence. "Um," he said. "Savina." He hesitated. "I, um—maybe I'm with Joska, and I don't necessarily like you killing people, necessarily. But—but you saved my life. On the ship, and then back here. I … I mean, I was the reason this all happened in the first place. If you'd just left me, let Yuur's people take me, you'd be back with the others right now." His voice was sincere, and she could almost picture his guileless green eyes watching her. "You didn't tell me much about what happened with our family, back when they—when you—" he trailed off, as if unsure of how to continue, then cleared his throat again. "But anyway. I've—Beni's told me enough. You and Beni risked a lot to keep me safe. And—" he laughed quietly. "And I guess I'm saying this wasn't all your fault, okay? And even the parts that maybe were —you were trying to help us."

Savina raised her head and stared at him blankly.

She couldn't make out his expression from across the room, but she was so stunned she wasn't sure she'd have been able to read it anyway.

"You killed the raider," said Joska, her wry voice cutting into the silence. "Without talking to any of the rest of us." She paused a moment, shaking her head. "It was probably stupid. But … Nicolau's right. I can't say blame you, necessarily. Because I'm going to assume you were doing the best you could with what you had. I wish you'd have said something. We could have figured this out between all of us, I'm sure of it. But could-be's won't fuel a ship. So, now that we know what happened, maybe we see if we can work something out."

"You—" Savina was having a hard time forming the words. "I thought you … you've been telling me this whole damn time how I'm a terrible person. Why aren't you damn well gloating?"

There was a moment's silence, then Joska chuckled. "You're a bad one, Savina. I know it, and you do too. But—I've seen how you care for Beni and Nicolau. And you didn't have to come with me to get Rafel, back on the ship. You could have left both of us. But you didn't. Doesn't make the things that you did go away, but—" she shrugged. "I guess what I'm saying is, perhaps you're not as entirely unredeemable as you appear at first glance."

Savina felt dizzy, disoriented. Her head was spinning, and there was an odd nausea in the pit of her stomach.

Where had this sympathy been when she was twelve years old? Where had it been when was crying in the compound, shoulders bleeding from a beating she'd taken? When she started her career as an assassin?

Sympathy, kindness, understanding—what the hell was the use of it, when it all came too late?

"You think I'm not so bad, do you?" she snapped, too angry to care about her words. "Do you know what I am? What Beni and I are? We're Old Believers. Corpus Dei. We're from one of the compounds in the Rim Mountains, the crazies. The ones the Orthodox church wants to wipe out. How do you feel about us now? What do you think about your siblings now, Nicolau?" She was spitting the words out through her teeth, trying to make them hurt. She was trying to shock them, hurt them enough they would hurt her back, because if they did, then the world would make sense again.

When she finished, there was silence in the small cell, for a long, long time.

Savina's heart was pounding, and despite the sickness in her stomach, she felt a vicious, ugly thrill of satisfaction.

Because this, she knew how to deal with. This, she'd grown up with—hate, and fear, and disgust.

"You're Old Believers?" Joska's voice wasn't angry. It wasn't even disgusted, just her normal curiosity, and Savina swore.

"Yes," she snapped.

There were another few moments of silence. At last Joska said, "I … am sorry if I disrespected your beliefs in any way. I haven't met many Old Believers, so if I said or did something offensive—"

Savina stared at her.

Joska stared back.

Savina could see in Joska's face that the woman was just as confused as she was.

"Don't you—doesn't your religion teach you that I'm evil?" Savina asked at last, when it seemed Joska had nothing to say.

Joska was still blinking at her. At last, she raised an eyebrow. "This was—you thought—" she gave a small smile. "I'm sorry, Savina. I thought you'd brought it up because I'd disrespected your faith somehow."

"You—you thought you'd—" Savina stared.

"You thought it would matter to me, for any reason other than that?" Joska's tone was a mixture of mild amusement and faint indignation. "Savina. I hope I haven't given you the impression that I allow bigots on my ship. Myself included. I'm not saying there aren't people who hate Old Believers, and I'm very sorry that you've run into it. But I've never allowed someone with those views to set foot on my ship. And I've never once cared what religion my crew were."

She paused a moment. "Or," she added wryly, "what religion my kidnappers and ship hijackers were, for that matter."

Savina felt her face heat, but she didn't have the mental energy to care.

This had to be part of some plot. Joska had to be telling her a lie, trying to lure her into complacency.

But she'd seen the expression on the woman's face when she'd mentioned her religion. It hadn't been antagonism, or craftiness, or anything but frank confusion.

"Well," volunteered Nicolau, "I was actually looking into—you know, some of the people on the ship were saying that there's a sort of religion where you pray to the spirits of the stars or something." He laughed a little self-consciously. "I don't know much about it, because, I mean, I just heard about it myself—but he said it was an old tradition or something, for sailors. And anyway, I thought about looking into it more, I mean, before …" he trailed off. "But anyway. Don't worry, Savina. You're not the only one who doesn't necessarily believe in the Orthodox Church."

Now it was Savina's turn to stare at him.

He was smiling, as if certain she'd appreciate his revelation. As if … as if this whole exercise had simply been a chance for everyone to share their beliefs.

As if the fact that she was an Old Believer meant—nothing.

"Listen, you idiot," said Rafel gruffly. "Like Joska said. I'm not saying there aren't people who hate Old Believers. I've seen plenty of it myself, in the military. It's never pretty, and some of it is damn ugly. But I told you—Joska doesn't let bigots on her ship. So if that's the worst you've got—if you think the fact that you believe the Mystery has a body is worse than the fact that you damn well held us at gunpoint and stole the captain's ship—" He shrugged.

Savina felt as if someone had hit her in the stomach, and she was still trying to catch her breath.

"I—" she began, then she stopped, because she realized she had no idea what she wanted to say.

Joska shifted from where she'd been sitting up against the wall. "You never actually answered our question, Savina," she said wryly. "But I assume from the fact that we've just been carrying on a conversation that you're not too badly injured."

"No," said Savina automatically, her lips answering without waiting for her brain to catch up. "I'm not hurt."

Joska gave a small sigh of what sounded like relief. "That's good." She paused. "Savina. It may not have escaped your notice that I've never particularly trusted Yuur or her people. And so I may have a way to get us out."

Savina stared at her.

They all stared at her, except for Rafel, who had a smug smile on his face.

"But," Joska continued, "I have no intention of being the reason for a number of unnecessary deaths. So I'm willing to get you and all the rest of us out of this, if I possibly can. But my condition is, you don't kill anyone who doesn't need to be killed."

Savina was still staring, but she managed an innocent grin nonetheless. "I never kill someone who doesn't need to be killed," she said, keeping her voice light.

Joska snorted. "Anyone who I determine doesn't need to be killed. You don't agree to this, Savina, and so help me, I will let all five of us die here."

Savina scowled at the woman, but Joska maintained her usual placid expression, only the quirk of one eyebrow and the almost imperceptible upward tilt in the corner of her mouth showing her amusement.

Savina swore under her breath out of habit. "So, you get us out, and I have to ask your permission before I do anything. What are you, my mother?"

Joska chuckled dryly. "Heaven forbid."

Savina glared.

Joska gave a small shrug. "Your choice, Savina. But I think we've known each other long enough that you know I'm not going to budge on this."

Savina sucked in a long breath through her teeth. "Fine," she snapped. "Fine, I'll ask your permission before I kill anyone. So when there's a knife at your throat, you'd better make sure you answer clearly so there are no misunderstandings before I take care of things."

Joska gave her an amused glance. "I'll make an exception for people who are actively trying to kill one of us."

"That's so very progressive of you," Savina muttered, but her scathing tone was entirely wasted on the captain.

"Fine," she snapped again. "I've bloody well agreed. So get us out of here, then."

Joska stood, and tried without success to reach into a pocket.

"Beni, would you give me a hand here?" she asked.

Beni rose to their feet and made their way over to Joska, and Joska directed them to pull something out of her jacket pocket. A moment later, Beni held up a small object.

"Those are the codes for the door locks. I stole them off one of the yibo when I was out bringing cargo back from the warehouses. Beni, do you know what to do with them?"

"Yes," said Beni, a hint of hopefulness showing through their tone. "If I have the codes, I should be able to get the lock open."

Joska smiled. "I hoped that would be the case."

Savina stared at her. "You stole something? The paragon of virtue stole something?"

Joska gave her a dry look. "If you're looking at me as a paragon of virtue, I'm afraid you're in for a disappointment. I believe that stealing is generally wrong. However, I also believe that locking someone up and keeping them captive against their will is wrong, and under those circumstances, I'm willing to bend a few of my general principles."

Beni was already working on the chip, their face creased in concentration.

"We're not free yet," Joska warned. "That chip might get us out the door. But I understand your friend the government agent is out there waiting for us. That, I haven't got around to solving."

Savina smiled, letting her dimple show. "I'll take care of Reka. As long as you give me permission to take care of her the way I see fit," she added sourly.

"Murder her, you mean," said Joska grimly. She sighed. "I suppose I can't argue with that. As justifiable as her methods may be, if she's actively trying to kill us, you can kill her. But if she's not, you'll leave her alive."

Savina spun on Joska in outrage. "If I leave her alive, the life of everyone here is in danger."

"And if we go to the Chief Justice and explain our position, and the Chief Justice calls Reka off, then none of us are in any danger. At least not until we get back to Colorida, and can stand trial for what we've done. I'm not going to countenance killing someone whose only crime is being good at her job. A job which," she added severely, "is perfectly justifiable and legal, unlike the jobs of some other individuals I know."

Savina glared at Joska, but it was only reflexive at this point—she knew bloody well that the only thing it would do would be to make Joska's mouth quirk up a little more at the corners in amusement.

The cell they were in was like all the other cells in the mob's building—a dark, cave-like structure with a wooden trapdoor above, no ladder. Savina stood under the trapdoor, looking upwards calculatingly.

If Reka was waiting up there, the woman would kill them before they got the trapdoor open so much as a crack.

She needed to find a way to get Reka away from the trapdoor long enough to let them out.

Which meant, unfortunately, that under Joska's stipulations, Savina may not be able to kill her.

For the briefest of moments, a memory flashed in her mind—Reka's face pressed close up against hers, the indifference in her eyes burned away by pure hatred.

It made her heart pound just a little quicker, and she refuse to let herself think about what that might mean. Because she might be stupid, but she wasn't that stupid.

"Wait," she said slowly. "Wait." She turned to the others. "Reka said that her employers will be showing up tonight or first thing tomorrow. I know Yuur. She's going to want to pump Reka for all the information she can get before the raiders get here. So I'm certain she'll ask her to come to a dinner. One of their ceremonial dinners, like they had when we got here. Reka won't be able to refuse, not without risking offending Yuur, and she can't risk that right now, not with us locked up in Yuur's prison." She gave a small, vicious smile. "We'll wait until she's gone. And then, with your kind permission, Joska, I'll kill the yibo guards left behind."

"Only if absolutely necessary," Joska broke in. "I hardly see how killing them is better than killing Reka, and they won't likely be any danger to us once we're out of their territory."

Savina gritted her teeth. "Fine," she snapped. "We tie up and restrain the yibo guards, and hopefully they'll try something so that we can actually kill them so that we can get away without being found out. And then we'll take their weapons, and we'll shoot our way through—"

"Actually," put in Nicolau, "I know a way out the back. They've had me going in and out of there a few times, bringing in cargo. I'll bet we can get out that way without shooting anyone."

Savina glared at him. "Thank you," she gritted out.

The entire damn universe was conspiring to keep her from doing anything she was actually good at. And after what had just happened, she really, really wanted to kill a few people. "Fine, we'll try this back way. But if it doesn't work, we shoot our way out."

Joska was smiling in undisguised amusement. "Fancy that. We've found a peaceful way out of the situation," she observed. "Well done, Savina."

Savina glared at her, then pointedly turned her back.

They waited until the time the dinner would likely be called, then a little while longer. From above, Savina could hear the low murmur of voices, the sounds of footsteps, a stool being pushed back. The heavier human footsteps leaving, although they were still impressively quiet.

Savina again had to fight back the memory of Reka, her hands twisted in Savina's collar as she shoved her up against the wall.

Damn it, she must have an actual death wish.

And then it was quiet, and Savina turned to Beni. "Let's go," she whispered.

Beni turned to her with their familiar smile. "Got it, sis," they whispered back, and for the first time in a long time, Savina felt a familiar, comfortable feeling settling back into her bones—of doing something she knew and was good at with people she trusted.

It had been a long time, and she hadn't realized how much she'd missed it.

28

Alba

The guards brought them to a heavily guarded building, and the guards at the door scanned Alba and Yosip for weapons before they let them in. They were led through sterile, echoing hallways to a bare underground room, damp and cheerless. There was a small cot that had been placed against the wall in one corner, and Feliu was sitting up on it. His face was still wan, but his expression was the familiar stiff irritation she'd grown used to over the last twenty years.

"Madam?" he asked in a hoarse voice as she and Yosip entered. "Do you know the reason we were brought here?"

"Apparently, it's for our safety," said Alba, sarcasm dripping from her tone as she cast a disparaging glanced at the interpreter.

The interpreter nodded respectfully. "We will ensure that your young lady, Ines, is brought back here as well, with your belongings."

Alba gave the yibo a chilly nod, and sat down on one of the small, hard stools.

Her mind spun aimlessly through the day's events.

She had the map. Even if Ines was able to find the plans, though —what good would it do now?

From the look of things, they weren't expected to live through the night.

They'd failed. They'd failed spectacularly, and she wouldn't be able to hold back forever the realization of what that might mean.

The cell door was shoved open, and Ines staggered in. Her arms were full of Alba's and Yosip's personal belongings, her face terrified.

When the door closed behind her, she gave Yosip a mutely pleading stare. She dropped the bundle of goods on the edge of the cot and fumbled among them until she came up with a piece of paper. "Yosip," she said, her voice trembling only a little. "I—I was wondering if maybe you could show me another paper animal. To—to keep my mind off things."

Yosip nodded instantly, standing to take the paper from her. "Come, let's move over beside Feliu. I'm sure he'd be interested in this one."

Once Yosip had settled into a steady rhythm, his hands creasing and re-creasing the paper, tearing and folding deftly, Alba said quietly, "Ines. What is it?"

Ines swallowed hard, and Alba could see now that the girl was trembling. "I—did what you asked. I found out which planet holds the mechanism for opening the portal. I don't know what good it will do us without a map, but I found it."

"That was well done," said Alba, her voice somehow gentle. Even though it hardly mattered now.

"I—but I also overheard the guards talking when they brought me back," Ines whispered, looking up at her. "They were talking about why you'd been moved." She paused, as if gathering her courage. "They—apparently, the price of Cavaco's cooperation is—is your death. And the ship's captain has demanded that he see your body before he goes forward with any final agreements."

There was a long, long silence.

The blood pounding in Alba's ears made her feel dizzy.

Physical danger was not something she was accustomed to. Nor was the way the thought of it froze her muscles, set her heart pounding, her pulse racing, made her breath roughen in her throat.

And after what had happened this morning, there was nothing academic about the threat.

It must have been one of Cavaco's people, then, who she'd shot that morning as she struggled for her life, attempting to hedge their bets by getting rid of her on their own.

"I'm sorry," Ines whispered, sounding on the verge of tears. "I wish I had better news."

Yosip's eyes flicked to Alba's face, searching. "What is Cavaco doing?" he said, almost to himself. "Why kill you? Killing you may give him a political advantage, but I'm not sure how—"

Feliu gave them both a grim look. "Madam," he said in a weak voice. "I've looked very deeply into Cavaco's files. He has … certain interests that rely very heavily on his ability to stay in power in the government. Favours he owes. If he were to fall from power, his influence is not the only thing he would lose. And as I've told you before, Cavaco is a dangerous man to underestimate. He has a reputation from his military days as a man who doesn't take the cautious route if a gamble might give him victory. The proposal that you presented, prior to the portal opening—that would put his influence, his position, his family, perhaps his very life in peril. He's desperate, Madam. And one must never underestimate the actions of a desperate man. Especially one as intelligent as the General."

Yosip nodded gravely. "I've never worked with General Cavaco personally. But from what I know of him, he'd take something like your proposal as an existential threat, and as licence to do whatever it took to defeat it." He paused. "I understand your proposal had significant support?"

"It would have passed. There was no question," said Alba grimly. "I am not accustomed to bring forth proposals until I am certain of my politics."

Yosip nodded thoughtfully. "And I'm sure Cavaco knew that as well as anyone." He paused. "That means Cavaco knew that even if you died out here, there was a high chance he'd lose his power regardless. The citizens' support for military action against the aliens does not necessarily translate into changing the Council's views on whether the Military Committee should remain in power. Even if you were dead, it would be all but inevitable that the proposal be brought up again."

Yosip's hands were still moving, folding and unfolding the parchment, creasing it here and tearing it there, the movements almost unconscious. A figure was taking shape under his fingers, and Alba watched it idly.

"He knows he can't convince the Council, even with you gone. And so instead, he sends his own people along on the diplomatic mission and instructs them to negotiate a separate arrangement. We don't know the details of this arrangement, but we do know it involves a promise of military aid from Cavaco, whether through legal or illegal means, and we know the yibo have promised him something in return." Yosip glanced up at her, catching her eye. "And if he's willing to take this much of a gamble for the yibo's support—"

Alba drew in a quick breath, ice forming in the pit of her stomach. "A coup. He's planning to use the yibo's help to stage a coup." She gave a sharp shake of her head. "It would never work. The people wouldn't accept it, and the military isn't big enough to deal with a large-scale rebellion."

"I—excuse me, Madam Chief Justice, I—" Ines's voice, normally quiet, was now at such a low pitch that Alba could barely make out the words. "I don't think the General needs to convince everyone, necessarily. He … he'd just need a distraction. Something to keep people too busy to worry about politics. He's been stationing soldiers in the Rim Mountains for a long time now, you know that. And there's a lot of discontent back where my family is from. A lot of the settlements are angry at the government already, and even more angry with the military after what happened at Swan River. All he needs to do is start ramping up the military presence on the pretence of preparing for an alien invasion. With how much resentment against the government there is already, that might be enough to spark a rebellion. And if that happened—"

Alba stared at Ines. "If that happened," she finished quietly, "all eyes would be on the rebellion. With the yibo behind him, he could stage a coup without anyone in any position to push back. He could take over the government in a matter of hours."

Ines nodded.

Alba met Yosip's eyes, and saw in them same horror she felt.

She glanced around their small cell, the bare walls and guarded doors, barred windows letting in the only light.

Cavaco would kill her here, on this forsaken alien planet. And then he'd take the government himself. And in one instant, the structures and institutions their people had spent centuries developing would be overturned, countless lives lost. And even if some remnant of humanity survived whatever the yibo had planned, who knew how long it would take to build that back?

"We can't let this happen," said Alba, her voice trembling just a little.

"If you and Ines have guessed correctly," said Yosip, his tone grave, "once the portal has opened, there's no way we'll be able to prevent it."

For a moment there was no sound but the rustle of the paper Yosip was folding between his fingers.

"There's no way, I suppose, to get word back to President Ander?" Alba asked, looking up.

Feliu scowled at her weakly. "Madam. If you've thought a way to get word back through a closed portal, I'm sure we'd all be delighted to hear it."

She stood abruptly. "Don't tell me there's nothing we can do," she snapped. "There has to be something."

Yosip looked up, and there was a weariness in his face. "I'm sorry, Alba," he said quietly. "I'm afraid Feliu is right."

She spun on him, almost relieved to have a target for her helpless anger. "So what's your suggestion, then? We simply let this happen? We have no idea what Cavaco will promise to the yibo in exchange for their help. And if Cavaco is able to take over the government—"

"Madam." Yosip's voice had an unbearable tinge of kindness to it, under the weariness. "I've followed your career, as have most of us on Colorida. You've done great things. But sometimes there's simply nothing to be done."

"There's always something that can be done," she snapped.

As she said the words, she heard their echo in her head—the same words she'd shouted at her father, as a twelve-year-old.

The expression on his face as he looked at her, and then down at the face of her brother, slack and still in the coffin.

If they'd made different choices, if the law had been sensible, if her mother and father hadn't bailed their oldest son out of prison time and again, turned a blind eye as he went deeper and deeper into his addiction. If the system that was supposed to keep criminals locked up hadn't let his supplier out on bail, had found a way to keep him from getting his hands on a pulse weapon.

If her mother and father had forced her brother to stay home, made him accountable for what he'd done. If the laws have been harsher, focused on justice rather than a wishy-washy farce of mercy

—

'If' so many things. So many things that could have been different. So many things that could have changed the result, could have made her memory of her older brother's face one of teasing laughter instead of that still sickly silence, his eyes closed, his face blank and dead.

She'd sworn to herself, at twelve years old, that she'd never use that excuse. She'd never moan that there was nothing she could do to change things. She'd never sit back and hide under the guise of supposed helplessness.

And yet in this case, had she done nothing—had she not tried to remove Cavaco and his dangerous ideology from the seat of decision-making, not tried to find a peaceful solution with the beings on this side of the portal, not suggested this mission to contact them —things could not possibly have gone worse.

She put out a hand and let herself sag against the wall for just a moment.

"Alba?" It was Yosip's voice, and then his hand was placed gently on her shoulder for the second time that day.

And for the second time that day, she didn't try to shake it off, although this time, it was less because of the unexpectedness of the gesture, and more because she no longer had the energy to care.

"Alba," he said again. "You've always been someone whose word has carried a great deal of influence. But you can only change what you can change. You do what you can, and then—" he gave a small shrug. "Then you wait, and hope."

Normally, she would have snapped at him, some cutting remark skilfully crafted to cut to the bone. But now she found herself too weary even for that.

She sank down on the low stool he offered her.

Yosip, after he'd make sure she was seated and comfortable, went to kneel beside Feliu, and soon the two were talking in low tones. On the other side of the cell, Ines sat rubbing her icon between her fingers, eyes closed, murmuring something under her breath.

There was a peace to her face that Alba hadn't expected, not with the circumstances they were in.

"Ines?" she said at last, trying to keep the habitual sharpness from her tone.

Ines looked up, startled. "Yes, Madam Chief Justice?"

"What are you doing?" asked Alba.

Ines gave her a tentative smile. "I'm—I'm praying, Madam. I—I expect you're more practiced at it than I am, since you're the Joint Head of the Council of Orthodoxy. But it—helps me calm down. When I'm scared." She paused, still with that tremulous smile. "I—I used to do it when I came to Vila Nova so Sol for the first time. I couldn't talk to my parents, and—and this made it better. A little." She gave a self-conscious laugh.

Alba just watched her.

Joint Head of the Church. It was funny, she'd hardly thought of the honorary title that came with her government position. She'd seen enough of religion—her fellow Joint Head of the Church was canny and intelligent, but just as much of an inveterate politician as any member of the Council.

Alba certainly knew fewer prayers than Ines did.

She sighed and turned away, a tight knot in her stomach.

It was all well and good for Yosip to talk about letting things happen. He hadn't been the one responsible for dealing with the consequences of every decision, and weighed down with the knowledge that not making a decision was a decision in its own right.

Alba had never simply 'let things happen' in her life.

Perhaps that had been what he was trying to tell her.

"You never thought to ask," Istvay had said.

She hadn't. She'd always been the one in charge. The one making the decisions. And now here she was. Helpless. Forced to sit and watch, while others made the decisions that would affect her life—perhaps end it.

It was a position she was not accustomed to, and it felt … excruciating.

At some point in the evening, the door opened just enough for some food to be shoved through.

They ate in silence.

A weary, resigned exhaustion had seeped through Alba muscles, lodging deep in her chest like a weight. She leaned back against the cell wall, wondering vaguely if their jailers would come to kill them before nightfall, or if they'd be forced to spend the night on the cold floor before being taken out to be shot.

And then there was a small tap on the door.

For a heart-stopping instant, she thought perhaps this was her answer.

But the knock was timid, and much softer than she'd expect from the guards. If they'd bother to knock at all.

She looked up, exchanging glances with Yosip.

They'd already been fed, and the dishes taken away. Perhaps they'd be given cots for the night after all?

Yosip was frowning, but he stepped forward to the door. "Yes?" he asked quietly.

"Madam Chief Justice," a soft voice hissed, the words heavily accented.

Alba frowned as well, pushing herself painfully to her feet. "Yes?" she asked, keeping her voice low.

"Madam Chief Justice, are you inside?"

"Yes, I am," she answered, a little peevishly. As if there was anywhere else she could be.

"Thank the stars." The voice outside sounded relieved. There was a faint clicking, and then the cell door swung open.

In the doorway stood one of the yibo, someone Alba recognized vaguely as one of Harroch's aides. The yibo woman looked supremely uncomfortable, and she was holding a small key.

"Hurry up!" The woman gestured impatiently. "We need to get out of here before the guards come back."

Alba and Yosip stared in frank astonishment.

The aide made an irritated noise. "Listen," she said. "Some of us who were listening to the negotiations believe you have the right of it. Going behind the back of your government in the hope of more favourable terms will be dangerous in the long run. We're not strong enough that we can afford to fight two enemies at once, and I and some of the others would prefer not to make an enemy of your people. You have influence. You must keep this from happening."

Alba just stared. At last, she nodded faintly. "I … will do my best," she said, her voice coming out strange.

The alien tipped her head to one side, her nervous impatience showing through the gesture. "Come on, then. We were able to get the guards distracted, but it won't last long. And if you're found, they'll shoot you. Don't think they won't."

"I harbour no illusions on that front," said Alba grimly. "Ines, Yosip," she said sharply over her shoulder.

Yosip was already standing, and Ines sprang to her feet. She and Yosip helped the groaning Feliu off his cot, and the four of them slipped out of the cell after the nervous yibo, and into the dark corridor beyond.

The aide led them out down a maze of corridors, and finally out into the courtyard, bathed in brilliant moonlight. She peered nervously over her shoulder, then stepped back. "You're on your own now," she said, her voice shaking a little. "You'll have to find your own way out of the city—I can't help you there. But—I hope the best for you."

Alba cleared her throat. "Thank you for your help," she said at last.

The sick ache in her stomach, the feeling of powerlessness, of being unable to do anything other than watch, had faded, and she was almost as grateful for that as for the opportunity to escape itself.

"Stop this from happening. Or at least, speak on our behalf to your government," said the yibo woman, stepping back in the shadows.

"I will do what I can," said Alba.

The woman watched her for a long moment, then tipped her head and disappeared into the darkness.

For a few moments, the ragged group of them stood there staring out into the unfamiliar streets.

"Well," said Yosip quietly. "Shall we, Madam?"

29

Savina

"You're going to have to lift me higher," said Savina through her teeth.

Rafel swore under his breath. "You're no damn lightweight," he grumbled.

Savina glared down at him icily. "I'll have you know," she said. "That I am very happy with my weight."

"Tell that to my back," Rafel muttered.

"I can help," came Nicolau's voice from behind her.

Savina swore again. "Beni, tell our little brother that if he lets that hatch fall on my head, I will personally stab him in the knee."

"Sorry, Savina. I was just trying to help," said Nicolau in an injured tone.

Savina gritted her teeth and ignored him, trying again to find purchase with her feet on the slippery shoulders of Rafel's pilot coat. "What do you do to this thing, grease it every day?" she muttered bitterly.

Rafel grunted as her foot slipped, and his face ended up in the joint of her knee. "Just get up there. You're a world-class assassin. I thought you be able to climb better than this, or at least pull yourself up."

"I'm a world-class assassin because I'm sweet and charismatic, unlike other people I could mention. And that's on purpose, so that I don't have to do things like climb on people's shoulders and pull myself up through a damn trapdoor hatch," she gritted. "If I'd wanted to be an athlete, I would have been a government agent like Reka."

Rafel grunted again, but, her feet scrabbling on his shoulder, Savina managed to catch the tip of the floor with her fingers where Nicolau held the trapdoor cracked open.

"Higher!" she snapped through her teeth. Rafel swore, but she felt the pressure of his hands under her thighs increase, and she pushed off him as hard as she could as Nicolau shoved up on the trapdoor hatch. Rafel stumbled backwards, but this time she caught the edge of the floor with both hands and managed to pull herself up.

Joska stepped forward, bracing the soles of Savina's feet, and Savina kicked off her, sliding up on her belly onto the floor above the trapdoor.

There were two yibo guards. They'd both turned to stare at her, a game of dice forgotten on the floor between them. One of them jumped to his feet, pulling out his weapon, as, with a final wriggle, Savina rolled out onto the floor.

They wouldn't just shoot her—if Yuur had planned to trade her to the raiders, they'd have to be desperate before they'd kill her.

Savina smiled, pushing herself to her feet. "Hello," she said in a soft voice. "Don't move if you want to live."

She had no idea whether or not they understood her words. But the threat in her tone was unmistakable.

"Don't kill them unless you have to," came Joska's sharp whisper from below.

Savina rolled her eyes.

Easy for Joska to say. She wasn't the one trying to do the escaping.

One of the guards reached for their communication device. Savina grabbed a small stool and crossed the room in a few quick strides. Before the panicked guard could call out, she slammed the edge of it into his temple, and he collapsed, groaning. The other guard was scrambling to her feet, lifting her weapon. Before she could bring it to bear, Savina swung the stool upwards, sending the weapon flying from the guard's hand, then swung it again, catching her across the back of the head. The guard slumped to her knees, blinking, and Savina shoved her over with her foot, planting her knee on the guard's neck.

"Either of you move, and I'll crush her windpipe," she hissed. "You know I can do it."

The other guard, who'd rolled over and was reaching for his own weapon, froze.

Savina gave a small smile. "Give me your weapon," she said. "Drop it on the ground and kick it over." She pantomimed the action, and the guard did as he was instructed.

Savina picked it up and straightened, brushing the dust off her knees. She kept the weapon trained on the two as she stepped back. "You can go ahead and shout an alarm," she said in a friendly voice. "And then I'll kill you. Or, you can tie each other up." Again, she pantomimed the action.

The two guards looked at each other, and then one glanced up at Savina hesitantly, miming untying the sash at her waist. Savina tipped her head impatiently, and the guard pulled off the strip of cloth and tied her companion, then, at Savina's impatient gesture, unfastened her companion's sash and looped it around her own wrists. Savina drew a circle in the air with her finger, and the guard turned, her eyes still wide with terror, her hands behind her back.

Savina stepped forward, inspecting the first prisoner's knots, then tied the second guard quickly and efficiently.

"You're smart," said Savina, coming around so the guard could look her in the face again. "You tied him up well. If you hadn't, I would have shot him, and then I would have shot you."

She plucked a knife from the guard's belt and sliced a strip off the woman's tunic, ignoring the whimper of terror, then gagged and blindfolded both guards.

Honestly, killing was a hundred times easier. If she'd had her preference, she'd have left them both dead.

But she could picture the expression on Joska's face. She wouldn't put it beyond the damn woman to sabotage their escape if she did that, or simply refuse to come at all.

She sighed, shaking her head, and crossed back to the open trapdoor.

Nicolau was on tiptoes, straining with all his might to hold the edge of the heavy door ajar, and she took it from him and pulled it back, letting it down as quietly as she could. "You're clear to come up," she called down. "And before you ask, Joska, I didn't kill anyone." She couldn't help a note of bitterness in the words.

Joska chuckled. "Well done, Savina. I'm proud of you."

Sabina scowled, then glanced around the room for something she could use to pull them up.

She ended up tossing down the stool. The cell had been made for people the height of the yibo, and Savina, the shortest human of their group, was several centimetres taller than the tallest of them. With the assistance of the stool, Nicolau was able to hoist himself out easily enough, and then reach down to help the others.

When everyone was out and brushing themselves off, Joska glanced around, surveying the guards. They both had bruises rising where Savina had hit them, and one of them had blood running down the side of her face, but they were unmistakably alive.

Joska nodded without comment, but Savina could still see that hint of amusement in her eyes.

"Nicolau, you know your way out from here?" the captain said.

Nicolau nodded. His face was paler than usual, but he was wearing an expression of stubborn determination, and it was clear he had no intention of being the first one to show fear.

Savina glanced around the room once more, and then her eyes caught on a small bench in the corner.

There was a jacket thrown casually over it, and she recognized it at once as Reka's.

She was unprepared for the surge of fury and hatred and— something else, something hot and disquieting, something that reminded her of the look on Reka's face as she'd pulled Savina to her feet, the pressure of her forearm against Savina's throat, the ease with which she'd held Savina still, even as Savina twisted and struggled.

The moment Savina had finally gotten through that icy indifference. The flash of anger in those cold eyes.

"I'll catch up," said Savina, a small, vicious smile forming on her lips. "I'm going to leave a little surprise for Reka."

Joska raised an eyebrow. "Savina. She's a government agent. I doubt even you could set a booby-trap that would—"

"Don't worry," said Savina, widening her eyes innocently. "This isn't for her. This is for whoever comes in with her, and finds us gone."

She smiled, pulled a knife from her belt, and then reached into the front of her tunic. She sliced off a scrap of edging from her bra as Nicolau averted his eyes, his cheeks going dark with embarrassment. Then she crossed to Reka's jacket and dropped the scrap of lace somewhere where it would be obvious both what it was, and that had it had been left on purpose.

She rummaged in Reka's pocket and pulled out a writing stick and paper. She scrawled, *'Reka, my love. Thank you. I will happily pay my debts tonight—in a hotel room, or in a back room, or on the ground in the alley, however you want to take it. Be quick, my obsession—I don't know how long I'll survive without seeing you.'*

She pulled out one of her needle-blade knives from a hidden pouch in her jacket and pinned it through the paper and the lace of her bra strap and into Reka's jacket.

Then she turned back to the others and gave them the full benefit of her dimpled smile. "I'm ready."

Joska gave a low whistle. "Savina. You're downright vicious."

Savina smirked. "I'd like to see her explain that to her employers." She blinked innocently. "A sweet girl like me, I wouldn't drag my reputation through the mud like that unless I was very, very in love."

Joska shook her head, but she had a look on her face that was almost impressed.

Nicolau led them quickly through the hallways of the safehouse. Once, they rounded a corner and Nicolau almost ran into a startled mobster. The yibo stared at them for a moment, then opened his mouth to call out, his expression turning to one of terror.

Savina shot him.

He vaporized.

She shoved the pistol back into her pocket and glared at Joska. "Permission?" she asked icily.

Joska sighed.

Savina didn't have to kill anyone else before they got up to the street, which in retrospect was probably a good thing. The way her mood was at the moment, though, she would have liked to kill a few people just to take the edge off.

The streets were darkening with twilight, the moons beginning to peek over the rim of the buildings. The air was still heavy with the wet, sticky heat of a jungle evening, the cool of the night not yet penetrating the thick warmth of the day.

"Where to now?" asked Savina in a whisper.

"The diplomatic compound," said Joska quietly. "From what I've picked up, the others are being housed in the government building near the centre of the city. We'll go there and turn ourselves in, say we're humans who just recently escaped the jungle if you'd like. I believe from there we'll be able to convince Alba that the better part of wisdom, in this instance, is letting bygones be bygones until we can escape this place. You do have a unique skill set, which could come in useful to everyone here." She paused a moment, clearly reluctant to continue. "And," she said at last, "if you could promise me that there would be no killing—I may find I lose control of my ship again on the trip home, before you're able to be taken back to Colorida in restraints." She shot a meaningful glance at Savina. "But that would only be a possibility if you could assure me there would be no deaths as a result."

Savina stared at her. At last, she shook her head.

Joska would never cease to surprise her.

They made their quiet way through the back alleys, Savina in the lead. She knew the streets well. She'd spent enough time on them, on her jobs. But it turned out Beni, who'd mapped out the jobs, knew them even better, and after about half a standard hour, Beni took Savina's place in the lead.

The streets were abnormally busy, and Savina frowned as the city moved around them. The people she'd expect on the streets—the petty thieves, the civilians from the poorer parts of town heading home after a long day of work, or heading somewhere they could intoxicate themselves enough to forget about their troubles for another day, weren't present. Those that were wore frightened looks, and walked with the swift, furtive movements of prey, rather than predators.

"What's going—" Savina began, then stopped, swearing under her breath. "It's because the raiders are coming," she finished through her teeth. "The whole city will be in an uproar if the rumours got out. These idiots are terrified of raiders."

Joska nodded grimly. "They'll be looking for anyone who sticks out. This isn't an ideal time for an escape."

"Well, I guess we could have stayed behind to get eaten," Savina shot back. "Come on."

The small party continued on down the streets, slipping through the dark alleys. Beni was in the lead, Savina behind them with the stolen weapon in hand. Nicolau took up the rear, as the most likely to be able to intimidate anyone following.

Savina glanced up at the sky as they crept along. The moons had risen higher, casting more light than she would have liked. Still, if her ploy had worked, it would be some time before Reka would be able to come after them. That was the best they could hope for, at this point.

And then they were there, and Savina stopped in shock.

The buildings in front of them were intricate, beautiful, ostentatious in the extreme.

They were also lit up like the Festival of the Dead.

Rafel swore. "Either they're having a hell of a party, or the diplomatic corps has managed to get themselves into trouble.”

A small group of yibo guards jogged past, and Savina and the others ducked back quickly into the mouth of an alley, concealed in the shadows.

In the moonlight, the guards’ faces were grim, and they all had their weapons drawn.

“I’m guessing the second option,” murmured Joska.

“What we do now?” Nicolau whispered. He looked worried, and despite everything, the look made something in Savina’s chest tighten with protectiveness. Even though her baby brother was at least twenty centimetres taller than she was, and probably outweighed her by ten kilos.

“Joska, this was your idea,” she said grimly. “What do you suggest we—”

A shout came from behind them.

Savina turned slowly.

Behind them, at the far entrance to the alley, stood another group of yibo guards, their weapons pointed at the humans.

“Permission?” Savina whispered sarcastically.

Joska sighed, and Savina chose to take that as a ‘yes.’

Savina shot the guards’ captain as he raised his gun, then shot the two closest behind him, and then put a knife through the throats of two others, grabbed the last, shoved them up against the wall, and slit their throat. She turned back to the others and smiled prettily, feeling a faint satisfaction at the sick look on Joska’s face.

“You did say I had permission,” she said.

“So I did,” murmured Joska. She sounded even more sick than she looked.

“They were about to kill us,” said Savina. “You may as well stop feeling guilty over it.”

"If only it was as easy as that," muttered Joska wryly. "Working with you feels like how I'd imagine summoning a demon would feel."

Sabina smiled at her. "Don't worry, it gets easier with practice."

Joska shook her head, pulling her gaze from the massacre. "Well, if the diplomatic party is in this much trouble, I doubt us finding them is going to do anyone any good," she said. "I suppose we'll just have to—"

"Wait," said Nicolau, frowning. He moved to the front of the alley and peered out into the open boulevard surrounding the diplomatic building.

"What is it?" Beni whispered, moving to stand beside him.

"There are people there, in the shadows," he whispered. "They look human."

Savina, Joska, and Rafel came to peer over his shoulder.

Sure enough, in the shadows of the high compound wall, Savina could make out a small party of figures, their shapes unmistakable even in the dim light.

"Savina!" said Nicolau, peering closer. "I know who that is!"

Savina swore quietly. "So do I," she muttered. "Joska, you'd damn well better be right about Alba not killing us."

She turned back. "Beni, pull up your scanner and let me know if I'm going to get into any trouble. In the meantime, I'm Vina to the rest of you, until we know what they want."

Then she slipped out of the alley and towards the small band of figures.

They looked up in alarm at her approach, and an old man, his face creased with smile-wrinkles, stepped forward. He was holding a pulse pistol, his grip steady, and beside him, a girl who looked younger than Nicolau, skinny and frightened with huge eyes and a cloud of black hair puffed in a soft halo around her head, held another.

"Don't shoot," whispered Savina. She could kill them easily before they had a chance to, but that wasn't likely to start things off on a happy note. "We're survivors from the ship as well. If you come with us, we may be able to keep you safe."

"And may I ask who you are?" The voice was old, and cracked with exhaustion, but there was an imperious note to it that told Savina exactly who the speaker was.

A shiver of something, half fear and half anticipation, buzzed through Savina's body as the woman stepped forward.

She managed looked regal even in the simple yibo shift, and there was the weary look to her face of someone who hadn't slept well in some time.

Alba Espina.

All it would take is one quick move, a throwing knife sent on its way, and then …

But … she could already hear Joska's voice. *"We need them, Savina, if we want to get out of this mess alive."*

Maybe that was no longer a possibility. But until she heard their story, she wouldn't know.

Savina gritted her teeth and forced herself to smile. "We were part of your group earlier, but we were kidnapped by some of the yibo before we got on the city transport. We escaped and came here to join the rest of you, but it looks like—"

"We may not be the ideal ones to join forces with," said Alba dryly. "We were planning on leaving, ourselves."

"But we've found a way to understand the yibo language," said the young girl, her voice trembling, her expression eager. "We could help you with that, at least."

Savina studied her carefully.

She didn't believe, honestly, that what Joska said was true—if Alba had any idea who Savina was, she would almost certainly be taken prisoner, and killed as soon as Alba could spare the time and resources.

But understanding the yibo language, and knowing what this diplomatic party had found out—all of it was important. All of it would help.

And there was no reason Savina couldn't simply kill the woman later.

"I'm so glad we ran into you, then," Savina said breathlessly. "We can help each other get out." She gave her widest, most innocent smile. "My name is Vina."

Alba and the old man exchanged a glance, and Alba nodded. "Very well, Vina," she said briskly. "Lead the way."

30

Aran

Alcohol, it appeared, affected yibo in much the same way it did humans. The translator in Aran's wavelink didn't translate the slur in their words, but the way the guards became progressively more talkative, and then, eventually, more and more maudlin, was familiar enough to make Aran and Istvay grin at each other in the darkness of their cell.

When the chatter had finally subsided into slow voices that were by this point slurred enough that the translator could only hazard a guess at what the guards were saying, Istvay gave Aran a quick nod.

Aran pulled Ani down from his shoulder and tickled her gently under the chin. "Hey there, beautiful," he whispered. "Are you ready?"

Ani gave an affectionate little chirrup and nuzzled into his hand, and he grinned despite himself.

Either Ani had sensed the urgency of what they were doing, or she was feeling cooperative. Either way, it was only a matter of minutes before there was a steaming hole in the walls of the prison, and a few minutes more until it was big enough to crawl through.

The acid, of course, would eat straight through skin, flesh, and bone if it got onto them, so Aran pulled off his much-abused jacket and tossed it over the spot they'd have to crawl over.

"Better be quick," he whispered to Istvay as he slithered through. "It'll only take a few seconds to melt."

Istvay, who was following close behind him, only grunted.

Both of them made it through before the first corrosive hole appeared in the jacket. Aran hesitated, but it was probably too far gone to be of any use now. He'd just have to find himself a new one.

"Come on," hissed Istvay.

The two guards were slumped against the wall of the small room outside the cell. One of them was still blinking her eyes slowly, the flask clutched between two loose fingers, but each blink took longer than the last, and it was less than a minute before her eyes fell shut completely, and she tipped over to join her companion snoring peacefully against the wall.

Istvay crept carefully to the unconscious guards and slipped their ID cards from around their necks. They handed one to Aran, then tapped their own against the door lock. It clicked open, and the two of them slipped out, closing it behind them, into the brightly lit corridors of the prison.

After a couple of wrong turns, and more than a couple near misses, they reached the passageway leading out to the courtyard.

A guard rounded the corner. His eyes went wide, and then Istvay stepped forward and landed a clean punch in the centre of his face. He staggered back, and Istvay hit him with an elbow to the jaw, then caught him neatly as he crumpled. They lowered him to the floor, clipped on a restraint, and shoved a gag into his mouth, then turned to Aran, grinning.

Aran tried very hard not to focus on how incredibly attractive

Istvay looked with their knuckles bruised and that crooked, mischievous grin on their face.

Istvay winked, and Aran almost suffered a cardiac arrest.

"Come on," Istvay whispered, turning away, and Aran forced his mind back to the more practical problem of getting out of the damn prison alive.

There was heavy security at the door, and the two of them hung back for a moment in the shadows.

"Ani?" Aran whispered, pulling her from his shoulder. "Do you want to play?"

She chirped, and nuzzled her bulbous body into the crook of his elbow.

"Alright, sweetheart," he whispered.

He picked up the gun Istvay had taken from the prone guard, took a deep breath, and stepped out into the corridor.

There was a moment of frozen shock.

"Ani," Aran whispered. "Chase."

She gave a little wriggled of excitement and launched herself off his shoulders, spreading her skin flaps so she soared across the open entranceway.

There was a moment of stunned silence.

And then the yibo turned and scattered like ants whose hill had been stepped on by an antbear.

Aran grinned, and beckoned to Istvay.

Ani had landed, and she gave Aran a questioning chirrup, staring at him piteously with her bulbous eyes.

He sighed. "I'm coming to get you!" He started after her, and she scuttled up the wall, spread her skin flaps, and launched herself toward the opposite wall.

Alarms began sounding, sirens wailing as someone finally realized what was happening. The guard in charge of the door gate was huddled behind the counter, trembling, but he'd managed to hit both the lock and the alarm.

Istvay started towards him. The guard jumped up as Istvay sprinted across the open floor, but Istvay vaulted over the counter and knocked the gun from the yibo's hand, then turned him around and shoved him, stumbling, out onto the floor.

He landed on his face and pushed himself up on his elbows. Then he noticed Ani, scrambled to his feet, and fled.

From down the corridors, Aran could hear the sound of running feet.

This entire place would turn into a damn gun battle in a moment here.

"Alright, Ani, you win!" he called, trying to make his voice sound light and cheerful, instead of on the verge of panic.

Behind the counter, Istvay fumbling with the buttons. "It should be somewhere in here—" they muttered. Then they swore, rolling their eyes and straightening. "There's a facial scanner or something, the ID won't work unless—"

Aran glanced around quickly, then snatched one of the guards huddled in the corner and dragged her over to Istvay. Istvay looked the struggling guard up and down, then snatched the card around her neck and held it to the device. It flashed green, then orange, and Istvay grabbed the yibo's face and shoved it against the screen.

The light flashed green again, and the doors to the jail slowly slid open.

"Go!" shouted Istvay, and Aran grabbed Ani, bundled her onto his shoulder, and followed Istvay out through the gates just as the yibo whose face Istvay had used to open the gates hit the controls.

The gates slammed shut, almost catching Aran's sleeve as he slid through, and then he and Istvay were out into the courtyard and running for their lives.

"This way," Aran hissed, grabbing Istvay's arm and jerking them after him. The two of them sprinted down the wide walkways between the buildings as guards shouted after them, yelling into their communication devices. It was obvious the guards had heard about Ani, because no one seemed anxious to get too close. But it would only be a matter of time before there were enough of them to hem Aran and Istvay in, Ani notwithstanding.

The prison walls loomed ahead of them, and Aran put on a final burst of speed, dragging Istvay behind him. Istvay's laboured breathing hissed in Aran's ears, and his friend stumbled once or twice as they ran, and the ever-present knot in Aran's stomach grew a little bigger.

Two years ago, Istvay would have been the one outrunning Aran.

He didn't have much time. He needed the cure, because Istvay didn't have much time.

When the two of them reached the walls, Istvay bent over, gasping, and cupped their hands, bracing themself. Aran stepped into their palms in a practised motion, and Istvay straightened as Aran jumped, flinging him upwards. They'd judged the distance well —Aran's fingers just caught one of the decorative mouldings on the top of the wall, and he pulled himself up by his fingertips, grunting with the effort. He got his elbow on the top of the wall, then scrambled the rest of the way up, turning quickly.

Below him, Istvay had straightened and turned, their back to the wall, facing the approaching yibo guards.

"Stay back!" Aran shouted, although he knew they wouldn't understand his words. "Ani, watch Istvay."

Ani gave a reluctant grumble, but swung down from his shoulder, catching herself along the way with her tentacles on the sheer wall to land in front of Istvay, hissing.

The guards drew back, and Aran reached into his pouch and yanked out a length of rope.

"Istvay!" he shouted.

Istvay glanced up, and Aran tossed the rope. Istvay grabbed it as Aran fastened it to the moulding on the wall top and pulled themself up, sweat standing out on their face at the effort. Ani swarmed up the wall after Istvay and reached the top before them, wasting no time in scrambling back onto Aran's shoulder, grumbling. Aran grabbed Istvay's hand as soon as it was in reach and pulled them the rest of the way up, then yanked in the rope and dropped it down on the other side of the wall.

Already, guards were swarming through the open gate, but it would take them a few moments to reach where the rope had landed.

"Ready?" Aran whispered, grinning a little in spite of himself.

Istvay nodded, and the three of them, Ani perched firmly on Aran's shoulder, slid down the rope almost quickly enough to burn the skin of Aran's hands, and dropped onto the street below.

He and Istvay brushed themselves off and took off down the street at a dead run.

The hue and cry after them faded quickly. He and Istvay were unfamiliar with the city, and so they probably weren't following any sort of logical route—just trying to get as far the hell away from the government compound as they could.

"Do you think Alba and the others are alright?" panted Istvay as they ran.

Aran give a quick shake of his head. "I have no idea. But she's smart. I'm sure she'll be able to take care of herself."

The streets grew dirtier and narrower as they ran, the buildings more dilapidated. Every so often they saw a cluster of yibo, but their movements were furtive, their expressions terrified.

"What's happening?" Aran asked over his shoulder.

Istvay shrugged, too breathless to comment.

"Where to, then?"

"Doesn't matter," gasped Istvay. "We'll reach the force-field eventually if we head in a straight line. Then we'll make our way around to the nearest gate. Unless you managed to get a city map, that's the best we can do."

There were more people in the streets now, but they seemed to be trying to get away from something, heading back towards where Aran and Istvay had come from.

Aran looked around uneasily. "Not sure if this is the direction we want," he panted.

Istvay gave a tight nod. "Maybe you're right. Turn due north then, we'll go that way. I'm pretty sure the city gates we came in on were on the north side of the city anyways."

Aran nodded.

They both slowed to a walk, more cautious about being seen, and crept along the alleys, keeping to the shadows.

Whatever was happening in the city, it was clearly enough that the yibo were fully focused on it—no one seemed to have attention to spare for two humans. But it wouldn't last forever. Eventually, the prison guards would find their trail, and then it would only be a matter of time.

They had to be out before then.

The first set of guards found them maybe ten minutes later. There were half-a-dozen of them, clearly following a sensor, because their footsteps followed Aran and Istvay's winding track unerringly.

Aran exchanged glances with Istvay and pulled a tranq dart out of his pouch, shoving the electric tranqs at Istvay.

The guards rounded the corner to the alley where Aran and Istvay were crouched, and paused.

"Come out," she called, her words heavily accented, but understandable. "Come out, and we won't hurt you, we'll just take you back to where you can be safe. Tonight is not the night to be out in the streets."

There was unmistakable fear in her voice.

Aran glanced at Istvay, then raised the blowpipe to his lips and straightened warily, just enough to get a clear view of the guard, silhouetted in the entrance to the alley.

He was well practised—three guards had been pricked by the tiny darts before any of them noticed him standing there. The first guard whirled, raising her weapon, as two of her companions slumped to the ground and a third swayed.

Aran got off one more dart, and then Istvay jumped forward, slapping electric tranqs onto the remaining two guards. The guards collapsed, and Aran jabbed them quickly with tranq darts. The moment their eyes fluttered shut, he knocked the electric tranqs off and shoved them back into his pouch.

Istvay looked at him questioningly.

He grimaced. "Emeric used one of those on me back on the ship," he said shortly. "Hurts like hell."

Istvay nodded with a small, fond smile, and then the two of them grabbed the guards' weapons, shoved them into their belts, and started off down the street again.

"It won't take long for them to figure out where we are after that," Aran whispered. "Things are going to get more exciting than we can handle pretty soon here."

Istvay give a terse nod. Their face was grim, and Aran realized with a start that they were shaking with exhaustion.

"Istvay," he said. "We need to take a break. Catch our breath."

Istvay's wry smile told him they knew exactly what he was doing, but they didn't protest, just slumped back against the wall, breathing heavily.

"How—how are you doing?" Aran asked in a low voice.

Istvay shrugged irritably. "Hardly matters, does it? I'll be doing worse if Emeric gets his hands on us."

Aran nodded, but he watched them in concern. They were slumped against the wall with the kind of weariness that generally would have taken a long day of exertion to provoke.

When Istvay looked like they were recovered enough to keep moving, Aran straightened, and the two of them started forward again, moving as silently as they could.

Aran had been right—it wasn't long before they began to see more and more guards. Thankfully, though, as long as they stayed to the alleys, the rest of the yibo hardly seemed to pay them any mind.

It was … an unsettling thought. Aran still wasn't certain how these aliens were so familiar with humans, but he had the strong impression that whatever it was, it wasn't something he'd be happy to know about.

Still, they'd have time to worry about that particular problem once they were outside the city gates.

Footsteps clattered in a run down the streets behind them, following their trail.

He and Istvay exchanged glances, and Aran nodded, yanking a detonator out of his pouch.

"Ready?" he whispered. Istvay gave a grim nod.

Aran waited until the guards were almost close enough to see them even in the shadows, then he tossed the detonator to land in the streets behind the guards.

It went off with a soft *pop* and a flash of light, and the guards turned on instinct. By the time they turned back, Istvay was already there, and dropped two of the yibo with electric tranqs. Aran tossed his bolas at a third, snarling her legs and bringing her down, and shot two more with tranq darts. Istvay disabled the final guard with another electric tranq.

The two of them disarmed the guards, retrieved the electric tranqs, and ran.

Aran could recognize landmarks now. They were almost at the edge of the city.

And then, booming through the city streets, presumably over some sort of amplifier system, came a voice so loud it startled Aran into stillness. Istvay stopped just in time to keep from running into him.

"This is an emergency message," Aran's wavelink translated. "Please pay close attention, as your very lives, and the survival of our city itself, may depend on it."

Aran and Istvay turned to look at each other.

"What the hell—" Aran began.

"A group of humans have escaped from where they were being held in government cells. They intended to betray us to the raiders. As we speak, there are raider ships approaching the city. The humans plan to let them in. If you see humans, you must detain them or kill them. They cannot reach the city gates."

Aran and Istvay stared at each other in wordless dismay.

"This has to be Emeric's doing," Istvay growled softly. "Damn him to hell."

Already the people in the streets were looking around them in alarm, eyes full of mistrust and suspicion.

"There!" Aran's wavelink translated in a pleasant voice as a yibo caught sight of him, and he dived to one side as a shot flared over his head.

Istvay yanked him to his feet, and the two of them took off down the alley at a dead run. But from behind them, Aran could hear the murmur of dozens of voices into communicators, alerting the government guards to their location.

"Dammit," Aran muttered as the two of them ran. "One of these days, I'm going to have a long talk with Emeric."

"You won't be the only one," Istvay panted.

The city force field loomed ahead of them through the alleys, and Aran let out a quick breath of relief.

And then Istvay slowed. "Aran," they whispered, their voice tense.

The street in front of them, where the alley came out, was crowded with soldiers.

He turned slowly.

The alley behind them, as well.

"I think they've caught us," said Istvay. "There's too many of them. Not even Ani can get us out of this one."

31

Alba

Alba watched the young woman in front of her suspiciously as the group of them started down the streets, moving as quickly as they were able.

Ines, to her credit, hadn't mentioned that the translator device was something she could give them outright. So whoever this girl was leading them to meet, they'd be motivated to keep the diplomatic party alive, at least for now.

And now that she looked at the girl, Alba realized she did look somewhat familiar—she'd either seen her on the ship, or in the group of survivors after they'd landed.

But she'd worry about that once they were out of the city.

Right now, they needed all the help they could get.

She recalled the small map tucked into her retinal screen.

The thought of what she'd have to do with that information still made her sick. But there was no way around it. There were many, many more lives than just their own hanging on their escape tonight.

Perhaps the fate of the entire Joias System.

The girl led them to a small group of people huddled in the alley.

Two of these she did recognize—the woman named Joska, and a tall, auburn-haired young man she was quite sure she'd seen on the crew of the diplomatic ship.

"Let's go," whispered Vina. "This is Alba Espina. And her friends have technology that translates the yibo language. They promised to show us once were all safe outside the city."

Alba didn't miss the sharp look Joska shot the girl, but the woman didn't say anything, just nodded and gestured them forward.

"The streets are a mess right now," said Vina. "I don't know what's going on, but we'll have to stay out of sight as much as we can."

It was quickly apparent that the girl hadn't been lying. The streets were crowded with panicked yibo.

Ines had gone back to help Feliu, and Alba noticed with some amusement that the young crewman had gone to assist her, and that he seemed somewhat more interested in Ines than he did in the old clerk.

"We need to move faster than this," said Joska over her shoulder. "I don't know what happened back there, but I'm guessing they'll have people after you as soon as they find out you're missing."

"And what exactly do you suggest?" snapped Alba. She gestured over her shoulder at Feliu. "Shall we simply leave the injured to fend for themselves?"

Joska's face softened a bit. "I'm sorry, Madam Chief Justice," she said quietly. "I know this isn't ideal. But if we don't figure something out, he'll die along with the rest of us."

She moved back to speak with the struggling trio, and Alba heard Feliu's irritated voice insisting he'd be fine, and he could move faster if they'd just give him a moment.

"Alright," said Vina. "Let's go." Her voice was sharp with

impatience.

In the distance, they could make out the shouts of the yibo guards. Alba and Yosip exchanged grim glances.

How long would these people be willing to stick with them once the guards caught up?

Joska caught their look and shook her head. Her expression was grim, but there was a trace of amusement in her voice. "We're in this together now. We won't leave you behind, guards or no. Come on."

They staggered on.

Alba's legs ached, her muscles burning with the unaccustomed exertion, but she forced herself to keep moving. Everything hurt, and she was exhausted enough that, had it not been for the copy of the small map in her retinal screen, she might have considered simply turning herself in.

At last, though, the city gates were ahead of them, visible in the distance through the buildings.

She breathed a shaky sigh of relief.

And then, over the city amplifiers, a voice shouted out in the yibo dialect, the cheerful translation by Alba's AI almost jarring in contrast.

"Can you understand them? What are they saying?" asked Vina in a sharp whisper.

Alba frowned and translated.

She didn't miss the sudden tension in the girl's face at the mention of raiders.

"There's a guarded checkpoint ahead. Once we're past it, we have a clear shot at the city gates," said Joska quietly.

Vina stepped up beside the woman and shot her a glance that carried just a hint of smugness, and Alba could see Joska's face tighten, just a little.

"With your kind permission, Joska," the girl began, but Yosip, who'd been watching down the street ahead of them, shook his head. "Please, Vina. Let me."

Vina glared at him, but Joska shot the girl warning look. "Go ahead," Joska said, and Yosip stepped forward.

He reached the guards, and Alba tensed, waiting for the yibo to spin and shoot him. But instead, Yosip touched the man's shoulder. "Kaar," he said in a quiet voice.

The guard spun, then his face relaxed as he saw who it was.

"Yosip. What are you doing here?"

"There are people trying to kill us. I'm sorry to ask this, but could see your way clear to looking for us over there for a few moments?"

The guard looked at Yosip, then back at the others, indecision clear on his face. From the corner of her eye, Alba could see Vina tighten her grip on her pistol.

And then the yibo man nodded. "Alright. But be quick." He stepped out into the street and beckoned his people after him, and they trooped off down an alley.

Vina was staring at Yosip in blank astonishment, and now it was Joska with the hint of a smirk in her expression.

When the entrance to the alley was clear, Yosip beckoned them, and they slipped hurriedly through.

And then they were standing in a narrow side-street, peering out into the broad boulevard that led to the city gates.

Joska looked almost weary with relief. "We made it," she said quietly. "I wasn't sure we would." She paused. "Alright. We'll have to —"

Whatever she'd been about to say was cut off by a bloodcurdling scream from one of the guards at the gate.

There were more screams, and then yibo were streaming from

their posts, running wildly into the city in panic.

Alba tensed, and even Yosip's expression was tight with worry.

"What—" Ines began.

And then something hit the force-field, and it shuddered. It shuddered again, and then it ripped apart, the gateway torn open as if by a giant hand.

On the other side of the gate, a ship steamed in the cool of the night air. It was blood red, spiky and angular, and clearly designed for war. And in front of the ship stood a band of aliens the likes of which Alba had never seen before.

They, like the yibo, were humanoid, but taller and more powerfully built than a human, and all of them wore long hair hanging down their backs, some down to the backs of their knees. Their features were as varied as humans, perhaps, but with blood-red eyes, and sharp, prominent canine teeth that were visible when they smiled.

And Alba realized, abruptly, why smiling on this world was considered a threat.

The newcomers' clothing was dark, a loose shirt and trousers that would blend easily into the shadows, and they moved with the smooth confidence of an apex predator.

Beside Alba, Vina gave a choked swear. She'd gone deathly pale.

Joska, too, looked worried. "Vina?" she asked in a low voice

Wordlessly, Vina nodded. "It's them," she whispered.

"It's who?" Ines whispered back.

"It's … another type of alien. Raiders, the yibo call them. They … hunt humans," Nicolau said in a low voice.

Alba almost staggered as the implications of this new development hit her.

The way Harroch had looked when he talked about another

sapient species. The way he'd squirmed when asked what had taken down the portal. The way the yibo had always seemed frightened of something outside their gates, the way Harroch said developments had forced his hand.

"Madam? Are you alright?" Yosip whispered.

"New plan," said Joska, turning abruptly. Her face was grim. "We have to get out of here, now. Nicolau, you—"

"Hello, humans," came a low, rich voice from behind them, accented differently than the yibo tones Alba had grown accustomed to.

Slowly, Alba turned.

One of the newcomers was leaned up against the wall of the alley behind them. There was a lazy smile on the creature's face, and a weapon in its hand, but it didn't look like it thought it would need to use it. "You took some hunting to find," the creature said, turning its attention to Vina. There was something almost indulgent in its voice, a parent humouring a child.

Or perhaps the better analogy, Alba thought, was a farmer grinning at the antics of a piglet she planned to slaughter.

"We've found her," the alien called.

Alba glanced over her shoulder.

The rest of the raiders had come in through the gates, and the group of them stood at the other end of the alley, watching the humans with an expression that was unmistakably hungry.

"Savina," their leader said. "How nice of you to bring enough for all of us."

32

Aran stared at the crowd of guards ahead of them, his heart pounding oddly in his chest.

This couldn't be happening. They couldn't have been captured just when he'd thought they'd finally got away.

"Istvay," he whispered. "Maybe if Ani—"

Istvay shook their head. "It looks like the yibo are more afraid of the raiders even than they are of Ani," they said grimly. "And they think we're going to sell them out, thanks to our friend Emeric."

Aran closed his eyes, trying to steady his breath.

This couldn't be happening. This absolutely couldn't be happening.

Istvay was dying. And whether Aran was killed here or taken back to the yibo prison, he wouldn't be able to do anything to help his friend.

He'd never wanted to die. But it had never been the thing that scared him the most. This was what scared him the most. And this was the second time tonight that he'd thought he'd lost it forever, but this time it was for real …

There was a hand on his shoulder, the weight of it grounding him.

He drew in a deep breath. "I'm … sorry, Pishti," he whispered. "If I'd listened to you, if we'd got out sooner—"

"Aran. Don't be an idiot."

Aran managed a small smile, and his heart broke all over again as he looked at his best friend, who he loved. Who he'd always loved.

This would be a hell of a lot easier if Istvay would just be a jerk about it.

Istvay glanced back into the alley, hesitating. "Listen," they said at last, quietly. "We can't get out of this, not both of us together like this. But if one of us could get to the escape pod, bring it back, we still may be able to get away. So—" they seemed to be bracing themself. "So you run. I'll hold them off while you get out."

Aran stared at his friend, too shocked even to speak.

"I can't do that!" he said at last, when he'd regained his power of speech. "I'm not going to leave you here in the middle of a group of soldiers who want to kill you. Who the hell do you think I am? You go first, I'll find a way to follow with Ani."

Istvay shook their head. "Aran." Their voice was fond, and a little sad. "Aran, I—" they hesitated, then looked down, as if they couldn't bear to meet his eyes. "I—don't think I'd be able to make it through the jungle back to the pod anyway," they said at last, quietly.

Aran stared at them, feeling sick to his stomach.

He could see now the way their legs trembled, how their breath still hadn't steadied even though they'd stopped running several minutes ago.

"I'm sorry," Istvay mumbled. "I—I'm sorry. This—this is the only way it'll work."

"I could carry you," Aran began, but Istvay was already shaking their head. They took him by the shoulders and turned him around so he was looking directly into their eyes.

"Listen to me. I know we haven't been at our best these last few weeks. But—" they paused, and swallowed hard. "But Aran." they hesitated again. "A few days ago, when you were angry with me, you … you said you didn't need a caretaker. And you're right. I thought I was protecting you. I thought I knew better than you did what you needed. And I was trying to pretend I was fine so you wouldn't worry, which was stupid, because I knew damn well you were worried, and you were right to be. I haven't been fine in a long time. But I—I think I finally understand. I finally listened when you told me how much it would hurt you if I was hurt. If I was killed. And Aran." There was something aching and vulnerable in their voice.

"Aran, if you don't believe anything else about me, please believe that I don't want to see you hurt. Please believe that I would do anything to keep you from getting hurt." They were still looking into his eyes, clearly fighting the impulse to look away at the confession, and Aran's heart stuttered painfully.

Istvay wanted him to leave them. They said they finally understood, but they wanted him to leave them to get captured while he ran off with Ani.

"Please." They were still looking into his eyes, their expression pleading. "I don't mean to sacrifice myself to save you. I promise. It's just—I can't make it like this. Get the pod, come back. Fire off a flare so I know you're out there, and I will find a way to meet you. I swear it. I just—I need you to trust me, one more time."

There was something in Istvay's voice, in the way they looked at Aran, that almost made Aran choke, and he found himself nodding.

Because in the end—if he couldn't trust Istvay, and Istvay couldn't trust him, what was the point of all this, after all?

"I—I trust you," he said quietly. "I'll go."

Istvay nodded, looking away quickly.

They blinked hard, and cleared their throat. "I'll need some of the supplies from your pouch," they said, their voice rougher than usual. Aran nodded.

Istvay grabbed a handful of flares and some detonators, as well as a tranquilizer dart and a stun gun.

"Is that all?" asked Aran.

Istvay nodded, face grim. "I still have the guns we took off the soldiers." They paused. "Do you know how to start the escape pod?"

Aran shook his head.

"Let me walk you through it, then," said Istvay.

When they'd finished explaining, and Aran had nodded his understanding, Istvay straightened, putting their hands on Aran's shoulder.

"Good luck," they said quietly.

"Pishti …" Aran began helplessly.

Istvay looked directly into his eyes. "I promise, Aran," they said. Then they squeezed his shoulders, and slipped away down a cross alley.

Aran stood where he was, eyes closed, hands clenched, trying to keep from another panic attack. His heart was pounding, his breath coming far too quickly.

Ani chirped in concern, pressing herself down on his shoulders and winding her tentacles around neck, and he reached up and stroked her with a trembling hand. "It'll be fine, Ani," he whispered, more to himself than to her. "Pishti will be fine. They know what they're doing."

And then there was the brilliant flash of a flare, and a loud bang, and one of the yibo captains was shouting something through her communicator that his wavelink translated as, "We've located them!"

Within a few confused moments, the street ahead of Aran was empty.

He took a deep breath, trying to keep his abject terror for Istvay from completely overwhelming him, and ran.

He made it out of the alley without being noticed, and down the street. He stayed to the shadows, but the shout had obviously been heard by more than just the government guards—it seemed had like half the city was streaming towards where the flare had exploded.

Another flare went off, and another detonator, a couple of streets further down.

Ahead of him, Aran could see a set of city gates in the force-field. They were unguarded, though, and when he reached them and clipped the largest detonator he had onto the mechanism, no one tried to stop him. He stepped back and hit the controller, and the detonator exploded with a loud pop. When the smoke cleared, the gate gaped open.

For half a moment he hesitated, looking over his shoulder to where he'd last seen Istvay.

And then he slipped through the gates and out into the darkness beyond.

33

Savina

"What the hell do you want?" Savina snapped at the raider captain ahead of her.

She knew the answer, but she couldn't stop herself from asking. It was something to say, at least. Something to stop the voice in her head that was telling her everyone here was going to die, and it was all her fault.

The raider smiled. "Savina, isn't it?" she said. "I think you know exactly what we want. Justice."

Savina glanced quickly over her shoulder at the others. "It's justice for you to kill all of us?" Her voice was harsh with fear.

The raider's smile broadened. "You're right," she said. "It would be justice to take just you. This—" she gestured at the ragged group behind Savina. "This is simply a delightful coincidence. But come. We need to get going before the yibo find their courage and ask us to leave."

"Stand back," hissed Savina. "Stay away from us." She had a gun in her hand, and her other hand hovered at her belt where three of her throwing knives hung. "You already know I'm dangerous. I killed one of yours without even getting a scratch."

The raider raised an eyebrow in amusement. "That only makes it more enjoyable. Hardly sporting if your prey is too easy to catch."

There was a moment's pause. Savina's breath was coming fast and harsh.

She knew what she should do. She'd known what she should do from the moment she first saw the raiders.

She should turn herself in. Bargain her cooperation to let the others go.

But …

Something was squeezing her chest.

She didn't want to die.

She'd already given up her entire life to save Nicolau. She'd given up everything she'd ever wanted, her freedom, Beni's freedom, to save Nicolau.

She wanted, just this once, to be selfish. To save her own damn life. She wanted it so badly.

She glanced back at her baby brother, standing protectively close to Ines, at Beni, standing between Joska and Rafel—

But she couldn't. She simply couldn't.

She took a deep breath, and opened her mouth.

And then Nicolau stepped up beside her, laying his hand on her arm. "No," he said in a low voice. "You're not going to give yourself up."

Savina turned, startled.

"Look, Savina. I'm not going to lie. You scare the actual hell out of me. But—" he paused awkwardly. "But I'm not going to lose the first sister I ever had, just a few weeks after I found her."

And then Alba stepped forward, her tone ringing and imperious, and addressed the raider captain. "I don't know who you are. I'm not sure I want to know, to be quite frank. But if you expect any of us to give up one of our company so that you can—" she waved her hand. "Eat them, or whatever it is you plan to do—" Her voice absolutely dripped scorn. "I will tell you now, you had best forget that idea completely."

Savina gaped.

Alba was looking at her, and honestly, the sentiment probably had less to do with Savina personally than it did with some stubborn, abstract Principle—and yet, regardless of the reason, she'd said it. The woman could have tried to save herself. And instead, she'd put all their lives on the line for … for Savina.

The raider captain frowned. "You, human." Her voice held the condescending disdain of an adult speaking to a very stupid child. "What's your name?"

Alba met the raider's gaze unflinchingly. "I hardly see that that's your business," she said icily, and as much as Savina hated the woman, she had to admire her sheer gall. "Now, unless you have an official reason to stop us—"

The raiders surrounding them stepped back, and another raider came forward through their ranks, pulling someone behind them.

Savina groaned inwardly.

The captive woman's hands were bound behind her back, and there was blood across the side of her face, a bruise rising on one of those sharp cheekbones. But Reka's icy, breathtakingly indifferent gaze was as cold and self-assured as ever.

Savina fought down the twist of inside her chest at the sight of the woman's battered face and bound hands, a mixture of guilt and elation.

She wasn't sure where either of those sentiments had come from.

Reka's eyes brushed past Savina with such disdain that it almost choked her.

Her gaze stopped on Alba.

"Reka Soler?" asked Alba, her voice astonished. "What are you doing here?"

Reka gave a small smile, still not deigning to look at Savina. "Madam Chief Justice," she said in that cool, rich voice that seemed to vibrate in Savina's very bones. "That person who you're traveling with is—"

Reka's next words would kill her, betray her to Alba, and Savina would die for it.

Savina stepped forward, yanking her pulse pistol out, and fired directly into Reka's chest.

Reka staggered backwards, her words choked off, and collapsed to the pavement with a soft thud.

For a moment, everyone stood stunned.

Then Joska turned to Savina, her gaze murderous.

"She was going to shoot us," gasped Savina in her most innocent voice. "She must have been working with them. Look, in her hand —"

Sure enough, Reka's hand lay half-open where she'd fallen, revealing a tiny, deadly weapon inside.

Never mind that the weapon had been pointing at the raiders, not them—that was for Savina to know.

From the look on Joska's face, she hadn't been fooled, but she couldn't exactly call Savina out at the moment.

"So she wasn't your lover after all," said one of the raiders, glancing down at Reka in amusement. "Very clever, Savina. Now—"

Savina turned to glance at Joska, raising her eyebrows in a mocking question.

Joska's face was set with anger, but she gave a brief nod.

Savina raised her pistol and fired into the face of the raider captain. As the woman staggered back, Savina yanked out her throwing knives, sending a handful in quick succession. Two of the raiders fell, the knives embedded deep in their throats, scarlet blood spurting up around the hilts. The other three knives caught on the flexible armour the raiders wore, sliding off to clatter to the ground.

But it distracted them, and by the time they regrouped, Joska and Rafel were beside Savina, weapons in their hands, and they were firing in a businesslike fashion.

"Nicolau," Joska called over her shoulder. "We'll hold them. Get the others out, we'll follow."

Nicolau nodded. His face was pale, but his hand on his weapon was steady enough. He supported Feliu with one arm and with his other steadied Alba while Ines helped Feliu, and they started off at a stumbling run as Joska, Savina, and Rafel set up a blistering covering fire.

Through the bloody mess of the scene, Savina could see the gates still open in a jagged tear.

"Come on," grunted Rafel. "Best get moving, or we'll lose our chance."

Joska nodded, and the three of them started after the others, still firing steadily to keep their path open.

The raiders' return fire hissed over their heads and pulverized the cement at their feet, but they kept to the cover of the alley walls, making a difficult target.

Savina peered around the corner of the alley. Nicolau was at the entrance of the city gate, waving frantically at her.

She swore. "We have to go, that idiot will get himself shot."

Joska nodded grimly. "Rafel?"

"I'm ready, Captain," he said in a tight voice.

"On my count, then," said Joska. "Three. Two. One. Go!"

They ran, dodging and ducking as the raiders' fire hummed around them.

They were almost to the gates, and Nicolau was starting forward, his own gun drawn, firing off covering shots.

And then, beside Savina, Rafel stumbled, grunting in pain.

Savina turned in time to see a bright stain of red blossom along his side.

Joska was a few steps ahead and hadn't seen, and probably wouldn't until it was far too late …

Savina swore and turned back, dodging the raiders' fire.

One of them had almost reached Rafel, but she got there first, skidded to a halt, and shot the raider in the face. It stumbled backwards, and she dragged Rafel to his feet, slinging his arm over her neck, and heaved him after her towards the gate.

And then they were through, and out, and running for the jungle.

34

Aran

Aran ran through the open fields surrounding the city, tripping and stumbling as he went. The moons were bright enough to illuminate the largest of the obstacles, but in the wispy shadows, it was hard to avoid the potholes and debris in the road.

And then he'd reached the edge of the jungle, and the branches were catching his sleeves, and Ani was hissing and growling at the world in general. A few steps in he tripped over a branch and fell flat on his face, but he scrambled up, heedless of the blood running down his forehead and into his eyes.

Ani growled again and launched herself off his shoulder, just in time to intercept a creature he'd never seen before, but didn't have time to stop and take note of. The fight was sharp, short, and one-sided, and Ani rejoined him almost before he'd got his feet under him again.

The branches slapped across his face, and he rolled his ankle more than once. After one such stumble, every step on his left foot shot pain all the way up to his knee.

It didn't matter. Nothing mattered except getting to the escape pod and getting back to Istvay before his friend was killed.

He paused a moment to set the directions into his wavelink, and he followed the cheery AI voice in his earpiece, stumbling blindly through the thick undergrowth. He yanked out his bush-knife to clear the way, hacking through thick, gnarled vines and heavy branches.

He had to make it. He absolutely had to make it. There wasn't another option.

And then, at last, he broke through into the clearing where the escape pod lay on its side like a bird shot out of the sky.

He gasped a sigh of desperate relief, slashing aside the jungle plants that were already creeping up the sides to claim the ship for their own, and shoved his way inside.

He hit the hatch closed behind him and stared helplessly at the control panel for a few moments. Cautiously, he reached down, flipped a switch, then another, then held down the starter, biting the inside of his lip hard enough to taste blood.

The ship choked a couple of times, and he thought he might pass out from a feverish mix of anticipation and terror. And then it grumbled to life, and he dropped into the seat, boneless with relief, and hit the controls to lift the pod off the jungle floor.

It strained against the vines and tangled vegetation for a moment, and then broke free, leaping up above the tree line, and Aran pushed the throttle, shooting the pod towards the yibo city.

The moment he passed the edge of the jungle, he grabbed for a flare.

And then he saw something that made his stomach lurch.

The city gate he'd come through was closed tight, and yibo guards were clustered around it once more.

Aran closed his eyes for a moment, pulling back on the throttle so that the pod hovered in place.

It wasn't what it looked like, it couldn't be. Surely Istvay could still get out. They had to have anticipated this.

But the pod couldn't get through the forcefield. If the gates were closed, and Istvay trapped inside—

Aran had known this would happen. He'd known the moment he'd agreed to leave. But Istvay had sounded so certain. Istvay had told him. They'd promised him they wouldn't sacrifice themselves. They'd promised they had a way out.

And … they'd lied.

The thought sat in his stomach like a stone.

Carefully, unsteadily, he got to his feet. He walked to the side hatch, pulled it open, and shot off the flare. He watched it for a moment as it rose and glittered against the black of the night sky. Then he turned his gaze back to the city, glowing under its force field.

There was something sick in his stomach. He felt a little like he wanted to throw up, but he couldn't seem to muster the energy to care.

Istvay had lied to him. This was the most important thing in his entire life, and Istvay had known it, and they'd lied to him.

Everything seemed slightly unreal. He knew he was focusing on the lie because it was easier than focusing on what would happen after. Easier than focusing on what his life would look like without Istvay in it.

Perhaps he could simply put the ship down, walk back into the city, give himself up. But that would mean giving up Ani, too.

He laughed, a quiet, hollow little laugh.

It didn't matter what he did, then.

He sank back into the seat, staring sightlessly out the window.

It had been—he checked his palmscreen.

Five standard minutes. Five minutes since he'd set off the flare.

But then, he'd known the moment he'd seen the closed city gates that it was hopeless.

He took a deep breath.

From the other side of the city there were shouts and screams, but it couldn't be Istvay—the distance was too great.

"Ani," he said quietly. "What should we do now?"

Ani didn't answer. Of course she didn't. She didn't care where they went, as long as Aran was with her.

He tried to smile, then choked on tears.

He hadn't cared where he'd gone, either, as long as it was with Istvay. His whole damn life, it hadn't really mattered—they could have been on the streets of Vila Nova do Sol, out in the Rim Mountains, on the bottom of the damn ocean, or—or in an alien prison.

It hadn't mattered, as long as he was with Istvay.

Something seared across the corner of his vision, and jerked his head up.

A flare.

He stared at it dumbly for a moment.

And then the gates parted, and there was a commotion of tiny figures running and yelling, and Aran shove the throttle on the escape pod forward, sending the ship swooping low over the fields.

The yibo scattered at its approach, all but one tiny figure, running towards him, waving their hands over their head.

Aran's eyes were blurry with tears, but he managed, somehow, to bring the pod down in front of them. He hit the hatch lock, and the hatch sprang open, and Istvay stumbled inside. They were panting, and there was blood staining their loose tunic and blood smeared across their forehead, and their face was tight with exhaustion—but they were the most beautiful thing Aran had ever seen in his life.

"Let's get out of here," said Istvay, stepping into the cockpit.

Aran jumped up, and Istvay slid into the seat, their fingers sure on the controls. They hit the hatch lock, then pulled back on the thrusters, and the pod rose smoothly in the air, spun in a neat circle, and shot back in the direction they'd come from.

"Aran?" Istvay asked, once they were out of immediate danger, turning to look at them. "Are you alright?"

But Aran simply stood there staring at them, and he couldn't answer. His throat was far, far too tight with tears, and if he opened his mouth, all that would come out was a wordless sob of relief.

35

The group of them stumbled across the uneven paths in the fields beyond the city. The roads were hard-packed, but in the dark, there were potholes that were impossible for the eye to make out in the odd shadows cast by the moons.

Alba's muscles ached, and her legs burned. Her whole body was trembling from the exertion, but she forced herself to keep going.

She had to keep going. There wasn't another option. They ran, or they died.

"We'll have to leave the roads," Joska hissed over her shoulder. "They can come after us too easily here."

Ahead of Alba, Vina nodded. She and Joska turned off the trail, and, leaning on Ines, Alba forced herself to follow. She was clenching her jaw so hard it hurt, and her breath ached in her lungs, and a sharp stitch stabbed through her side at every step.

A quick glance over her shoulder, though, confirmed the need for haste—the raiders, whatever they were, were after them, streaming out through the city gates and down the open road.

Alba's foot caught in a depression, and she stumbled, falling hard.

A sharp, breathtaking pain shot through her knee, and she bit back a scream.

"Madam! Madam, are you alright?"

Ines was hovering over her, but her face was blurry through the haze of pain. Alba tried to answer, but the only thing that came from her lips was a moan.

"Let me help you up," came Nicolau's voice, and then she was lifted to her feet. She tried to put weight on her injured leg, and the pain crashed into her, almost overwhelming her consciousness.

"Lean on me," hissed Ines in a low voice, and somehow, hobbling and stumbling, pain shooting through her body at every step, Alba stumbled after the others, leaning heavily on Ines. She was lightheaded with pain, breathless with it, but she forced her body to keep moving.

She would not slow up the others. She wouldn't allow the others to be captured.

But—

But she couldn't go much farther. She knew that much. The pain was an awful thing, cutting through her like a knife, and she caught herself wondering if a quick death at the hands of the raiders could possibly be worse than this …

"Come on, Madam."

She glanced over at Ines's face through the fog of pain.

There were tears running down the girl's cheeks. "Come on, Madam. We have to keep going."

From behind them, the raiders' voices were getting closer.

A shot hissed over their heads, and Joska swore. "I don't think much of our chances," the woman panted. "We're not going to make the trees at this rate. And from the looks of the bastards, they'll be faster in the jungle than we are anyway."

"What the hell do you want to do?" hissed Vina. "I can't kill all of them." But she slowed, reaching into her jacket, and it looked like she was thinking of at least trying.

"Madam."

It was Ines' voice, thick with worry, but it sounded distant and far away. Alba realized, in a detached, clinical way, that she was on the verge of fainting.

She'd never fainted in her entire life.

Ahead of her, Joska was slowing as well, pulling out her own pistol, and Rafel, leaning heavily on Vina, had his own gun out. Alba saw, hazily, that she and Ines had finally caught up to the others.

Joska glanced over as if to tell them to keep going, but when she saw the shape they were in, she just shook her head. "Weapons out, if you have them," she said in a low voice. "May as well make a stand here, if we're going to."

Alba closed her eyes for a moment, too exhausted and sick with pain to answer.

"I have an extra," said Nicolau, and Alba could feel Ines shift to take the weapon from him.

The raiders were slowing now, their quarry cornered, moonlight glinting off their sharp canines as they smiled.

And then, overhead, there was the loud hum of a spacecraft.

Alba jerked her head up reflexively, saw the others doing the same.

The craft dived, heading towards the other side of the city, and was skimming low to the ground.

Alba frowned.

It was one of the escape pods from the diplomatic ship.

"Is that—" Nicolau began.

And then the raiders were shouting and pointing as well. For a moment they hissed a quick argument, then they turned, running back towards their own ship.

The tiny, exhausted group of humans stared after their erstwhile pursuers.

Then Joska snapped, "Come on! I don't know what the hell that was about, but I'm not waiting around to ask questions. Let's get out of here."

Alba tried to take a step, and hissed in pain.

"Madam?" Ines' voice was worried. "Madam, are you—"

"Since I won't be permitted to die in peace," said Alba sourly, trying to keep the strain from her voice, "I suppose we shouldn't waste any more time talking about it."

Ines nodded, a spark of relief in her eyes, and Alba leaning heavily against her as they started off after the others.

36

Alba

The trek through the jungle felt never-ending, a constant fog of pain, exhaustion, and terror. With each step, agony jolted through Alba from her injured leg, until she began to wonder if perhaps she'd died, and this was some torture from the Void—forced to keep moving eternally, through eternal pain and eternal night and eternal exhaustion.

Finally, her leg simply collapsed under her when she tried to take a step. She lay where she fell, too spent and dazed to even consider trying to get to her feet.

Joska turned back to her, concerned. She bent and examined Alba's leg, and when she looked up, her face was grim. "You broke something, it looks like," she said. "Honestly, I'm not sure how you made it as far as you did. But—" she glanced around them. "We'll have to find a way for you to make it farther. We can't leave anyone and come back for them later, not out here."

They'd seen the raider ship take off as they entered the jungle. It hadn't come after them, and as long as she knew that, Alba wasn't sure she cared where it had gone. But the recollection of the night she'd spent in the jungle when she first arrived on this planet was vivid in her memory, and the raiders weren't the only things to fear. Although honestly, with the dull pain pulsing through her body and numbing her thoughts, she wasn't sure she cared.

"Vina," called Joska.

The young country girl with the wide eyes and dimpled smile came over and knelt beside Joska.

"You're better with a pistol than I am," said Joska shortly. "I'll carry the Chief Justice, you and Ines take guard. Nicolau is carrying Feliu. Can Yosip support Rafel?"

The look that Savina shot Alba was brief, but there was a sharp, shocking spark of what looked like hatred in it. And then it was gone as quickly as it had come, leaving Alba to wonder if, in her pain-fogged state, she'd imagined it.

"Of course, Captain," said Vina. She pulled out her gun and stepped to the front. "Ines, you take the rear," she called over her shoulder.

Joska examined Alba again, shaking her head, then said, "You'll have to excuse me, Chief Justice. I don't imagine you'll like this, but it's better than being left to die."

In any other circumstance, Alba would have protested. But here in the jungle, with a broken leg, fleeing for her life from murderous aliens, on a desperate, ludicrous mission to trap herself and her companions here permanently, dooming themselves and thereby saving the entire Joias system—she realized, suddenly, that she had no room for dignity, not at the moment.

"I would be grateful," she said stiffly, and Joska hoisted her up onto her back, grunting at the effort.

When they reached a clearing with an old, battered ship at the centre, Alba was no more than half conscious. Pain from her broken bone, pain from her aching muscles, pain from scrapes and scratches too numerous to be counted—it felt as if her entire existence had become nothing but pain.

Vaguely, she realized Joska was stumbling with exhaustion, breath coming short and heavy.

"Madam Chief Justice," the woman said, and it took Alba a moment to realize she was being addressed. "I'll let you down here, and Nicolau will carry you into the ship."

"Thank you," murmured Alba, too exhausted and spent to worry about her dignity or anything else.

Joska let her down gently, but Alba's one good leg wouldn't hold her weight. And then Nicolau was beside her, and he caught her and carried her gently up the ramp and into the ship as if she were a child. He placed her on a cot on the main deck, concern sharp on his face, but she was too weary and in too much pain to pay much attention.

As he left, Alba noticed Feliu in an adjoining cot on the deck. Yosip and Rafel were there as well, all of them looking as exhausted as she felt.

Joska stepped onto the deck a few moments later. "Chief Justice. I'll have a look at your leg and Rafel's injury as soon as we get off the ground," she said. "But I think we'd best get off this planet as quickly as possible if we want to live through this."

"It would seem a pity to die, after all that," said Yosip, with a wan smile that still managed to hold a bit of a twinkle.

Joska chuckled. "There's painkillers in the med kit, anyway. I'll send Beni back with it." She paused. "Beni's blind, so I'll leave you to find the dosage yourself, since I assumed they haven't memorized it."

Alba nodded, too weary to speak.

When the person who must be Beni arrived, Alba took the proffered painkillers and leaned back against the wall of the tiny deck, closing her eyes.

She was too exhausted for this. Too weary, too old, too weak.

But at the end of the day, she and the tiny, ragged group with her were all that were standing between the Joias system and an alien war. Between Cavaco and ultimate power.

How many Joias citizens would die in this war that Cavaco would thrust them into in exchange for power?

How much would Cavaco care?

The ship hummed as it started up, and then her stomach dropped as they shot up into the atmosphere.

"Madam," said Yosip quietly, when the harsh noise of their escape from the confines of the planet had settled to the sullen silence of near space, and she'd reoriented herself to the weightlessness of zero gravity. "How are you?"

Alba turned to him and managed a wry smile. "I'm exactly as alright as I appear to be," she said.

He smiled back, just a little.

Joska came in a few minutes later, Nicolau behind her. They examined Rafel, and Joska bound up the injury, and then she turned to Alba.

"Let's take a look at you, then," she said.

Alba had to fight back a whimper of pain as Joska examined her knee gently. When the woman looked up, she was frowning. "Your kneecap is broken in a few places," she said. "I know basic first aid, but this is beyond my skill. I can try to set it temporarily and put a splint on your leg, but that and painkillers is the best I can do. And I doubt it will be enough, unless we can get somewhere with a doctor."

Alba took a deep breath, then pushed herself gingerly into a sitting position. "I had wanted to speak with you about that, Captain," she said. "Where are you planning to go from here?"

Joska shook her head slowly. "It's not only up to me. But I hadn't made much of a plan. We'd originally hoped to find you in the government compound and join up with the rest of the survivors, but …" She shrugged.

"If you would be open to my advice—" Alba began.

Joska gave her a wry smile. "At this point, I'd be open to anyone's advice."

Alba closed her eyes for just a moment.

She couldn't tell this woman what they were planning. Not until she knew her better, and could predict what her reaction might be. It was entirely possible—likely, in fact—that if these people knew what she planned—to find a way to destroy the mechanism that opened the portal, trap them here permanently—they would do anything in their power to stop her.

But at the moment, with her leg broken and on a stranger's ship, she was entirely at this captain's mercy.

"The yibo, it appears, have decided to open negotiations with the mutineers from the diplomatic ship," she said at last, opening her eyes. "That is what led to our rather precipitous departure from the government compound. However, while I was still engaged in negotiations with the yibo diplomats, I was able to obtain a map of the system. There is a small agricultural planet not too far distant from here, and from the size of the cities shown on the map, it's likely they'll have a medical centre. I believe that would give us an opportunity to regroup and make our new plans."

Joska raised an eyebrow. "You don't think a group of humans showing up on a small agricultural planet will cause comment?"

Alba hesitated. This was the point that had been worrying at her ever since they'd reached the yibo city.

"I … believe that they are far more familiar with humans in this system than we've been led to believe," she said at last. "I believe they've had contact with one of our fellow generation ships not too far in the past."

Joska watched her, her gaze sharp, but at last she nodded slowly. "That's the sense that we got, as well," she said. She sighed and pushed herself to her feet. "As far as I'm concerned, that seems like a sound plan. I'll have to consult with rest of my crew, but at the very least, I think I can promise to set you down there, if you'd like."

Alba nodded. She was almost too weary to offer the captain her thanks, but Joska seemed to understand.

When Joska left, Alba glanced around the small deck.

It looked like a refugee camp—cots strapped down to the floor, almost everyone wounded and exhausted. Feliu was already sleeping, and Yosip's eyes were closed as well, his face drawn with weariness.

In one corner, Nicolau and Ines were deep in conversation. Nicolau was grinning enthusiastically, speaking with his hands as much as with his words, and Ines' gaze was as earnest and intent as her voice.

Alba couldn't help a smile, watching them.

"Alba?"

She looked up, startled, to see Vina. The girl had come over and was crouched on the floor with her mag boots next to Alba's cot.

"You have quite a bit of information on the layout of this system, Joska said," the girl began. There was something about her voice, the way she talked, that was very different from that of the innocent, wide-eyed country-girl she'd appeared when they'd first met.

Alba glanced at her sharply.

This girl, whoever she was, was much more capable than she

wanted anyone to know.

"I did get some information while I was speaking with the yibo ambassador," Alba said cautiously. "Not as much as I would have liked, but something."

Vina nodded, turning to watch Nicolau and Ines.

"And Ines—" the girl continued. "She's figured out how to translate the yibo language?"

Alba nodded. "She's a talented linguist."

Vina nodded again, absently. Her attention seemed to have been caught by the two young people in the corner, and there was a hint of a smile on her lips. "They seem happy," she said at last.

Alba looked over at her in surprise.

Vina gave her a broad, innocent smile that showed her dimples. "I worked with Nicolau for a while. He seems nice. They'll probably be good for each other."

Alba nodded without speaking.

"Maybe it would be a good idea for us to travel together," said Vina at last. "You don't mind, I hope? I'm afraid I can't offer much insight on the political situation, or the geography, or anything like that. But—" she shrugged. "We have a ship, and, if you'll pardon me for saying it, none of you look like you're in any shape to travel far on your own. At least we'd increase your numbers, so it's not just the four of you."

Alba watched her from the corner of her eye.

She didn't trust this girl, wouldn't trust her with a cut penny. And if Vina found out what Alba and the others intended, Alba was certain she'd stop at nothing to keep them from it.

But ... she was right. Their small remnant of a diplomatic corps wouldn't survive a day on their own, not injured as they were.

"I believe that could be mutually beneficial," said Alba at last. "As

I told Joska earlier, I do have a map, and information that could be useful. When we find somewhere to get our injuries treated, we can decide on our next move, but for the moment—"

"That's an excellent plan, Madam Chief Justice," said Vina brightly. "That's what we'll do, then. I'll talk to Joska." She stood, and turned to go.

"Vina," said Alba quietly.

The girl paused, and Alba caught the quick, inadvertent jerk that belied her nonchalance.

"What is it?" Vina's voice was even more innocent than it had been a moment ago.

The girl was unlikely to tell the truth. But her reaction might be edifying, at least.

"That government agent. Reka Soler," said Alba slowly. "Do you have any idea what she wanted? I had been under the impression she was out after a warrant."

She was watching Vina closely.

Vina. A pretty girl from the Rim Mountains.

And Reka had been sent out after an assassin-for-hire. A pretty girl from the Rim Mountains, named ... Savina, if Alba remembered correctly.

The same name the raiders had called her.

Vina's smile widened, her eyes large. "That woman was a government agent? I thought she was one of the people you were telling us about who'd been working with the mutineers. But whoever she was, she'd sold us out to the raiders. They knew who we were, and where we were." She shivered. "I'm glad I was able to shoot her before she shot you."

Alba nodded.

It was a lie, of course.

The raiders themselves had mentioned a connection between Reka and this girl. Something about thinking they'd been lovers.

Alba shivered. She'd heard rumours about this particular assassin—vicious, and deadly, and completely ruthless. And she'd seen the calculating look in the girl's eyes, in the moment after she'd pulled the trigger and shot Reka Soler dead on the street.

Still … right now, Savina and her friends held Alba's life, and the lives of the entire diplomatic party, in their hands. Perhaps the fate of the entire Joias system. And for now, it seemed, the girl intended for them to stay alive.

"I see," said Alba.

As long as Alba had the star map and Ines had the translation program, they were probably too useful to kill. At least for the moment.

And 'for the moment' was as far as she could see ahead of her right now.

Savina dimpled prettily. "I hope you'll excuse me. I should go see if Joska needs anything."

Alba nodded again, and Savina moved away. Alba watched her go, a hot spark of unease burning bright in the back of her brain.

37

Savina stepped back into the cockpit, looking around quickly.

There was something restless buzzing in the back of her brain, and she couldn't seem to make herself sit still.

She needed to be alone. And Rafel, for all his faults, wouldn't try to talk to her.

When she glanced over at the pilot's seat, though, it was Joska, not Rafel, seated there.

Of course. Rafel was still in the sickbay, barely conscious.

She tried to ignore the unpleasant jolt at the recollection.

She hesitated in the doorway, but Joska had already glanced over and seen her.

The captain's mouth took on that thin, angry line that Savina knew far too well, the one that left her feeling like a scolded child. She scowled, and turned deliberately to leave.

"Savina?"

She was tempted to simply walk out. But she was too tired. Too tired to let the anger flood over her like it would have any other time. Too tired to try to wriggle her way out of the inevitable confrontation that would follow, when Joska at last forced her to sit down and talk.

"What?" she snapped. "You want to yell at me for what I did? Fine. Go ahead."

Joska's lips were still pinched, but she studied Savina for a few moments before she spoke. "I think you know what I'm going to say," she said at last.

Savina's scowl deepened. "You're going to ask why I killed Reka. Why I killed the woman who's been hunting me for the last three weeks. The woman who's the reason we all ended up behind this portal, the reason why we got caught by that damn Yuur in the first place."

Her voice was choking just a little, and she couldn't tell if it was anger, or that odd, sick feeling that had flooded her stomach, half vindication, half horrified shock, to see Reka sprawled on the ground, face bloody and bruised, blood welling from the wound from Savina's pulse gun.

It wasn't something she wanted to think about. Which only made her more irritated.

"For all we know, she wasn't going to hurt us. Not then. She obviously wasn't on the raiders' good side," said Joska, still watching her.

"She wouldn't have hurt you, you mean," Savina spat. "She was going to tell the Chief Justice who I was. And then my life, and Beni's life, and Nicolau's life, would have been worth nothing. Yours too, for all you like to pretend you're so holy and self-sacrificing."

Joska's mouth quirked up at that, and Savina narrowed her eyes.

"You know damn well that what Reka was going to say would have killed me. And maybe you can laugh about it. But I can't. I'm trying to protect my younger siblings. So I ask you, Joska—why the hell do you think I killed Reka?"

"Trying to protect your younger siblings? Or yourself?" asked Joska.

Savina scowled. "Fine. Myself too." She had to bite off her words quickly, and it was a moment before she could speak again. "I'm tired of sacrificing everything to save someone else," she said at last, in a low voice.

Joska was still watching her. At last, she said, "While we're on the subject—why did you go back for Rafel? He told me what you did."

For a moment, Savina just stared at her. "We were running, and I didn't want him to slow us down," she said finally.

"You could have left him," said Joska, still watching her. "The raiders would have taken him, and maybe that would have slowed them down from coming after you."

"Well, believe me, I won't be doing something that stupid again," Savina muttered.

Joska smiled just a little, a faint, knowing smile.

"You want to talk all night?" Savina snapped. "Because if you do, I'm going somewhere else. I was looking for peace and quiet."

Joska gestured to the copilot's seat without speaking, and at last, warily, Savina strapped in.

For a while, neither of them spoke. Joska was bent over the controls, calculating out their route, most likely, and whether they'd make it with their current fuel and supplies.

Savina just stared out the cockpit window at the endless black of space around them.

They were pointed away from the planet, and until they rounded their orbit and started towards the planet Alba had indicated, she could see nothing ahead of them but the bright, fiery glow of the stars. They could have been standing still, for all the movement you could see from inside the cockpit.

"We'll stay with the Chief Justice for now," said Savina at last, shortly.

The corner of her eye she saw Joska glance over at her. "I believe that's a wise course of action," the captain said. "She has information that would help us survive, I think."

"Yes," of Savina. "I need to know more about the politics of this place. Not to mention that linguist girl."

Joska nodded again.

Savina sighed. "With any luck, she'll know enough to keep us from being killed. At least until we don't need her anymore."

Joska had looked up from the controls now, and was watching her. "Do you still plan to kill Alba?" she asked at last, quietly.

Sabina scowled. "I doubt you'd give me permission," she said sarcastically.

Joska smiled, just a little.

Savina sighed again, and looked back out the window. "Not as long as we can use her. I make no promises after that."

They were silent again for a while.

"Is there anything else we need to talk about?" asked Joska at last.

There was. There was so much more. And again, just for a moment, Savina was hit with that sick, overwhelming need to talk. To tell Joska about what she'd done to save Nicolau. To tell Joska what it had been like living in the compound, asked the woman if it was true — ask her if it was really true that outside the compound, no one thought about the holy wars anymore.

She wanted Joska to understand why she'd done what she'd done, and she wanted her to tell Savina that it was alright. That it would all be alright, that Beni's strange mood wouldn't last, that Nicolau would stop being afraid of her, and scared of who he might have been. That she was right to hate Alba—or that she wasn't, because Alba wasn't a danger anymore.

But it was too much. Too much emotion, too much tied up inside her head that she didn't think she'd be able to tell even if she'd wanted to.

And even if she did, Joska wouldn't be able to give her the answers she wanted, because they weren't true.

Savina could justify what she'd done. But the cold hard fact was, she'd done it, and she'd have to deal with the consequences. And someone like Alba wouldn't be appeased with a pretty apology.

She was still fighting for her life, whatever Joska might want to believe.

"No," she said at last, when she realized Joska was still waiting for her answer. "No, I think I should probably get some sleep."

Joska nodded. "May as well. Who knows what's coming up? You may not get any sleep for a while."

Savina left the cockpit and made her slow way back to the main deck.

Nicolau and Ines were still huddled in the corner talking, but the conversation seemed to have petered off.

Alba was asleep, thank goodness, and most of the rest of the diplomatic party. Even Nicolau's eyes were drifting shut, and Ines kept covering her mouth to stifle a yawn.

Savina strapped herself down against the far wall and stared up to the ceiling, smiling to herself just a little.

Beni came in a few minutes later and joined her.

"Looks like our little brother found a friend," Savina whispered after a moment.

"Ines?" asked Beni. "She seems like a nice girl."

"Yes," said Savina.

They sat in the comfortable silence for a few moments, the kind that came when you were weary and exhausted, and safe, just for the moment.

Savina glanced back over to where Nicolau had leaned back against the wall, his eyes finally fallen closed. Ines' eyes had drooped as well, and she was curled against his shoulder, breathing slowly and steadily in her sleep.

"He's happy, isn't he?" asked Beni, their voice small and plaintive.

Savina nodded. "As happy as he can be, I suppose. And he was happy, I think. I think his life was good."

Until she and Beni had arrived, and dragged him away from everything and everyone he knew and cared about.

"That's good," said Beni.

Savina leaned against the wall beside Beni and let her eyes fall shut.

She didn't know who she was anymore. She didn't know what to believe, or who to trust. She had no idea how to get out of here alive, and she'd just formed a tentative alliance with the person she hated most in the entire system.

She'd finally killed the woman who'd been trying to kill her, and she couldn't get rid of the cold, sick ache in her chest at the thought of it.

But whatever it had cost—whatever it would continue to cost— saving Nicolau had been worth it. No matter what else she'd let herself regret, she wouldn't regret that.

She took a long breath, and let herself drift, finally, into sleep.

38

Aran

The lights of the yibo city had long since faded in the distance. The motion of the escape pod was quiet and steady under Aran's feet, and he leaned back in one of the pod's small seats, watching Istvay.

The pod was far out over the jungle now, and there didn't seem to be any pursuit, and at last Istvay put the controls onto autopilot and turned to Aran.

They looked exhausted, but there was a spark of exhilaration in their eyes, just like there always was when the two of them had gotten out of a hopeless situation yet again.

And looking into Istvay's familiar brown eyes with their absurdly long lashes, the mud and blood ground into their skin, their shadow of a beard and their hair pulling loose from its ponytail, Aran was almost choked yet again by the sickening sense of mingled relief and gratitude.

Istvay had made it. Somehow, they and Aran had both made it out of that alive.

"I—wasn't sure you were going to get out," said Aran finally.

Istvay chuckled, then sobered when they saw the look on Aran's face. They leaned forward, putting a hand on Aran's shoulder, and looked directly into his eyes. And just like always, Aran found his gaze caught and held, and he was unable to look away even if he wanted to.

"Aran. I promised. I'm not going to start lying to you now, after however damn many years we've been friends. Okay? Maybe you're right, maybe I am a self-sacrificing idiot. But what I told you was the Mystery's own truth—if I've been overprotective, which I probably have, it's because I don't want to see you hurt. So I'm not going to start hurting you myself." They cleared their throat. "I realized a few things these last few days. And I … Anyways, I …" Their voice cracked, and they broke off, blinking hard.

Aran managed a shaky breath, and Istvay released their grip on his shoulder, and finally he was able to actually breathe again.

"How did you get out, anyways?" he asked, his voice a little shaky still.

Istvay grinned. "Do you remember that time on the Opal Plains where those snouted whirligigs were after us?"

Aran raised his eyebrows. "You mean—"

Istvay's grin widened. "Yes. I got them coming after me so you could get out, but the way they were running around panicking, I got to thinking maybe the rumour of the raiders was more than just a rumour. So I use my sensors and figured out where in the city there was the most chaos, and I led them that way. They were pretty close on my heels, and I won't say there weren't a couple times things got a bit sticky. But the closer I got to where the raiders were—if there were raiders, mind you—they more of them decided they'd rather avoid whatever the hell was over there than recapture me, Emeric or no. Once I lost them, I circled back around to the city gates, and when I saw your flare, I shouted to the gate guards that the raiders were inside, and it was everyone for themself.

"They dropped everything and left, and I got the gates back open and headed for your flare. A bunch of yibo guards must have seen me, because they took off after me, and—" they shrugged. "And that's where you found me. They must have been terrified of the ship swooping down, because as soon as they saw you, they were gone. They're damn scared of those raiders, whatever they are." They give a soft chuckle. "I'll be honest, I wasn't sorry about that. I don't know how much longer I could have stayed on my feet."

Istvay and Aran were both quiet for a while. At last, Istvay turned back to him. "So," they said. "What's the plan now?"

Aran bit his lip, staring out the window of their small craft. "The same plan as before," he said quietly. "I need to find that cure, Istvay. I have to."

Istvay nodded. "I know."

"Do—do you think the raiders were really in the city?" Aran asked.

Istvay gave a soft chuckle. "If they were, I doubt very much they'd have been in the mood for talking. But ..." They bent over their palmscreen. "I've got a copy of the map here. We know where to find them. If that's—if it's still what you want to do."

Aran glanced over at him, eyebrows raised, and Istvay chuckled again, shaking their head fondly. "Okay, okay, that was a stupid question." They paused a few moments, looking down at the map on their palmscreen. "It means going back into space, unfortunately. It doesn't look like it will be more than a three- or four-day trip, but ..."

"I don't care," said Aran.

Istvay took a deep breath, and then grinned. "Well," they said, turning back controls, "I guess this is just like old times, then—you and me and Ani, flying off to look for something that might kill us."

"But it'll be interesting, at least," said Aran. He found he was grinning too, just a little.

Istvay leaned their head back against the pilot seat. "That's one thing, I guess—we've done a hell of a lot since we graduated, but we really haven't been bored, have we?"

"No. No, I guess we haven't," said Aran.

And looking at his best friend sitting beside him in the cockpit of the tiny, beat-up craft, on their way to a place that no one from their system had ever seen or explored or experienced, with no idea what lay ahead—Aran found himself smiling, despite the sudden, familiar surge of terror at the thought.

He was with Istvay. And as long as he was with Istvay, it didn't really matter where he went—he'd be home.

39

Epilogue

Emeric swore softly to himself as he strode down the halls of the alien hospital.

Everything had gone wrong this whole hellish trip. And it had all started with that damned Aran. Yes, there was Alba as well, but they'd planned for her. They'd made plans to keep her from causing trouble. And while their plans may have been modified, how much harm could a seventy-three-year-old woman on an alien planet do?

He'd had a plan to take care of Aran, as well.

And it hadn't worked. Somehow, that bastard and his trained bear Istvay had gotten away again.

He gritted his teeth, tasting the impotent fury in his mouth.

They were both gone. They'd made it out of the city despite his best efforts, and his superiors were furious. Yes, Cavaco could pull off a coup without the cure, but not in the same way. The cure was the bait he'd dangle, available to those who pledged themselves to his side. A demonstration of how badly they needed Cavaco in power, and what he could do to save the system if they'd only let him.

They'd need some justification. Something to build goodwill.

Maybe those other idiots weren't considering that, weren't thinking ahead, but Emeric was. And for once in his damn life, that stupid Aran wasn't going to get there first.

Ever since Emeric had met the quiet, desperately poor pity-case in his first year of university, and Aran had somehow, using some blend of skill and social standing that was an absolute mystery even to Emeric, managed to rise into the top tier of the university students, Aran had been the one everyone talked about. The one everyone bragged that they'd gone to classes with. He had that quiet, bewildered air, that mock humility that everyone seemed to swoon over, but Emeric could see through it. Even if no one else could.

Aran was far craftier than he appeared.

And now the bastard had gotten away. Even at this moment, he was out trying to find that damn cure, the thing Emeric desperately needed. The thing he'd sacrificed everything for, come on this damn mission for. Given up his place at the University, his chance at advancement, everything. His one breakthrough.

And Aran was going to come in in his quiet, awkward, self-effacing way, and take it. Just like he'd taken every damn other thing that Emeric wanted.

Except this time, he wouldn't.

Emeric touched the small sphere in his pocket.

This time, Aran wouldn't be able to simply take it away.

The yibo ahead of him pushed the door open to a hospital room. "You can go in. She's awake now," she said in her heavy accent.

Emeric gave her a short nod, and stepped inside.

The human woman on the table looked as if she'd barely escaped death. If the reports Emeric had heard were correct, that was true. But even bruised and battered as she was, face drawn and ghastly with lack of blood, bruises written across her face and body, she looked dangerous.

She looked like someone who wouldn't hesitate to kill.

Emeric took a deep breath, and smiled.

This was exactly what he wanted.

He strolled over to the edge of the cot and looked down at the woman.

Her eyes were open. They followed him steadily, and a faint prickle of fear buzzed at the base of his skull. He shook it off.

"Reka Soler," he said.

She just watched him, and made no effort to respond to his words.

He took a deep breath.

So it would take some patience. Not his forte, necessarily.

"I know why you're here, Soler," he said. "We have access to all the files the Chief Justice had aboard the ship. We know everything about you."

"You work for Cavaco."

It was the first thing Reka had said to him.

He nodded. "Yes. But—"

"I intend to pay him for what he did to me," she said, in a voice that was terrifying for its very casualness. "If I have to kill you to do that, I will."

It wasn't the words themselves that were frightening. It was the utter emotionlessness behind them. As if she wasn't making a threat, simply stating a fact.

"If that's your attitude, you'll have a difficult time making it far enough to get revenge on anyone," he said coldly.

She just looked at him, with an expression of utter disdain.

He cleared his throat. "I understand you're upset with Cavaco. But I have authority to promise you that he will clear your name, if you help us."

This did get a reaction—her eyebrows twitched, as if in grim amusement. "I trusted Cavaco once. It led to me losing my career. Why do you think I would trust him again?"

Emeric blew out a breath in frustration. "Because," he said patiently, as if speaking to a child, "it's the only option you have at this point." He glanced around. "The raiders aren't going to work with you again, if I understand correctly. And the yibo—if I ask, they'll kill you here and now, change out the saline solution pumping into you for something more toxic. They want what Cavaco is selling."

"But you can't deliver on your promises to them without someone who walked through the city gates not too long ago." Despite the fact that the incident in question had left Reka bleeding her life out in the streets, there was a trace of amusement under her words.

Emeric narrowed his eyebrows. "We can deliver what we promised. But it will be easier if we have Alba."

Reka was still watching him with that thoughtful gaze, so he continued. "I know you want Savina. She's the one who set you up, if I understand correctly. And she's the one who were you were after when you got dragged through the portal. So go after Savina. But right now, it appears she's travelling with Alba. All I'm asking is that you bring Alba back with you when you return. You don't need to kill her, just bring her back. It's for her own safety, really, as much as anything—it's dangerous here, especially for a helpless old woman. I'll send some soldiers to help you."

Reka was still watching him with that small, amused smile on her face. "Very altruistic," she said at last. "Then tell me—Alba was the one who promised to restore my good name and my reputation. She was the one that gave me a warrant for Savina in the first place. Why would I bring her in?"

Emeric snorted. "Loyalty, Reka? I know very well you don't bear any love for Alba Espina. There are those who respect her, but I doubt there's anyone who loves her. She's bowled you over to forward her agenda just as much as she's done to any of the rest of us, hasn't she?"

Again, Reka didn't answer, just studied him with those hard, icy eyes.

"You're working with her because you want what she offered you. All I'm asking is that you work with Cavaco for the same reason. Once you've brought back Alba, I don't care what you do with Savina. You can take her alive if you want, you can kill her—" he shrugged.

Reka was still watching him. "Very well," she said at last. "As you say, I don't have much of an option." She paused a moment. "But as for Savina—I must be permitted to use my own judgement."

Emeric raised an eyebrow.

Up until now, Reka's voice had been flat and emotionless. But at Savina's name, he could hear the hiss of absolute loathing in her tone.

"Of course," he said, spreading his hands. "I have no interest in some Rim Mountain assassin. Do with Savina as you like."

Reka nodded, slowly. "You will let me free," she said at last, quietly. "The moment I'm well enough, you will set me free. I will find Savina. And I will kill her." Again, he could hear the snarl under her tone.

There was something in her hand, something black and lacy—a scrap of material, from what he could see. But the way she was holding it, it could have been a lit match.

"And then, after I finish with Savina, I'll bring Alba back. I will be working on the specific instructions of General Cavaco. And I will not harm Alba, because I don't intend to have those politics on my head. You'll write me a warrant, duly signed, stating exactly that. If you don't, I won't agree. And I'll have that pardon you promised written and signed, contingent only on my successful completion of my mission."

Emeric nodded. "All that is eminently doable. Before we left, Cavaco specifically authorized Captain Mattin to act in his name, and we have documentation to show that."

Reka nodded again, then turned her flat gaze to the ceiling. But he could see her hand clenching the bit of black lace as if she wanted to atomize it by her grip alone.

He left the room, shivering involuntarily as he stepped out the door.

Reka Soler was not someone he'd want to cross. She wasn't someone anyone would cross lightly.

If he could have sent her after Aran and Istvay—

He shook his head.

No point. They were gone. And Reka may have been able to bring them back, although Aran's stupid land-devil pet made that questionable, but the captain was probably right. Despite Emeric's personal interest in the cure, they needed Alba more urgently. If she somehow made it back through the portal before they did, she had the power and influence to possibly ruin everything.

But he wasn't about to forget Aran.

He smiled a little as he walked.

Maybe this wasn't so bad after all.

Aran and Istvay were almost certainly going after the cure, somehow. Aran was obsessed with it—had been even before that worthless nobody, Istvay, had started showing signs of the defect.

So. Let him do the hard work. No matter how much Emeric hated

Aran, he had to admit there was some justice to the idiot's reputation.

Let him go. Let him confront those raiders, the ones that hunted humans. If he was killed, it would be no great loss. And if he was successful—well, once he'd gotten the raw materials and data, they'd still need someone with the laboratory experience to turn that raw data into a cure. And who better than Emeric?

Their yibo allies kept very close track of the movements of the raiders. It would be easy to get word of where Aran had gone and what he was doing. And as soon as they'd found the cure—the soldiers who were following him and Istvay, on Emeric's orders, would step in and take it away.

Emeric drew in a long breath.

And finally, he'd be able to do what he'd wanted to do ever since he'd first laid eyes on that soft, helpless-looking boy in too-short trousers and a ragged shirt, standing the door of the common rooms in their university looking lost, his attack-dog Istvay at his shoulder.

He'd crush Aran. Take away what he'd dreamed about and worked for his whole life, just like Aran had so effortlessly taken away everything Emeric had dreamed of and worked for.

The thought made him smile a little.

Maybe, if he was feeling generous, he'd dedicate the cure, not only to Istvay, the last person to die of the defect, but to Aran, who'd perished heroically searching for the cure.

There was a spring in his step as he started back down the corridor.

And behind him, in the hospital ward, Reka closed her eyes and dreamed of revenge.

This time, there would be no warnings, and no mercy.

Book three, Uncertainty Principle, available now!

You might also enjoy The Ungovernable series, also by R.M. Olson.

A mouthy ex-smuggler pilot, a grumpy demolitions expert, a tech genius and a hacker. They're pulling a job on the most dangerous weapons dealer in the System. They're stealing tech that could change the course of history. And every one of them has something to hide.
What could possibly go wrong?
"Spectacular and thrilling! Olson's debut novel is filled with compelling characters and endless excitement." -SD Simper, author of the Fallen Gods series

You can order book one, Zero Day Threat, on Amazon.

I also have a Patreon, where I post character art, short stories, sneak peaks, and other fun stuff. You can get in on it for only $3/month, so if you're interested, check it out here!
https://www.patreon.com/rmolson

www.ingramcontent.com/pod-product-compliance
Lightning Source LLC
Chambersburg PA
CBHW050853210726
48290CB00004B/1206